Two Feet
Under

Charlie Cochrane

RIPTIDE
PUBLISHING

Riptide Publishing
PO Box 1537
Burnsville, NC 28714
www.riptidepublishing.com

Two Feet Under

Cover art: L.C. Chase, lcchase.com/design.htm
Editor: Carole-ann Galloway
Layout: L.C. Chase, lcchase.com/design.htm

ISBN: 978-1-62649-682-8

First edition
January, 2018

Also available in ebook:
ISBN: 978-1-62649-681-1

Two Feet Under

Charlie Cochrane

RIPTIDE
PUBLISHING

To the Deadly Dames—Mesdames Carol Westron, Nicky Slade, Eileen Robertson, and Joan Moules, not forgetting our occasional chevaliers L.C. Tyler and Peter Lovesey—who inspire me to keep turning to crime.

Table
of Contents

Chapter One

"And this is our safeguarding checklist. If you'll just sign it to show you've read it and agree to abide by it . . ."

Adam nodded, read the sheet of paper, then signed and dated it at the bottom.

Adam Matthews, deputy headteacher. 10th April.

He fancied writing the job title again, as it had felt so good the first time. His first deputy headship, and a real chance to put a feather in his cap, given that Culdover Church of England Primary School officially "required improvement." He'd been recruited to help the new headteacher light such a firework under the staff that by the next time the Ofsted inspectors popped their cheery heads round the door, they'd rate the school as at least "good."

Before any of that could happen, though, he'd have to go through the standard induction procedure, almost all of it necessary, some of it boring, and some elements—like safeguarding and the location of the men's toilets—vital.

Soon everything was done and he had the chance to familiarise himself with the place, including sitting in with his year-six class, which he'd be taking two days a week and who were at present under the beady eye of Mrs. Daniel, the teacher who'd have them the other three days. The pupils seemed a cheery enough bunch, eager to show their new deputy just how good they were at maths. He sat down at one of the tables, where they were mulling over fractions, although it wasn't long before they wanted to bombard him with questions, a new member of staff—and that rare thing in primary education, a man—being much more interesting than halves and quarters. In the end, Adam, Mrs. Daniel, and the pupils came to the arrangement of making the last five minutes of the lesson a question-and-answer session, in return for which the children would work like billy-o up to that point. The plan worked.

"Which team do you support, sir?" opened the official interrogation.

"Saracens for rugby. Abbotston for football."

"Are you married, sir?"

"No." Until he had an idea of how mature his class were, he'd better keep quiet about the exact nature of his relationship. "But I've got a Newfoundland dog called Campbell."

"Wow! Will you bring in a picture of him?"

"Of course. I'll put it on the desk so he can keep an eye on you all." One day perhaps he'd also be able to bring a picture of Robin in to show the class, but that was probably wishful thinking. Children had open minds, yet too often they got filled with an imitation of their parents' prejudices.

"I interviewed you, sir," one spiky-haired lad piped up.

"I remember." The school-council part of the interview process had been trickier than facing the headteacher and governors. "You asked me to sing a song."

"Yeah. And you made us sing one instead." The boy chortled, his classmates joining in.

"I remember. No point in getting old if you can't get cunning." Adam grinned. "Right, one last question."

One of the girls—with an expression more serious than normally came with her age—raised her hand among a sea of others. She waited for Adam's nod before asking, "Which school did you used to teach at?"

Adam forced his grin to keep going. "Lindenshaw. Lindenshaw St. Crispin's, to give it its full name."

"Oh." The girl turned pale. "My dad told me they had a murder there. Is that why you left?"

Adam paused. So the school's reputation was preceding it?

Mrs. Daniel, obviously flustered, said, "I don't think we should talk about things like that."

Adam pursed his lips. "I think I disagree. It's better to have stuff in the open, and I'd have hoped this class is mature enough to discuss matters like that sensibly." How best to describe what had happened? Simply stating that there'd been a murder in what had been the children's kitchen, where the pupils had once learned to make semi-inedible fairy cakes, might put these pupils off cookery for life. "Somebody was killed, which is a really rare thing to happen in a school. None of the children were ever at risk, and the police found the killer very quickly."

And he'd found a partner in the process, which had been the best outcome from a wretched time.

The spiky-haired lad chipped in again. "*My* dad says that you probably can't go anywhere in Culdover without walking over a place where someone's died. What with the Romans and the air raids and—"

Adam raised a hand. "I think that's where we'll leave it. Time for lunch."

The class left their chairs, lined up at the door, and waited for Mrs. Daniel to let them out to their pre-lunch play. Just another first day of term for the children at Culdover, but for Adam it was that cliché: "the first day of the rest of his life." He'd miss Lindenshaw school—that went without saying, especially as it was starting to show a real improvement under the new headteacher—but his regrets would be few. The place held far too many unpleasant memories and associations now, and not simply in terms of the murder. Just last term a young teacher had thrown away the chances of a good career because he couldn't keep his fists to himself.

Worst of all, but predating Adam's sojourn at Lindenshaw, it had been Robin's school, where he'd been subjected to continual bullying.

Adam had promised to keep in touch with those of his colleagues who'd become genuine friends, but the building itself . . . The sooner Adam could shake the dust of the place off his shoes, the better.

He decided to spend his lunchtime mingling in the Culdover staffroom, getting into the normal school routine as soon as possible, then he'd give Robin a quick bell, and he wouldn't need to wander a quarter of a mile to do so. Another thing he wouldn't miss about Lindenshaw school was the mobile-phone black spot it sat in, which made reception a hit-or-miss affair unless you braved the women's toilets, where the signal was said to be perfect. Adam had always opted for the quarter-mile walk.

"How's it going?" Robin said when Adam had done his mingling and reported in.

"Much as expected." What was there to say about a typical first morning? "Friendly place, good team, interesting pupils."

Robin sniggered. "Interesting as in potential psychopaths?"

"Do you think of everyone as a potential criminal?"

"Only if they come from Culdover."

"Don't let them hear you say that." Culdover was a typically English small town, one that had been distinctly posh in its heyday although it had gone downhill post-war, and parts of it were looking rather ropey. Regeneration had made a difference in some places, but the preponderance of charity shops on the high street showed there was plenty still to do. "Busy today?"

"Usual sort of stuff. Spate of upmarket car thefts. Case of dognapping too. I won't tell Campbell."

"Make sure you don't. He'll have nightmares." At work one of them may report to a headteacher and the other to a chief superintendent, but at home the roost was ruled by a large, black, wet-nosed Newfoundland dog, whose self-estimation had been swelled by his having saved both of his masters' lives on separate occasions.

"Got to go. Villains to nick. See you tonight."

"Yeah. Don't forget the milk."

"I won't."

Adam smiled. Their house was well stocked with semi-skimmed, but "don't forget the milk" and its response "I won't," or some slight variation on them, had become code for "I love you" and "I love you too," which couldn't always be used. Even if Robin and Adam were no longer in the closet, sometimes common sense had to prevail.

Robin ended the call, finished his sandwich, and got back to his paperwork. He glanced up at the clock, only to find that it wasn't where he'd expected. How long was it going to take him to get used to this new office and new location?

Abbotston nick wasn't proving so bad in the wake of chucking out the rotten apples. It was better still, Robin believed, now that he was the acting chief inspector with every prospect of that position being made permanent in the months to come, so long as he kept his nose clean and his clear-up rate healthy. It was a pity Anderson hadn't come with him, but his erstwhile sergeant had been bumped up to acting inspector back at Robin's previous station, Stanebridge. He'd miss the man's spiky sense of humour and his sudden bursts of enlightenment, if not his driving style.

Crime was crime anywhere, from big city to leafy village—the Lindenshaw murders had proved that—but the sheer scale of things came into play at Abbotston. It was larger than Stanebridge, much more sprawling, and so there was extra everything, from industrial estates to coffee shops to drug dealers, even if murder was still thankfully rare. It had grown bigger than Kinechester, which was the county "capital" and had been since the time of the Romans, who'd made their base there and left their stamp in the layout of the streets, although Abbotston lacked the history which had secured Kinechester's importance. At least Abbotston was a step up from Culdover, which might give Robin some bragging rights over Adam if they were into that kind of new-job-related one-upmanship. But they weren't.

Campbell would never tolerate that, anyway.

A rap at his door—thank goodness he remembered where that was—made Robin look up from the papers on his desk. "Yes?"

"Got a bit of an odd one, sir." Pru Davis, also newly promoted and blossoming in her role as his sergeant, poked her head round Robin's door, her brow wrinkled in bewilderment.

"Go on." Robin had always had a lot of time for Pru. She'd been a keen-as-mustard and deadly efficient constable at Stanebridge, and when the chance to bring her along to Abbotston presented itself, he'd snapped it up. While the pair of them had to make sure they didn't form an ex-Stanebridge clique—there was history between the two stations that wouldn't make for an easy ride initially—she'd be moral support for him. The fact she was so good at her job, not something that could be traditionally said for Abbotston coppers, made her presence a win all round, although it carried the risk of alienating the pair further from the locals.

They had a subtle path to walk and a lot of diplomacy to deliver.

"Got a dead body turned up at an archaeological site."

Robin frowned. "Is this a wind-up? Abbotston city slickers trying to put one over on the yokels?"

"I wish it was." Pru entered the room, notepad at the ready. "It came from Lewington, down on the front desk, so I doubt it's a wind-up."

Lewington appeared to be an old-fashioned sort of career copper, and he had a reputation of not suffering fools gladly. His son was something to do with the BBC sports department so allegedly always had a bit of inside gossip on who to put your shirt on for the Grand National.

"Added to which," Pru continued, "I recognised the name of the bloke who rang it in, so it seems legitimate. Up at Culford Roman villa."

"You'd better take a seat and tell me all about it." Robin jotted down notes while his sergeant gave a brief but pertinent outline. They'd been contacted by Charlie Howarth, who was the bloke at Kinechester council in charge of historic sites, and who'd apparently pulled Pru's pigtails when they were both only five, back in Risca.

"Risca?"

"Near Newport. Land of my fathers and all that."

"'Cwm Rhondda' and 'Delilah'?" Robin grinned. "How did you both end up here?"

"Took a wrong turn off the M4." Pru rolled her eyes. "Charlie was bound to end up by here, given all the history in the area."

Robin winced at the Welsh argot, which had a habit of coming and going in Pru's voice. She was right about the history, though; the local area was awash with it. He'd learned back in school that Culdover had been occupied for thousands of years because of its abundant natural resources. Even Kinechester wasn't as old as Culdover, which had been knocking around since the Neolithic. Like so many places throughout England, it retained evidence of its previous occupants, and many of the local schools made the most of that fact, focussing their trips on both the Iron Age hill fort and Roman villa not five miles from the town centre.

School trips. Please God there'd not be a connection to Adam this time.

Robin refocussed. "What did this mate of yours have to report? It's not one of those routine 'found a body; we're pretty sure it's from the time of Cromwell, but we have to call it in just in case' things?"

"Looks unlikely. They've had the doctor in." Pru's eyebrows shot up. "To declare that this poor soul really is dead despite it being obvious she must have been there months."

"It's procedure. Is Grace there too?" Grace was Robin's favourite crime-scene investigator. If anything had ever evaded her notice, he wasn't aware of it.

"On route, at least."

"So what do we know?"

"A routine, planned dig started up earlier today, exploring an area near the villa where somebody reckoned they'd found a new range of buildings. New as in unexcavated."

"I understand that. I *have* watched *Time Team*." It was one of his mother's favourite programmes.

"Better you than me, sir, but don't tell Charlie. He's at the site, if we want to drive down there."

Robin fished out his car keys. "Let's go and hear what he's got to say."

There was no easy route directly from Abbotston to Culford; the main roads made two sides of a triangle, and the third was formed of winding country lanes. The old Roman road, which ran straight and true through Tythebarn and other villages and which formed the foundation of Culdover High Street, was the wrong side of the site to be of help.

When they arrived at the car park, Charlie Howarth was already waiting for them, chatting on his phone while trying to sign off some paperwork.

"Sorry about that," he said in a deep Welsh accent as he ended the call. "Pru, you don't age, do you?"

"Got a picture in the attic." Pru's voice reflected its roots more than normal. "Chief Inspector Bright wants to know all about what you found."

"Not me who found it. One of the diggers, poor girl." Howarth—what sort of a Welsh name was that?—winced. "I was going to send her home but thought you might want to interview her."

"Quite right." Robin nodded. "Tell us what you can."

"We started digging the area this morning. Just by hand, nothing mechanical. This is supposed to be a virgin bit of the site, excavation-wise, so we had no idea what we'd turn up."

"Why here in particular?" Robin asked.

"The university got a grant to do a geophysical survey of the whole area. Do you know what that is?"

"Of course," Robin snapped. "We're the *Time Team* generation. Did you think you'd found a plunge pool?"

Howarth inclined his head. "Sorry. I was being patronising."

"Apology accepted." Robin could be gracious when required.

"We weren't sure what we'd found, to be honest, only that there were signs of underlying structures. Unlike the people on *Time Team*, we don't make assumptions until we've exposed the archaeology."

"So what did the digger expose?"

"Part of a mosaic to start with. Bit of a small panel, with some sort of substrate for the tesserae to be embedded in, just lying in the topsoil." Howarth indicated the size of the thing with his hands. "Very unusual, which is what got Kirsty—that's the digger I mentioned—so puzzled in the first place. She'd barely raked off anything else when she found black plastic. A sheet or a large strong bag. It was slightly ripped, and hair was protruding through the tear."

"We'll get her to supply the details." Robin couldn't shake off an instant, and uncharacteristically unprofessional, dislike he'd taken to this witness. "You said this was virgin ground, but if somebody buried a body, then the area must have been disturbed. Did nobody notice?"

Howarth shrugged. "That bit of ground's been used for all sorts of things over the years, because people didn't think it was important. There used to be a children's play area there, but it was taken out. Health and Safety." He rolled his eyes. "It's been a right mess since then, so if somebody was careful enough, they could cover their tracks."

"Hm. How easy is it to get into this place out of hours?"

"The main building's locked and alarmed." That made sense, given that the mosaics and hypocaust ruins were in great condition. Culford wasn't Fishbourne, but it remained impressive. "The rest of the site just has a fence. We weren't aware of anything that needed protecting." Howarth gave Pru a rueful smile.

She returned the smile, then adopted her most professional air. "You'll appreciate there are questions we'll have to ask you, and statements to be taken, both now and as the details emerge. For a start, are you aware of anyone associated with the site going missing?"

Howarth shook his head. "No, all women accounted for."

"How do you know it's a woman we're concerned with?" Robin interjected.

"Oh, sorry. Kirsty said she reckoned the corpse was female, from what she could see of the hair. Have I spoken out of turn?"

Robin narrowed his eyes. "We don't make any assumptions about identifying the victim until we hear from our experts."

"I apologise once more. Thing is, our staff here is predominantly female. We only have one paid employee, Clare, who runs the administration and just about everything else. She gets helped by volunteers so we can have the site open as much as possible."

"I'll get a full list of names from Clare, thank you. In the interim, I'd like to talk to the student who found the body. Kirsty, did you say?"

"That's right. She'll be up in the staffroom, which is our posh term for that Portakabin." Howarth pointed towards a dingy green building. "Do you want to talk to her now?"

"After we check in at the scene. Thanks," Robin added, remembering his manners.

"Shall I take you . . . ?"

"No thanks, Charlie." Pru cuffed his arm. "You'll be busy enough putting off the school trips and the public. This place needs to be shut to everyone for the time being."

Howarth's face dropped. "Hell. I never thought. I'll get onto it."

As Robin and his sergeant made their way from the car park to where a white tent indicated the victim's last resting place, he cast a glance over his shoulder. Howarth was on his phone, talking animatedly. "Is he always like that?"

"Like what, sir?"

"Gets up people's noses and they can't work out why."

Pru laughed. "Yeah, that's him. Or at least it is if you're a bloke. They find him a bit smarmy."

"And what's he like with women?"

"A charmer. No harm in him, though. He's always struck me as happily married." They halted at the point where they'd have to slip on at least gloves and overshoes if they wanted to get closer to the shallow grave. "I suspect if a woman misread the charm and made him an offer, he'd run a mile."

"Hmm."

The appearance of Grace, emerging from the tent with a cheery wave, focussed their attention away from smarmy site directors towards the gruesome minutiae. "Coming over for a look, sir?"

"When we're kitted up. Want us in bunny suits?"

"Please. Whole kit and caboodle. This isn't *Midsomer*." Grace had no time for television crime dramas and the way they played fast and loose with crime scenes and forensic matters. Shoddy procedures and the depiction of seemingly limitless budgets; both riled her. "The doctor has been, to say that she's definitely dead. He'll do the postmortem tomorrow."

"How long has the body been there?" Robin asked once they were inside the tent and had their first glimpse of the corpse. The dismal sight of somebody's child, somebody's loved one, cut off in their prime was one Robin would never get used to.

Grace wrinkled her nose. "She's been there months, rather than days. I'll be able to give you a better answer when all the tests are done."

"Definitely a she?" Pru clarified. She waited for Grace's nod before continuing. "Any idea how old she was?"

"About twenties or thirties, from what I can see of the body and clothes. Although what I can expose has been restricted by the plastic she was wrapped in. We'll confirm everything as soon as we can, along with cause of death and all the rest of it. I suspect she's had blunt trauma to the forehead, but she's in a pretty bad way. The doctor didn't like the state of the bit of her face that's visible."

"Series of blows?"

Grace shrugged. "Can't tell as yet. Maybe something that happened postmortem. When I know, you will."

Robin, with a quickly hidden shudder, glanced at the dead woman again. "Do we have a name for her?"

"Not that I've found yet. But it's going to be a slow process. Don't want to miss anything by rushing." Grace sighed. "Poor lass."

"Poor lass, indeed." Robin forced a rueful smile. "Get all the information you can. She deserves it."

"I'll do my best. And then we'll see what Greg and his pals can make of it."

"We'll leave you to it." The sooner Grace could collect the samples, the sooner they'd be off to the lab for examination.

Once they'd left the CSI to get on with her job and were heading off to find the digger who'd uncovered the body, Pru—pale faced—rubbed her hands as though ridding the grave dirt from them.

"First corpse?" Robin asked, not unkindly. Death took some getting used to.

"First murder, assuming it *is* a murder. Seen a couple of RTAs." Thank God that was still the most likely way the local police came across dead bodies. "I imagined it would be the same."

"But it isn't?"

"No, and I can't work out why." She halted. "Ditch me if I'm being a sea anchor, sir. There must be some of the Abbotston team who've got more experience than I have."

"There are. And they'll have plenty to exercise that experience on, especially if there's no ID on our victim. At least you didn't puke all over your shoes, like Anderson did."

"Did he?"

"Do you think I'm lying?" He was, but it wouldn't hurt for her to believe the story for a while. "Fancy a cuppa? Your pal must be able to rustle us up one."

"No, thanks." They'd reached the Portakabin door. "He'd only try to find somebody with two X chromosomes to do it. He wouldn't know one end of a kettle from another."

Robin grinned, then immediately changed his expression for one suitably serious for interviewing a witness.

Kirsty—they guessed it was her from the name emblazoned on the back of her sweatshirt—was sitting at a table with what appeared to be a colleague. Both had their hands clenched around mugs which somehow looked far too large for them. The Portakabin was comfortably enough decked out, having—apart from the table and chairs—several more comfy armchairs, a sagging sofa, a tiny kitchenette, and another section which appeared to be set aside for the cleaning and sorting of artefacts. A couple of PCs, surprisingly modern, completed the contents. The windows provided a scenic view of the car park, which could be blocked out by blinds when the sight of school coaches and snotty pupils became overwhelming.

The inevitably edgy introductions were made, and Kirsty's colleague, Abby, offered to make them all a fresh brew, which Robin readily accepted.

"Nothing like this has ever happened before," Kirsty said, without being asked. "I mean, I'm used to turning up burials or cremations, especially on the edges of Roman sites, but I knew as soon as I saw it that this wasn't old."

"Can we take this from the beginning, please? Assume we don't know a thing," Robin said in what he hoped were soothing tones. The girl was clearly nervous, and some important element might be lost if they didn't go through things logically.

"Okay." Kirsty gave a little background to the dig, which matched what Howarth had said. She and Abby had arrived that morning as the advance guard of a team from Kinechester University, and they'd barely got a couple of inches down when they'd come to the mosaic.

"Where's that now?" Pru enquired.

"In a finds tray, up by the trench. We lifted it whole, didn't we, Abby?" she called across to where her colleague was doling teabags into a pot.

"We did." Abby gestured with her teaspoon, miming the procedure. "After we'd recorded it and everything. It was obvious it wasn't in situ, so we thought it must have been backfill from some previous dig we didn't know anything about, or maybe from when they put the play park in."

"Yes"—Kirsty nodded—"we knew before we started that the ground had been disturbed time and again, and who knows how careless people had been."

Robin wasn't sure that the contractors who put in or took out the play equipment would have been allowed to be so gung-ho with any artefacts they turned up, but he let it ride. "And then?"

"And then we cleared back a bit more and found the plastic. I wondered at first if it was from landscaping. You know, people put down black plastic to inhibit weeds. I made some stupid joke about how it wasn't typically Anglo-Saxon or anything like that, and then I called Abby over. She spotted the tear in the bag and the hair sticking through, so she said we should leave everything as it was."

"Quite right." Pru smiled encouragingly. "Did you turn up any other finds before you shut digging down for the day?"

"No. We weren't expecting to, given how little we'd got down into the soil. If the archaeology is at the same level as the villa, we'd have expected to go down another three feet."

"Why didn't you use a mechanical digger to take off the top layers?" Robin had seen that on *Time Team* too.

"Because we knew the top layers were likely to have already been disturbed and didn't want to risk missing artefacts in the topsoil." Abby brought over the steaming mugs of tea, to a chorus of gratitude. "Just as well, isn't it?"

"Indeed." Robin blew on his tea, then risked a semi-scalding sip. "Why didn't you ring *us*? Protocol?"

"Lack of phone signal. You know what it's like round here." Kirsty, taking a draught, didn't seem to notice how hot the tea was. Maybe she had it milky enough to counteract the heat. "I came down to the office, where Charlie was. Mr. Howarth. He came up to double-check, then went to ring you. You can get signal in here."

"What did he double-check?" Pru asked.

The students rolled their eyes. "That we hadn't made a mistake and misidentified a body that was too old to be of interest to you. As though the Romans used plastic."

"I thought you had to report all bodies, unless they were found properly interred in a burial ground." Pru looked to Robin, who both shrugged and nodded.

"Always best to call us in." He took another sip of tea. "Have you any idea of who the dead woman might be?"

Abby and Kirsty shared a *How the hell are we supposed to know?* glance before shaking their heads.

"I know, it sounds a daft question." Robin smiled. "But you'd be surprised. People hear things, about somebody who's gone missing but not been reported to the police, or rumours about odd happenings. Office gossip that turns out to have a basis in truth."

"Sorry." Kirsty shook her head again. "Nothing."

"That mosaic's a bit off, though," Abby remarked. "I took a picture of it to send to my tutor. She reckons it's totally the wrong design and era for this site. She said it looked like a Victorian antiquarian might have hacked it out of somewhere else."

"Seems fishy," Robin agreed. "It was definitely on top of the sheeting? The dead woman couldn't have been holding it in her hands or anything?"

"I doubt it." Kirsty frowned. "Not unless the plastic had all been disturbed already."

"Thank you." Robin took another swig of tea. He'd never be able to manage the entire mug. "We'll get a constable up here to take formal statements from you both, as well as anybody else who's on-site. You'd think somebody would have seen or heard something suspicious."

Abby snorted. "Don't count on it. I can think of people in my department who'd notice a flint flake three metres away but not spot a bollard until they walked into it."

"Let's hope you're wrong." Robin had an awful feeling she wouldn't be.

Chapter Two

A dam had just put the house phone down as Robin trudged through the front door. Campbell must have heard the approach of his "other" master well before Adam did, as he was ready and waiting to pounce.

"I wasn't expecting you to be home so early," Adam said, then gave his partner a kiss.

"Sorry about that. You'd better tell your sugar daddy to skedaddle." Robin, dog in tow, edged towards the kitchen. "Was that him on the phone?"

"No. The usual 'We're from Microsoft and there's something wrong with your computer.' I always say, 'Microsoft? That's very interesting,' then clam up. They panic and put the phone down."

"Good tactic." Robin yawned. "I told the team to make the most of this evening. Once we have an identification of the dead woman, it'll be all hands to the deck."

"Dinner won't be long. Saturday's chilli con carne from the freezer."

"Sounds like heaven." Robin kicked off his shoes. He'd texted earlier, from the site, to warn Adam a new investigation was afoot, although Adam had already guessed that was the case, as the incident had been on the local news feed. Once the folks from Culford villa had cancelled the school trip which was due the next day, and the characteristic blue-and-white police tape had appeared, word had spread.

"Want to talk about it?"

"Not a lot to say at present." Robin stroked Campbell's ears.

"What's that on your sleeve?"

"Where?" Robin twisted about.

"Left elbow. Looks like oil. Or rust. Or both."

"That's because it *is* oil. Sod."

"Take it off and I'll put something on it. There's a can of Stain Devil under the sink."

Robin slid the jacket off, grimacing at the smear on what he'd always described as one of his favourite items of clothing. "This cost me a small fortune. Got it in a little shop down an alley in Bath."

"No wonder it cost so much." Adam started work on the stain. Little domestic tasks such as this formed part of the process of bringing them closer and keeping them together. It was like being a married couple, only not quite.

"That jacket's almost as precious to me as Campbell, even if it's never saved my life." Robin peered over Adam's shoulder. "I rubbed up against some rust bucket of a truck in Culford car park. Must have done it then."

"No wonder the people on *Time Team* always look like they've borrowed their outfits off the local scarecrows. Perhaps it's an occupational hazard."

"Don't you start. I feel like I've spent all day fending off daft 'of course you've found a mosaic at a Roman site' type quips."

"Mosaic? There wasn't anything about that on the news." Adam, having performed first aid on the jacket, opened the fridge and pulled out a bottle of beer and one of sparkling water.

"Just the water, please. I'll keep the beer for when I really need it. Thanks." Robin took the bottle. "And yes, we've kept the mosaic quiet for the moment."

He gave a résumé of what they'd found out about that morning: the ground-penetrating survey, the possible bathhouse, the university students beginning to dig.

Adam winced when he reached the part about finding the body. "Poor girls. Do you think it's worse to find a fresh corpse or an old one? Or are they equally gruesome?"

"You should ask Pru Davis that. I thought she was going to lose her breakfast, although she held it together in the end. Anyway, this bit of mosaic was on top of the body, a whole section of it embedded in whatever Romans used to hold their tesserae. I suspect the archaeology mob is more puzzled about that than about the dead woman. Wrong era, wrong place, wrong everything."

"Sounds odd."

"Sounds bloody peculiar. And who knows how it links to the murder."

"It'll make sense in the end." Adam began to plate up their food. "Like a jigsaw when you can't see where a particular bit goes until you've got the ones that fit round it. Then you say, 'Bloody hell, I never realised it went there!'"

Robin grinned. "Are you always so aggressive when you do jigsaws?"

Adam made a face. "You know what I mean. Ooh, and before I forget, your mum rang. Must have heard about the case on the news and knew you'd have your nose stuck in it."

"You leave my nose alone." Robin chuckled. "Mum says I've got a cute nose."

"She'd say you had a cute nose if you were Cyrano de Bergerac, though, wouldn't she? Mums do. Anyway, she sends her love, says she'll be thinking of you and you're not to work too hard."

"Fat chance of that."

They gave the next few minutes over to eating and preventing the dog from stealing anything from their plates.

"It'll upset your tummy, young man," Robin said, fending off a furry snout. "Basket. Go on."

Campbell grudgingly obeyed, curling up in his basket with a mortally offended look on his face.

"You can have a biscuit in a minute if you're good. You as well," Adam added, turning to address Robin rather than the dog. "Sandra got in some Abernethys from Waitrose. And Bonios for 'himself'."

"I have no idea how I survived in the past without a cleaner cum Jill-of-all-trades to pander to my every biscuit whim."

"Oi!" Adam snorted. "What about me? How did you survive without a handsome teacher in your life?"

"I've no bloody idea about that, either." Robin scooped up the last bit of food from his plate with a satisfied sigh. "Good cook, good lover, sympathetic ear. What more could a man want?"

"A quick solution to this case?"

Robin blew out his cheeks. "Too true. Not sure we'll get it, though. Nothing useful showed up on the initial trawl through missing-persons reports, despite the description we have. Grace says she's a slim thing, size eight or ten, perhaps, and that the clothes are standard UK brands like White Stuff and Fat Face. Preliminary thoughts are that she isn't a visitor from abroad. Auburn hair, seems natural."

Adam cleared away the plates, then put the kettle on. "Now we've finished eating, can I ask whether she's recognisable?"

Robin winced. "Grace has a feeling the body was originally not wrapped in plastic. Something got at the face and had a gnaw."

"Ew." Adam raised his hand. "I get the picture. Don't say any more or you'll put Campbell off his Bonio."

"I'll get him one while you make a cuppa."

"Deal." Everything seemed more manageable with a cup of tea in one's hand. "You said, 'originally.' Was she reburied?"

"Seems like it. Grace's guess is somewhere around six months ago, give or take a bit either way. That supports what the site administrator said—they had a Community Payback group in to weed and dig over some of the tattier parts of the site. That would have been best part of a year ago, and she wasn't in the ground then."

"May sort of time?" Adam nodded. "And leaving a nice turned-over piece of ground for somebody to make use of. Who'd notice another bit of disturbance?"

"Indeed. Especially out there. They'd think it was a fox or badger having a poke. Look at the mess Campbell can make if we let him."

The dog raised his head at the sound of his name, clearly decided there was no food involved in the conversation, and snuggled back down again with the remains of his biscuit.

"What are your thoughts on the mosaic?" Adam asked.

"No thoughts, simply questions, like how it entered the scene. Has it always been with the body? Was it put in the second time, or just lying around in the topsoil and got interred by accident or what?" Robin watched as the dog nibbled his biscuit. "I've never seen a hound who eats so daintily when he wants to."

"He's smart. He's learned it makes the food last longer." Adam couldn't help but smile at the two beings he valued most. Campbell could easily have been envious of Robin suddenly appearing in his master's life, but from the start he'd been as besotted with the policeman as Adam had been. "Smart but sentimental."

"Then he takes after you."

"Guilty as charged." Adam kept an old mobile phone upstairs, SIM card intact, because it had saved the last text his grandfather had ever sent him. When he'd first told Robin about it, they'd both been in tears— He should get back to talking about the murder, or he'd be getting sentimental again. "Why did nobody notice that the area had been disturbed twice?"

"It wasn't necessarily disturbed twice. The body might have been somewhere else the first time and moved because Culford was a better spot. That's up to Grace and her cronies to work out. I get the impression the area was overgrown and ignored. They've had to clear a mass of weeds already."

Adam nodded. "If you'd enough nous to choose your spot behind a bush and pick your time, I suppose you could get away with murder. Sorry. Didn't mean to sound flippant."

"I know. We all use those expressions too casually." Robin strolled over, put his arms round Adam's waist, and leaned into his back. "Next few days are going to be busy. If I forget to say 'I love you,' you won't forget that it's a fact, will you?"

"I promise." Adam, thoughts heading trouser-wards, caressed Robin's hand before the arrival of a pair of massive paws and a cold, wet nose broke the romantic moment.

"Yes, and we both love you too." Robin stroked Campbell's head. "Now hop it to your basket so Daddy can give Daddy a kiss."

Eventually the dog got the message, but the kiss had barely started before the unwelcome tones of Robin's phone interrupted it.

"Oh, hell. Sorry." Robin grabbed it off the breakfast bar and managed, "Hello?" before heading for the hall. It had to be work, given the snatches of conversation Adam could hear; developments on the case, no doubt. Chances were Robin would have to go in to work again, just as the evening was looking promising. Hopefully the traffic wouldn't be too bad at this time of the day so he could make a swift journey there and back.

Commuting from their house in Lindenshaw to both Abbotston and Culdover was viable, albeit logic kept telling them that a move would reduce travelling time for both. With the money from the sale of Robin's flat, they had a sizeable deposit to lay down on another property, although it would have to be exactly the right place to warrant selling up their Lindenshaw home, especially given the house's history. It had belonged to Adam's grandparents, and it had been the site of all the significant moments in their romance, even when it hadn't been an actual romance, simply an illicit longing between detective and witness.

Didn't people reckon that moving house was a stressful experience at the best of times? So shouldn't any potential move have to be worthwhile? And, of course, any prospective property would have to pass the most stringent of tests, specifically that of Campbell, who'd need to sniff every bush and tree in the garden to assess its suitability for leg cocking. And the residents of Lindenshaw wouldn't appreciate having their favourite hound—much petted and fussed over by locals when he was taken out for walks—being relocated to a place where other lucky so-and-sos would be able to ruffle his fur and have his wet nose stuck on their legs.

"Sorry about that." Robin's reappearance in the kitchen roused Adam from his thoughts.

"You really don't need to apologise about work calls any more than I do about the interminable marking and planning. It goes with the job." Adam wrinkled his nose. "Time for that cuppa before you go?"

"Go?" Robin frowned. "Oh, no, this can wait until morning. We've had a report of a missing archaeologist. Right sort of age, although not from this area. London. Somebody saw the story on the BBC news website, remembered the lass disappearing, and got in touch. I'll have to go up there, assuming that a more local or viable connection doesn't turn up."

Adam nodded. "I guess it's dangerous to assume this poor lass is anything to do with Culdover."

"I wish you'd tell that to some of the constables at Abbotston. Two plus two always makes five for them." Robin, sighing, rubbed his eyes. "I hate it when there's no identification. I'm going to double- and triple-check what we know about the missing woman against what we know about the corpse. Imagine if we go up there and spook her family and it turns out it's not her?"

"God, that would be awful. They must be twitching each time the phone rings or the doorbell goes. Like she dies again every day, if that makes any sense." Adam poured the tea—they needed it more than ever. "How can so many people simply go missing?"

Robin shrugged. "They're not all abducted by loonies, certainly. Some of them must take ill and die when they're miles from nowhere and don't turn up for months or years. Thanks."

They took their drinks and the packet of biscuits into the lounge.

"That can't be many people, though, can it? To go unfound for so long? Britain isn't exactly full of unpopulated areas."

"True, but it does happen. More likely they decide to go off somewhere for whatever reason."

"Made a break for freedom?" Adam, having got himself comfortable on the sofa, and Campbell comfortable—if a touch peeved—on the floor, managed to open the biscuit packet without too much damage to the contents and without intervention from black canine noses.

"Could be. People are complex. They do illogical things because it seems like a good idea at the time." Robin dunked his biscuit for the required amount of time, then ate it with evident pleasure. "Maybe it gets to the point you can't face returning home because of all the fuss and the shame, so you stay put and it just gets worse with every day that passes."

Good point. Putting off dealing with matters only made them worse, and it would surely get to the stage where it made them impossible. "What if she's missing and hasn't been reported, though? That happens, doesn't it?"

"It does." Robin's brow puckered. "Even in these days of social media overkill and constant communication, people quietly disappear or are made to disappear. If this girl was here illegally, we might have the devil's own job of finding out who she is—was—despite doing facial reconstructions. The fact that she had no ID suggests somebody didn't want her name coming to light in the event that her body did."

"Unless she was killed in a robbery that went wrong. Purse and whatever taken for their contents as opposed to anything else."

"True, oh genius." Robin took another swig of tea. "They host lots of school trips at Culford, I understand."

"Yeah. Most of the Culdover schools use the place for trips, and there's an activity centre near Tythebarn that always takes the kids over for a day."

"Ever taken *your* class there?"

"No. Culdover Primary uses it for a year four visit, but Lindenshaw never utilised the place, I'm afraid. Too infra dig, if you'll excuse the pun. Oh." The penny dropped. "I get it. You want to know if I have a connection to *this* case too."

"Well, I have to ask." Robin grinned sheepishly. "Just promise me you won't let yourself get involved this time."

"You make it sound as though I deliberately try to. I don't. Your cases want to embroil me no matter how much I attempt to keep out of things."

Campbell opened one sleepy eye, as though agreeing that Robin's murder investigations seemed to want to involve them all, him included.

"If you do end up finding you have a connection to Culford, I'm not sure if I'll want to know. Even if it turns out you dropped a ring pull in the play area and it has your fingerprints on it."

"You can count that out, for a start. I visited the villa when I was a boy, but I've not been there since, and I don't think any ring pull would be mine. Mum would have killed me if she'd caught me dropping litter. And I didn't see anyone burying a body." Adam paused a moment, feigning deep thought. "No teachers of my acquaintance gone missing, either."

"Pillock." Robin slapped his arm. "You never went out with any archaeologists? Sat on a committee with one? Did jury service when one was on trial?"

Adam rolled his eyes at the reference to two of Robin's previous cases, both of which had been a bit too close to home. Even before they met, they'd both derided those television shows where friends of the detective—or his daughter, in one case—were always linked to the corpse or the suspects. Neither had dreamed that could apply in real life, but Robin's two recent murder cases had disproved that, although technically that connection had been the outcome of the first case. Still, random events clustered, didn't they? So hopefully they'd had their cluster and could move on safely.

Adam hadn't expected that murder would never cross their paths again, given Robin's job and the fact that the villages of England were as full of jealousy and other fiery emotions as the cities. And the prevalence of legitimately held and used shotguns—or golf clubs or any other potential implements of death—gave means as well as motive or opportunity. Probably easier to hide a body, welcome to that, which was just what this case showed.

"No, no, and thrice no. I swear," he replied at last, hoping that vow wouldn't come back to haunt him. He'd seen one dead body and was in no hurry to repeat the experience.

"Right." Robin grabbed another biscuit and held it in mid-air, pre-dunk. "Not another word about this case until we have some proper evidence to go on. And what's so funny?"

"Sorry." Adam managed to get the word out despite the laughter. "You reminded me of an old joke. The one about all the loos being stolen from the cop shop, so the police had nothing to go on."

"I'll give you bloody nothing to go on." Robin laid down both mug and undunked biscuit, pounced at Adam, and tickled him mercilessly down the sides of his ribs.

"Hey! Stop! You'll spill my tea."

"That's not all that will spill if I get my way."

"Promises, promises." Adam put his mug on the table. Might as well take advantage of the offer because who knew when they'd have the chance again? Murders meant long hours, late nights, and knackered policemen whose thoughts were too tired to descend to their pants. He leaned in for a smacker of a kiss.

"That was good. For starters." Robin's lascivious grin could have turned the iciest libido to butter. "What about—"

Once more Robin's phone interrupted them.

"Sorry," he said, picking it up off the table.

"I told you to stop saying that." Adam forced a grin. A second call so hard on the heels of the first couldn't be good news and surely meant Robin's return to the station.

"Oh, hi." Robin halted halfway to the door. "How's life?" Not the station, by the sound of it. "Yes, if we can. Depends what it is." Robin turned to mouth what looked like the name "Anderson." Hopefully this was just a social call from his old sergeant that could soon be dealt with, letting them get back to the matter in hand.

"Bloody hell!" Robin sat down heavily in the armchair. "When? Why?"

Adam, infuriated at only hearing half the conversation, helped himself to a consolatory biscuit. The worried expression on Robin's face and the way he'd settled into his chair suggested he was in for the long haul. As it turned out, though, the call was surprisingly short, with Robin saying, "Okay, I think that'll be all right, so long as it's short term," then making a helpless gesture at Adam.

"What the hell's going on?" Adam mouthed, but his partner simply gritted his teeth and rolled his eyes. Things must be bad.

"I guess you got that was Anderson," Robin said after the call ended.

"Yeah. Sounded ominous, whatever it was."

"It is. Helen's chucked him out."

"What?" Stuart Anderson had been living with his teacher girlfriend for years, and everyone at Stanebridge seemed to regard them as an old married couple, even if they hadn't actually tied the knot. Although Robin always said he wouldn't have been amazed if it turned out they'd been married years ago, and Anderson hadn't mentioned the fact to any of his workmates. Helen never wearing a wedding ring seemed to argue against that, though. "What's he done?"

"According to him, he didn't do anything. She's been edgy for days, and this evening it all exploded." Robin retrieved his tea, took a sip, then winced. It had no doubt turned tepid. "She says he can pack a bag and hit the road."

"But surely she gave some sort of explanation?"

"Apparently, she said that if he didn't know what he'd done, she wasn't going to tell him."

"Ouch." Adam gave Campbell, who looked distressed at the goings-on, a conciliatory pat. "What a mess. What's he going to do? Ah." The sheepish expression on Robin's face answered the question. "He's staying here, isn't he? Presumably he cadged a bed, seeing as I didn't hear you offer."

"You should be a detective." Robin patted his arm. "He hasn't got any family around here, and I suspect we're the people he trusts most, in this area. It'll only be for a few days until he sorts himself out."

"Or works out what he's done and apologises for it?" Adam remembered the penultimate assembly he'd attended at Lindenshaw school, how it had centred on the Good Samaritan; that's how they were being called to act. "I'd better get the spare bed ready. You can find him some towels."

Robin started to clear away the remains of their tea and biscuits. "Sorry about our romantic night in being spoiled."

"You can make it up to me when *he's* gone or when the murder's solved. Whichever comes first. Hopefully the former." Adam halted halfway out of the lounge door. "What does he eat for breakfast?"

"Whatever we put in front of him. Beggars can't be choosers."

Beggars. Adam shivered. "Maybe that's how it started with your dead woman. Row with the other half, or with her parents. Sofa surfing until her mates got fed up with it. Nobody realised she'd slipped out of the loop until it was too late."

"Now who's putting two and two together and getting five?" Robin edged over to give him a hug, encumbered by mugs and plate— and a dog that wanted to be involved—but a hug nonetheless. "We won't let him end up on the streets."

"Good. Only I wouldn't want him to end up living here permanently, either. I mean, he's a nice bloke and all that, but three's a crowd. Four . . ." he added, glancing at Campbell.

Robin grinned. "Yeah. Better get practicing our relationship advice."

Chapter Three

The rest of the evening had passed without event, Anderson being extremely sheepish when he'd arrived—with a bag only big enough to last him a few days, Robin had noticed with relief—and not really wanting to get into explanations. They'd given the bloke a beer, chatted about Abbotston Alexandra's prospects for the football season, watched the news, and then gone off to bed. Very British, playing things on the principle that if one didn't mention them, they might just go away. Only Campbell had made some allusion to the problem, nestling by Anderson's legs and putting his head in the man's lap, looking up at him with eyes that seemed to say, *You poor bloke. Would you feel better if you gave me a pat or two?*

They'd gone to bed, slept, got up, had breakfast, all being terribly polite to each other, and then set off to their respective places of work, with Anderson promising—as he left the house—that this was only a temporary arrangement and that they'd talk more about it that evening.

When Robin arrived at Abbotston station, he was whisked off to talk to the assistant chief constable, his immediate boss being on holiday. By the time he escaped and made it to the incident room, Pru was already at work, as were a team of constables, two of whom had been sent to complete the last of the interviews with the Culford staff, leaving another two to trawl through missing-persons lists and various reports which had come in from members of the public, although it appeared the latter were of little use. People saying that they'd always thought there was something odd about that play area, how their kids said it gave them the shivers, how they'd seen odd-looking blokes hanging around there ten years ago, looking at the children. Those, and similar stories which didn't link up in terms of time frame or content, were politely noted and filed away.

Robin didn't entirely ignore them, of course. There was no way to tell in advance when some disregarded scrap of information might turn out to be crucial. It was just possible that the odd-looking blokes might have been sussing out a potential crime scene, although it was more likely they were myopic metal detectorists in an attempt to work out the best place to locate a coin hoard, or even forgetful types who were simply trying to work out where they'd left their glasses.

Something concrete on the scientific front should come in soon. Abbotston was the location for the county's forensic department, and although many of the tests were outsourced, they could still handle a lot of the routine stuff internally, and Grace could call on a wider range of experience than some of her contemporaries in other counties. What she couldn't do was make tests results appear instantaneously.

"What's the latest on Becky Bairstow?" Robin asked when he'd called Pru into his office. The missing London archaeologist had to be top of his priority list.

"There's nothing so far to stop her and our corpse being one and the same. No obvious conflicts of age or hair colour or whatever." The "whatever" would have included scars or tattoos. "We could get some DNA from a relative or compare dental records. Sorry," she added, raising her hand apologetically, "teaching my granny to suck eggs, there. I've been spending too much time recently talking to students on the forensic course at the university. I go into over-explain mode."

"You're forgiven." Robin looked out of the window, at rooftops and scudding clouds, thinking of the person—a worried boyfriend— who'd rung the report in. That wasn't going to be an easy interview. "No other leads on identification?"

"Not so we've heard."

As if on cue, the phone on Robin's desk began to ring. Hearing Grace's cheery tones down the line, when he answered, brightened his day.

"Let me put you on the speakerphone," Robin said. "Save me repeating everything."

"Cool beans." Grace went on to relate that the doctor who'd done the postmortem was dealing with a traffic-accident victim, so they'd have to put up with her initial feedback if they wanted information now. Robin was secretly delighted; Grace told it in layman's terms and had a nose for what was important. She reported that they still had no idea who the girl was, so they might have to do a facial reconstruction if other leads petered out. The teeth would provide a good matchup, though, as she had three crowns and some other fillings.

"Everything suggests she was in her twenties, had never been pregnant, and was placed there between June and October of last year."

"Any indication that she *had* been somewhere else originally?" Robin asked.

"Balance of probability. Sorry to be so vague, but we've got various tests going on and we won't be sure for a while. All those things we used to believe about patterns of blood settling aren't as definitive as we held them to be, but my gut instinct is that she's been moved, in the first few days after death. After rigor mortis passed off and after the face got nibbled a bit."

Robin, watching appreciatively as Pru jotted all of this down, enquired, "Have you identified the cause of death yet?"

"Yep. She'd been hit with that old favourite of crime stories everywhere, the blunt instrument, at least twice, front and back of head. Where the face had suffered some damage, it was hard to see the other blow at first. There's a hint of bruising round the neck, but not enough to cause death, and no obvious indications of much else, including no signs of disease. We're running toxicology tests too, but—again—don't hold your breath. Could just be a simple belting."

"If such things are ever simple." Robin rolled his eyes at Grace's choice of words. She pulled no punches. "Anything in her pockets? A bus ticket or a receipt stuffed away in a corner?"

"No. I suspect they've been completely cleared out. Not even a scrap of jewellery on her. No evidence of recent sexual activity, either, so this doesn't look like a sexual assault that turned nastier, or a night of adventurous fun that went wrong."

Robin didn't think there was anything adventurous—or alluring—in some of the games people played in bed, but in view of the bruising, they had to consider it. He thanked Grace and ended the call.

Pru glanced up from putting in a final full stop. "So, day trip to London?"

"Looks like it, although in an ideal world we'd get the dentistry compared first, just in case it isn't her. But chicken and egg."

Pru nodded. "We won't be able to get the name of the dentist without talking to the relatives, so I guess there's no way of avoiding it. Do you want me to ring the person who reported her missing?"

"No, I'll do that. Unless the statements from the people at Culford villa contain something more promising in terms of an identification."

"Probably too early for that. Ben's collating them, and I think the last few have only just got in. Give him ten minutes."

"That's time enough for a loo break and a coffee."

On Robin's return, he paused at the entrance to the incident room, watching his new team. They didn't exude the same air of quiet purpose that the constables at Stanebridge had, although he'd wait to see their results before judging them. The fact that they stirred into animation as soon as they spotted him wasn't encouraging, but he gave them a smile as he made his way to his own office, which led off the main one. A fresh-faced constable, bearing a pile of paper—he seemed about fifteen, so who knew how young he'd appear to the public—followed him, slipping through the inner office door, which was ajar. Robin had made it plain from the start that he really did have an open-door policy and hoped it would be made use of.

"You wanted an update on these, sir?" the constable asked.

"Yes. Now all the team are back in house, it'll be time to brief them, and if there's anything in those statements I should know about beforehand . . ." He didn't need to add, *I should bloody well know about it.*

"Not so far as I can see. No names of potential victims cropping up. Nobody's noticed anything odd in the last year, either." Ben shrugged. "I haven't gone through all of these twice over yet, as I've focussed on getting an initial impression. Clare, who you took a statement from yesterday, is by far the best informed, as you'd imagine, although she didn't have a lot to add to what we know."

Robin nodded. She'd been friendly, obliging—providing a comprehensive list of everyone involved with the site and thereby facilitating a quick start to the legwork—but she'd not been able to shed any light on anything to do with the burial, apart from the information about when the play area had been dug over. It sounded like the volunteers had been equally unenlightening.

"Nothing catching your eye?"

"No. I'm not turning up any inconsistencies apart from what you might expect with the natural vagaries of memory." Ben grinned. "One of the volunteer guides swore the Community Payback people had been up to no good, but everyone else said they were very helpful. Sian something or other—she's a local librarian who covers on holidays so Clare can have time off—said they were absolute sweeties."

Robin took an appraising look at the constable. He was still sussing out his team, working out their strengths and weaknesses. You always needed someone who could go through piles of stuff without getting bored and missing a crucial detail. Would Ben—with his strangely avuncular approach, appreciating the nature of the people behind the words of their statements—be the person for that role? "Did you think all the statements would tally?"

Ben narrowed his eyes. "Would it sound daft if I said I'd be worried if they did? Agree one hundred percent, I mean."

"Not daft at all." That reflected Robin's viewpoint. "Tell me more."

The young constable visibly bloomed under the endorsement from his new boss. "Do you watch football, sir?"

"Yes, although I prefer rugby."

Ben, clearly wrong-footed by having chosen the wrong sport, quickly rallied. "Same thing applies. Four people watch the same game and they all remember it a bit differently, especially when you get into why people did whatever they did or whether they played well overall. If I had four people who agreed down to the last detail, I'd think they'd prepared their stories in advance."

"So would I. You carry on with those statements, and then we'll see if we can find you something a bit juicier to follow up." Robin left his chair, clapped Ben's shoulder, and set off to brief his team.

The main office, now the incident room, had a display board dominated by all the usual trimmings of photos, locations, and time.

He'd often wondered how much use the things were, apart from acting as a visual aid when addressing people; did they really help solve a case—a constant reminder of the victim and the justice owed to them—or did they just become wallpaper?

Robin shared what he'd heard from Grace, listened to what—very little—else had turned up, and let Pru both pin up the picture of the missing woman, Becky Bairstow, and relate the meagre details they knew about her.

"If no better bet has turned up by late afternoon, I'll make arrangements to see the boyfriend today." Robin scanned the faces in the room. "Meanwhile, we carry on eliminating other possible identifications. Any questions?"

"Cowdrey's going to be delighted when he comes back off his holidays to find this on his plate." The glee in Constable Alison Cosgrove's voice was unmistakable. Chief Superintendent Cowdrey had come over from Stanebridge after the Abbotston night of the long knives, in order to steady the ship and root out any existing pockets of less-than-exemplary practice. While Robin was ninety-five percent sure they'd got rid of all the truly rotten apples, the not-trying-hard-enough atmosphere, added to the residual mistrust and sense of feeling hard done by, would take longer to rectify. The most difficult part of any job was changing attitudes.

"Chief Superintendent Cowdrey to you. Or *sir*," Robin snapped. "I don't want to hear different. And he *will* be delighted if he finds you lot have got off your arses and are putting your backs into things. By which I mean all of you," he added, eyes once more scanning their embarrassed faces, "not just Cosgrove."

Robin ignored the faint rumble of dissatisfaction around the room. He didn't mind if people didn't like him, but that was a privilege to be earned. Time-wasters and time-servers didn't have it, and sitting round on their arses doing sod all earned them nothing.

"Yes, sir," Cosgrove muttered at last, and Robin left them to it. He planned to take Pru back to the site, to get a better feeling for the area and talk to the contractors who'd removed the play area, before dealing with the Becky Bairstow thread. They'd get a decent coffee en route—better than the one Robin had got from the station machine—so the caffeine could perk up their brains.

He'd just pushed his chair back from his desk when Ben, eyes as bright as Campbell's when he'd found a piece of cake under the breakfast bar, poked his head round the office door again. If Ben's acumen matched his enthusiasm and willingness to please, something might be afoot.

"I may have saved you a trip to London, sir. To see Becky Bairstow's boyfriend."

"If you have, you'll get my gold-star-of-the-day award."

"You'll make my head swell, sir." Ben, obviously trying to hide a grin, cast a glance over his shoulder at his colleagues, more than one of whom was eyeing him warily. "We've already got her dental records. Or at least we will have when they get here. I've been running a few checks, and a body turned up in January in Nottingham—some backwater of the Trent, I think—which they thought was her. So the Nottinghamshire CID spoke to Andy Hales, who's the boyfriend, got her dentist's name, and were able to eliminate her."

"Good work." And what a relief.

"It will be when the records get here. Apparently they only had a paper copy—the dentist was a bit of a dinosaur and a stickler to boot, so either didn't have, or wouldn't send, an electronic record."

Robin, aware there was a problem which wasn't being made clear, said, "But that wouldn't stop the Nottinghamshire boys and girls scanning the paper and sending the scan, surely? What's the hold up?"

"They can't find the records." Ben rolled his eyes. "They think they've been misfiled. I got them to give me the dentist's contact details, but I haven't managed to get hold of him yet, either. I'll keep trying."

Robin nodded, appreciative of an officer who didn't just bring problems, but engineered solutions. "Okay. Keep me informed. Good job."

"Ta." Ben slipped back through the door, before his head became too large to get through it. Robin gratefully got his gear in order and waited for Pru to return from the ladies' loo. Andy Hales could wait until they knew whether they'd found his girlfriend—meanwhile, they'd see what else Culford could tell them.

Sam Pryce, the contractor's representative, was already at the villa site when they arrived at the car park, chatting to a uniformed policewoman who was both holding all the access keys to the site and keeping rubberneckers at bay. Pryce appeared to be happy enough passing the time of day with her, although Charlie Howarth, sitting in his car with a face like thunder, seemed less than impressed at events.

"Pru!" he yelled from the window as she and Robin got out of the car. "This officer won't let me on the site. Can you work the oracle for me?"

"I'm afraid not. We've shut the site down entirely so we can go over it with a fine-toothed comb." Pru sounded friendly but firm. "Didn't you get my email?"

"Yes, but I thought you'd make an exception." Howarth's unctuous smile got Robin's fists twitching.

"No exceptions, sorry," he snapped. "Why do you need to get in?"

"I left some paperwork there, and now I need it. Head like a sieve."

Easy enough to test the truth of that statement. "Tell us where you left it, and we'll get it for you."

"Not sure. Either in the main office at the villa or where the diggers had their bolthole. Big blue file." Howarth was out of the car, as though he intended to keep them company.

Robin could be incredibly unhelpful if he wanted, making a case for not interfering with anything until all the forensic work was done, but Howarth would have to be incredibly thick not to see that he was being unnecessarily obstructive. Time had passed and any subtle clues would surely have been trampled under a parade of feet or been swept away into the bin months ago. He'd offer to get the file—assuming it existed—and he'd have a quick look through it as well.

"I'll fetch it if I can find it. Wait here, please."

With a glance and a raise of the eyebrows at Pru, Robin set off to introduce them to Pryce and obtain clearance from Grace to visit the site. He left his sergeant to get the interview with Pryce going, then went to the main office, where he was amazed to discover that there was a big blue file on the desk. He flicked through the contents, but they all appeared to be financial: a pile of invoices along with some notes about Culford villa and its profitability. Income from school trips and the like was matched against outgoings, the bottom line being that the place was struggling to break even without external funding, none of which was a surprise.

He took the file back to the car park, where Howarth was chomping at the bit, and returned it with a smile and a slightly acid, "No wonder you wanted that back."

"Eh?" Howarth flinched. "What do you mean?"

"I couldn't help seeing the tabs on the file dividers." Robin pointed at the one labelled *finance/confidential*. "Not the sort of thing you'd want people poking about in."

"No, very true." Howarth forced a laugh. "Saved my bacon. Thanks." He held out a limp hand for Robin to shake, then retreated to his big flash car. Robin narrowed his eyes: that reaction had been interesting, to say the least. Was it simply that Howarth would have got into trouble for leaving confidential information around, or was there something else in the file he didn't want people to know about? If there was, it hadn't been obvious. And where did Howarth get the money to buy a Merc?

Robin rejoined Pru, who brought him up to date on the discussion with Pryce. He'd been with the company for years, which was why he'd been appointed to help the police, and could talk about all the work they'd done at the site. The play area had gone in ten years previously, as part of a campaign to make the villa a better tourist attraction, a plan that had included a more effective perimeter fence—to ensure people paid for the privilege of seeing the walls and mosaics—and a café. The latter had closed following a disastrous outbreak of food poisoning, had never reopened, and had been demolished not long after.

"That would be two years ago." Pryce's brow crinkled. "They've got a fridge for soft drinks in the shop, and they sell snacks as well, although these days a properly run café can be a bit of a gold mine."

Robin nodded. He'd spotted a line about shop sales on the accounts overview, and a pencilled note against it—there'd been several notes on the page—that simply said, *Café?* so maybe Howarth had been thinking of reopening a catering facility. "We heard it was Health and Safety that got the play area shut as well."

Pryce, slowly shaking his head, gave a frown of distaste. "Only after the vandals got at it. The equipment was fine up until then.

This place went through a phase when youngsters used to love climbing over the fence and getting up to all sorts of mischief here."

"The swines." Pru frowned. "Why do people want to spoil things for others?"

"Beats me. They'd plead boredom, I suppose, but I call it selfishness. Anyhow, what with the damage they did and the glass and God knows what else they left around—let alone the damage they kept doing to the fence—we decided to clear the area and leave it." A sly grin crossed his face. "May have encouraged the nettles and brambles to grow, while we were at it. Cooled their ardour a smidge."

"When was all this?"

"Eighteen months ago." Pryce scanned the site. "I'd love to see the county make a real go of this place. Maybe if these students turn up a bathhouse, then it'll kick a bit of life into the attraction. But Howarth"—he jabbed his thumb towards the car park, even though the man concerned had left—"faffs about. The local sites need a vision, but he plays about at things."

"A case of 'don't tap it, whack it,' would you say?" Robin asked.

"Along those lines. But he doesn't want to speculate to accumulate, to use another cliché. Here, let me show you something." Pryce led them to a spot ten metres away from where the body had been found. "They get a lot of the university students working up here, and not just digging. One of them did a project about viability of heritage sites, focussing on this place. Bright girl, thoughtful. She emailed me about some of the technical stuff. Sent me a copy of her finished work and it was full of good ideas, with some innovative suggestions about funding. I spoke to Howarth about them, but he wasn't interested."

"Why was that?"

"He had a dozen reasons. Most of them based on this lass not being a professional and how, if she lived in the real world, she'd understand what the problems really were. Which was a load of crap, if you'll excuse the expression."

Robin suppressed a grin. Pryce seemed to possess the same unimpressed view of Howarth as he did. "What's your take on it?"

"He didn't want to be shown up by what he regarded as some chit of a girl. And he's cagey about this site. Like it's his particular baby." Pryce drew his finger through the air. "I suggested we could knock up a viewing platform right here for the public so they could watch the diggers. People are interested in that sort of thing. *Time Team* effect."

"Not only that. Think of every time somebody's digging a hole in the road—they always attract onlookers."

"Natural curiosity, sir," Pru agreed.

"Exactly. Only Howarth wouldn't have it. Said it lowered the tone of what was an important archaeological excavation." Pryce winced. "Made it like something off reality television."

Funny how the more Robin learned about Howarth, the less he liked him. "Maybe it's just as well you didn't, given what happened."

"True, but Howarth couldn't have been expecting that, could he? Or maybe he was, do you think?" Pryce echoed Robin's thoughts on the matter. "Although if he knew there was anything dodgy about the site, why allow the dig in the first place?"

"What do you know about Howarth and his connection to Culford?" Robin wasn't going to get into idle speculation with a witness, but if the remarks about Howarth were based on other than just dislike or mistrust, he wanted to hear them.

Pryce spread his hands. "Not a lot, apart from the fact he seems to . . . overdo his official role, if that makes sense. When we've been on-site, he seems always to be hanging around. Even out of hours."

Robin gave Pru an encouraging glance, urging her to take up the questioning.

She picked up her cue. "Out of hours?"

"Yep. One of the blokes I work with dropped his mobile in the car park but didn't realise until he was halfway home. When he brought the van back, it was well past the usual closing time, but Howarth's car was still here. You can't help but notice it. Bloody great Mercedes. Not sure how he affords that on council wages."

"I had the same thought." Robin rolled his eyes.

"Maybe he's got a rich aunty." Pryce didn't look as though he believed that.

"Maybe. When was this?"

"Sometime last summer. I'll talk to Frank and get back to you."

"Thanks for that." Robin made a note to follow the point up with Howarth. "Just one more thing. Do you know anything about the Community Payback people who came to work here?"

"A bit. Why?"

"We've heard conflicting stories." Robin left it there, not wanting to lead the witness.

"As far as I'm concerned, they worked a damn sight harder than some of the people we pay do. I dropped in at the start and the finish, and they'd done a really good job of clearing out stuff. They took down a mass of brambles and stripped the ivy off the fence." Pryce nodded favourably.

"They cleared this area too?"

"Yes. They— Ah, I'm with you. You're wondering if one of them could have something to do with the dead woman? Preparing the ground, quite literally?"

"We have to consider that." Even if it seemed supremely unlikely. How thick would you have to be to return to where you'd very visibly dug over a piece of ground in order to hide a body there? Unless it was a brass-necked example of a double bluff.

"I guess so. But loads of people saw those lads at work. Just about anyone who visited the site would have noticed what was going on and could have made a note to take advantage of the situation."

"Or remembered it afterwards," Pru chipped in, echoing Robin's thoughts.

They concluded the interview with the usual question about anything to add, Robin not expecting much else to be gained, but he was wrong.

"There is one thing I thought of, on the way up here, although I don't see how it relates. Do you know about the letters to the paper?"

"What letters?"

"Anonymous ones, to the *Culdover Echo*. They started couple of years back, and cropped up again again last autumn, all of them saying that people shouldn't be digging at the villa because it was a sacred site. That if they poked around here, it would come back to haunt them."

Haunt them to the extent of murder? "Any idea who wrote— Sorry, you said they were anonymous."

Pryce grinned. "Yeah. I suppose the paper might have a contact address for them, although the reaction from other correspondents suggested they thought this 'sacred site' stuff was a load of tripe.

I'd agree. Nobody gave us particular instructions about this site, and they would have done if it were special, believe me."

"You're probably right." Evidently, any suspicions Pryce had centred around the site director; still, Robin would get on the trail of those letters.

Once he and Pru were on their own, Robin voiced his concerns about the flash car. "Does Howarth really have a rich aunty?"

"Nah, sir. Ordinary family. He'll be the first of them to have a Merc." Pru wrinkled her nose. "Something fishy going on, do you reckon?"

"That's what my nose tells me, but whether it's murder . . ." Robin shrugged. "He's been hanging around out of hours, he has access to the site, and he's surely one of the people who could hide a body there."

"Bound to know all the wrinkles," Pru agreed, "but why mess on your own doorstep, particularly if you know the area's going to be dug? And if you'd already buried the body before the decision was made to look for the bathhouse, why not move the body from the shallow grave in the interim?"

"Exactly. And everything we say about Howarth could apply to Pryce, or another one of the contractor team, or the person in charge of the Community Payback team, even." This wasn't a closed-room mystery, where the murder had to have occurred in a small area within a small window of time. They had no definite time or place of death, nor a name for the victim or any hint of a motive.

It was going to be a hell of a case to solve.

Chapter Four

Here we go again.

Adam took a deep breath as he entered the staffroom on Tuesday morning before lessons started. The place was already awash with talk of the murder, including wild speculation about who the victim might be and why somebody would bury a body on the Culford site. He made himself a coffee, listening in on the chat only to discover that there were a few amateur archaeology enthusiasts among the parents. One of them had apparently brought his metal detector into the school to show the children how it worked just the previous term, and they'd asked him to make regular visits, so there would likely be some uneasiness among the school community even if their connection to the murder was several steps removed.

Jim Rashford, the headteacher, hovered around being both soothing and sympathetic to all and sundry. Although Adam hadn't yet got to know the largely female staff team, he suspected they'd be naturally concerned for their own safety, especially in the early days when nobody really knew what was going on, and whether there would be a risk to them. Any similar parental anxiety could easily transfer itself to their children.

Just before they dispersed to their classes, Rashford called for quiet, reminded his staff members not to discuss the discovery of the body where the pupils might overhear, then encouraged them to let him know if they noticed children showing signs of upset. He'd dealt with something similar in his previous school, and a string of nice, reassuring whole-school assemblies and the odd forceful reminder to parents to watch what *they* said could make all the difference.

Adam swallowed hard, took another deep breath, and made the announcement he'd been putting together in his head while driving in, just in case it was needed. "I think you'd better know that my partner is in charge of the investigation. That doesn't mean you can't discuss it while I'm around, but it does mean you can't pump me for inside info." He forced a grin, then pressed on. Better to get everything in the open. "*He's* got experience of tackling murder cases, and a one hundred percent clear-up rate, so it's in safe hands."

There were one or two surprised expressions—and one of distinct horror—swiftly hidden among those present, but generally Adam's revelations were taken well.

"It's like having Cully from *Midsomer Murders* here!" Dilys, one of the learning-support assistants, a blue-rinsed woman old enough to be Adam's mother and someone he'd already identified when he'd come for his interview as being a real asset to the children's learning, gave him a wink.

"So long as Adam doesn't cook like Joyce Barnaby and poison us all at the PTA barbecue, we'll be fine." Jim, with a smile at Adam, gently set his staff about their business proper. The pair of them were due to spend the morning in a conflab about rapidly improving teaching standards in the school, something which would involve Adam working alongside a number of the teachers to improve their lessons. It wasn't an enviable task, but somebody had to do it. The meeting in Jim's office would be followed by a learning walk round the school, which was making a few of the staff, especially some of the long-in-the-tooth ones, more agitated than the talk of murder.

"That was a brave admission," Jim remarked as they reached the office and he closed the door. "Were you 'out' at Lindenshaw?"

"Not at first. But it's hard to stay 'in' when you get spotted walking along a towpath holding hands with the policeman who was all over the school like a rash only a few months before." Adam took his seat. "Your governors all seem to know about the murder there. As you'll remember from my interview."

Jim rolled his eyes. "I have no idea why he raised that. I've never felt more like murdering him. Sorry." He raised his hand. "Poor choice of words, given the situation."

"Poor but probably apt." It had been a sticky moment, the then-chair of governors asking Adam outright what it had been like having somebody killed while on school premises. Adam had taken the question at face value and described dealing with the impact on pupils and staff, the practicalities of keeping the media off the site, and working with the police, but he'd clocked the headteacher's annoyance at the interview going so wildly off script.

"I wondered if it was one of those trick questions," he continued. "You know the sort of malarkey. 'What would you do if you got to school and found two teachers were stuck in a queue on the motorway, an irate parent was in reception, and the headteacher couldn't be contacted?'"

"I'll make a note of that one. Good question." Jim grinned. "Actually, your answer to being interrogated about the murder was one of the things that tipped the balance in your favour. We had a strong field and you were neck and neck with that woman who was relocating from London. I insisted we throw her a curveball question as well, in the interests of fairness, but she didn't think on her feet like you did."

"Not sure what to say to that, except 'thank goodness.'" Adam had known it had been close, but not so skin of the teeth.

"You're clearly good at dealing with the unexpected. Well done for getting the bit about your partner . . ."

"Robin," Adam replied, to the obvious, if unspoken, invitation.

"Getting Robin's job out in the open. The longer you didn't say something about him, the harder it would be. The whole kit and caboodle."

Adam hid a shudder at the echo of his conversation with Robin the previous evening about missing persons. His discomfort soon turned to puzzlement as Jim began to chuckle. "What's so funny?"

"I was about to say Jane and I should have you over to dinner so you can meet her brother and his partner, who's also male, but then I realised that was daft, if not downright offensive. Labelling you as probably wanting to meet each other because of that one common feature."

"Thanks for that as well. It happens too often." Adam shook his head. "Like we're Freemasons or whatever."

"Our ex-chair of governors was a Freemason. Didn't he give you the dodgy handshake?" Jim got out his files, signalling a return to proper work. "But I would like you—and Robin—to meet Jane, anyway. She's a Newfoundland fan."

A pastime of taking Campbell on long walks had been mentioned on Adam's application, and commented on during the interview. "Then she has great taste. Is *her* cooking better than Joyce Barnaby's? Or are you the household chef?"

"You'll have to come round to find out."

They got their heads down over the school improvement plan and the deputy's role in delivering it, although something that had been mentioned in the staffroom nagged at the back of Adam's brain. Amateur archaeologists among the parents? Was this case going to drag him in too? If so, perhaps better to take the bull by the horns, just as he'd done that morning. Whether Robin would welcome it or not was a moot point, but his conscience persuaded him that if it helped to get the case sorted sooner rather than later, it had to be done.

By lunchtime it was apparent that the older children had heard about the dead body. Years five and six had been to Culford on a school trip when they were in year four, so their ears had evidently pricked up when it was mentioned on the news or by their parents. Jim called a special assembly for the upper school that weaved expertly between the proper concern for the pupils' sensibilities and reassuring them that they were under no threat. Bad things did happen in the world, but that was why they had people like the police to keep them safe.

One of the year six girls—Sophie Baxter, who'd asked where Adam had taught previously—lingered behind afterwards, obviously wanting to talk to them. Jim beckoned Adam over with a subtle tip of the head so he could be involved.

"My dad's a metal detectorist, sir." She fiddled with her cardigan cuff.

"Yes, I remember, Sophie. He came to visit us before the Easter holidays, Mr. Matthews, to show the pupils the tricks of his trade." Jim's soothing tones clearly eased the girl's anxiety.

"Yes. He was great." Her anxiety couldn't stem her obvious pride. "It's just . . . I don't want to get anyone into trouble, but you told us at the end of last term that we had to do the right thing wherever we could."

"Well remembered. We had a series of assemblies about the Good Samaritan," Jim explained to Adam, who nodded. The diocese had been encouraging all the schools to explore the story. "So what do you want to tell us, Sophie?"

"Dad was saying last night that he was worried. He only joined the detectorists club when we moved here, and now he says he wishes he hadn't. Too much infighting." Sophie looked about her, as though checking whether they could be overheard.

"Sophie's family moved into Culdover in January," Jim clarified for Adam's benefit, and thereby possibly for Robin's; the headteacher was nobody's fool and he'd recognised they could be steering into tricky waters. "Who are you afraid of getting into trouble? Your dad?"

"No." Sophie appeared outraged at the suggestion. "The other people in the club. Some of them have children here. My friends."

Adam put on his best reassuring smile and tried to ignore the voice that said Sophie's dad had also told her about the Lindenshaw murders. Surely it was local gossip fodder and signified nothing? "I'm certain the police understand those sorts of things and can deal with them sensitively. They were at school themselves once."

"I suppose so." She still didn't appear convinced.

"They do understand how hard it can be," Adam assured her. Robin had experienced a rough time when he was this girl's age. He knew how cruel children could be and how families could manipulate them to fight *their* fights, so he'd do his best not to let her get embroiled. "Tell us what's concerning you, and we'll pass it on to the right people. They won't let on that it came from you."

"Thank you." Sophie produced a nervous, horsey grin, her face not yet grown to accommodate root teeth properly. She looked terribly young and vulnerable, like Robin must have done when he was being bullied. "Mum told Dad to go to the police himself, but he says there's nothing to tell them."

Adam raised his eyebrows. "Your mother clearly doesn't agree."

"Yes. She says the police would want to know that the detectorists club had a right old barney with the archaeologists, even if Dad hasn't got to the bottom of what it's about. He says that they all hate each other, on top of being a cross between *The Big Bang Theory* and *Coronation Street*." Sophie frowned. "I'm not sure what that means."

"Don't puzzle over it. We'll tell it to the police and they'll sort it out." Jim gave Adam a sidelong glance, obviously suggesting that he was the one who should pass on the information. "Let's go and get you a 'helping hand' sticker. You've earned it."

Adam returned to the staffroom, where he had some data to finish analysing, although his thoughts about the case kept interfering with his thoughts about assessing maths skills. If Sophie's family had only moved to Culdover recently, that should mean they couldn't be complicit in the crime, but that wouldn't apply to the rest of this detectorists club, or any other parents with a connection to the villa site. He forced his mind back onto the job; the sooner he worked through this stuff, the sooner he could ring Robin and see what he made of things.

Fate, which clearly wasn't satisfied with having connected Adam and his school to the latest murder, decided to intervene with his plans in the form of a lorry shedding its load outside the school just when the pupils were due to go home. By the time they'd assembled the children on the school field, marshalled traffic—the school run had caused gridlock—and got everything back to normal, Adam decided he'd simply save the news for when he got home.

As the afternoon had worn on, the potential importance of the information had appeared to diminish, although a discussion with Dilys over a post-crisis cuppa gave him pause, as well as giving him something juicier to report. Still, fallings-out happened all the time, didn't they? They didn't inevitably lead to murder, surely?

Adam was first home, grateful not to see Anderson's car already in the drive. He'd a bundle of things to read through, the incident with the lorry having put everything back, but those could wait until he'd had a bite to eat. Robin had texted to say he'd be home at a reasonable time, so Adam wouldn't have to make awkward how-do-we-not-mention-Helen conversation with their guest once he arrived.

Adam had barely got tea out of the freezer and into the oven when Robin came through the front door, greeting Campbell before looking for Adam, who'd returned to spreading his paperwork all over the table in the lounge.

"Glad to see you home in one piece. I heard about the lorry." Robin ruffled his hair.

"It was like the M25 on Friday evening. Total chaos until your mob turned up and started organising people. I mightn't have got home until Friday."

They shared a kiss before Robin went upstairs to change his clothes, and Adam headed off to make them a cold drink and get ready for the daily debrief, albeit that wasn't quite the debriefing he'd like to get involved in. The sound of Anderson's car pulling up, then the arrival of the man himself, fiddling about opening the front door with the spare key, put an end to all chances of smooching.

Once Robin was inside a clean shirt and outside of a glass of diet cola, and they were both sitting in the garden enjoying the evening sun, he tapped Adam's arm. "You look thoughtful. Out with it."

"Out with what?"

"Whatever you're trying not to tell me. Or want to tell me, but not quite yet. Even Campbell knows you're hiding something."

"Is it tattooed on my forehead?" Adam smiled, then knocked back the rest of his cola—this detective business was thirsty work. "You know the way your cases seem determined to drag me in? No matter how much I want to keep out of them?"

"Part of me wants to say 'I don't want to hear this.'" Robin rubbed his temples. "But go on."

"The staff were talking about Culford Roman villa today. Not only the safety element. The two year-four classes are due to go there on a trip in a fortnight, and the teachers were getting their knickers in a twist about whether it would be cancelled and how they'd explain it to the kids."

"That's no surprise. Everybody in Culdover's probably talking about it."

"Yeah, it's all over the playground too, so Jim held an assembly about it this afternoon. Cleared the air."

"And?"

"And it turns out that one of the pupils is the daughter of a local metal detectorist."

"Oh yes? Working on the Culdover site?"

"No, I don't think so. It seems like there's history—excuse the pun—there." Adam rolled his eyes. "A bust-up between the detectorist community and someone else."

"That could be useful information. It's the first hint we've had of anything being awry up at the villa."

"I think it's more awry in the town." He gave a résumé of what Sophie had told him, including the bit about *The Big Bang Theory* and *Coronation Street*, as it had seemed picturesque and was probably accurate. "I had a word with Dilys, who must have worked at the school since the Romans sent their kids there, and she says there are two groups in Culdover: the metal detectorists and the amateur archaeologists. There was a big falling out between them just before Sophie's family moved here. Maybe the same sort of time that your victim was buried."

"Right." Robin nodded. "Thanks for that. I'll get onto the trail first thing. We can set him"—he jerked his thumb in the direction of Anderson's room—"to work this evening. Earn his keep by getting onto Google and seeing if he can find a contact name. Assuming these societies are up to date enough to be contactable via the web?"

"Hey, not everybody in the sticks is a techno-Neanderthal. They even have electricity in Culdover, believe it or not."

"And they know how to use it? You amaze me. Hello!" Robin waved as Anderson appeared at the kitchen door. "Fancy a drink?"

Anderson eyed the cola bottles, then shook his head. "I'm okay, thanks."

Adam pointed at a chair, encouraging their guest to pull it over. "There's a cottage pie in the oven, Stuart, if that works for you."

"Perfect." Anderson plonked himself onto the chair, flicked through his phone messages, sighed, and put the device away again. If the pantomime had been for his hosts' benefit, the message got through loud and clear.

"Any news from Helen?" Adam asked.

"No. Deafening silence."

Robin put down his drink with a *thump*. "Why don't you take her a big bunch of flowers and a box of chocolates? Then tell her you're a total bloody idiot who doesn't know his arse from his elbow, and if she'd only tell you what you've been such a prat about, you'd apologise fifty times over."

"Do you think that would work?" Anderson shifted in his seat. "It sounds too easy. I think she'd prefer I walked over hot coals."

Adam, having spotted the signs that his lover was getting ratty at Anderson's fecklessness, chipped in with what he hoped was a helpful, "Can't you have a word with one of her friends, or somebody in her family? She might have vented to one of them, and you could get an inkling of what she's angry about."

Anderson winced. "Been there, done that. A few years back when she got miffed that I'd forgotten the anniversary of the day we met."

If that was the sort of thing that caused ructions, no wonder the sergeant felt he was walking on eggshells. Before Adam could make any soothing noises, however, Robin snapped, "Oh, for goodness' sake. Talk about mountains from molehills."

"Look, she was going through a stressful time at work, and everything was getting on her nerves. She didn't talk to me for two days, and when the dam broke I got a right rollicking, not just for the original offence—for which I'd apologised and produced said choccies—but for going behind her back and talking to Rosie, her best mate." Anderson leaned forward, head in hands. "I'm damned if I do and damned if I don't."

To Adam's surprise, Robin moved across to give Anderson a hug, the first time Adam had ever seen more than a handshake or a friendly punch pass between them.

"Sorry to be a pain. You've got enough on your plate." Anderson took a deep breath, clapped Robin's shoulder, and disentangled himself. "Media briefing tomorrow?"

"I was trying to put that out of my mind." Robin groaned. "Still not got a lot to tell them. I'm going to state that we have a possible identity for the dead woman, but that at this stage we're not ruling anyone or anything in or out. Ask for the public's help in working towards something conclusive, albeit without making ourselves sound like ineffective wimps."

Anderson nodded. "Whatever I can do to help, let me know."

"Funny you should say that." Robin explained the task he had lined up. "Find me a contact and you can have an extra helping of cottage pie."

"It's a deal. I'll do it now. Take my mind off . . . you know." Anderson grimaced, then headed back into the house.

"Poor bloke," Adam said once he was out of earshot. "I can't help feeling sorry for him. He's like a rudderless ship."

"Yes. He's not his usual ebullient self, is he?" Robin rubbed Campbell's head. "But don't feel too sorry for him. We don't want a permanent lodger, do we?" He glanced over at Adam. "This is my safe place. Am I being a pain in the arse to him if I don't want him—or anyone—sharing it for too long?"

Adam winced. "You're a pain in the arse about plenty of things, but not this. We'll give him till tomorrow, and if there's no sign of progress, we'd better start the marriage guidance."

"Deal."

But would it prove harder to mend Anderson's relationship or find the Culford villa killer?

Chapter Five

R obin ploughed through Wednesday morning, checking in with his team before addressing the press about Becky Bairstow and neatly avoiding answering their inaner questions. He tried to contact Howarth to talk about the late-night site visit he'd made, but the man was at a conference in Paris for a couple of days and Robin didn't want to tackle this by phone, wanting to see his face when he was confronted.

The time spent in the incident room was less productive, all the strands of the investigation being brought together but yielding little that was new. The lack of properties in close vicinity to Culford villa meant that house-to-house enquiries had produced very little, apart from vague mentions of vehicles using the lane to the site at odd times. The usual lines of enquiry also seemed to be drawing a blank.

Ben had talked to the editor at the *Culdover Echo* to get an address for the writer of the anonymous letters, but his initial success had turned out to be a bit of a red herring. The house in question had been demolished between the dates when the two sets of letters were written—a fact not picked up by an overstretched editorial team. The name they'd been given would no doubt turn out to be fictitious, the unnamed writer clearly having wanted to preserve that anonymity when they'd moved house, perhaps as a result of some of the reactions to the first batch of letters. Whoever it was wouldn't have enjoyed an accusation of being a lunatic.

"Right. A . . . couple of contacts of mine gave me some interesting gen on Culdover." Robin decided not to mention to his team that both Adam and Anderson had come up trumps; that would likely cause more resentment. "There are two societies in Culdover: one for archaeologists and one for metal detectorists."

"Are either of them involved in the university dig, sir?" Ben asked.

"I don't believe so, but Pru and I are meeting a contact for the detectorist society later, so we'll find out. There's been some sort of a fallout between the groups. Ander— And some of that's been fought out online." He'd been about to say that Anderson had dug up the dirt. "There are discussions in which a number of the comments have been deleted and odd references made." He stuck a Post-it note with *If we want doors opened, we'd better stick to doing it ourselves* onto the board.

"Any idea what that means?" Alison asked with a barely hidden sneer.

Pru looked daggers at the constable. "That's what we're off to find out."

Robin encouraged everyone to keep going because they were certain to get a break soon, although he wasn't sure he believed that himself. He distributed some routine jobs, including getting Ben to identify and make contact with the student who'd done the dissertation about the villa, then set off with Pru to talk to the contact Anderson had turned up for the Culdover detectorist society.

Harry Tuckton—neat, bespectacled, wearing a tatty leather jacket and incongruous bow tie—resembled one of those middle-aged academics (or vicars) who tried to look trendy. He greeted Robin very correctly, treated Pru with exaggerated if somewhat wary gallantry, then offered them a chair. They'd arranged to meet in the foyer of the engineering company where he worked, out on the new industrial estate at the back of Abbotston. That openness suggested he had nothing to hide—or was pretending he had nothing to hide—and he certainly gave off an air of being pleased to help the police, perhaps benefiting from some sort of cachet of doing his civic duty.

They went through the introductions, and then Robin got stuck straight into the questions. "Have you had anything to do with the excavations at the Culford villa site?"

"No." Tuckton almost snorted, clearly affronted at the fact. "It seems like none of the local 'amateurs'"—he made the speech-mark signs with his fingers while deepening his disdainful look—"can be trusted with the place. So they bring in a busload of inexperienced youngsters who are probably high on heroin and leave them to make a mess of things. Such a waste."

Robin, who'd not got that impression of the students, who'd seemed eminently sensible, totally sober, and very knowledgeable, wondered if Tuckton had actually met the people he was so quick to insult. "What's a waste?"

"Not making the most of our local knowledge. We have extensive maps of the local area, showing where items have turned up and into what eras they fall. We haven't been allowed on the villa site, but we've conducted metal-detecting surveys of several of the local fields and dug test pits in a number of gardens, to put context to our finds."

Tuckton might have an understandable grievance; that appeared, to Robin's inexpert eyes, to be helpful information. "Didn't they want those?"

Tuckton shrugged. "They took them, but I doubt whether they've made any use of them. They'll have their own detectorists, I suppose, whom they'll trust more than they trust us. Mind you"—his mouth crinkled into the hint of a smile—"in the case of the Culdover Archaeological Society, you'd be wise to have no confidence in them. Might as well get advice from the Culdover Allotment Committee, because at least they get some sort of useful output from their digging." Tuckton smiled at his joke.

"We understand they—the Culdover archaeologists—meet at the Peatcutter's Arms." Pru, sharing more fruits of Anderson's labours, smiled sweetly. "Do you meet there as well?"

"No." Tuckton's own smile vanished.

Her eyes widened, a picture of ingenuous ignorance. "Are the detectorists not part of that organisation?"

Tuckton, face drawn tight, sniffed again. "No. We once associated with them, having joint meetings and the like, but not anymore. Not since The Incident with The Woman. Now we drink at the White Hart. Proper beer. Proper food. No deconstructed bouillabaisse on a bed of whelk droppings."

Robin and Pru shared a glance. What can of worms had they opened?

"I take it you don't get on with the archaeological-society members?" Robin remarked innocently.

"You take it correctly." Tuckton remained thin lipped. "All connections between us have been severed."

"Why?"

"As I said, because of The Incident. The Woman. We'd had our doubts about them before that, and we certainly couldn't trust them afterwards."

"The woman? Irene Adler?" Pru's flush revealed her immediate regret about making the quip, but Robin's thoughts had gone down the same lines. God forbid there was some sort of Sherlock Holmes element to muddy the waters. The works of Arthur Conan Doyle produced their fair share of nutty enthusiasts.

"That's not funny, Sergeant." Tuckton drew himself up to his full five foot five, which was still three inches shorter than Pru and lost some of its effect as they were seated. "We were infiltrated, and I don't use that word lightly, by an imposter. A female, and please note that I don't say 'lady', member of the Cads and Scoundrels."

"Cads and Scoundrels?"

"CAS. Culdover Archaeological Society." Tuckton smirked at what he clearly thought was a brilliant play on words. Robin could think of stronger nouns for both C and S, but either the Culdover Detectorists thought they were being daring enough or Tuckton was bowdlerising the expression for Pru's benefit. The quickly hidden grin on his sergeant's face suggested she was having similar thoughts.

"You'd better tell us all about this incident." Pru's manner was at its most pacifying. "It could be important."

Tuckton fluffed up like a gamecock at her interest. "We used to work closely together, CD and CAS, if you're happy for me to use the acronyms."

Robin nodded. Better them than the excruciating nicknames.

"There are many local sites still to be explored properly," Tuckton continued, "with modern techniques, not just the villa itself. If only we didn't have distractions—distractions like Lydia Oliver."

"We're listening." Robin nodded; he'd been half expecting Tuckton to say The Woman was named Becky Bairstow, so he was now rapidly re-evaluating where the interview was going. There was clearly a flood of information Tuckton felt the need to discharge, so better to simply let that happen.

"She joined us last summer, just after we started having extra get-togethers away from the CAS. We had business we wanted to discuss that there never seemed to be the opportunity for at our joint meetings. Too many people wanted to squeeze the metal-detection side of things out. Said it wasn't proper archaeology." Tuckton shook his head. "Lydia was rather a breath of fresh air at first. Very up to date. Had some modern tweeter account called Trowelgirl or something."

Robin noted the possible Twitter handle and smiled encouragingly.

"She wasn't the world's greatest detectorist, but I suppose I have to say she was a productive member of the society. Up to a point. I mean, she helped us get to grips with social media, but it was at a heavy price."

Robin took a punt, based on a note in the witness's voice and the look in his eye. "Was she pretty?"

"One might say so. In a rather flashy way." The admission seemed to cost Tuckton a lot in terms of pride. The man was either making no effort to hide his feelings or was incapable of it; as a drama queen, he could have taught even Anderson a trick or two.

"You mentioned her productivity. Was it also in opening doors?" The comments Anderson had found—and the possible contents of some of the deleted ones—were making sense.

"It pains me to say so, but yes. She had contacts, or said she had contacts, at all sorts of places, like the university. We were hoping she'd use those connections to create some opportunities for us. She could charm"—Tuckton winced at the words—"the birds out of the trees. She certainly charmed us."

"So what soured things?" Robin spoke sympathetically, appealing to the "us males against the monstrous regiment of women" side that evidently lay in Tuckton's nature.

"Not only did none of these 'mythical' opportunities come to anything, it turned out she was a mole. For the Cads and Scoundrels. Sent to infiltrate our ranks and report back."

"Report back on what?"

Tuckton drew himself up again, gaining a whole quarter of an inch in height. "Have I not conveyed to you the tensions there are between the two societies?"

"I'm beginning to get a good idea of that." Tensions enough to commit murder, though? And could it be that Lydia Oliver, rather than Becky Bairstow, was the victim? "I'd be grateful if you could give us all the information you have on Lydia Oliver. We need to talk to her."

"I'll do my best. I have her application form at home—perhaps I could send you a copy?"

"If you could scan it and send us it by email, that would save time." Robin noted, with pleasure, Tuckton's fleeting look of horror at the notion of scanning a document.

"Application form for what, by the way?" Pru asked.

"Joining the detectorists' society. We can't let anyone just stroll in. Mind you," he added conspiratorially, with an arch glance over his shoulder, "we've tightened up security no end since Mata Hari conned us."

Robin, mind boggling at whether a prospective detectorist would now need to provide three character references before being allowed to join this merry band, simply nodded. He waited as Pru gave a contact email for Tuckton to use, and let her beat him to the sting-in-the-tail questions.

"Have the detectorists been involved at all up at Culford over the past year?"

"No. Much as we could add a lot to the process, we've been banned."

"Not even unofficially?" Pru smiled winningly. "I mean, somebody must see the value of *your* input."

Tuckton snorted. "Charlie Howarth from the council doesn't. I wrote to him offering our help, but he dismissed us out of hand. At least he also turned down the CAS."

"So you have no idea of who the woman in the grave is? Or how she got there?"

"No. If I did have an idea, I'd say. It's not every day that a young woman goes missing, is it? I—" The colour drained from Tuckton's face. "Lydia went off somewhere. Is there a chance the dead woman is her?"

"We don't know who she is. That's why we have to follow up every lead."

"Good God." If Tuckton wasn't genuinely surprised, he was a consummate actor. "It never occurred to me. We thought she'd just ..."

"Just what?"

Tuckton squirmed in his seat, clearly weighing up the relative merits of the truth and a lie. From the pained expression he wore, he appeared to have opted for the truth. "Just run off with one of the club members." If he'd been a dyed-in-the-wool racist describing how his daughter had eloped with a member of the West Indies cricket team, he couldn't have appeared more disgusted. "He'd been in charge of organising the Christmas dinner, so we had to cancel it."

That cancellation appeared to be the biggest problem of all. Although the possible coincidence of dates between Lydia "running off" and the burial of their dead woman meant this had to be taken seriously.

"Was the bloke she ran off with married?"

"No, but he was going out with someone else. Sian. Nice girl. She used to be quite keen on archaeology, but after Lydia went off with her man, Jerry, she quit. She took up line dancing or samba or something," he ended lamely.

Robin wondered whether he'd meant zumba rather than samba. He also wondered whether Sian's new hobbies had included finishing off love rivals.

"Was Sian part of the group?" Pru asked.

"Not officially. She came along with Jerry a couple of times, but she didn't say a lot. Quiet, unassuming type. As I said, a nice girl." "Nice" seemed to be the pinnacle of praise so far as Tuckton was concerned.

"We'd better have a word with her. Can you get us her contact details? In fact," Robin added, "can you give us the contacts for all your members? I assume you won't be able to do the same for the CAS?"

"You assume correctly." The impact of such curt words was lost; Tuckton's voice no longer contained the edge of bluster. Whatever he'd said about The Woman, he was clearly concerned about her well-being. "Will you let me know? If it is her in the grave."

Robin thought about answering with a terse, *You'll know soon enough, as it will be all over the news*, but the detectorist's reaction had touched him. He'd developed a bit of a nose for a villain—that facility had played a part in their last case when there'd turned out to be something rotten in the state of Abbotston—but nothing about Tuckton made him smell a rat. "We'll be in contact, I promise. And I take it that you'll make sure to let us know if there's anything else you can think of that might link to this case, even if it's the most bizarre rumour of goings-on up at the villa."

"I will. I wish there were more I could tell you, perhaps to the discredit of the CAS, but there isn't."

And if Tuckton couldn't find even that tiny bit of dirt to hurl, there was no point in continuing the interview.

Back at the station, Robin got his team to work on this new line of investigation—those of his officers who weren't out trying to finish the last of the door-to-door enquiries, all of which had been drawing a blank. Now they had coincidence of gender and timing with the victim and a possible motive in the rivalry between the groups. But the faint streak of optimism about Lydia Oliver being the dead woman kept being dampened by the lack of a missing-persons report in that name, assuming the Abbotston team hadn't been so negligent as to miss the obvious. Meanwhile Pru, who'd acquired a contact number for the student who'd done the dissertation and had the subsequent fallout with Howarth, got on the blower to her while Robin chased up the forensic team.

When his call ended—to little avail—Pru knocked on his door, then came in to plonk herself on the chair on the other side of Robin's desk. "I've spoken to Ros Butler, the girl who did the dissertation on maximising the use of the Culford site."

"I know who she is." Robin was in no mood for pussyfooting about. "And?"

"And not a lot. She couldn't shed any light on the dead woman and hadn't noticed anything suspicious at the site. Apart from Charlie Howarth, of course."

"She thinks he's suspicious?" Robin liked the sound of that, especially if it was based on fact rather than instinct.

"She thinks he's a smarmy, slimy git. Her words, not mine." Pru grinned. "Sexist to boot. He wasn't interested in any of her ideas about increasing profitability of the site, or similar sites, and part of that seemed to be because she was 'just' a girl."

"We knew that already."

"What we didn't know was that she came up with a scheme for selling reproduction antiquities. You know, coins and jewellery and things. She'd done a fully costed commercial plan and reckoned that as a small business, it would create a regular income so long as the scheme was rolled out at shops over all the local sites, as well as on eBay and the like."

Robin nodded appreciatively. "Seems eminently sensible. What was his problem with it?"

"He had a list of them, although Ros said they all were surmountable and it seemed like he was clutching at straws." Pru consulted her notes. "Taking up staff time, the need for upfront investment in technology and training, blah blah. Ros reckoned that the admin staff on-site had plenty of time to spare and that investment needed would be minimal. Her take on it was that he didn't like it because it wasn't his idea and he couldn't wangle a way to get the credit. Sounds like him," she added with a snort.

It sounded odd, but was that simply because Howarth was a dinosaur? There was nothing to connect him yet to the dead woman—whether she was Becky or Lydia or whoever—and they couldn't go down the route of investigating the bloke just because he had the sort of face you'd like to punch, although that late-evening visit to the villa needed explanation. Especially if Pryce had got back to them to say that Howarth's car had been spotted on-site sometime during the previous summer, so within the broadest window for the body's interment.

"Ros also reckons that Howarth tried to stop this dig happening. Said there were more important sites, ones that hadn't been investigated at all, and if the university had the resources, they should throw them at those."

That was interesting. "When was this?"

"I'm not sure. I asked her, but she didn't know. It was a rumour going round the department. The people there aren't keen on Howarth, either. Think he's a jobsworth."

"He may well be. I wonder if he wrote those letters to the paper?"

"Doubt it. Anonymous isn't his style. Anyway, he's up to something, even if I don't know what," Pru said with finality. "Blimey, when I think of all the times me and my pals were taken in by his crap."

"Well, maybe—" Robin was interrupted by Ben knocking at the office door. "Yes?"

"Would you like the good news or the mixed news, sir?"

"I'd like people to stop arsing about. Sorry." Robin held up his hand. "No call for that. Take a pew and tell me what you've got."

Ben sat a touch gingerly, avoiding Robin's gaze. "We've got the dental records for Becky Bairstow, so I sent them over to Grace."

"That is good news." Robin was pleased to see Ben look up and give him a cautious smile. "What's the other bit?"

"I can't find anything about this Lydia Oliver woman. Not yet. If you ask me—" Ben stopped, clearly worried that he was at risk of another tongue-lashing.

"I *do* ask you," Robin encouraged him. "I always want to hear my team's ideas."

"So long as they're not daft!" Pru chipped in over Ben's shoulder.

"You can't always tell if they're daft, though, can you? Not at the time." Robin didn't want Ben or any of the other constables sitting on something that turned out to be vital, just because they were scared that their idea was too off beam. "Anyway, you should have heard Pru when she was first in the job. Gold medal in daftness."

"I thought that was Anderson, sir." Pru's eyebrows shot up. "You can't be as inventive as him, Ben." She'd obviously taken the young constable under her wing, no doubt recognising in him the same qualities she possessed.

"Inventive but effective. He should go far. You all should," Robin added. "You don't want to find yourselves being career constables."

"Like Lew—" Ben, flushing, clammed up.

"Like who? Come on." Pru tapped her fingers together.

"Sorry, sir. I just don't want to end up like Sergeant Lewington, on the front desk. I mean, he's good at his job, but he could have done a lot better. I—"

Robin forestalled him with a wave of his hand. "I suggest if you want to make progress, first thing to learn is not to comment on your fellow officers. Unless you're whistle-blowing."

Ben, red to the ears, nodded. "Noted, sir. Sorry."

"Apology accepted." Robin sighed. Another example of shoddy Abbotston practice? No wonder the place was so low on morale. "I know you won't do it again."

"I won't." Ben swallowed hard, then brandished some paper. "Lydia Oliver. I think she might be a sock puppet, sir. Somebody creating an online identity that hides her own. It's easy enough done if you've got several email addresses and a bit of nous."

"Why would she do that, though?" Pru asked. "Was she trolling people?"

"Not that I can see. It's just that she appears from nowhere."

"And disappears equally rapidly? Sometime last summer or autumn?"

"About that." Ben nodded.

"If she *was* a spy"—Robin rolled his eyes at the notion, but they had to consider it—"for the other side, then she might have wanted to hide her name. Makes you think about what sort of shenanigans we've stumbled on."

"I might be able to help with that." Ben, evidently growing in confidence again, waved a slip of paper. "I've been poking about online, and you know what it's like. You click a link and then another . . ."

"You need to take care." Pru wagged a finger. "You'll see things you'll never unsee. Or end up with a Russian bride. You didn't in this case, I hope?"

Ben flapped his hand. "Leave off, will you? Russian girls aren't my scene, anyway. I—"

"Sian!" Robin clicked his fingers, then jabbed them at his notes. "Sorry. You said Russian, Pru, which reminded me of the woman Lydia Oliver cuckolded."

"Cuckolded?" Ben glanced at Pru, *What the hell does that mean?* writ large on his face.

"Had it away with her boyfriend," Pru explained.

"You should have made him look it up for himself. Anyway," Robin continued, "isn't there a Sian who volunteers on the site? Do you think it's the same one?"

"It's a common enough name, but it could be," Ben agreed.

"Tuckton said she'd gone off archaeology, though," Pru pointed out.

"She may have done, and then gone back on it. Tuckton's persona non grata up at Culford, so he probably wouldn't know." Robin turned to Ben. "Can you add that to your growing list of jobs? Or get someone else onto it."

"Will do." Ben made a note. "Now, what I found online . . ."

"I'm all ears."

Ben took a deep breath. "Okay. Some bloke was blogging about the rivalries in archaeology and how daft they were when there were more important things to consider. He mentioned Culdover in passing, along with some other places, and though he didn't point the finger at anybody in particular, he riled people. They thought he was taking the piss. You should have seen a few of the comments."

"Any from Lydia Oliver?"

"Not that I could see. Tuckton had given his two penn'orth, though. Anyway, this guy with the blog is called Richard Agnew, and he's quite an authority on Roman sites. He did a bit of work at Culford ages ago."

"You think we should see him?"

Ben's brows creased in thought. "Yeah, although it's nothing other than a hunch based on one of Agnew's replies to a comment. About everything not being rosy in the archaeological garden and the lure of filthy lucre. He does tend to what you'd call purple prose."

Robin nodded, appreciating the constable's erudition as well as his nous. It wouldn't hurt to talk to Agnew if nothing else turned up, not least because it might help to scratch the itch he'd developed; there were dodgy goings-on at Culford, irrespective of the murder. "Okay. That's good. Carry on with the digging around, and let me know if you turn up anything else even vaguely suspicious."

"Will do." Ben scuttled out, hiding his delighted smile.

"He's showing promise," Pru said once he was out of earshot.

"Reminds me of you." Robin steepled his fingers in thought. All day he'd been waiting for something significant to happen. A stupidly superstitious feeling, one that would probably come to nothing, but it meant that when the phone rang, he immediately snatched it up.

"Got a call for you, sir." The front-desk sergeant's solid tones came down the line. "A woman, and she's being cagey about her name, but she insists she has to talk to you and you alone, being the officer in charge of the case."

Robin blew out his cheeks. Would his "something significant" turn out to be nothing more than a nuisance call from a person who brought little to the mix other than sharing a vision she'd had, or relaying a message from beyond the grave? "Okay. Put her through."

Pru pointed at the door and made a phone gesture with her hand, then slipped out to take a call in the incident room.

"Sorry, sir. The bloody line's just gone dead." The desk sergeant huffed. "The system's been a pain in the arse since they started the road works outside. I'll try to ring her back."

"Thanks." Robin put the handset back, got up from his desk, stretched his legs, then peered out at his team. Alison, catching his eye, immediately jerked her computer mouse, maybe caught in the act of viewing something she shouldn't. The others appeared to be doing what they were supposed to, although from Pru's expression, he guessed her phone call wasn't what she wanted to hear. When she'd put the phone down, he strolled over and perched on her desk. "Bad news?"

"Sort of. That was forensics, coming through to me as you were occupied. Whoever our dead woman is, she's not Becky Bairstow. Dental records show no real similarity."

Robin drummed the desk. "Bloody brilliant. Back to square one." The harsh ringing of his phone rescued him from the ensuing discussion, as people began moaning about a case that seemed to be going nowhere.

"Hello?"

"Got the lady back again." The desk sergeant sounded pleased with himself. "Second time lucky."

"Inspector?" The voice was brisk, efficient, and younger than Robin had expected.

"Speaking."

"I'm Becky Bairstow. I believe you've been looking for me."

Robin swallowed hard. "We have indeed." But clearly in the wrong place.

Chapter Six

Becky Bairstow had been en route to Abbotston—and to present herself live and kicking for inspection—when she'd rung to ensure somebody of appropriate rank was there to see her. She'd been briefly apologetic and had promised to explain everything when she arrived. Robin and Pru waited for her in reception, hoping that the odd representatives of the media who'd been lurking about on and off wouldn't spot and recognise her until they had the answers they needed. That mop of auburn hair could be a giveaway.

When she did appear, the hair wasn't the only striking part about her. Dark eyes, legs up to her armpits, she was the sort of woman capable of making a pair of jeans and a T-shirt from White Stuff look like haute couture.

How had she managed to hide herself away for so long?

They made the introductions and took her to an interview room, where Robin assured her she wasn't being interviewed formally.

"Thank goodness for that. I seem to have caused you a lot of trouble, for which I apologise, but I didn't realise what was going on until yesterday when I saw something on the web. I'd have rung, but face-to-face is better. I've just flown in from Stuttgart." She paused, leaving Robin with the feeling he'd been steamrollered by words and force of personality. He resisted saying that it wasn't only them she owed an explanation to, not wanting to risk putting her back up, but he couldn't drag his thoughts away from Andy Hales and how the bloke must be feeling, and *would* feel when he knew the truth.

"Have you been in Stuttgart all this time?" he asked with a smile he hoped didn't look too forced.

"No, although I'm likely to be there a while longer, as my partner's doing some work there. I've been travelling to the places I had on my bucket list, ending with the Mercedes Benz museum."

"You're lucky to be able to do that."

"Lucky's the word, all right. Believe it or not, I won the lottery."

"Lottery?" Robin and Pru shared a disbelieving glance.

"Yes. Enough to buy myself a sabbatical. Easy when you're self-employed." Easy to check too. "I opted for no publicity, though."

"Didn't want friends and family to come calling?" The sarcasm in Pru's voice rang through.

"That makes me sound rather harsh. I'm not, I promise you." Ms. Bairstow shook her head bleakly. "Look, I have no immediate family—I was orphaned in a car crash when I was fifteen—and my relationship with Andy was in the doldrums. It came at an ideal time to break free."

"You didn't bother to say goodbye to him?" This beggared belief. "Has he spent all this time thinking you were dead while you were living the life of Riley?"

"No, it's not like that." She drummed the table. "I didn't say goodbye at first. He's very clingy and I didn't want him trying to dissuade me from going. We didn't live together, so I decided I should simply pack up where I was renting and send him a letter after a few days to say I'd gone for a short break. Those days turned into weeks."

"During which he reported you missing and the police wasted time trying to find you? Don't you think we have better things to do?" Ms. Bairstow was winding Robin up almost as much as Howarth did, and with more valid reason.

"Of course. When I found out he'd reported me as missing—I guess he couldn't believe that I'd ditched him—I rang to say I was safe and told him to get off my back."

"Then why the hell didn't he tell us so we could take your name off the list?" Pru, clearly fuming, slammed her notebook on the table.

"You'd have to ask him that. I assumed he'd done so, up until yesterday."

It sounded unlikely, but was it true? Even the most rational of people could act irrationally. They'd have to let the Met know so they could pursue a charge of wasting police time—if the CPS felt it was worth it—although Andy Hales would be the one in the firing line, not Becky Bairstow.

Robin was convinced they hadn't been told everything. "Okay, I'm finding it really hard to believe that in this age of social media, you didn't make a single post or comment about your bucket-list tour. Or put a single photo on Instagram."

She snorted. "I've done social media, and I'm fed up with it. If it isn't nastiness, it's people tweeting about being on the bus going past the baker's or what they're having in their sandwiches. Pathetic trivia."

Robin, much to his disappointment, had to agree. He despaired about the constant stream of pictures of people's cats that friends were supposed to drool over, or posts giving every little detail about their wonderful children.

Pru rolled her eyes. "Tell me about it. As bad as Christmas letters. You know, 'Our Olivia is taking her A levels though she's only eight.'"

Robin let the conversation carry on. Pru, who appeared to have calmed down—or at least pretended to—had put on her most sympathetic smile and was evidently taking this somewhere, even if he couldn't immediately identify the destination.

"Them as well." Ms. Bairstow groaned. "I thought I was the only one in the world who hated those things. People boast in a way they never would face-to-face. Because you're not there to give them a mouthful."

Had Andy Hales got a "mouthful" from this evidently belligerent woman? And maybe he'd kept the missing-persons report active as some sort of revenge at being dumped in such a casual, heartless manner? She certainly provoked strong reactions, and Pru's thoughts were clearly running down the same line, given her next remark.

"True. And it's the same with the negative stuff. People make remarks in a Facebook comment they'd never say face-to-face."

"Tell me about it." The interviewee winced.

"Have you been trolled?" Pru's voice, calm and considerate, would have put the wariest person at ease.

Ms. Bairstow shrugged, wrinkling her nose and obviously trying to find the right words, or at least attempting to give the impression that was what she was doing. "A bit. Also subjected to a bit of unwanted interest. When you enter the land of the nerds, you come across some weird people."

"Enough to make you want to disappear for a while?"

"No!" The reply verged on the lady protesting too much. "I can look after myself."

Robin intertwined his fingers, then clenched them to the point they hurt. Why was his sergeant asking about things which didn't seem relevant to the case? He had a dead, still-unidentified woman to find justice for and a living, named woman in front of him.

Named. Of course. *That's* where Pru was going.

"Anyway," Ms. Bairstow continued, "I've always used a username online rather than my real name. It's easier."

"A username like 'Trowelgirl'?"

Ms. Bairstow flinched as though she'd been slapped, looking from Pru to Robin and back again as though following a rally at Wimbledon. "How the hell did you know?"

If this was The Woman, Robin could understand why she'd got the metal detectorists in a flutter. Just because he was gay didn't mean he couldn't recognise a pretty face or a good figure or undeniable sex appeal. Having seen the investigational light on the road to this particular Damascus, he picked up the questioning. "How do you think we know?"

"Charlie sodding Howarth, I guess. Can't keep his big gob shut."

Robin caught Pru's astonishment, swiftly hidden, out of the corner of his eye and hoped their interviewee hadn't registered it. "He's certainly voluble. Let's have *your* side of the story."

"I'd be glad to. I suppose it isn't quite what he told you." She raised a quizzical and immaculately shaped eyebrow. "He's an old pal. Friend of mine used to go out with him, back in uni days. He got in touch and asked for a favour. Culdover's not so far to get to on the train, and I thought it would be a laugh. He wanted to know what was going on among the amateur community."

"But why would he need a spy in their camp?"

"He didn't trust them. Suspected they were at risk of spoiling some of the local sites, poking around where they shouldn't. Somebody has been digging at a couple of scheduled sites locally, and he had his money on it being the Culdover mob."

Trying to catch somebody digging would be an explanation for why Howarth had been up at Culford out of hours, although it could equally be an effective cover story. And it would have been imperative to put people off if he'd been planning to put a dead body there.

They had no evidence of a connection with the dead woman, Robin reminded himself. Whoever she was. "And was it the Culdover mob who were poking about where they shouldn't?"

"Not so far as I could tell, and I had my ears wide open." There was no shifty flicker of the eyes to suggest dissemblance. "And anyway, that wouldn't be their style. They're all too obsessed with playing by the book and the proper way of doing things. They take themselves far too seriously. Rules and regulations and procedures—those are the things they used to argue about most."

"Before they argued about you?" Pru chipped in again. "Or should I say about Lydia Oliver?"

Ms. Bairstow flicked her hand. "Okay, okay. It was all part of the game, all right? I didn't want to use my own name. Just in case I had to ditch—I didn't want them trying to find me."

"They'd have had every right. You would have left a lot of people wanting answers."

"Only among the detectorists. That Tuckton bloke's a right nerd, and he winds the others up. Some of them aren't so bad." The innocent air in the witness's voice, belied by the flush on her cheeks, might have fooled a child, but Robin and his sergeant were one step ahead in this game.

"You mean Jerry?" he asked. "Was part of the game running off with him?"

The flush deepened, suffusing Ms. Bairstow's face. "That wasn't meant to happen. I swear. I didn't anticipate that they'd actually have somebody fanciable involved with them. Howarth said they were all anoraks. You know"—she rallied—"types who like to watch the trains going past, although they'd never have the courage to hop on board one."

"Jerry clearly did."

Ms. Bairstow wriggled her shoulders, bridling at Pru's bluntness. "Well, he's a nice, normal bloke."

"And are you still an item?" Pru asked, a touch waspishly.

She bridled again, giving Pru an old-fashioned look. "Must you use that word? It sounds like something you buy at a car-boot sale. We're living together, very happily."

"Does Sian know that?" Robin cut in.

"Sian? Oh, *Sian*." Ms. Bairstow didn't seem to be a good actress. How she'd managed to fool the Culdover detectorists about her motives was becoming a mystery, although maybe her being so attractive had deflected any suspicion. People did still judge by appearances. "She's cool about it. I mean, she was upset at the time, but she settled down. She volunteers at the villa now, I believe, so she must have come to terms with things."

"You've not exactly made yourselves popular, have you? Exes everywhere." Except making those enemies hadn't led to her being killed, nor her boyfriend, one assumed. "So you and Jerry have been living the life of Riley on your lottery win?"

"That's putting it crudely too. I prefer to think that the money meant we could buy ourselves some space. He worked on a contract basis, so we just packed up and went."

Robin looked at the witness, then studied his notes, letting her stew in her own juice for a moment, but the strategy didn't produce anything. He'd have to get the team to check all the details of this story, but the only crime that he could pin on Becky Bairstow or any of her men was the wasting of police time.

"One last thing," he said, keeping his eyes fixed on his notes until the conclusion of the question came, "perhaps the most important. Have you any idea who the dead woman might be?"

He caught the tail end of something—guilt? Shock at his abrupt introduction of the murder?—in her eye.

"No. No idea. I'd have told you if I had."

"Hm." Robin let her squirm some more, but nothing further emerged. "You say that you took the advantage of coming into money to make a new life for yourselves?"

"I don't think I quite said that," Ms. Bairstow corrected him. "Just that it was a well-timed opportunity for us to go off and lie low for a while. Away from pressures from other people."

"Not a case of lying low because you'd killed someone?" Robin noted her renewed look of unease. "You see, I don't like the coincidence of dates. Somebody got buried at Culford, a place you have connections to, around the same time as you did a runner."

"I understand your suspicion; I really do. Maybe. But I'm not the kind of person who'd be daft enough to come back when the body was found. You didn't know where I was, so I could have simply maintained that state of affairs. Unless you think this is some elaborate double bluff?"

"Perhaps you had no choice. We'd already linked the case to you, so guilty or not, the wise course was to get in contact." Robin let her squirm further before continuing. "So we're to believe that the timing is just coincidental?"

"Look." She leaned forwards, jabbing her finger at him. "There's a world of difference between playing spies and running off with some woman's bloke and committing murder. I swear to God I know nothing about this girl."

Even though he'd heard witnesses lie through their teeth with a huge degree of credibility, this sounded depressingly like the truth, so why had she reacted? He stared her out until she had to look away, then said tartly, "We'll be back in touch."

They concluded the interview with some formalities, including getting contact details for Jerry, whom Robin—perhaps unfairly— suspected would say anything his girlfriend told him to. After she'd gone, he and Pru went back to the interview room to compare notes, the sergeant having also spotted Ms. Bairstow's shock at Robin's question.

"Guilt, do you think?" Robin asked.

"Not quite." Pru frowned. "But she knows more than she's letting on."

"I agree." Robin, yawning, stretched like Campbell did after a hard day of gnawing bones and cocking his leg. "Well done for making the connection. I was about a minute behind you. Coincidence of dates?"

"Not just that. You'll laugh."

"I won't."

"You know I like old movies. She reminded me of the sort of femme fatale you get in black-and-white pictures. Veronica Lake type."

"I have no idea who you're talking about, and I don't need to be enlightened. Well done for taking a punt." He stifled anther yawn.

"Can you arrange for me to see Sian tomorrow? I still want to interview her. Hell hath no fury and all that, so maybe there's lingering resentment and she'll be willing to dish a bit of dirt on Becky Bairstow."

This wasn't clutching at straws. No way. Copper's instinct that something was amiss, and he was going to find out what.

"Will do, sir. She does have a surname, by the way. Wheatstone."

"Like the bridge?" Robin, amused at his sergeant's blank look—didn't they teach people proper physics down in Wales?—ploughed on before he was asked to explain. "And then there's an itch I need to scratch at the first convenient moment. An itch called Howarth. Would you be offended if I took Ben with me instead of you?"

"Cut out the personal connection?" Pru grinned. "Of course I wouldn't. So long as I've got something juicy to get my teeth into while you're gallivanting."

"Oh, yes. I've got plenty of juice for you. I want the other side of the Mata Hari story."

The grin widened. "The CAS? You'll have it, sir."

"Good. Ben tells me they meet tomorrow—same night as the detectorists, so nobody can attend both." Robin rolled his eyes. "Even if they haven't got an inkling about the dead woman, they may know who's been digging where they shouldn't dig or what 'Lydia Oliver' is hiding."

"Apart from her identity?" Pru blew out her cheeks. "Which brings us back to our dead woman, doesn't it?"

"It does indeed."

Robin was barely through the door before Campbell pounced on him for a hug. "I'm pleased to see you too. Any chance you can solve my case for me?"

Adam, hot on the dog's heels, came up to get some affection of his own. "He's clever, but he's not Sherlock Holmes."

"Are you sure he's not the canine equivalent?" Robin remarked after the obligatory welcome-home cuddle. "I wonder what goes on in his head?"

"Something like 'food, basket, food, garden, food, sleep, food.'"
Adam grinned. "Bit like you, really."

"Leave off." Robin raised his arm and sniffed. "Ugh. That's horrible. I'm going to change my shirt."

"Yeah. That's a real passion killer."

Robin paused halfway up the stairs. "Is Anderson back yet?"

"In and back out for a run." Adam grinned. "He had to wait for me to let him in."

"Good. A bit of discomfort won't hurt. Don't give him his own key, right?"

"Believe me, I won't." The arrangement whereby Anderson had to pick up the spare key from the neighbour would work well enough for days he was home before either of his hosts. "He's already started to treat the place like a hotel. When I let him in, he just sauntered past me into the kitchen with a 'Smells good' and an appreciative look at the saucepan. Not a 'Hello, Adam, how was your day?' or even a pat for Campbell."

It was rare for Adam to vent quite so much, but this grievance clearly needed to be aired. Robin nodded and let him continue.

"There was a pile of stuff on the breakfast bar, waiting to be laid out or put away, but there was no sign of him bothering about pitching in. Okay, he keeps his bedroom tidy and there's not a lot of mess in the bathroom, but I'm not the kitchen slave."

"I know you're not." Robin gave him another hug. "If he was like this at home, no wonder Helen lost her patience with him."

"Maybe. Although it's got to be more than that. A good shouting at and a kick up the backside would have been better punishment for that offence. Ugh." Adam gently pushed Robin away. "Go and change that shirt."

Once changed, freshened, and sufficiently deodorant-ed, Robin made his way to the kitchen, where Adam sat flicking through the local free newspaper. He avoided hovering over the saucepan and saying how good the stew smelled—even though the aroma was delicious—for fear of slipping down the slope Anderson was on.

"I see your missing woman turned up." Adam glanced over, grinning—a grin which shut off as he saw Robin's expression.

"Hold on. How did you know? Is it in there?"

"No." Adam closed the paper, then held up the front page so Robin could see for himself. "I heard it on the local radio when I came in. I'm guessing from that look in your eye, that story didn't come from an official briefing?"

"Too right it didn't. We weren't due to tell them until their update tomorrow." Robin slumped into a kitchen chair, where a consoling Campbell came to let him have a soothing rub of his canine ears. It helped, but it didn't change the facts. "What did the news story say?"

"You don't want to know." Adam exhaled loudly. "It was that clown of a bloke who covers when the usual woman is on holiday."

"The one who was taken off air for offensive comments?"

"Yeah, him. I'd have turned him off, but I wanted to hear the weather forecast. Anyway, matey was chuntering along the lines of the police being astonished when their dead woman walked through the door. Their crime correspondent came on, saying she had an exclusive story. It was on about six o'clock if that's any help."

"Hmm, might be." Robin rubbed absent-mindedly along the dog's back.

"Do you think someone from Abbotston snitched to them?"

"It's a possibility I have to consider." And there were a couple of people he still didn't feel able to trust. "Although it might be Becky Bairstow herself, going to the press to make sure she's presented in a good light rather than as a lying cow."

"That bad?"

Robin shrugged. "Maybe." He gave Adam a brief outline of what had come to light during the interview.

Adam shook his head incredulously. "That's like the plot of a TV show."

A ring of the doorbell—Anderson back from his run—ended further speculation. Robin let his colleague in, then gave him five minutes to get down to the table, with the threat that he'd give Anderson's portion to Campbell if he didn't keep to time. He returned to the kitchen, where he and Adam pored over the wonderfully inane items of local news before serving dinner.

Eating in the kitchen was always easier than using the dining area, which was a part of the lounge and ideal for intimate tête-à-têtes but not suited to entertaining ever-so-slightly unwanted guests. It was also more advantageous to cleaning up spills, especially as the dog usually made a beeline for any unwanted scraps. Tonight's offering—a slow-cooked beef stew with a hint of cloves and chilli—wasn't conducive to the proper workings of canine stomach, though.

"Careful with your dinner," Adam warned Anderson. "Campbell will be looking for any smidgeon that drops on the floor, and it's not good for his digestion."

"Oh, bless." Anderson, putting on the infuriating sort of voice that people tend to use when addressing children or old people, turned to face Campbell, who was sitting placidly in his basket. "Does he like a bit of chilli and it upsets his tummy-wummy?" Anderson waved his laden fork, at which the Newfoundland leaped onto his feet and bounded towards the breakfast bar.

"Basket!" Adam ordered the dog back to his rightful place. "Don't tease him like that. It's not fair."

Anderson flapped his hand, sending sauce flying. "I wasn't teasing him."

"Hold on." Robin jabbed the air with his forefinger. "You're still our guest. And you'll stick to house rules, okay?"

"Okay." Anderson gave the dog a sidelong glance—not a contrite one—then loaded his fork again, although he laid it back down before eating anything. "Sorry. I'm not myself at the moment. And I know I'm being a burden to you."

Robin tentatively cuffed his colleague's arm. "We understand." He held back on saying, *Stay as long as you like*, though; that would have been making a rod for their backs. Funny how, now that they had a chink in the conversation, into which they could wedge some exploration of how best to move towards Anderson's moving out, they couldn't face making the most of it. Too bloody British by half.

"We can make it work, short term." Adam's voice had never sounded so waspish.

Anderson opened his mouth, then just smiled as though he couldn't trust himself to say anything. Robin *did* feel sorry for him, but the sooner they sorted this out, the better.

After dinner, Anderson's offer to make a cup of tea for his hosts and then do the washing-up was both unexpected and welcome.

Robin and Adam retired to the lounge, taking Campbell—whose normally friendly eyes still burned with annoyance—with them.

"He seems to have taken the hint," Robin whispered, nodding towards the kitchen.

"Hm." Adam rubbed the dog's ears. "I won't have him annoying Campbell, though. It's bad enough that *we* have to put up with him."

"I'll make it up to you when the case is done. Dinners out, chocolates. Long walks along Abbotston canal." Robin grinned, and was delighted to get a grin in return. He leaned closer. "I could make it up to you tonight, assuming the phone doesn't go off."

Adam's grin disappeared instantly. "No. I couldn't face doing *it*. Not with him here." He shuddered. "It would be like doing it at Mum's house, in the bedroom next to hers."

Robin bit off the *Oh, for goodness' sake* before it left his lips. Adam was correct. This wasn't a university hall of residence where things going bonk in the night were just part of the soundtrack.

He remembered Adam's reluctance to occupy a particular room in this house, because it had been the one his grandparents had slept in when they owned the property before they bequeathed both it—and an infant Campbell—to their grandson. Even now that both dog and property were his own, he believed there were still proper observances to be made.

"You're right," Robin conceded. "Which is an extra incentive to ensure this doesn't go on forever."

Adam cast a glance at the door, but the sounds of washing up were still in full swing. "What are you—we—going to do about sorting matters out? Can you talk to Helen?"

Robin would once have vowed that he'd walk through a pit of snakes for his lover, but in this instance it felt a demand too far. "Must I? You know how I hate that sort of thing. It's much more in your line, dealing with those awkward school governors."

"Yeah, but you know her better. Anyway," Adam added, while stroking Robin's arm, "you've got the knack too. All that practice coping with witnesses and angry relatives. I only get to talk to ten-year-olds."

"And their parents. If you can deal with the average Culdover family, you can manage Helen." Robin sighed. "Please. I've got a dead woman to identify and a murderer to catch."

"Okay." Adam raised his hands in surrender. "I'll do it from the school, tomorrow, if you can give me Helen's mobile number. I've only got his."

"Deal. You can tell them you're helping the police."

"Helping the police with what?" Anderson's voice came from the doorway. How long had he been there and what had he heard? "Is your school involved with the Culford murder?"

"No, it bloody well isn't." Adam bridled. "Excuse me. I have stuff to plan for tomorrow."

He left the room, taking the dog with him, evidently headed for the study they'd set up in the smallest bedroom.

"You were a loss to the diplomatic service," Robin snarled at Anderson. "Watch the telly or something while I make peace."

He headed after Adam, ready to offer an olive branch, although Anderson's comment about the case involving the school had produced a pang of guilt. On the way home he'd been playing with an idea, but that ill-timed remark meant he'd have to tread carefully if he wanted to implement it. If Pru was going to get the inside story from the CAS, it would be useful to get some gen from the rest of the detectorists. Adam would have an ideal connection there through Sophie's father. Nobody would know of Adam's connection to the police—not unless the gossip machine worked really effectively—and he could present himself as a genuine candidate to join the society. After that it would be just a case of keeping his ears open.

And maybe getting himself killed like he nearly did last time?

Robin halted at the closed study door. Pru was paid to put herself into difficult situations, and she'd had training on dealing with them. Adam hadn't, unless you counted stuff like "don't go into a small room alone with one of your pupils."

Desperate times called for desperate measures, but were things that bad? He headed for the bathroom to create an alibi for why he'd come upstairs, hoping that a breakthrough would soon come which would make his bright idea redundant.

Chapter Seven

Thursday morning, Adam drew into the Culdover Primary car park, pulled on the handbrake, got out his phone, and readied himself to face the ordeal. This would be much worse than tackling little Olivia's mother about why her daughter was such a nightmare at playtime or why Kyle never had his PE kit in school.

He looked at the handset, hoping that when he got up the courage to ring, Helen would answer and he wouldn't have to leave a message—a situation which would be even worse than speaking to her direct. Better to do the deed now than fret about it all day. And if he was faced with the answerphone, he couldn't just cut off the call and *not* leave anything, either—given the nature of Anderson's job, any unknown call could be a source of worry, and Helen wouldn't recognise Adam's number. He needed to avoid causing a panic; despite the fact she'd chucked Anderson out, surely she retained affection for him?

Helen was a nice woman; on the occasions Adam and Robin had met up with her socially, they'd enjoyed her company. She was funny, liked sport, and managed to control some of Anderson's flights of fancy, so she seemed an ideal match for him. The pair made what his mother would have called a lovely couple and had never, to his knowledge, shown any signs of cracks in the relationship.

He dialled; time to bite the bullet, or else he and Robin might as well become monks for all the romantic action that was happening.

"Helen?"

"Yes?"

"It's Adam. Robin's partner."

"I thought I recognised the voice. Are you ringing because you're sick of Stuart already? He texted to say that he was staying with you two. You have my sympathy." Her spiky tone didn't bode well.

"You've got me bang to rights." Why pretend? She wasn't daft. "Robin and I were worried about you, actually. Are you all right?"

"Why shouldn't I be?" Her voice got tetchier. "I'm happy as Larry, apart from the fact my personal life has fallen apart."

The admission that not everything was rosy in the garden gave cause for hope. "I've got to ask. What the hell happened between you two? I'd always admired how you two got along."

"You should ask him what happened."

"I have. Robin has. Stuart has no idea what he's done."

"Really?" Helen sounded unconvinced.

"Really. Robin's worked with him long enough to know when he's lying."

"Oh. And does he lie very often?"

Hell. Was everything he said going to be twisted? "According to Robin, not often and usually only when he'd nicked somebody's chocolate." Or, apparently, in an effort to get a suspect to give themselves away, but Adam wasn't going to pass that on in case it was twisted too.

"He does that a lot. Nick chocolate." For the first time in the conversation, Helen appeared to mellow, although Adam wasn't dropping his guard at this point.

"I'm sorry it's not Robin ringing you himself, but he's up to his arse in this murder business. Who knows how long that's going to go on for."

"Oh, so it wasn't simply a case of getting you to do the dirty work?" She paused. "Sorry, I didn't mean it like that. Robin's a good bloke, and he must be working all hours God sends. I appreciate your calling." Another hesitation. "Can I tell you something in confidence?"

Maybe they were getting somewhere. "You can."

"I'm talking about total confidence. If you tell Stuart, I'll thump you. I swear."

"I believe you." He'd heard worse threats from irate parents. They rarely meant it; hopefully the same applied here. "Okay, so long as you're not confessing to murder, I'll keep shtum."

"I'm pregnant."

Adam managed not to say, *Bloody hell!* Instead he hid his shock with, "Congratulations. Assuming it *is* a matter for congratulations?" And was it horribly sexist to assume that state of affairs might account for the change in her usually equitable temper?

"As far as I'm concerned, yes. Not sure about Stuart." Helen's voice was stoic but carried a suggestion of tears in the offing.

"Have you asked him? Does he even know?"

"Of course not, you clown, or else why would I have sworn you to secrecy? Sorry." Helen sighed. "I'm really snappy at the moment. And don't you *dare* put that down to my condition."

"Never dreamed of it," he lied.

"Anyway, Stuart's made it plain he doesn't like children. Every time we're out he makes a remark about other people's badly behaved brats. His words, not mine."

"But wouldn't he change his tune if they were his own?"

"Maybe. But I'm not sure I should give him the chance to find out. He's worn me down with his attitude, and I'm scared to tell him."

"The longer you leave it, the worse it'll be." While Adam had some sympathy for Helen's situation, her attitude was exacerbating the problem. And he still couldn't get to the bottom of what Anderson had allegedly done, apart from making a string of tactless remarks. "Look, tell me to mind my own business, but you've always struck me as being too sensible to create a drama. Is there more to it than that?"

"How long have you got? My father doesn't really approve of him, although he's a fine one to judge anybody because he ran off with a woman of my age, so he's not going to be enamoured of any child of Stuart's. Let alone the fact of his becoming a grandfather. That's no good for his 'young and trendy' image."

"What about your mum?" Adam remembered meeting her at a barbecue. She'd been loud, overtly maternal, and a barrel of laughs.

"She's thrilled. Sworn to silence too, but thrilled about the baby itself. Trouble is she'd like to see us get married before it's born, although she won't press matters. Dad wouldn't give two figs, as usual. Since he found his fancy woman, he keeps going on about what a waste of money all these big flash weddings are and how if he had his time over again now, when there's no shame, he'd not even bother getting married."

"Very modern." Very tight-fisted, as well. "Sorry, that wasn't a dig at you and Stuart. This isn't the 1950s."

"I know it's not. And I don't want to get married in a rush simply because of the baby."

Good to hear that she hadn't discounted marriage—and therefore by implication Anderson—entirely. "Bit of a mess, isn't it?"

"Oh, Adam, you have no idea. Thanks for listening, though. I haven't got anybody else I can talk to who doesn't want to take sides."

"We'll always be strictly neutral. I promise." The only side Adam wanted to take was one which got Anderson out from under their feet. "You should talk to Stuart. He'd listen."

"Would he?"

Adam tried to sound convincing. "I'm sure he would. You can't keep up the wall of silence forever. That's just being silly."

"Don't call me silly." Helen's voice had tightened again, the angry edge—never far off—returning with a vengeance. "I'm not one of your pupils."

"I know. I wouldn't dare call them that. All I'm asking is that you talk to him."

"I'll think about it." That seemed to be the best she was going to offer. "Don't you dare tell him about the baby, though. I swear to God, it'll make things worse."

"I promise." He'd tell Robin, though. "Take care of yourself. And the baby."

"Okay, mother." It came across like a jokey exit line, but the abruptness with which Helen ended the call didn't fill Adam with confidence. Were he and Robin any nearer getting rid of the unwanted lodger? He doubted it.

The day promised to be a hectic one. Culdover Primary always held "meet the teacher" evenings at the very start of the academic year so information could be shared and expectations laid out. As Jim Rashford averred, you could make more of an impact spending an hour with parents than a day with pupils; it was the next generation back who proved so often to be feckless, lacking in discipline and common sense.

Adam had still been at Lindenshaw school when those evenings had happened, so he'd missed a vital part of establishing the right relationships with the parents of his charges. So he was looking forward to this morning, when they'd be holding open class sessions for the first hour. Parents would be able to drop in informally before they set off for work, see what their children were learning about, join in themselves, and bend the teachers' ears if necessary. His enthusiasm continued until Sophie's father appeared, wearing an expression that signalled he wanted to talk.

Best to start on the front foot; Adam waited until his target had spent some time looking at Sophie's work, then drifted over, hand outheld. "Mr. Baxter. Good to meet you."

"And you." Baxter shook the proffered hand vigorously. "Sophie cried all evening when she heard her old teacher was leaving, but you know what kids are like. Fickle. She thinks the world of you."

"Oh, Dad." Sophie, blushing, studied her shoes. "Stop it."

"That's me told." Baxter didn't appear bothered. They shared some pleasantries about how well Sophie had settled in, Adam stating that he'd prefer to talk about things like progress when it was the proper parents' evening and he had all the information to hand.

"Suits me." Baxter nodded while Sophie breathed a sigh of relief and got back to her work. "I wanted to nab a word about something else."

Adam, heart sinking, forced a smile. "Now?"

"Yeah. It's nothing the children can't hear."

That at least was reassuring. "Okay, but excuse me if I keep part of my attention on the class."

"I get that." Baxter dropped his voice. "I've just chatted with Mr. Rashford. I wanted to thank you for passing on what Sophie told you about the detectorists. I should have done it myself, but it made less trouble that way."

"She's a sensible girl."

Baxter snorted. "I wish the detectorists were half as sensible."

Adam, keeping an eye on one of his charges, who seemed to be contemplating poking his pal with a pencil, then thinking better of it when he saw he was under observation, said, "I used to have a hankering to do that when I was a boy. Metal-detecting, not sticking a pencil in other people."

"You should join us! We could do with some younger blood."

"I wish I could," Adam backtracked, regretting the confession, "but you know what it's like with teaching workload. I'm up to my eyeballs."

"Tell me about it. My boss would have me work all hours God sent." Baxter halted. "I can say that, right? I mean, this being a church school."

"You're okay." Adam smiled. Baxter seemed like a genuinely nice bloke, and in any other circumstances Adam might have been glad to take up the offer. He could do with a new hobby, one that was nothing to do with either school or Robin, and his early interest in metal-detecting hadn't been feigned. But if there was any risk of getting caught up in the Culford case, that would put the kibosh on things.

"You could just come along for a meeting, see what you think. If you hate it, you wouldn't need to come again. You might get put off by the paperwork, anyway."

"Paperwork?" That had Adam intrigued.

"You should see the palaver you have to go through to become a bona fide member"—Baxter wagged his finger—"but I won't tell you about that, or I'll definitely put you off. We're meeting tonight, if that's not too short notice. It can't hurt to meet the locals."

Adam, about to pretend he was too busy, noticed Sophie out of the corner of his eye. She appeared tickled pink that her dad and her teacher were getting on so well. "I'll come along the once," he offered. "Although I need to check it with Mr. Rashford first. There's a proper protocol about teachers socialising with parents, although this is probably okay. So long as we don't become pals on Facebook and start making comments about the pupils."

Baxter looked aghast. "I hadn't thought of that. Mind you, if you're used to working with strict protocols, the detectorists will love you. They have more red tape than the Department for Education."

"Don't you believe it." The arrival of another parent gave Adam the opportunity to escape. "Sorry. Duty calls. Leave me the details of when and where to meet, and if I can, I'll be there."

"Cool beans," Baxter replied, at which the class burst into laughter and Sophie, groaning, hid her head in her hands.

Jim Rashford had no objection to Adam going along to the detectorist's meeting, so long as he used his common sense about what he could and couldn't talk about. There was a hint, in his agreement, of suspicion that this was more about Robin's case than Adam's potential new hobby, but Adam pretended not to notice. He'd need all his energy and wits to explain this one to his partner, and the sooner the better. A call at lunchtime would be preferable to leaving his thoughts to stew.

As it turned out, Robin appeared cautiously positive about Adam's plan. He was convinced something was awry at Culdover, over and above what had emerged so far, but he couldn't get a handle on it, and anything that might lead to the lucky break was worth a try.

"Do you think you can act dumb?"

"I'm certain I can." Adam chuckled. "Not sure it'll do much for my reputation with the parents, though. Why?"

"Just thinking that if you keep quiet and smile, it's amazing how many people want to tell you things—the sort of stuff they're probably not supposed to tell anybody." Robin sniggered. "They need to fill the conversational void."

"I can make that happen. You have no idea how many little old ladies have regaled me over the years with tales of their operations. Everyone wants to pour their heart out to me."

"That's your natural charm. Let's hope it doesn't run to some nasty great villain telling you how they did someone over round the back of Victoria Station, because one case is enough, thank you. Keep to Culdover stuff."

"Will do. And while we think of it, do you want me to join the detectorists?" Adam offered. "I mean, I will if it'll help. I can always leave again once we've got what we need."

"No. You don't have to go through with the whole malarkey, unless you suddenly decide that's the life for you. Dip your toes in the water and keep your ears open. Show enough interest and you might get under their skins."

"Shall I take Campbell with me? To be my bodyguard?"

Silence reigned at the other end of the line.

"Hello?" Had the connection been lost?

"I was just wondering whether you should send your apologies. Look, forget it seemed like a good idea." Robin, voice shaky, must have been thinking of the last murder case he'd been involved with and the almost disastrous end it had come to.

"We'll be in a pub. I promise I won't let any of them lead me down a dark alley."

"Like I did, you mean?" Robin's reference to getting himself beaten up seemed light-hearted enough, but the underlying message remained.

"I'll be careful, I swear. And if it would be helpful, I'd be happy to do it, unless I hear from you that it's a no go." They both needed to think this through; time to change the subject. "How was *your* morning?"

Robin groaned. "I'll tell you about it later. How did you get on with Helen?"

"About the same level of success as you've had, by the sound of it. I'll explain that later too. Remember the milk."

"I'll make sure not to forget it. I love you too."

"No," Adam insisted. "We really *do* need milk. Stuart's gone through all of it, and I've had to open the long life I keep for emergencies."

"Oh, gotcha. I'll ring him and make sure he buys some en route to ours. He can get me fish and chips in too. Pay his way a bit. We're not his parents."

"Don't let's get started on them."

"Sorry?"

"Conversation with Helen. All will be revealed later."

Robin sniggered. "Promises, promises."

"Daft beggar." Adam snorted. "Have to go. See you sometime tonight."

Adam got back to work, preparing for the afternoon ahead, only half his mind on the task. Had he made the right call? He made a mental note not to let himself end up alone with any of the detectorists—or anybody who might be involved with the case—and he definitely wouldn't get in any cars until he was absolutely sure the driver was innocent, and maybe not even then. He'd learned his lesson twice over.

Although given that Robin still couldn't identify the dead woman, how could Adam know who was in the frame for being the murderer?

Chapter Eight

R obin's Thursday morning had started with a showdown. Having
managed to calm down overnight—if he'd been in a position
to speak to his team the previous evening, he'd have gone off like a
rocket—he still needed to get to the bottom of the leak. How had the
media known about Becky Bairstow? The morning update seemed
an ideal time to deal with attitudes, as well, so he'd got the troops
together, lulled them into thinking this was a briefing like any other,
then dropped the grenade.

"Before we get our heads around developments in the case, I
want to investigate developments here." Robin scanned the faces of
his merry men and women, not that they looked particularly merry.
He'd been fighting off a deep suspicion that some of them were
deliberately being less than effective, maybe in an effort to discredit
him personally. He was forcing himself to believe it was more likely
they were simply feckless, suffering from having poor role models over
the last few years—even Ben had shown signs of that. But the situation
wasn't helped by being served with a side order of antagonism towards
Stanebridge and anyone associated with that place.

"I'm due to brief the media at ten. I was going to start by telling
them that Becky Bairstow had been ruled out from being our dead
woman. I don't need to do that now. Do I? Seeing as they already
know." He drew the words out, watching his team's discomfort visibly
increase.

Ben—of course it would be him—responded first. "Some of them
were hanging around outside yesterday. Maybe they saw her leave the
building, vaguely recognised her face, then connected her with
the picture we'd put out. She's not changed much."

"Could be." Robin acknowledged Ben's remark. "But I heard the local bulletin on catch up, and there was too much in that report that couldn't have come from simply matching a face to a name." He scanned the room again. "Has one of you been talking where you shouldn't have been?"

"We wouldn't talk directly to the press." Sarah, a constable who hadn't overtly blotted her copybook yet in Robin's eyes, even if she didn't seem to be putting her whole effort into her job, appeared outraged at the suggestion. "Look, sir, we may not have got off on the right foot with you, and I know that Abbotston earned itself a reputation, but *we're* not stupid."

"So you say, but can I be sure of everyone sitting here?" Robin paused, scrutinising each team member in turn—with the exceptions of Ben and Pru. He wanted to make it clear who was being addressed and who wasn't. "This case is important. Not only for your careers, and God knows you're not covering yourself in glory where they're concerned, but for the people involved. We have a dead woman and she deserves justice. She also deserves people to try their utmost best for her." Out of the side of his eye he caught another constable, Alison Cosgrove, squirming. That wouldn't hurt. "Given all that happened here, I don't expect you to like me. Or like Chief Superintendent Cowdrey. But I do expect that you'll do what I ask you to, when I ask you to do it, and that you won't jeopardise a successful outcome by talking to people you shouldn't be talking to. Am I making myself plain?"

A murmur round the room and all eyes firmly fixed on the ground proved as infuriating as an out-and-out argument would have done. Robin, who'd kept his tone even so far, raised his voice to a level he'd never had to use at Stanebridge. "Am I making myself clear?"

"Sorry, sir." Alison broke the silence. "There's still a bit of bad feeling between the two nicks, and it's hard to shake off."

"I'm well aware of that. But if you were being professional, you'd do your damnedest not to let it affect your work. It isn't Stanebridge versus Abbotston. It's us versus whoever bludgeoned that poor girl and denied her a decent burial."

"You're right, sir." Sarah, clearly willing to risk what might appear to be siding with the enemy, sat forwards in her chair. "We haven't all been putting in as much effort as we should. There are people at this nick who'd love to see you and Mr. Cowdrey come a cropper. No"—she raised her hand at the rumbles of protest—"what's the point in denying it? And if it's delaying this case being solved, what's the bloody point at all?"

"Yes, but—" Alison protested.

"When you've quite finished." This must be how Adam had to talk to his class. "Right, I've said my piece, and I expect you to act accordingly. Now, let's get down to business."

Pru and Robin got everyone up to speed with the latest developments—such as they were—and listened to what the constables had to report.

The Community Payback line had turned out to be a bit of a blind alley, the three men who'd been involved at the site all having been interviewed and effectively ruled out. One had been arrested and held on remand within days of finishing at Culford, one had been abroad on business—dodgy-sounding business, but he'd definitely been out of the country—at the crucial time, and the third had moved back to Scotland to live with his parents as soon as he'd discharged his sentence, which was for driving offences.

Andy Hales had been put through the wringer by the Met, eventually confirming Becky Bairstow's story. Whether he'd face charges for wasting police time was up to the Crown Prosecution Service.

Ben had the most intriguing piece of information to share. "When we got the news back from the Met, I started poking around about Becky Bairstow. As far as I'm concerned, her story doesn't hang together, despite what her boyfriend says."

"I'd agree." Robin waited for the rest of it.

"She told us she was orphaned. Have I got that right?"

Robin nodded.

"Well, she wasn't. Isn't. Her parents are both alive. Why would she lie about that?"

"Maybe she hates them," Alison suggested, her first real contribution to their bank of ideas. "She took her chance to get away from them as well as the ex-boyfriend. Anyway, what's that got to do with the dead woman?"

"I don't know," Ben admitted, "but I don't like factual inconsistencies."

"Neither do I." Robin gave Ben a thumbs up. "If that turns out to be a lucky hunch, you can give me the lottery numbers. Pru, can you make a note to follow this up with Ms. Bairstow?"

Progress made, of a sort, but there was no getting away from their biggest stumbling blocks: who was the dead woman, why had all ID been taken off her, and why had the body been relocated after death? "Is there nothing more on a possible identification? Are we going to have to look for her worldwide?"

Sarah raised a tentative hand. "Ben and I have been going back through every viable option on identification from the UK database. We've not yet turned up a name, but we have run across something odd."

"Go on." Nice to see some proper intra-team cooperation. Maybe he'd underestimated Sarah, tarring all of the Abbotston crew with the same brush.

"A girl called Philippa Palmer was reported missing at a similar time to when our girl was killed, but we'd discounted her because she then turned up again, sort of."

"Sort of?" Alison quickly suppressed a sneer. Just as well, given Robin's inclination to get her transferred as soon as convenient.

Ben, bridling, said, "She'd gone travelling round the world, like Becky Bairstow."

"Another one?" Robin ran his hands through his hair. "I've come across a lot of coincidences in my time, but this is unbelievable."

Sarah shrugged. "I know, but apparently it's a fact. She's been posting on social media and assuring everyone she's okay, simply in need of some time out. As a result, the file got closed."

Robin nodded. "Right, well, you need to check whether she and Becky Bairstow have any connection."

"Already made a note to, sir." Ben pointed—superfluously—at his pad.

"Good." Having given his constables a bollocking, Robin was pleased he hadn't scared them all stiff in the process. "What more do we know?"

"Not much," Sarah responded. "It only came up because the officer who sent us Becky Bairstow's dental records mentioned it. They'd considered Philippa Palmer as identification for their dead girl. The fact she had a degree in archaeology made them mention it to us."

"There are hundreds of women with degrees in archaeology. We're back in the realm of coincidence." Pru stared at the incident board. "And if she isn't dead, she can't have been buried at Culford."

Robin's mobile phone began to ring, signalling a halt to proceedings. As soon as he saw who was calling, he mouthed, "The boss," and went into his office, then shut the door behind him.

"Chief Inspector Bright." He tried to convey a tone both professional and friendly. "How are things, sir?"

"Better for me than you, I guess." Cowdrey's usually asthmatic tones sounded clearer and healthier for his break. "No murderers on the loose here. Or if there are, I don't have any responsibility for catching them."

"It must be heaven." Once they'd dispensed with a few further pleasantries about his boss's holiday, Robin could give the man an update on the case so far.

"Sounds like you have it all under control. And you've had plenty of practice by now. Two years ago I might have felt the need to dash back, but I'm confident it'll all be going well without me."

"Thanks, sir. Much appreciated." Robin wished he could feel so positive.

"I'll be back home the day after tomorrow, unless you feel you need me before then."

"Your Fiona will kill me if I drag you back early." One domestic drama with a colleague was enough to deal with. "If there's a problem, I'll let you know."

"Good. Anything else I should know about, or will it all keep?"

Robin tossed a mental coin. Heads he'd leave reporting back about the less-than-brilliant Abbotston team until the boss was in the office once more, given that their underperformance was hardly a matter of urgency. Tails he'd give the boss a bit of a heads-up right now because he wanted the bloke to know what he'd be returning to.

Tails won; if things blew up, then Cowdrey would have wanted to know as soon as the fuse might have been lit, even if it were only smouldering.

"Just something bubbling with the team. Young Ben's turning out to be a real star, and Sarah's got potential to be one too, but the other two needed a rocket and I've been delivering it. You'd have thought they'd see this case as a chance to make their names, especially given the cloud this nick's been under."

"Still resenting us? They'll never forgive the Stanebridge yokels for solving their last murder case for them."

"They'll bloody well have to learn how to." Robin snorted. "And it's not only that. I suspect somebody—may not have been one of my team directly—has been leaking to the media. I've spoken to them about it, and if I get wind of who's involved, they'll be speeding along the disciplinary route before their feet touch the ground." Robin glanced out of his office window, but everybody appeared to be hard at work.

"I've got your back on that if it's needed. Maybe we haven't chucked out all the bad apples."

"You could be right."

The call ended with a bit more chit-chat about Cowdrey's holiday, after which Robin gave himself a few minutes of thinking time before opening the office door once more. Thirty seconds later, Pru appeared—a pair of very welcome coffees and some biscuits in hand—and no sooner had she got herself settled than Ben stuck his head through the door, with Sarah in tow.

"Got a minute, sir?"

"Yep. Take a pew if you can find one."

Ben looked uneasily over his shoulder, at his other colleagues, then lowered his voice. "They'll probably think we're trying to be teacher's pets."

"Sod them if they do," Sarah countered before making a point of shutting the door and addressing Robin and Pru. "We think some of the team took their feet off the gas. You know, when we believed the dead woman was Becky Bairstow."

Robin, who'd just about calmed down again about the media, felt his hackles rising once more. "Am I dreaming that I asked Alison to carry on the search?"

"You're not dreaming." Ben, squirming, appeared torn between covering his colleague's back and loyalty to the new regime.

"Ben tried to nudge her about it. Yesterday," Sarah confided.

Pru sighed. Robin knew from experience that she'd not have let that sort of task slip if she'd been in the same position as Alison. "You had a hunch she'd not come up with the goods?"

Ben shifted uneasily. "Maybe. I mean, there are a lot of missing-persons reports to get through."

"You're too nice for your own good." Robin shook his head. He'd let Cowdrey deal with Alison when he got back from his holiday; it was the kind of task the boss enjoyed.

"He needs to be hard as nails, like you." Pru grinned.

"Right. Before this becomes a Robin Bright character-assassination session, I want to bat a few ideas back and forwards. Get some momentum again." This was where Robin missed Anderson. He'd been great for brainstorming, even if some of his suggestions had been way off beam. Out of their interaction new ideas had tended to spring. Pru hadn't yet demonstrated quite the same facility, although that might be due to the relative newness of their working relationship. "Back to the basics of the case. Why do you strip all the ID off a body?"

"Because you want to delay identification so you can get as far away as possible before somebody twigs who it is." Trust Pru to state one of the most obvious—but nonetheless valid—explanations. "Maybe only a day or two's delay while the police put out a picture or a photofit might be crucial."

Sarah nodded. "And if you're fairly confident the corpse won't be found before nature does her bit in making a photo impossible and a photofit less accurate, that gives you further breathing space."

Robin, still haunted by the notion that something had likely been feeding on the newly dead girl's face, pressed on. "If that's the case here, the strategy's probably worked. What else?"

"Spite?" Ben suggested. "You know, murder not being enough. Maybe wanting to wipe away any trace of the person. Like you somehow claim their identity by stripping it from them."

"Then why not go the whole hog and take off the hands so you take the fingerprints away too?" Sarah asked.

"Because you can't actually eliminate someone's identity entirely that way. Not in the age of DNA sequencing." Ben shrugged. "And anyway, maybe the killer wasn't that sadistic."

"Shame our dead woman hadn't got a twin sister who was on the national database," Pru said. "Then we'd have got somewhere."

"If wishes were horses, beggars would ride. Oh, what is it this time?" Irritated by the interruption, Robin grabbed the phone on his desk. "Hello? Ah, my favourite CSI."

Ben eased out of his chair. "Want us to go, sir?"

"Hold on, Grace." Robin put his hand over the mouthpiece. "No, you can all be in on this." If it put the rest of the team's noses even further out of joint, so be it. They needed to see how effort was rewarded, and they'd get updated in due course. "Sorry about that. Just making sure the children keep quiet while you're talking."

"Give Pru my love." Grace chuckled. "Okay. They're working on a reconstruction of our lass's face, but you won't have it for a while. The doctor was right about postmortem changes. Some creature either dug into the grave and had a gnaw, or did so before she was reinterred. They seemed to have liked the nose."

"Steady on! You'll be putting me off my snack." Robin ruefully eyed his uneaten biscuits.

Grace snorted. "Such a wimp. Anyway, all the evidence points to her having been stored in a garage, wrapped up in a carpet. Curious mixture of fibres, oil, and other chemicals on the clothes. Maybe one of our furry friends got in and had a nibble during that period. Cat or a rat or—"

"I get the picture." Robin shuddered. "Was she killed there?"

"I can't say. She was in the garage for only a short time—a few days maybe—before she was moved. Want all the technical bits about how I reached that conclusion?"

"Might as well have all the works. I don't think I can face a custard cream anytime soon. No chance she was wrapped in a rare type of carpet that only three people in England have bought?"

"Not quite. It's upper end of the range, though. Chinese wool. Not the sort of thing most of us would have offcuts of lurking in the garage to soak up a leak from the sump."

At last, something tangible. "True."

"Yeah. Not even in posh places like Lindenshaw. I'll email everything over to you. Then you can go through the details when you're not feeling so squeamish."

"Oh, haha. Thank you, Grace. Over and out." Robin put down the phone, then gave his eagerly waiting listeners the low-down.

"That carpet could be useful. Chase the money." Pru tapped her notepad. "Not that we've come across anybody unusually well off yet, apart from my mate with his Mercedes."

"You don't have to have won the lottery to buy a decent Chinese rug. And that doesn't imply I'm making a connection to Becky Bairstow." Robin rubbed his hands together. "While we're in a brainstorming mood, want to look at why somebody moves a body? Apart from the fact it soon stinks to high heaven?"

"I think you just answered your own question, sir." Sarah stifled a snigger. "And you'd be constrained by rigor mortis, wouldn't you? Easier to manoeuvre the body if you wait until it's floppy. I wouldn't want it hanging around my garage for too long."

Robin noted from the corner of his eye, and not without satisfaction, that Ben appeared a touch green round the gills, although the young constable still managed to contribute his thoughts. "He—or she—the murderer, I mean, doesn't seem to have been that organised. Assuming it was premeditated. Wouldn't they have planned a better way of getting rid of the body? Short and long term?"

"You'd have thought so." Robin nodded. "Perhaps it was simply an accident or self-defence and the culprit panicked. Hid the body in the nearest convenient place until they could work out what to do. It happens." How many crimes hadn't come to light because the culprit had executed some simple plan for disposing of the body? There were plenty of nice deep holes left in the countryside to stick a body down if you could transport it there, so why choose Culford?

"If it was self-defence, why not report it straight away?" Pru's question roused him from his thoughts.

"Because people are stupid and illogical and prone to panic." Robin picked up the custard cream and absent-mindedly nibbled a corner. Biscuits always made things better. "And once you'd made a decision not to report it immediately, the worse it would look if you didn't report it until later. To the point you'd maybe not be able to report it at all."

"Is that what you think happened here, sir?" Sarah chipped in.

Robin wagged a finger of the hand which wasn't occupied with his biscuit. "Don't go jumping to conclusions."

"I wonder if the murderer is kicking themselves," Pru mused. "They might have assumed the body could have lain undetected at Culford for years, not knowing about the risk that the students would relocate their dig."

"Unless they wanted the body found there," Ben pointed out, to snorts of disbelief from Pru and Sarah.

"He's got a valid point." Robin flicked a biscuit crumb off his cuff. "Shallow grave, for a start, and the mosaic placed as though it was meant to signify something. Any news on that, by the way?"

Sarah, glancing through the window, muttered, "Don't hold your breath. Alison was supposed to follow that up too."

"You take that task over, then. It'll be right up your street after you've gone with Pru to the archaeological society meeting tonight." Robin clocked the delighted twinkle in Sarah's eye at being given the new responsibilities. "Okay, how did they move the body from garage to site? Car? Van? Somebody must have spotted a ruddy great truck if it went down there."

Culford was down a road designed to take one car in each direction—and barely that—so anything much larger than a minibus would have attracted attention, surely. A coach might escape notice given the prevalence of school trips, but a large vehicle moving around at night? The police would have expected that to be reported, and they'd seen nothing of the sort in the statements.

"What if the vehicle was driven up to the site during the day, when comings and goings are just routine? And then the body disposed of later that night?" Ben suggested. "And before anybody says one of the on-site staff would have noticed a vehicle left there overnight, it could have been done one of the days when the villa was shut."

Pru looked up from her notes. "Shut? I thought it was open every day bar Christmas and New Year?"

"Normally, yes." Ben opened a file and produced a piece of paper which he laid on the desk. "Do you remember the storms we had last

July? They had to shut the villa for three days because they couldn't guarantee safe access to visitors."

"Really?" Why had nobody mentioned that? Although given the problems in the area at the time—including a partially collapsed bridge on a trunk road and a landslip on the railway line which had caused transport chaos—minor problems at minor archaeological sites had probably escaped most people's notice. Robin scanned the article, which had been screen-captured from the local newspaper website. "The dates could work out, just about. Somebody could have had that site to themselves for several hours."

Pru voiced what they all might have been thinking. "Especially if they looked like they had legitimate reason to be there."

"Yep." Robin ran his finger around the picture on the page—a fuzzy image of Charlie Howarth that appeared to be linked to a video. "Let's see what your smarmy mate has got to say about it."

Chapter Nine

B en proved to be a better driver than Anderson, Robin not feeling the need to keep one hand clamped onto his seat as they negotiated the lane up to Culford villa. Howarth had suggested they meet at the council offices, but the police had insisted they wanted to be on-site.

If Howarth's expression of disappointment—hidden quickly, but not quickly enough—indicated he was upset at not seeing Pru, his cheery greeting was clearly an effort to show nothing was wrong.

"Inspector! I see that your missing woman wasn't who you thought she was."

Robin forced a smile. "We were pleased to find her alive and well and were able to eliminate her from our enquiries."

"Um, yes, indeed. How can I help you?" The offer, superficially cooperative, was made with such a smarmy smile that it stung worse than an insult.

Robin introduced Ben, made a few pleasantries about how they'd hopefully soon be letting him have his site back, then opened the gate—the constable on duty having been stood down—and manoeuvred them towards the taped-off area where the body had been found. If it made Howarth uncomfortable, all the better.

Robin got out his notepad, more for show than use. "Can you tell us why you didn't mention that the villa was forced to shut at around the crucial time?"

"Shut? Oh, yes. The storm. I thought you'd be aware of that. It was a big deal, having to disappoint so many people."

"A big deal for you, perhaps, but the police had plenty of other important matters to deal with then." Ben evidently was as little satisfied with the response as Robin. "Didn't you realise the date was significant?"

"I'm afraid I never connected the two, but—"

Robin cut in. "Did you visit the site during that time?"

"No. Well, yes, but only when we were about to reopen. I was on holiday with my family when everything happened." Howarth smoothed his tie. "You can check."

"We will." Although chances were the alibi would check out. Though it only counted as an alibi if they were sure that was the crucial period. "Becky Bairstow. Turns out she's a friend of yours?"

A wary tone replaced the cheery one. "Yes. Why?"

"I was going to ask you that. Why the hell didn't you tell us that you knew her when we linked her to the dead woman?"

Howarth cast a glance over his shoulder, although there was nobody else on-site to overhear. Guilty reaction? "Can I speak confidentially?"

Robin nodded.

"I asked Becky to do me a favour, one that I didn't want word getting around about."

"Infiltrating the local archaeology group?" Ben asked, earning himself a dirty look from Robin. Why lead the witness down that line? And was Robin imagining the fleeting expression of relief on Howarth's smarmy face?

"Yes. I didn't think it was relevant to the case, seeing as none of the people involved have gone missing, have they?"

"How can you know what is and isn't relevant? Especially when the chaos she caused amongst that group happened around the same time our dead woman was killed?" Robin, losing patience, moved closer, forcing Howarth towards the crime scene.

"I didn't realise that when you interviewed me. I was in shock about what had happened here."

Valid point, but not one that reduced Robin's desire to punch him. What was it about the bloke that made him so angry? A sudden recollection of one of the teachers at school, Mr. Brideman, who'd not quite connived at the bullying Robin suffered but who'd turned a blind eye to it, flashed through Robin's mind. Howarth could have been his twin. Maybe Robin should hold back and let Ben lead on this interview, although would the constable be confident and experienced enough to ask the right questions at the right points?

"Strikes us that there have been lots of odd things happening here." The timing of the question suggested Ben could read minds. "You've been seen at Culford villa out of normal hours. What were you doing?"

Good to see the smarmy expression disappear from Howarth's face. "When was this?"

"When? Is it a regular occurrence?"

"Oh"—Howarth waved his hand—"you know what it's like when you're busy. Sometimes I have to fit bits of work in whenever I can. If I'm passing by and need to call in, I make the most of the opportunity."

"Why would you need to call in when no other staff are on-site and the place is locked up for the night?"

"Well"—the airy wave again—"there are sometimes tasks to do which are much easier to get done when I'm on my own, with no annoying wom—people hanging around."

"Is your boss aware of your working practices?" Robin pulled out his phone. "Shall we ring him and ask?"

"Her," Howarth clarified feebly.

"Her." Robin flicked open the phone cover. "I'm sure visiting sites in the dark can't fit in with the council's lone-working directives. Probably breaks a host of other rules too."

"Okay." Howarth ran his finger around the inside of his collar. "I wasn't here officially. It's to do with why I asked Becky to ingratiate herself with the archaeology society. I suspected somebody had been poking about up here. We've had isolated incidents all across the county, and further abroad, with people—amateurs, with their latest toy metal detectors—causing damage. A proper, professional dig was needed, and I didn't want anybody arsing around beforehand. I used to drop up here on the off chance that I might catch them red handed."

"And did Ms. Bairstow find any evidence that they *were* red handed?"

"Alas, no." Howarth stared at the turned-over patch of ground and shuddered. "I guess we should count our blessings. We might have stumbled over this happening."

"We?" Ben had picked up on the key word.

"Ah, yes. I didn't always come here alone. Becky kept me company. So, you see, I wasn't lone working."

Pru had talked about Howarth being a charmer. To what extent had he tried that charm on "Mata Hari"? "Was that all there was to it? Really?" Robin asked. "We weren't born yesterday."

Howarth hesitated, clearly weighing something up, before answering. "Very astute, Mr. Bright. I won't try to justify myself because I suppose there is no justification, but Becky and I had other reasons for meeting here."

Ben stopped scribbling in his notebook. "Like what?"

"What do you think, Constable? We weren't playing Monopoly."

Ben's turn to squirm. "You were having an affair?"

"I wouldn't call it anything as grand. I used to pick her up after their meetings, and she'd brief me on what had happened."

"Which meetings?"

"Archaeologists, detectorists, anywhere she could inveigle herself in. We were very careful not to be seen together, and I guess with all the subterfuge, one thing led to another; we'd had a fling at university, and the circumstances made it flare up again. A brief flame but a brilliant one."

Ms. Bairstow had said Howarth had gone out with a friend of hers, but that wouldn't have precluded *their* having got it on. "Doesn't strike me as romantic, coming up here in the pitch dark."

"Pitch dark means you can't be seen." Howarth leered.

"But where—" Ben cut off his own question, much to Robin's relief. There was a line between legitimate questioning and sheer prurience.

"Not in the car park! Mind you, that Portakabin sofa isn't as uncomfortable as it appears."

Robin shuddered, remembering the sagging item concerned and wondering if the damage to the springs was related to Howarth's girth. "You said a brief flame. What extinguished it?"

"She started chatting up that bloke. The one she ran off with." Howarth frowned. "Sian's boyfriend."

"Ms. Bairstow seems to have had an eye for the men. She had a boyfriend in London too."

"I know, Inspector. But you're a man of the world. Scandalous what women get up to."

"*Chief* Inspector." Robin resisted giving Howarth a lecture about sauce for the goose being sauce for the gander. He had more important things to say. "Given that you've just told me your boss is a woman, I'd have thought you'd have exercised some care about using sexist language. I don't want to hear any 'all boys together' stuff."

"I—" Howarth opened his mouth, then shut it with a *snap* as Robin launched into his next question.

"Why didn't you take up Ros Butler's suggestions?"

"Ros Butler?"

"The student who did a report on how to increase profitability of the county heritage sites. I hear she had some sound business proposals, but you rejected them."

"Oh, her." Howarth may have been a flirt where women were concerned, but he was consistently giving the impression of not liking them. And the way he'd suddenly found his shoes to be of immense interest suggested he was less than comfy with finding a convincing answer to this question. "Typical student. No idea of the real world. Good proposals in theory, but in practice the whole thing would have been a nightmare. Not least asking some of the people who work at these sites to get up to speed with selling online or anything like that. Some of the younger ones like Sian would probably be fine, but my older lady volunteers—"

Tired of Howarth's ageist, sexist, probably everything-ist ramblings, Robin cut in. "Talking of Sian, is she the woman who's coming through the gate now?"

Howarth swung round. "Yes. What's she doing here?"

"Helping us with our enquiries." Why did the man seem so edgy at the sight of her? "Is that a problem?"

"No. No, I was just thinking that we'd been discussing Becky, and Sian might be upset if you mentioned her."

"That's a risk we have to take." Not that Robin believed Howarth's explanation. "The university dig. We believe you tried to have it stopped."

A flicker of unease registered in Howarth's eyes before he calmly replied, "That's true, but it wasn't so much about having it stopped as using resources wisely. The county's strapped for cash, as you can imagine, whereas the university seems to be awash with it. Foreign investment to take foreign students. If they've got the capacity to organise large-scale digs, then I believe they have a duty to serve the local community by targeting those digs where there's the most need."

Robin wished Howarth would get down off his soapbox, but the man seemed a sight too fond of his own voice for that to happen anytime soon. "Where would you have targeted an excavation?"

"On the plain the other side of Tythebarn, of course. There's a suspected banjo enclosure there which showed up as a crop mark during the last hot summer we had. The whole area's criss-crossed with ditches and trackways. It would make for a brilliant exploration into the Iron Age, but no, the university wouldn't have it. Culford wasn't even the first choice."

"You'd better explain that."

"There's a wonderful Roman site right on the county border, in the fields by Stockford. Only been dug the once, a hundred and fifty years ago. Loads of artefacts turning up in the plough soil and intriguing crop marks. They'd planned to dig there, but the site got contaminated by an overflow from the sewage farm next door, and they had to make a last-minute change." Howarth snorted. "The banjo site was dry as a bone, but the university department wanted Roman and Roman it had to have, and when *it* wanted it."

There was no doubting Howarth's enthusiasm for his subject, and the explanation was plausible. That last bit had been said with added venom, though. "Was there some issue with the timing, then?"

"Eh?" Howarth, brows knitted, might have been reviewing exactly what he'd said. "Only that it's terribly inconvenient to accommodate people at the last moment. They spoke to my boss, and she gave them the go-ahead to come here."

"Why didn't they speak to you?"

"I was on holiday." Howarth seemed to force himself to wear a more positive expression. "It's not that I object. Only it causes a bit of awkwardness for the schools we have booked to visit. They want to be able to see the whole site, not be constrained by a load of students. *My boss*"—he wore the momentary look of distaste that seemed to accompany every mention of the woman—"doesn't understand the implications. These things can't just be rescheduled without causing a lot of disruption to staff and visitors. I suppose they're bottom of her pecking order—"

Robin cut off any potential rant before it could develop. "Right. We'll be making sure your story checks out, and then we'll get back to you. Ben will be in touch to take a proper statement. And you'll know if your story doesn't check out, because *I'll* be back, with further questions."

Before Howarth could shake off his astonished expression and frame a reply, Robin had turned on his heel and headed for his next interview.

Sian Wheatstone looked like the sort of woman who wouldn't stand for any nonsense. Tall, dark-haired, with an athletic frame, she resembled some of the girls who'd made Robin's life hell on the sports field— Mixed hockey had to be the invention of a sadist. Sian proved much more welcoming than Howarth had been, opening the Portakabin so they could sit inside, then putting on the kettle for a welcome cuppa. Robin took a glance at the sofa, then opted for a chair at the table.

"Terrible business, this," she said over her shoulder.

"It is indeed." Out of the corner of his eye, Robin noticed Ben eyeing the sofa with suspicion and mouthed, "I know what you're thinking. Behave."

"I'm afraid it's only 'plastic' milk." Sian waggled a basket of small cartons, the sort they stocked in hotel rooms.

"So long as it's strong, I'm happy." Ben positioned himself to help carry the mugs when needed. "How long have you been volunteering here?"

"Oh, months and months." She busied herself with tea-making; had Ben's move been a master stroke, allowing him a clear view of her face? "I stopped for a while when I split with Jerry, because I was in a right huff, but then I thought, 'Okay, Sian, no point moping. Pull yourself up by your bootstraps.'"

"Didn't working at an archaeological site risk, um, stoking up memories?"

Sian's shoulders tightened almost imperceptibly, only enough for an experienced copper like Robin to spot. "No. I felt it was almost like raising two fingers to him. I was well rid of the toerag."

Ben spooned some sugar into his mug. "Why was that?"

"His true colours were starting to show. I hadn't realised before just how much of an eye he had for other women."

"Bit of a player?"

"Probably." Sian snorted. "Anyway, at the time it all happened, I'd have happily belted Lydia one, but I reckon she did me a favour. I hoped he was Mr. Right, and the sooner I knew he'd be off with the next pretty face, the better." Sian seemed much more reasonable than most jilted girlfriends would have been; a truly mature personality or just putting on a brave front? Although not many witnesses would so freely admit to the police that they'd entertained thoughts of thumping somebody.

"How long had they known each other?"

"Long enough." Sian waited until they were all settled with their drinks before continuing. "I met Jerry . . . hmm . . . maybe June or July of last year. I definitely started going along with him to the detectorists' meetings in July. There was a big debate about whether they should have a summer break in August because of all the holidays, and they decided not to and some people didn't like it. They're an opinionated bunch."

"So we believe." Robin blew on his tea, always a useful strategy for getting his thoughts together. "When did Lydia enter the picture?"

Sian knitted her brows. "Sometime in August? She'd only been around for a few weeks before she started getting in with Jerry. Then they ran off together back end of September. Quick worker, that girl."

Ben, who'd been happily knocking back tea which must have been too hot for any normal person to drink, asked, "And you started volunteering here . . .?"

"Around July, I think. About the time I met Jerry. Sorry to be so hopeless with dates. Not my forte. You'd be best to talk to Tuckton about when the detectorist meetings happened. He's probably got a note of the very second we arrived or left each time. Anyway, my main job is at a library—not that I actually need to work—but they can't offer many hours and I don't want to be bored, so taking on extra volunteering stuff is useful."

Robin took another fortifying swig of tea; he'd not realised just how thirsty he'd got. "You said that you don't actually need to work. How did you get to be in that lucky position?"

Sian's smile disappeared. "I came into money."

Robin hoped that wouldn't be because of a lottery win; there was enough replication in this case already. "I'm sorry to have to press you, but when we're investigating a murder, we need the full picture of anyone who might have been involved, however incidentally. You inherited the money?"

"Yes. My dad died. He was a widower and I'm an only child, so I've never been short of a bob or two, but now I've more than I need, so I can choose what I do. I know I should count my blessings, but . . ." Her bottom lip began to quiver. "I'd rather have Dad than any amount of money."

Ben, leaning over, pressed a handkerchief—Robin hoped it was clean—into Sian's hand. "I'm so sorry for your loss."

"Thank you. On both counts." Sian blew her nose. "Poor Dad. He'd made money in the city—which is rather a dirty word these days—but he was a good man, and when he retired early he was looking forward to the years ahead. Not just to enjoy himself, though. He would have had time to do voluntary stuff."

Quite a hagiography. Irrespective of whether the real Mr. Wheatstone matched up to his description, his daughter clearly felt his loss deeply. "How long ago was this?"

"A couple of years, now. It still feels like yesterday. His death changed everything for me."

This was beginning to be more like a counselling session than an interview, but Robin let it run. "How did he die?"

"He had a terrible accident. He loved walking, even though he could be a bit reckless at times. I used to warn him to take care, but if he saw something of interest—an unusual bird or a lump of old stone wall—he'd be there like a shot." She welled up again. "The silly idiot went too near a cliff edge and slipped. He broke his neck on the boulders they'd put in to protect against erosion, and then his body slipped between them. They didn't find him until the next day, although they assure me he died instantly."

"That's awful." Robin could imagine the guilt that would build up after such an event. Wondering if you'd only insisted the person concerned took special care or if you'd gone with them, perhaps the accident wouldn't have occurred. "Where did this happen?"

"Up near Gorleston, on the east coast." Sian dabbed her eyes. "We had a flat there. For family holidays, or for when he simply wanted some space to clear his mind of work. I can't bear the thought of ever going back there, but I can't bear the thought of selling it, either. It's probably a dust heap by now."

Ben offered her a clean tissue. "Take your time. We can wait."

"Thank you. Well, that was only the start. There was an inquest and then the estate going through probate, none of which I'd any experience of." She blew her nose. "Sorry, I'm getting in a right state."

"Nothing we haven't seen before."

"You're extremely understanding." Sian trumpeted into the hankie again, then had another draught of tea. "I got myself into a right tizzy, especially when the family started playing up. My uncle. He wanted some stuff from Dad's collection—Roman coins and stuff—saying he'd always been promised them. We had a blazing row, and I told him he could have what he wanted and after that I didn't want anything more to do with the family. That's when I moved to Merritt's End, about a year ago. Best thing I ever did. Fresh start."

Ben put down his mug, smiling sympathetically. "It must have come as an awful shock when they found the body here."

"Oh, yes. Like reliving Dad's death again, in a way. But everybody was so nice. Sarah—she took my statement—wasn't at all like you imagine the police to be." Sian blushed. "Present company excepted too. I only wish I could be more helpful."

So did Robin. Sian's life history was interesting enough, but it wasn't getting them any further forwards. "There are a couple of things you could help with. Keys to the site. Who has them?" That was another thing the Abbotston constables should have obtained, yet hadn't.

"I'll copy the keyholder list for you, but it's basically Clare, me, Mr. Howarth. And there's a spare set we can lend to contractors."

"Is the spare set kept securely?"

"As securely as it can be. It's in the small safe we have in the office, but any keyholder also has access to that." Sian shrugged. "It's not like we have anything here that's worth stealing."

True. And, as Robin had suspected, any keyholder could have copies of the keys made, maybe to give to their girlfriend to access the sagging-sofa love nest, although anyone—like a contractor—who'd legitimately borrowed the keys might have done the same. This was hardly a sealed-room type of crime.

"Okay. So, access outside of normal hours. Does anybody come here when they shouldn't?" Ben asked.

Sian hesitated, showing for the first time a degree of uncertainty. Robin shot a warning glance at his constable; they had to give the witness space to answer. At last, she said, "Oh, dear. I don't want to get people into trouble."

"If you know something, you must tell us. If it's not relevant to the case, we won't pursue it." How many times had Robin cajoled witnesses using similar words?

"There was one day I'd got all the way home and discovered I didn't have my phone. I hoped I'd left it in the office here, so I came back to check. Mr. Howarth's car was parked in the car park, the gate to the site was open, and there were lights on in here." She indicated the Portakabin with a sweep of her hand.

"It would be reasonable," Ben said gently, "to have come over and checked that nothing was amiss. In the circumstances."

Sian, flushing slightly, nodded. "That's exactly what I thought. As you can imagine, I'm a touch wary of people having had an accident and not being discovered until it's too late."

"Entirely understandable," Ben agreed.

"I got as far as the steps, and I heard voices. Mr. Howarth and . . . a woman. She was saying that they had to stop, that it wasn't right." Sian's gaze flitted between the door, the sofa, and the policemen. "He said they weren't harming anybody. It was just a bit of fun."

That seemed to bear out Howarth's story.

"Do you know what they were up to?" Ben immediately reddened at the reaction his question provoked.

"What do *you* think they were up to? Having a cup of tea and a biscuit?" Sian snapped. "I didn't look through the window to confirm—I didn't want a front-row seat. I dashed straight over to the office, got my phone, and legged it."

"You said 'a woman.'" Robin picked up the questioning. "Who was she?"

"I'm not sure. I thought it sounded like Lydia Oliver, or Becky Bairstow or whatever she's called, but it couldn't have been. She was making eyes at Jerry around that time."

Which probably wouldn't have stopped her, given what they knew of Becky Bairstow.

Back at the station, Robin and Ben were halfway up the flight leading to the main entrance when Pru came through the door.

"Just getting some sandwiches for me and Sarah, sir." She jerked her thumb in the direction of the team's favourite café. "No idea if we'll get fed tonight."

"Good thinking. You can't work on an empty stomach." Robin's own guts were grumbling like mad at the mere mention of food. "Got a minute to hear what Howarth had to say?"

"Always time for that."

Robin brought her up to speed, aided and abetted by Ben, who had a knack of imitating Howarth's voice for all the juicy parts.

"Having an affair?" Pru's eyebrows nearly hit her hairline. "I don't believe it."

"That's what he says," Ben confirmed.

"Yeah, well, he's always been a bit of a one for tall tales."

Robin had a further question to ask, one that needed privacy. "Ben, could I meet you back in the office?"

"Of course, sir." The constable gave a knowing look and disappeared into the building.

Pru fiddled with her handbag. "This feels ominous."

"It's not meant to be, but I've got to ask. Was there anything romantic between you and Howarth? Even back when you were snotty five-year-olds?"

"God, no, sir!" Pru, closing the handbag clasp with a decisive *snap*, made a moue of distaste.

"Sorry, but you know that if there was any strong personal connection between you two and it ever turns out he's in the frame for something..." Robin made a "cut off" gesture with his hand across his neck. "An old friendship might still mean you should come off the case."

"I understand that, sir. Given the history at Abbotston, we have to be seen to be acting with absolute probity. I'm not offended. Well, only at the fact that you think I could have fancied him." She grinned. "He really was only a friend, and that's all. He chatted me up at school, but he chats up all the women."

"So if he chats up all the women, why don't you believe he was having an affair?"

"Like I've said before, he's all talk and no action. He'd like to be thought of as a Casanova, so maybe he embroiders the truth."

"But isn't it taking a terrible risk to lie about your love life? Word gets out and his marriage could be up the spout."

"*You're* not going to tell anyone, are you?" Pru narrowed her eyes, obviously puzzling it through. "If he'd been sleeping with Becky Bairstow, her reaction in the interview—when *she* mentioned him before we did—would have been different."

That might be so, although Ms. Bairstow struck Robin as being pretty convincing at dissembling. "So why tell such a whopper? Unless you're trying to hide something worse."

"That's certainly more in character for Howarth. Like covering up a murder?"

"No. I wouldn't trust him as far as I could throw him, but I don't think he's a killer. He reminds me of some of the con men I've nicked. Smooth, smarmy, always a bit too quick with an answer and a change of direction."

But what con he was putting over, Robin couldn't tell.

Chapter Ten

Adam's unease had grown from car park to town-centre pub. Not that he thought somebody was going to try to deck him—he'd have brought Campbell for protection if he'd been that worried—but at what the evening would hold. Robin's description of Tuckton and his fallout with the archaeologists didn't inspire confidence in the detectorists' club, but Baxter seemed a decent enough bloke, and surely he wouldn't hang around with a crowd of costive jobsworths?

Fifty yards from the pub door, he caught sight of Baxter, who stopped to let him catch up.

"I thought you'd chicken out!"

"I nearly did," Adam admitted, "when I saw what you had to do to become a member." Adam's research on joining the organisation had been an eye-opener. "It's almost as arduous as the process for getting a job in a school. Why would you need to produce two character references?"

"Are you worried nobody would vouch for you?" Baxter laughed. "Tuckton—he's the bloke who runs the group—wanted to ask about people's credit history as well, but he got shouted down."

"Isn't it all a bit over the top?"

Baxter shrugged. "They got stung, and it knocked their trust for six. Maybe they'll ease up when they get over it. And some of the stuff's sensible. Did you see the terms and conditions of behaviour?"

Adam recalled a hefty downloadable PDF. It didn't fill him with optimism for the evening ahead; if it proved as miserable as the paperwork suggested, he'd have to find an excuse not to attend any further meetings. "Yeah, but I didn't read it. I'd have still been there."

"Not small, is it?"

"I wondered if it was a wind-up. Something to do with their getting back at the local archaeologists."

"No, it's deadly serious. And once you get past the enrolment bits, it's useful information. Really clear details about what constitutes a hoard, and the law about treasure trove. We're all dead keen not to give detectorists a bad name, so we need to act in accordance with all legal requirements." They walked on. "Nobody wants to break the law."

"That's good to hear." Hopefully that included steering clear of murder.

Once in the pub, Adam would have been able to identify Tuckton simply from the word portrait Robin had given him. Neatly turned out without being dapper, the man was marked out by a fussy air and slightly exasperated expression. Baxter made the introductions, explained Adam's potential interest in joining them, then led him to the bar, where Baxter got himself a beer and Adam a shandy before they made themselves comfortable and waited for business to begin.

Adam had anticipated something like a school governors' meeting, but the proceedings opened with one of the members giving a fascinating account of the Jersey hoard, which she'd observed being processed when on her holiday. She presented well, with an interesting range of slides displayed on her laptop, to the point that Adam started to think the evening might exceed all expectations on the enjoyment front—a sentiment which fizzled out when they got down to what Tuckton described as "business proper."

Out came the screeds of minutes and other stuff, and then Adam got effectively yellow-carded, asked to sit out as he wasn't a member. Baxter, rolling his eyes, mouthed an apology, at which Adam mouthed back, "No worries." He moved to another table, where he was joined by another newcomer to the group—a dark-haired, handsome bloke dressed in a style he'd have described as shabby chic and which his mother might have called expensive clothes worn beyond their shelf life.

"Blimey, they love the sound of their own voices, don't they?" The posh voice fitted the attire. The man held his hand out to be shaken. "Richard Agnew. Another newbie, like yourself."

"Adam Matthews. Glad to meet a fellow outcast."

Agnew grinned. "Been detecting long?"

"Never done it. Just dipping my toe in the water."

"Careful you don't get it bitten off." Agnew lowered his voice. "They're a funny lot. They get their knickers in such a twist."

"I thought this was your first meeting?"

"It is, but I've run across them before, here and there. I'm doing some work at Kinechester Uni, so I thought I'd drop in. You never know if there'll be a fracas to gawp at."

"Fracas?"

"Do you not know about their falling-out with the local archaeologists? Who refer to this lot as 'the defectorists,' by the way."

Adam chuckled. "I'd heard there was no love lost between them. Something about a woman running off with somebody else's boyfriend."

"Was that the same woman the police thought was the victim of the Culford murder?"

"Culford?" Adam, glass halfway to his mouth, nearly spilled his shandy.

"It's all over the news and social media. I suppose that some of what's said has to be true."

"What they get from the proper police channels will be." Did that sound too much like he had a vested interest in the case, or was it the normal reaction that any local might have had?

"And the rest is what people make up? Quite likely. I feel so sorry for the girls who were digging up the 'bathhouse.'" Agnew made an inverted commas sign. "They must have had a hell of a shock."

Adam didn't have to feign a shiver. He knew what it was like to come across a dead body; a fresh corpse was bad enough, but a long-dead one didn't bear thinking about. "That could put them off for life." He took another drink. "The bathhouse bit. Don't you think it's one?"

"Hmm, not sure." Agnew shrugged. "Some people struggle to accept that their local site is just a common or garden villa. Culford's a posh one, granted, with decent mosaics, probably something the local native bigwig Iron Age family built."

"Iron Age?"

"Upwardly mobile natives. Wanting to make themselves into good solid Roman yeomen—forgive the rhyme—they moved into the villa from the hill fort, or one of the local farmsteads, to show how they were in favour with the new ruling power. Looking down on people who lived in the old-fashioned round houses."

"That sounds a rather modern notion. Was it like that back then?"

"Do you think people were any different in those days? Human nature doesn't change."

"You're right there." Adam waited—Agnew seemed voluble enough that useful information might emerge without him having to obviously pump the man. "The bathhouse is a figment of their overactive imaginations?"

"There may well be one, because that would have been 'one up' on the locals too, but even that isn't enough for some people." Agnew tipped his head towards the rest of the group. "They always want a site to have a ritual element or another thing that's out of the ordinary. 'Our site's better than yours' sort of annoying rubbish."

"You prefer things simpler?"

"Every time. If someone destroyed all the records we have of our era and a poor soul two thousand years in the future finds a Rubik's cube, they'll say, 'Aha! That's for a ritual purpose,' rather than simply being an activity nerds passed the time with."

Adam grinned; chatting with Agnew was making the evening bearable, although things might change after he asked his next question. "Wasn't there a bit in the local rag about this being a sacred site?"

Agnew rolled his eyes. "Anonymous letters, or so I understand. Lunatic fringe wanted to have their say-so."

"Could be." People did get agitated about local matters. "So why are you here exactly?"

"I'm curious. I've always suspected something odd was going on locally, by which I don't only mean the fallout between the groups." Agnew leaned closer. "Can I trust you? Given that you're not one of 'them.'"

"It depends what you want to trust me with. I'm not likely to snitch to anyone—except my partner. He's running the investigation into the Culford murder."

"Bloody hell!" Agnew put his hand to his mouth, then lowered his voice again. "Are you here on official business?"

"No. Honest. As Baxter said earlier, he invited me along because I teach his daughter. Anything I hear of interest I'll pass on to my other half, although I'm no Hercule Poirot."

Agnew appeared to weigh his options before continuing. "Okay, well, you'd better tell your bloke that there's a trade in faked artefacts, and it can be linked to this area. And that if he hasn't got somebody looking at the mosaic which the press say was found with the body, then he should."

"Hold on." The conversation appeared to have jumped a line or two. "Pass that by me a second time."

"In words of one syllable?" Agnew grinned. "I'm based at a slightly more reputable university than Kinechester, and in the course of my work I've run across a couple of faked Roman items. So I've been doing some digging, no pun intended, and I think there's an organised racket. Not making huge amounts of money, but that's not the point. I also developed a suspicion that Culford may be somehow tied up with it. When I saw the story about the murder, I had to dig further."

"Why didn't you report all this to the police?"

"Because I have no proof, apart from the faked articles, and they could have been made at any place at any time. Forgery isn't a newly minted crime."

Valid point. Robin—or one of his team—might just have listened to Agnew and then filtered out the information as being irrelevant. He was about to ask if Agnew thought the mosaic found with the body might have been faked, then held fire, remembering that element wasn't supposed to be in the public domain. "They'd still be interested, proof or not."

"I'd be happy to help."

"Can you give me a contact number, please? I'm sure the police will want to pick your brains."

"They can pick to their hearts' content, for all the good it will do." The words may have been self-deprecating, but Agnew's air made it plain he was confident of his own abilities. Like many truly clever people, he was clearly happy to play down the capacity of his grey cells. "I thought that if I could get in with this lot, I might hear something, but I'm already beginning to doubt it. I made the stupid assumption that getting some of these"—Agnew waggled his glass—"inside them would let me see what makes them tick, but it just appears to make them more up themselves."

"You need soppy drinkers rather than bolshy ones." Adam's shandy had all gone, but he couldn't be bothered to get another. He'd no doubt learned all he was going to learn. "Anyway, they're probably wary of newbies. Once bitten twice shy."

"Oh. The Woman? Yes, I heard about her." Agnew leaned closer. "What I'd like to know is whether she was trying to find out about this forgery business as well?"

A bookie might give ten to one on for that to be exactly what Robin would ask.

By the time Adam got home, Robin was sprawled on the sofa, flicking through the TV channels, and Anderson had gone to bed to watch something on Netflix. A thorough debrief on what Helen had said—interspersed with both amusement and amazement from Robin, and his being sworn to secrecy—took place before Adam could follow the revelations of the morning with the revelations of the evening.

"Faked artefacts?" Robin's eyes lit up.

"That's what Agnew said."

"Agnew? Ben's run across that name somewhere. Hold on." Robin reached for the notepad and pen that lived on the coffee table shelf, waiting for one of them to have an idea they needed to jot down. "Just give me the key points of that again so I haven't forgotten them by morning. I'm too knackered to retain everything."

Adam patiently went through things again as his partner took notes. "Interesting, isn't it?"

"More than interesting. It could fill some annoying gaps. Pru's not convinced by what Howarth says he's been doing at Culford."

"Eh?"

"Sorry. I forget you're not with me on investigations." Robin ran his hand along Adam's arm. "It's because I think of you all the time."

Adam grinned. "Stop slinging me a line and explain what you're on about."

"Long story short, this bloke's been hanging around Culford after hours and said it was because he was getting his end away. We suspect that story's a smokescreen."

"A smokescreen to cover up dodgy dealings in fakes?"

"Could be. I was going to talk to this Agnew bloke, but it didn't seem a high priority." Robin sighed. "Looks like it goes to the top of my list. Thanks."

"Glad to be of help." If this led in some small way to a solution, then Adam would have a less tired lover sitting next to him, one with another feather in his cap, to boot. "Are you guessing these forgeries are linked to the murder?"

"No idea, but it's something a bit more tangible than inter-society feuds. If I'd been conned into laying down a pile of cash for what turned out to be old tat, I could be feeling murderous. And"—Robin, eyes suddenly glinting, tapped his notepad excitedly—"if that dead girl was involved, then the choice of burial place could be symbolic. It could also explain why they chose a shallow grave, as though she was meant to be found."

This was starting to make sense. "With a piece of fake mosaic as another symbol?"

"We don't know it's fake, but that's not an unreasonable surmise." Robin ruffled Adam's hair. "We'll make a detective of you yet."

"No, thank you. I have quite enough to do."

"Shame. I'd like to have you on my team. Actually"—he leaned closer—"I'd like to have you, full stop, but I suppose there's no chance of that until Stuart's gone?"

Footsteps overhead formed a theme track to the answer. "No bloody chance at all."

Chapter Eleven

Agnew didn't sound surprised to be contacted by Robin so hard on the heels of the detectorists' meeting. He arranged to meet the police over coffee later that morning, at one of the university cafés. The police could arrive armed with the Culdover archaeologists' viewpoint on things, as a debrief with Pru and Sarah was first on Robin's list, before the Friday morning meeting with the rest of the team.

"How did it go with the CAS?" Robin asked once the three were in his office. "Are they as painful as Adam reckons the detectorists are?"

"Not a bit. We had a hoot of a time." Pru, grinning, gave an encouraging glance to Sarah, who took up the story.

"Yes, sir. Part of it was a brief formal meeting, following up some actions from last time, but mainly the evening was about networking and sharing ideas. And there didn't appear to be any constraint because we were police. It's been a long time since I was offered so many top-ups of my glass."

"Drinking on the job. Whatever next?" Robin shook his head theatrically.

"Leave off, sir. We kept strictly to the lemonade. Diet at that. And we got lots of information." She held up her official notebook, pinching a wodge of numbered pages between her fingers.

"Blimey."

"They like to talk," Pru chipped in.

"But do they like to say anything useful?"

"I'll have to work with Ben and compare all this to the other information we have. Painstaking, but seeing as we're so short on leads, who knows what could help." Sarah opened the notebook, then flicked through it.

"Actually, we might have got a lead, but I'll leave that until the team briefing." Robin, amused at the disappointed looks his statement produced, waited for them to continue.

"Spoilsport," Pru said, no doubt reflecting what Sarah was thinking too, although she'd have been too polite—or wary—to say it. "Couple of things came out. This'll amuse you. They call Tuckton's lot the 'defectorists.'"

Robin chuckled, not wanting to give away that he'd already been informed. "I like that."

"You'll like this too. They feel as cross about Lydia Oliver as the detectorists did. The two groups used to get on like a house on fire, and they think she caused the great rift. They've been spitting nails since it emerged that she's really somebody else; nobody likes being conned. And at least one of them says they've heard rumours about her and Howarth, although how accurate the rumours are or where they started, who knows." Sarah came to something in her notes that raised a smile. "They describe Charlie Howarth as a slimy creep."

"They've got good judgement. Howarth and Bairstow seem to have put plenty of backs up." Maybe it was just as well Ms. Bairstow's name had leaked, even if Robin wished he could have controlled the flow of information. If people started to talk, so much the better; the police could sift rumour from fact.

"Yeah. They were furious when they discovered the detectorists thought the CAS were behind the 'spying' thing, that one of them had put Becky up to it. But now they think it's a huge joke, and they're delighted to have severed all connections." Sarah consulted her notes. "'Good riddance to a bunch of pretentious twits.' The actual words they used weren't as complimentary."

"No, I bet they weren't."

"And they're much more concerned about the dead girl and who she might be than most of the people we've talked to seem to be. They say that if there's anything they can do to help us work out who she is, we've just got to ask."

"Go back and ask them about fakes."

"Fakes?" Pru's head shot up from where she'd been bent over her notes.

"Yes, they're my new lead. So look surprised when I tell the rest of the team, eh?"

"Will do, sir." Sarah gave Pru a wink.

"Becky Bairstow isn't the only person who's been doing some spying." Robin consulted his own notes. "Adam met a bloke called Agnew—remember Ben coming across that name?—at the detectorists' meeting. He's on the trail of faked artefacts, and he's convinced that trail takes in Culford. We're seeing him later, Pru, to get the details." He halted, puzzled at his officers' mischievous expressions. "Okay, spill the beans. What do you know that I don't?"

"Well, we might have heard about the fakes before you did," Pru explained. "One of the blokes we met last night works at Kinechester Uni, and he'd seen the picture that student took of the mosaic. Apparently, the place is awash with the story."

Damn. He'd forgotten about that photo.

"So he suspected it was dodgy, just by looking at the picture," Pru continued. "Maybe Agnew might give us an expert view."

"It's on my list of questions for him. Anything else you're one step ahead on?"

"All the theories the CAS have about what happened. Some of which are weirder than others." Sarah rolled her eyes.

"Go on; hit me with them." Robin eyed the thick pile of notes. "For elimination purposes."

"Okay. There's a view that the villa might be built on an older site of occupation, one that was used for ritual purposes. What's so funny, sir?" Sarah asked.

"Ritual. It's what they always used to say on *Time Team* when they didn't know what something was for."

"This has got evidence to back it up, though. Apparently, when the villa was first excavated in Victorian times, they found the body of a small child in a ditch. Bronze Age, maybe." Sarah hesitated a moment. "Its head had been stoved in and a flint scraper placed in the grave with it."

"Like our dead woman?" Robin took a deep, calming breath. "They reckon this murder is somehow linked to that one?"

"That's about the size of it, although I don't see it myself," Pru confided. "This doesn't feel like the work of an obsessive. If we'd known who the victim was from the start, we'd have plumped for something like an argument that went wrong, and a hurried, unplanned attempt to hide a body. *You* always look at the domestic angle first, don't you, sir?"

"Yes. You're more at risk from your nearest and dearest than any stranger. Although those sorts of murders don't usually involve dodgy bits of mosaic." Robin scratched his head. "Hold on, though. What about those letters to the local paper, saying that future digging at Culford should be banned because it was a sacred site?"

"Yes, sir. We asked the CAS if they'd seen them, and whether they mentioned this small child. They said they had read them—for a laugh—but the child wasn't referred to." Sarah rubbed the side of her nose, like one of Adam's pupils might have when puzzling over a tricky sum. "They had no idea who'd written them, although they suspected it was just a loony."

And they were probably right. "Any other theories get aired?"

"Remember the Community Payback people they had working at the site?" Pru glanced through the office window at the rest of the team.

Robin took the hint. "We effectively eliminated them. Are you suggesting somebody cocked that up?"

"Not sure. Tom, who we met last night, knew one of them. Jamie Warnock, the bloke who's supposed to have moved back to Scotland. Tom reckons that he comes back here visiting, pretty regularly."

"And your contact thinks Warnock might be involved?" Heads might have to roll if they'd let a vital thread unravel. The impression he'd got from his team was that Warnock had moved permanently north of the border. "What was he done for in the first place?"

"Driving offences, I believe." Pru checked her notes. "Yep. And Tom said he's seen him three times out and about here; each time Warnock's been acting out of character. Blanks him. And it can't be that he's mistaken somebody else for Warnock, because the bloke's apparently got a distinctive scar under his right eye."

"Blanking somebody's not a lot to build suspicion on, let alone a case." Albeit this whole investigation was built on thin foundations. "This Warnock might feel embarrassed that he's got a criminal record."

"*This Warnock* used to go out with a girl called Philippa Palmer."

"Really? Our Philippa Palmer?"

"I didn't know she was ours, sir." Sarah cheeked the boss a bit. "I don't know how common a name it is, but they said she was an archaeologist. That's one of the reasons why Tom mentioned her, because Warnock used to go on and on about how clever she was and how she'd have loved the Culford site."

"That sounds like she'd never been there." Or at least Warnock believed she'd never been there. "You said 'used to go out with.' Did Tom say anything about why the couple had split?"

"No. He didn't appear to know. Just that she'd been on the radar and now she wasn't."

"We made a point of asking them if they knew of any women who'd mysteriously disappeared," Pru clarified, "even if we didn't put it quite as dramatically. No leading the witnesses."

"I should hope not." Robin pushed back his chair. "Time to update everyone."

The morning briefing and brainstorm had a better, positive atmosphere; Robin's outburst had evidently had an effect. Alison even volunteered to follow up on the Warnock angle, although Robin gave that job to Sarah, as she'd been the one to first light on it. He gave Alison the ritual aspect to follow up—they couldn't ignore the possibility of this being the work of some lunatic—encouraging her to look for any evidence of other peculiar happenings at Culford on any other occasions since the Bronze Age.

"If it is a lunatic, one obsessed with ritual, surely that'll make matters worse, sir." Ben addressed Robin, but his eyes scanned the team. "People who pick up victims at random and do despicable things to them are usually the ones who get away with it longest, aren't they?"

"Then we'll have to hope, Alison's best efforts notwithstanding, this isn't that type of case."

Robin should have been grateful to hear the murmur of agreement run round his team—the first time he'd heard them be united on anything—but he couldn't shake off the depressing thought that they might never identify the victim, nor her killer.

When Robin and Pru arrived at the café, Agnew proved easy to spot from Adam's acerbic description of, "Brooding demeanour. The kind that people might describe as smouldering if it belonged to a Spaniard, and would probably call miserable if it belonged to a Scotsman."

From the firm handshake and the brisk welcome, Robin immediately classified him as a person who wouldn't tolerate any arsing about; no wonder he'd been so harsh online about the shenanigans between the two rival Culdover groups. He'd certainly struck Adam as being the sort of man who, once he'd decided you knew what you were talking about, would take you into his confidence.

Robin couldn't help warming to Agnew, in the same way as he'd taken against Howarth, even though he'd taught himself not to be affected in any interviews by how he reacted to the witness or suspect—didn't they call it the horns and halo effect? An easy trap for young coppers to fall into, interviewing a witness they took to and assuming they were telling the truth, especially if they reminded said copper of their Uncle Fred, who was a bastion of probity. Too easy to go the other way, as well, and give that witness a hard time while you made a deliberate effort not to let your bias affect you.

While Robin reckoned he was savvy enough to identify his biases and remain objective, he'd probably been a touch too heavy on Adam during the Lindenshaw murder when they'd first run into each other. It had been entirely necessary, not letting sexual attraction to a potential suspect cloud his judgement.

"Sir?" Pru's voice knocked him out of a fond memory of those days.

"Sorry. Copper's brain—always darting off somewhere." He took a swig of coffee.

"Occupational hazard, I'd have thought." Agnew gave Pru a dazzling smile. "I'm glad I met your partner last night, Chief Inspector. He seems very switched on. I guessed he'd have you hot on the trail."

"He knows how important it is to pass on information in a timely manner." Bloody hell, how toffee-nosed did he sound? He should simply let his pride in Adam shine through. "So you think somebody is making pretend Roman artefacts and selling them on as the real thing, dodgy provenance and all?"

"I don't reckon, Chief Inspector. I'm ninety percent certain. Mind you, I don't have an audit trail of who and where, or else I'd have got in touch with you before now." He laid a large brown envelope on the table. "This is what I have so far."

"Thanks." Robin opened the flap, then whistled at the volume of paper. "I've got a nice, keen pair of constables who'll enjoy ploughing through this."

"Good. I wish you every success in pinning the swine down."

"When did this start?" Pru asked.

"Hundreds if not thousands of years ago, although not—obviously—this particular racket." Agnew gave a shiver of evident distaste. "As long as there have been gullible people with a bit of money to spend, there have been people willing to take it off them. It's an ancient and not very noble business."

"Really?"

"Absolutely. Faked relics for pilgrims, animal bones masquerading as saints' bones in shrines—I wouldn't be at all surprised if there was a burgeoning market in faked carved mammoth tusks being sold out of the backs of caves to unsuspecting Neanderthals."

Pru chuckled. "You're probably right. Villainy's as old as the hills. So, when does *this* outbreak date to?"

"I'd say a couple of years. Not that it was picked up at the start." Agnew consulted his notebook. "I got called in about eighteen months ago, when somebody was changing the insurers for their collection of artefacts. I had to give some expert opinions on valuation." He grinned self-deprecatingly at the word "expert." "The stuff in this collection would have graced any museum—most of it came from antiquarian Victorian relatives who'd dug it up hither and yon. But there were a few other pieces that had been acquired recently. The last two were definitely 'off,' and some of them appeared to be a bit dodgy."

"How could you tell so rapidly?" Robin had seen the experts on *Time Team* study a bit of old pot and date it to within fifty years; it always seemed like a magic trick. "I mean, what did you see that he didn't?"

"She." Agnew grinned. "For a start, one of the objects in question was an almost exact copy of an artefact I'd inspected only a few months previously. And not a mass-produced Samian Ware bowl.

A distinctive statuette. I won't go into the details, but it rang all sorts of bells, and not tuneful ones. When we looked further, it turned out her version had been manufactured by the wrong kind of iron-production process."

Now they were getting somewhere. "Had all the dodgy items come from the same source?"

"That's a good question. And one to which I couldn't get a decent answer. She was distinctly cagey about where they'd come from. I suspect she thought they'd been smuggled off a site somewhere rather than turning up legitimately in somebody's back garden."

"Does that happen? Artefacts turning up in back gardens, I mean?" Pru clearly wasn't a fan of *Time Team*, or she'd not have had to ask that.

"Surprisingly often. Sites get used, forgotten about, reused . . ." Agnew waved his hand. "Dig up your own garden and see what you find."

"I'm afraid I live in a flat. There won't be any stray Roman roads in my window box." Pru gave Robin a sidelong glance.

Time to produce the Culford mosaic? Robin got out the evidence bag which held it; maybe the piece not having been dispatched for identification would turn out to be a blessing in disguise. He encouraged Agnew to slip on disposable gloves, even though the item had already been found to be without fingerprints. Better to be safe, rather than risk Grace's wrath. "What do you make of this?"

"Hm." Agnew turned it in his hands, then brought out a small eyepiece to inspect it in more detail. "It appears to be set in opus signinum."

Pru snorted. "Opus what?"

"Opus signinum." Robin grinned. "Roman cement."

"Very good." Agnew nodded. "Did you study ancient history before you turned to enforcing the law?"

"No. I just watched an awful lot of *Time Team*. One of my mother's favourite programmes."

"Then you'll know that you don't usually get tesserae set in this stuff. It happens, but as a rule it's one or the other. Cement floor or mosaic." Agnew studied the piece again. "Is this what was found in with the dead girl? Before you ask me how I know, it's the talk of the Kinechester archaeology department."

"So we understand."

Agnew raised an eyebrow. "That must be galling when you're trying to control flow of information. For what it's worth, the sensible opinion is that the picture she shared told us little, although it rings alarm bells."

"Wrong era for the site?" Robin recollected what they'd been told that first day.

"Yes. On the face of it. So either this piece has been imported from somewhere else or Culford has a different history than we presently believe. And there's a third option." Agnew studied the piece again. "I'd say this was not only brought in from elsewhere, but probably knocked up within the last year or so. I said *appears* to be set in opus signinum. I'm not convinced this is the real thing, but I'd need to take it away and check."

"Thanks for the offer, but we have to follow protocol on that. We were going to send it to Kinechester, although using an expert out of the area might be better."

"How sensible. I'd get two or three opinions on it too, just in case you ask somebody who's up to their necks in fakes."

Robin nodded. "Is there any way of telling if this came from the same source as the forgeries you've identified?"

"I doubt it. I don't remember seeing any faked mosaics, although that doesn't mean they aren't about." Agnew knocked back the remainder of his coffee, then set down the mug with a snort. "Oh, I see. Are you thinking that the dead woman was somehow caught up in this racket and the mosaic was put into the grave as a kind of symbol of guilt?"

"It's a possibility." And one that Robin himself had just been mulling over.

Pru, who'd appeared slightly miffed at not being able to contribute to the archaeology talk, was back on more familiar ground. "You suspect this fakes trade links to Culford. Why?"

"It's all in here"—Agnew tapped the envelope he'd handed to Robin—"but the gist is to do with IP addresses. It's hard to follow up this stuff directly, not least because you don't want to scare people off while you're on the trail, so we went round the houses. My wife's a whizz-kid at all things online, so she and I have been rooting about, using a lead we got from another disgruntled customer. Not everybody wants to keep shtum and avoid admitting they were 'had.'"

Valid point. "So this stuff is sold over the web? Darknet?"

Agnew chuckled. "A lot of the people I work with can hardly manage a smartphone, let alone get into the deeper recesses of the internet. No, we found what looks like a legitimate site connecting buyers and sellers. You could call it an artefact 'lonely hearts' business, selling mainly genuine stuff with a few forgeries hidden amongst it. Emily—my better half—registered under an assumed name so nobody would see 'Agnew' and get rattled. She then had the bright idea of following up on a few of the comments on the forum and seeing where these people were located. Some of them, allegedly from a variety of usernames, all came from the same IP address. Which appears to be the Culford site, and seeing as the occupants of the villa wouldn't be online, it must be the office."

Robin recalled the PCs he'd seen there, then had a revelatory vision of Howarth and Bairstow *not* romping on sofas but chatting online, dealing in dodgy artefacts. Ms. Bairstow infiltrating the Culdover meetings before the great split, to find out whether anybody suspected their game. "Do you think the stuff's actually being made at Culford?"

"No, they haven't got the capacity. It could be being churned out anywhere—maybe even at the university, although I've not seen any evidence of that yet, and I've been on the hunt, believe me."

Robin didn't doubt him. "Does this link to our dead woman? Have you come across anybody really suffering because of the faked antiquities? Losing a stack of money, or maybe losing their reputation and being out for revenge?"

"Does loss of life count?"

A prickle of excitement shot up Robin's neck. His question had felt so thin in the asking, so much like grasping at straws, he'd despaired of getting a useful response. "Exactly."

"Yes, although not a woman, I'm afraid. If I'd come across the merest hint of anyone disappearing, I promise I'd have been in touch. There *is* a story, which I suspect is worth looking into, if you don't mind me suggesting it. It must be a pain in the arse when members of the public try to tell you how to do your job."

"It is, believe me." Robin couldn't help chuckling. "I can usually work out for myself what to follow up and what to ignore."

"Glad to hear it. Well, among her many talents, Emily's a fine-art expert, so she's your girl when it comes to making sure provenance is spot on." The self-deprecating, jokey tone turned serious. "She said that there was a collector of antiquities—guy who'd made his mint in the city, absolutely rolling in it—who died under mysterious circumstances two years ago. Chap called Eric Wheatstone."

Robin, suppressing a thrill at the mention of the surname, hoped Pru would be equally cautious and not let on they recognised it. "How mysterious? Murder?"

"I don't think so. He was supposedly out for a walk and strayed off the path. The 'supposedly' being that Emily's heard he might have chucked himself over the cliff, rather than it being an accident. All covered up. Assuming people *can* cover up that sort of thing."

"In theory no, but if you had a sympathetic coroner and there wasn't any implication in terms of life insurance, I guess it could happen." Robin tried to hide his disappointment that the information hadn't quite been what he'd hoped. "No chance he was pushed?"

"I'm not sure. Reliable witnesses saw him heading off on his own, seeming as happy as Larry, and the cliff path is said to be dangerous."

"Nobody raised the alarm when he didn't return?" Sian had said her father's body lay undiscovered until the next day.

"Apparently not, because nobody was expecting him to be at any particular place at any particular time. His daughter said he'd a habit of setting off on the spur of the moment for a few days' walking. Sorry to disappoint you." Agnew shrugged.

"It's never a problem to establish the facts." Robin's bland words covered a mad whirl of thinking. "Why was suicide suspected in the first place?"

"Emily says the rumours arose because of Wheatstone's distress at some faked artefacts he'd bought. Nobody likes to be made a fool of, especially if they've got a bit of a reputation for knowing what's what."

"Agreed." Robin realised he'd been running his fingers along the table edge, as though they were chasing his thoughts. He clamped his hands together. "But is that enough for somebody to take their own life?"

"Who knows why anybody commits suicide? I had a cousin who did, and the family have beaten themselves up ever since." Agnew winced. "We've come to the conclusion that these things are rarely logical, which is why there's no point in us puzzling over what we should or shouldn't have done to prevent it. In cousin Gary's case, it probably would have made no difference."

Chilling but true. "Did Wheatstone's family beat themselves up?"

"His daughter did. She got herself into a terrible state over his death, making all sorts of wild accusations of fraud and the like. How she'd see the perpetrators in court and how they'd never be able to work in archaeological circles again."

All this bore out Sian's version of events. "Do you know the daughter's name?"

"Alas, no, but it would be easy enough to find out."

Although to all intents and purposes, the police already knew.

Pru, still busily taking notes, asked, "If she talked about bringing them to trial, did the police get involved?"

"I don't think so. Emily heard she was mainly sounding off to friends, although there may have been some offensive comments on social media. All taken down now and *not* to be used in evidence."

"Did the threat of prosecution work? Has the fakes industry stopped now?"

"It may have worked, initially. At least something must have given them cause of thought, because it all went quiet, but they started up again last year and it's been ticking over, ever since."

"Still operating out of Culford?" Which might explain why Sian had moved to the area and why she'd volunteered to work at the Roman site.

Agnew shrugged. "Can't tell."

"Okay." No point flogging that horse further for the moment. "I've got some names to put to you. Tell me if they mean anything. Lydia Oliver."

Agnew, brows knotted, shook his head. "Nope. Not ringing any bells. Should she?"

"There's a Culdover connection." Best leave it at that. They couldn't entirely rule out the possibility that Agnew himself was somehow caught up in this, unlikely as it may seem. "What about Becky Bairstow?"

"Surely we've all heard of *her*. The missing woman who wasn't missing. I'd not come across the woman before I saw the local news story, although Emily—I have no idea how she finds out these things—has heard on the grapevine that she's either about to sell her story to the tabloids or is getting a spread in *Hello* magazine." Agnew's face showed what he thought of either of those prospects.

"Great. Just what we need." It was a judicial nightmare, having information related to cases all over the media; it made finding untainted jurors difficult. But was this an indication of Ms. Bairstow having nothing to hide? Or sheer brass neck, getting her version of the story out in advance? Another name, out of left field. "Philippa Palmer?"

"I've come across a Pippa Palmer. Same girl?"

"Could be. Archaeologist?"

"I think so." Agnew leaned forwards, lowering his voice. "I'm intrigued to ask why her name cropped up, because a Pippa Palmer was connected with hawking these fake artefacts about."

"Selling them?" Was Robin jumping to conclusions thinking that Palmer's "going travelling" was connected to threats Sian had made? His mind ran on to the problems of questioning her; surely it wouldn't be that easy to get an extradition warrant for a suspect just because they'd been hawking fake statuettes, and there was no clear connection to the dead girl.

"No. She appears to have been providing 'expert' opinions that these things were real. Her provenance was almost as dodgy."

"Fake expert on fake artefacts?" This was getting more bizarre by the minute.

"Not entirely. She has a first in archaeology, even if she was doing her PhD on representations of the ancient world in modern media. Brad Pitt's Achilles, Colin Farrell's Alexander, and all that." Agnew rolled his eyes at the mention of the film, although maybe it was simply the PhD topic he found distasteful. "She's just rather over-egged the pudding in terms of her qualifications, even if what she said about authentic artefacts seemed spot on. The whole business was pretty clever, to be honest. All the verifications—for fake and real—were couched in terms that strongly implied the object was genuine, without guaranteeing it one hundred percent."

"Is there anything about her in here?" Robin tapped the bundle of material Agnew had given them.

"Indeed there is. Nothing in terms of an actual name or face, however. Apart from Miss Palmer, who did use her real name, as she probably had to be seen to be the genuine article, the main players generally hide behind icons and usernames."

That sounded familiar. "Is one of them 'Trowelgirl'?"

"Not that I recall. There is a 'Trowelboy,' though." Agnew grimaced. "I remember thinking how corny that was."

Robin nodded. Though if that turned out to be Howarth, corny was just his style.

Robin and Pru sat in the car after pulling into a convenient lay-by, watching the Kinechester traffic pass by and considering what they'd heard. Had they reached a crucial point in the case?

"What if Howarth and Becky Bairstow are in this together?" Robin proposed. "Running a dodgy business out of Culford rather than indulging in rumpy pumpy?"

"Rumpy pumpy? Is that what they're calling it?" Pru made a disdainful face. "Maybe. It could explain why he was so determined not to take up some of those business ideas that student, Ros, put forwards. Wanted to keep anybody with a bit of nous out of Culford's computer system."

"Yep. And the timing of that suicide is interesting. I could imagine Sian Wheatstone tracking down the people who'd conned her father, maybe following them here. What if Becky got scared off at that point and did a runner with her fortuitously timed—and absolutely genuine—lottery win? Her legging it would have slowed down business for a while, but now Howarth's got it up and running again. Maybe." That mysterious file of Howarth's, which he'd been so keen to recover; if only Robin had been able to have a proper look through it, would there have been some clue to his nefarious dealings?

"Hmm." Pru stared out of the window. "Trouble is we still have no objective evidence to link them to the forgeries, or to the dead girl. We're back there again."

She turned and gave Robin a long, thoughtful look. "I know you don't like Howarth, and I don't blame you, but we can't let our opinions blind us to other possibilities here."

Robin took a deep breath before answering; his sergeant was right. "Point taken. If Howarth's not up to his neck in fakes, who at Culford is?"

"One of the CAS? Or the detectorists? Or Jamie Warnock if he used to be involved with Palmer. Maybe Howarth didn't suspect people were just digging up stuff illegally, but digging it up and selling it on. Or manufacturing it and selling it on. Or both." Pru waved her hands. "Running some sort of operation out of the Culford site. That's what he asked Becky Bairstow to look into."

Robin could think of several arguments to counter that, but didn't want to be accused of further anti-Howarth bias. "Okay. How would they have accessed the site?"

Pru spread her hands. "As you found from interviewing Sian, it would be easy enough to get a set of copy keys made. Or perhaps they've got their own mole on the inside. Warnock, for example, who might have had the opportunity to make an imprint of the keys when he was working at Culford."

They sat in silence again, mulling over thoughts, until Pru said, "You didn't ask Agnew about ritual killings. Is that because you don't want this to be a replica of that Bronze Age burial?"

"No. I don't think I'm that blinkered." Robin gave his sergeant a smile; she seemed much more able to guess what he was thinking than Anderson had been able to. Was it sexist to put that down to female intuition, or did the fact simply reflect her empathetic personality irrespective of gender? "I haven't got much—if any—experience of darker cases, if you want to call them that, but this doesn't appear to fit the bill. Not weird enough."

"That mosaic isn't weird enough for you?"

"No, oddly. It feels far too prosaic." Nothing seemed to make sense: Robin longed for just a spot of clarity in this case's muddy waters. "I've got a question for the forensic team about the window of time in which our victim was buried. We've been focussing on when Becky Bairstow disappeared, but have we been too narrow minded? We need to go back to first principles—what if the timescale were either shorter or longer than that? Back a couple of months to when Pippa—assuming she's the same girl as Philippa—Palmer initially fell off the radar."

"But she's still alive, sir. Like Becky bloody Bairstow. There's a total lack of dead women associated with this case." The line sounded so much like it might have come from a Monty Python sketch that they both giggled.

"Indulge me."

"You think she's our unidentified corpse? Really?"

Was it such a ridiculous idea? "I think we have to examine the possibility, and we'll start by seeing if the timings work."

"Okay. If we're taking it back to first principles, let's take it all the way. Means, motive, opportunity." Pru counted them off on her fingers.

"Motive." Robin tapped the dashboard. "Revenge. Sian, or another family member, avenging Wheatstone's death by physical action rather than just naming, shaming, and prosecuting."

Pru put her index finger down, eliminating one objection. "I'll grant you that. Nearest thing we've come across to a motive in this case."

"Means—well, anybody can lay their hands on a blunt instrument, especially in the heat of a domestic argument. But not everybody has access to an archaeological site."

"I'll half give you that. And not everybody has posh Chinese rugs, either." Pru tried to hold her middle finger halfway down, then gave up the attempt. "Opportunity?"

"Opportunity aplenty for burying her. We've seen how easy it was for Howarth to get into Culford out of hours without attracting notice from the locals. It was sheer luck we found out he'd been there after dark." Little events on which successful solutions hinged; if the workman hadn't dropped his mobile and had to return, they'd never have picked up on that thread.

"It doesn't narrow matters down much, although I suppose there's no real chance of that until we know who the dead girl was."

"I suspect you're right." Robin rubbed his knuckles together in frustration. "You say I'm biased against Howarth, but if he's innocent, why didn't he—or Becky Bairstow—tell us what they suspected was going on at Culford?"

Pru sighed. "Because he's an idiot. The sort of idiot who'd like to claim all the glory for uncovering something. That's what he was like at school, anyway, and I'm not convinced this leopard can change his spots."

Well, irrespective of that, Robin was relishing the prospect of bearding that particular leopard in his den—or whatever leopards liked to live in—to see what the bloody hell he was playing at.

Chapter Twelve

A dam's day started well, with most of his class understanding what he was trying to get across about shape symmetry, but the note from Baxter he found in his pigeon hole at playtime unsettled him.

"Hope you enjoyed the meeting last night. Sorry about all the 'business' stuff, but Tuckton said he'd been contacted by someone from the local radio to give the detectorists' point of view on this murder up at the Roman villa. He's forbidden any of us from talking to the media."

Adam grinned. He could imagine the members being threatened with excommunication should they disobey.

"Thing is, this researcher from the BBC has been in touch with a couple of us—they must have known they'd get nowhere with Tuckton— and we're thinking of talking to him. Show we're not all stick-in-the- muds. Anyway, if we didn't put you off, come along next time."

It wasn't the bulk of the content or the direct contact which was so disconcerting—school rules meant that social media or telephone contact was frowned on, so good old-fashioned pen and paper was the only way to send a message—but the mention of the media. Why did that ring an uncomfortable bell?

A school-related question from one of the teaching assistants brought his mind back to more pressing matters, so he stuffed the note into his pocket and returned to his work.

That evening Adam wasn't as pleased as he should have been to see his partner home at a reasonable time. He'd got halfway through a pile of marking with some other stuff to do afterwards, and he wanted to shift the majority of it so he could enjoy the weekend. Robin would understand—in the same way as Adam understood *his* job pressures—but it would still be a shame they wouldn't be able to spend more of the evening just chilling. Time together was always at a premium, and the continued presence of Anderson made relaxation a challenge, even on occasions such as this when he'd taken himself to the pub after work.

"How goes it?" Adam asked after they'd shared a welcome-home kiss.

"Not sacked yet." Robin slumped into a chair.

"As bad as that?"

"Nah. At least I could make a positive report to Cowdrey when he touched base this afternoon. Looks like there may be something worth pursuing in that fakes element." Robin sat up again. "Which means that if you have any ideas about joining the detectorists, I suggest you wait until we've cleared this case up."

"You think one of them might be involved? Don't answer if it's all under wraps. I can take a hint. Oof!" The arrival of Campbell, bashing against Adam's legs before he made a dash for Robin, set some of the books flying. Picking them up, he admired once again the way the two most important characters in his life seemed besotted with one another.

"Don't worry. I don't even tell this lad my secrets." Robin stroked the dog's ears. "And no, I don't at present think one of them is involved, but this case is so incestuous I can't be sure. So can you put any interest on hold, please."

"After last night, I can't imagine many things I'd like to do less than attend another meeting. They made the governing body at Lindenshaw look like Morecambe and Wise." He laid the marking to one side; it could wait an hour or two. "Any luck with Agnew?"

"Yes. In spades. I've got the team following up the fraudulent artefacts industry. I'm trying to keep as objective as possible, but there's one bloke in particular I'd love to pin it on."

"What's he done to rub you up the wrong way?"

"Just been generally smarmy." Robin, still caressing Campbell, shut his eyes. "This bloody case is driving me bananas. I've told all the team to get a decent rest tonight, and we'll come to it fresh tomorrow. I need a definitive answer on how big a window we've got for that body being put into the ground. We've been focussing around the time Becky Bairstow went off, but if we can push the envelope back a couple of months or so, we might have another chance at an ID."

"Sounds good."

"It does. First sniff we've had of somebody being threatened, anyway. Except that although said person may have been reported missing at around the right time, they appear to be alive and well." Robin took Campbell's face in his hands, addressing him as though he were a crucial witness. "How do you pretend someone's still alive if they're dead?"

"That dog may be a genius, but he can't answer that one. It doesn't involve food, for one thing." Adam watched the pair with continued pleasure. "It would be almost impossible if they were impersonating somebody outright and in the flesh. Anybody who turned up at Culdover saying they were me would be seen through straight away."

"Ah, but she's supposedly off travelling. All the contact is on social media—at least with friends—and nobody's cried foul."

Adam stroked his chin. "Pretending to be somebody else on social media would be easy enough, if you'd got hold of—I'm assuming we're talking about your victim—her passwords. Some people use the same one for everything, so if you'd even got one of them, Bob would be your uncle. Then you reset the whole lot to make yourself a secure little cyber shell."

Robin sat forwards again, temporarily ignoring Campbell's demands for more petting. "Yeah. I guess if you had access to their main email account, then you could probably reset any passwords you didn't know. Play the 'forgot my details' card."

"True. The murderer could pretend the victim was still alive for long enough to muddy the waters. Assuming you could explain why she's not appearing in person. That would be the stumbling block."

"She's *said* to be travelling." Robin's eyebrow shot up. "Which sounds highly suspicious to me."

"Like that Bairstow woman was?"

"Exactly. Too much of a coincidence. Although there's a bigger difficulty to overcome. The pictures she's been posting of herself." Robin addressed the dog again. "Let's see if your 'dad' can come up with an answer to that."

"Hmm." Adam drummed on the pile of schoolbooks. "Okay, what if somebody got access to her photo files as well? On Dropbox or whatever? You could use those."

"Wouldn't somebody spot that the pictures weren't new?"

"Maybe nobody had seen them before. What if the impersonator also nicked a camera with a mass of pictures on that your victim hadn't yet shared?" Adam warmed to his theme. "If you post a snap with a comment like 'Cocktail time in Amsterdam,' other people wouldn't necessarily be able to spot that it had been taken in a bar in Bradford. Not if it was generic enough."

"Your dad's clever, isn't he?" Robin sought Campbell's agreement, which came in the form of a lick to his face. "And there's always a chance people would soon get bored with holiday snaps and skim over them. Could it work?"

"It's possible. People are really gullible online. We warn the children about internet safety all the time, telling them that the people they're communicating with may not be who they say they are." Adam shuddered at the thought of some of the cases they'd heard about in training sessions, where horrible old men had pretended to be teenagers to lure their victims. "And then the credulous adults quite happily accept everything they're told at face value and fall for a—what do you call it?—catphishing scam."

"Something like that." Robin, staring into the distance, obviously considering some element of the case Adam wasn't yet privy to, had gone into thinking mode.

"Dinner?"

Campbell's reaction—a bolt for the door—struck a sharp contrast with Robin's. "Um? Sorry?"

"Dinner?"

"Please."

Adam moved into the kitchen, then busied himself with a couple of ready meals to bung into the microwave as Robin appeared in the doorway. "Thanks for that," he said, nodding at Adam's culinary efforts. "I've been worse than useless on the domestic front these last few days."

"You can make it up to me. Once you solve the case, straight back onto being chief cook and bottle washer." Adam got out plates and cutlery, then laid them in a neat but welcoming manner on the breakfast bar.

"If I ever solve this bloody case." Robin slumped onto one of the kitchen stools. "This catphishing lark. Why would anybody bother to do it?"

"To get money, for a start, like most other cybercrime. Create a sob story and set up an appeal. You know, 'We're in the USA and we have a major medical emergency. We can't afford to pay, so please donate to my PayPal.'" Adam waved a fork as though conducting an orchestra. "Like I said, the same adults who warn children to be careful fall for it and fork out."

"Okay. Is it always about making money?"

"Probably not. I guess some people do it to get emotional support. Lots of hugs and kisses and fuss. Like Campbell when he feels he's being ignored." Adam had another couple of minutes before the stuff in the microwave needed attending to. Enough time to rub his lover's shoulders. "Is this what you think is happening with your 'travelling but not travelling' woman?"

"Could be, although it seems far-fetched." Robin leaned back into the massage. "And that's very good, by the way."

"Thank you." Adam worked on a tensed-up muscle. "Although why would your murderer—and no, I'm not mind reading, simply applying a bit of logic—pretend the dead woman was still alive? Especially when they put the body somewhere it was always going to turn up?"

"That, Sherlock, is the big question." A loud *ping* had Adam glancing at the microwave and Robin grabbing for his phone. "Sod it, what now?"

Time to go into "prepare to change all plans" mode, although if the news was really bad, it would probably have come in a call, not a message. "What's up?" Adam asked when his partner laid the phone down. "You're looking distinctly smug."

"That was a text from Sarah. She's been doing some extra homework on Pippa Palmer. That's the woman we were just discussing."

"The one you thought might be being impersonated online?"

"The very same." The self-satisfied grin Robin was obviously trying to restrain broke out fully. "Sarah's been studying her social media profile, and it seems our Pippa's quite camera shy. She says she'll explain more at the team briefing tomorrow, but the gist of it is that there are not any pictures—pre-travel or current—that give a clear view of her face."

Another *ping* indicated that dinner was ready. As Adam filled the plates, he pointed out, "That's not unusual. Lots of people don't want to have a recognisable picture online, for all sorts of legitimate reasons. And that would be a boon to anyone trying to pass themselves off as her."

"My thoughts exactly." Robin—appetite evidently whetted by this welcome piece of news—set about helping himself to dinner. "Now I need to work out a subtle way of identifying whether the dead woman *is* Pippa Palmer without either spooking her family or making a right tit of myself."

"You can do it!" Adam did an impression of the worst kind of motivational speaker. "Failure is all in the mind."

"Pfft." Robin pretended to stab him with his fork. "Yeah, I can do that. I just wish I could solve the other problem as easily." He pointed the fork in the direction of the spare bedroom. "The unwanted lodger."

"That sounds like a Sherlock Holmes case. Maybe we'll have to end up murdering Stuart. Surely there's a simple, undetectable method for disposing of annoying sergeants?"

"Steady on. I don't want to be investigating you. Not in that way, anyhow." Robin smirked.

"No smut in front of delicate young ears." Adam jerked his thumb towards Campbell, who was far more interested in cleaning his tail than any romantic talk. He got to hear plenty of it, and as it didn't concern food, it wasn't likely to be of importance. "How long do you think Stuart is going to be here?"

"God knows." Robin groaned. "I feel sorry for the bloke, and I don't want to just kick him out on the streets, but he can't stay here forever. Can he?"

The question had been asked with a bleakness Adam rarely heard in his lover's voice, unless he was referring to the bullying which had blighted his childhood. Adam reached across the breakfast bar and squeezed Robin's hand, giving him a reassuring smile, although he didn't feel reassured himself. It could be so easy to slip into a routine whereby Anderson became a paying guest, always chipping into the domestic pot and always looking for other accommodation but never quite finding it. "We won't let that happen. I'll have a word with him this weekend. To hell with Helen's swearing me to silence. We've got to do something."

Robin forced a smile. He looked desperately weary, bags forming under his eyes; the fine crows' feet round them only appeared when he was in the midst of a difficult case. They gave him an air of gravitas, which had its attractions, but Adam would rather not see them there. Robin was hot stuff, anyway, even covered in mud and dripping with sweat from when he'd been digging the garden.

"Maybe we should get the pair of them in a room," Robin suggested, "and knock their heads together until they see sense?"

"While I'd usually applaud that kind of idea, the vibes I got off that conversation with Helen stick the tin lid on it. I wouldn't put Helen past knocking *our* heads together instead." Adam eyed his dinner bleakly, appetite waning.

"Eat up. You can't mark books on an empty stomach." Robin returned the hand squeeze. "We'll find a way to solve the problem. We've faced worse."

"And in this very kitchen, in your case."

The best that could be said for Anderson was that he didn't brandish any deadly weapons, although if Adam broke the vow of silence he'd made, he wasn't sure the same was going to be said of Helen.

Chapter Thirteen

Next morning, the team briefing was buzzing, despite it being a Saturday and the usual weekend leisure activities having to go on hold. There was plenty to get their teeth into: fakes, threats of prosecution, an inkling of a chance that Pippa Palmer was being impersonated online. Surely there had to be a key lead amongst those?

Her picture, such as it was—a face almost entirely hidden under the shadow from a large-brimmed black hat—had been put up on the incident board, but they were trying to source a better one. The forensic department had been asked about dates, and they had confirmed that the dead woman could have been killed even as much as ten months previously.

There was plenty to do: Ben and Alison were detailed to talk to Warnock, who'd come back to the Culdover area just the day before, or so he said, while Sarah and the other constable, Fraser, were set the task of working out how they could quietly check if the body might be Pippa Palmer. Robin emphasised that they couldn't risk egg on their faces twice over, going to the media with another possible identification only for her to turn up on their doorstep. He and Pru were off to see the Culdover version of Mata Hari.

Becky Bairstow had wanted to meet the police in a café in Normanton, twenty miles the other side of Kinechester. That was where Jerry's parents lived; she'd explained that she was staying with them until she got police permission to fly back to Germany. Robin refused to agree to that arrangement, although he did deign to meet her at the local police station, even if it meant a bit of a hike for him; the witness had to understand that the ante had been upped.

Ms. Bairstow was late arriving and appeared flustered, searching her handbag for her keys and then finding them in her pocket. Normally, Robin would have settled a witness with a cup of tea, but this time he resisted—being disturbed might allow a chink in her armour to appear.

He began with the usual introductions, thanks for her seeing them again, and an explanation that they'd be recording what she said this time. She took a long appraisal of the setup, asking what exactly would be involved, although—to Robin's surprise—she refused the offer of legal representation. He'd already primed the duty solicitor, just in case she was needed, but Becky Bairstow appeared determined to face this situation alone.

Robin voiced his gratitude at her cooperation, then explained that the case had moved on since last they spoke.

"For example, you and Charlie Howarth were seen late at night at the Culford villa site." That was stretching the truth, but by the slight flinch on the witness's face, it had hit home.

"Seen by whom?"

"I'm not prepared to divulge that at present. What were you doing?"

"What does he say we were doing?" Becky was evidently regaining her composure.

"Again, I'm not divulging that. I want to hear your side of the story."

The witness glanced at Pru, then back to Robin. "We were having an affair. It was a convenient place to meet."

"Is that the truth?" Pru almost spat the question out. "Or is it just what Howarth asked you to say?"

"Why should I lie? Why should *he* lie?"

"You're staying with Jerry's family?"

The change of questioner—and Robin's change of tack—took the witness by surprise. "Yes. Is there a problem with that?"

"Not that we can see. It's odd that you didn't stay at your own parents' house."

"I told you, I'm orph—"

"No, you're not. You asked us what reason you should have to lie about Howarth; we'd suggest you're a habitual liar."

Becky raised her hands. "All right, you've got me on that point. My parents are still alive. They live in Inverness—got relocated with Dad's work—so it's too far to be staying up there and being at your beck and call."

Pru ignored the sidestepping. "So, we're back to why you keep telling us lies. And we're quite happy to sit here until you decide to tell us the truth."

Becky slumped back in her seat. "About my parents? Or about Howarth?"

"Both."

"Hm. Maybe it is time we stopped pussyfooting around." Becky, glancing at the recording equipment, was clearly quite relieved.

"I appreciate your cooperation." Robin nodded. "Will you tell us what you and Charlie Howarth were actually doing at Culford out of hours?"

"Operating a business. As I suppose you already know."

"A legitimate business?" Pru took up the questioning as Robin sat back to observe the witness. The Becky Bairstow who'd swanned into Abbotston police station had been immaculately turned out and wonderfully self-assured. This version was less well-groomed and carried an air of hesitancy. Something had obviously spooked her. She eyed Pru, then Robin, and finally the recording equipment once more before answering.

"Have you had any complaints made against us?"

"Just answer the question. Was it legitimate?"

There seemed to be an ounce or two of fight left. "We sold honestly sourced artefacts. Things people had turned up legally. We were simply a means by which those things could reach an appreciative market."

Robin resisted making a snide comment about how it sounded like she was suggesting they provided a public service. "What about the fake artefacts?"

"Fakes?" Her innocent expression took in nobody.

"Yes. The recently manufactured items you were passing off as old." Robin waited for an answer; they'd take as long as necessary to winkle the truth out of this particular shell.

"If there were any items of a dubious provenance, we weren't aware of that." Becky was evidently choosing her words with care.

"We used an expert to verify them, but sometimes even a specialist can't be entirely certain."

"You're telling me you had no idea that you and 'Trowelboy' were dealing in fakes?" Pru's use of Howarth's supposed online name brought a brief flicker of recognition from the witness. "You're an intelligent woman, and given your record of spouting lies to us, I'm finding it hard to believe you."

Becky slapped the table, making Pru flinch. "What do you want me to say?"

"The truth, the whole truth and nothing but." Robin forced his body to relax, forced himself to put on a friendlier face. "It'll be better for all of us, not least you. You can't run forever."

Somehow he'd found the right words to pierce the armour. The witness put her hand to her face. "Do you know," she said in a tremulous voice, "I'm so tired of having to hide."

"Take your time." Robin rose, said what he was intending to do—for the benefit of that all-important recording—then walked to the door and called for the constable on duty to get them all a cup of tea.

"Thanks. This is going to be thirsty work." Becky, who'd produced a hankie, dabbed her eyes before continuing. "I knew Charlie Howarth at uni. Not 'knew' in the biblical sense. He got back in contact best part of three years ago, saying he was in my neck of the woods and suggesting we meet up. It turned out he wanted to make a business proposition: selling legitimately sourced items online—everything from bits of Roman glass to World War II-era helmets. Part of my role would be to verify what was being sold, either directly or via one of my contacts. It was, as they say, 'a nice little earner.' We should have stuck with that."

"So what happened?" Pru asked.

"One of Charlie's 'big ideas.' He started getting enquiries about whether we could provide certain specialised items for certain collectors. When we couldn't obtain them legally, he thought it could be an idea to provide a substitute. The way he sold the notion to me was that we would be making these clients happy."

Pru gave a snort. "You fell for that?"

"Yeah, I did. I'm not proud of it, but I was at a low point. Mum had been diagnosed with cancer—she's in remission now—and I wasn't thinking straight." The answer appeared to be an honest one, although it could simply be a convenient excuse to use; nobody would be heartless enough to question it. "And once you're in these things, it's hard to get free. You tell yourself you'll do something about it, and then you chicken out. It goes on, getting worse and worse."

Robin, mind never far from the Anderson situation, was beginning to appreciate how people ended up in that sort of a mess, almost impotent to deal with it. "We'll need the details of what went on—names of anybody who bought a faked item, for a start—but those particulars can wait. You can either come into Abbotston to make a full statement or the duty officer here can take one. First, I need to know who was involved apart from you and Howarth."

"There was a girl called Pippa Palmer. She was another friend of Howarth's. I guess he inveigled her into working with us, just like he'd inveigled me."

Robin had difficulty imagining Becky Bairstow being coerced into doing anything she didn't want. "You're saying that neither of you wanted to be involved in this business?"

"I'm saying that neither of us realised what we were getting into until it was too late. Anyway, Pippa provided the independent verification for artefacts. Only it wasn't really independent, was it?"

When no more was forthcoming, Robin nudged the witness with, "You'd better tell *us* that."

"It wasn't entirely independent," Becky conceded. "She didn't make huge amounts out of it, though."

"Enough to go travelling?" Pru cut in. "Like you did?"

"Hardly." Becky gave the sergeant an old-fashioned look. "There wasn't that much money in the business, although Howarth had plans to make a big coup. I suspect he was hoping for a 'Hitler Diaries' moment. He can whistle for that, now."

"Were you threatened by any of the people you'd conned?" Robin wrested the questioning back.

"Eh?" Becky, clearly flustered, screwed her hankie into a ball.

"Please answer the question." Pru tapped the table. "Were you threatened with prosecution for fraud?"

"Yes." The answer came with a hint of relief; had Becky expected a different question? "Albeit the threats never amounted to anything.

Not enough evidence for a prosecution, although I suppose our reputations could have been sullied. People will persist in believing there's no smoke without fire."

"But that wasn't enough to make you want to do a runner, was it?" An inkling of an idea had formed in Robin's mind. "Exactly what threats were made? Apart from seeing you in court."

The witness hesitated again, evidently weighing her options once more.

"We know there's more to it than that," Robin said, keeping the pressure up.

"All right, all right. There was a relative of someone who bought an item from us. Several items, about two years ago, when we started on the faked stuff. A couple of months later he had an accident, but she seemed convinced it was suicide, brought on because he couldn't believe he'd been scammed." Words were tumbling out now, as Becky seemed to be getting her version of the story onto the record. "She started with saying she wanted to ruin us, but when we wouldn't respond, the intimidation got worse. She made comments online, saying what she'd like to do to us."

Now they were getting somewhere. "For the record, will you detail precisely what those comments were?"

Becky screwed her eyes shut, shuddering before proceeding. "She said she was going to strangle us with her bare hands, then smack us over the head with a real piece of stone from a Roman villa, before burying us alive with one of our own faked artefacts. It sounds really silly, and we didn't take it seriously at first."

It did sound like a ridiculously overworked threat, although it possessed a chilling edge. Had Pru—who was keeping a remarkable poker face—noticed what Robin had? "You said 'at first.' What changed?"

"Howarth counter-threatened. Said he'd report *her* to the police, given that physical threats were much worse than anything we were accused of doing, so she took the online comments down. Last year it started again. She'd managed to find a contact address for us— Howarth's on LinkedIn, so it was easy enough for her to write to him via the council. She repeated the threats. Said she knew where we lived and was just biding her time. Fortunately, I won the lottery and got away before she had any opportunity to make those threats reality."

A knock on the door heralded the arrival of the local bobby with steaming mugs of tea and an unexpected plate of biscuits. Robin pressed his stomach, constraining the rumbling, although once he'd got a biscuit inside him, he was straight back into the fray.

"Did the person who made the threats have a name?" Stupid question. Everybody had a name. "I mean, who was it?"

"I don't have absolute proof, but I think it was Sian Wheatstone. Jerry's ex. He had a hell of a shock when I told him my suspicions. That's partly what threw us together." Becky took another sip of tea. "He was sorry for me, and scared for himself. They'd not long been going out—only since she moved here, obviously—and he didn't want to be hooked up with a psycho."

Quite. At last some of the elements in the case were pulling together. Robin took a drink—not the best cuppa he'd ever had, but it was warm, wet, and welcome. "So why did you say earlier that you were having an affair with Howarth?"

"I was caught between a rock and a hard place. I don't mind taking the rap myself, but it's different dobbing in your colleagues. Especially when you've been asked to keep up the pretence."

"Who asked you to keep up the pretence?"

"Charlie, of course. He rang me yesterday, saying that things were getting a bit hairy. He couldn't work out how you'd got onto us."

"A lot of hard graft." And a bit of luck, with Sophie Baxter and her father, and the line of enquiry they had led to, although he wasn't going to mention that. "Going back to that first interview you gave—"

"Which I came and gave voluntarily," Becky clarified, no doubt for the benefit of the tape.

"Which you did," Robin confirmed, "even if you weren't entirely candid with us. Why did you tell us you were orphaned? And get your 'ex' to back up that part of the story?"

"Isn't that painfully obvious?"

Pru sniffed. "Answer the question for the tape, please."

"Because I was scared for my parents' welfare. If we were being threatened, then they might have been at risk too. We were told it wasn't just us in the firing line."

That might be so, although the fact that "being orphaned" would have added credence to her disappearance story couldn't have hurt, either. Still, Robin wasn't convinced the story of these threats and her reaction to them hung together. Anybody *that* hell bent on revenge would surely have been able to track down any living relatives? "So why did you come back at all? Weren't you safer staying away? Your parents must have known you weren't the woman found at Culford."

"Don't you think I considered all that? But I'm tired of running and hiding. Okay, Jerry's got the job in Stuttgart, but at some point we'll want to move back here—now seemed the right moment to begin that process."

That could also be the truth, given Becky's apparent tendency to seize an opportunity and make the most of it, although there were several elements which continued to make little sense. Pru's thoughts must have been on the same lines, given her next question. "If Sian was the one making the threats, why is she working at Culford? I'd have thought Howarth would want to keep her at arm's length."

"He didn't know she was working there. The woman who manages the day-to-day stuff at the site—Cathy? Clare?—took her on as a volunteer." Becky knocked back the last of her tea, then plonked the mug down decisively on the table. "Can you imagine the shock he got when he came across her?"

"I can, except that you and he were still operating your business out of Culford after she began volunteering there. Wasn't that taking a huge risk?"

"It was, in retrospect, but—as I said—when we restarted, he didn't know she was there. He'd planned to lie low, and then resume only the legitimate side of the business once we thought we were safe. I wouldn't be surprised if she'd been keeping an eye on him all that time."

It was certainly suspicious that Sian had come to Culford; maybe she still had an agenda to work through. Becky's explanation that Howarth had been shocked to find Sian on-site might be the truth, depending on the exact timing and sequence of events. It would also further strengthen the rationale for Becky and Jerry having left the country, getting out of the way of somebody they regarded as unstable.

"Okay. We'll talk to Howarth and might have to come back to you on that point." Robin pretended to check his notes, letting the witness stew for a moment. "We know the dead woman was buried at Culford around the time you and Jerry left. Who do you think she is?" He glanced up and caught an uncomfortable flicker across Becky's face.

She lowered her eyes. "I don't know."

Pru's snort would sound loud and clear on the tape. "You're an intelligent woman. Do you expect us to believe that you haven't any suspicions?"

Becky closed her eyes, although whether to compose herself or get her story together, Robin couldn't tell. "I did wonder if it could be Pippa Palmer," she said at last. "She was a lynchpin to our business, on several fronts. Really good, actually, where *genuine* items were concerned. She came up with a lot of supporting evidence for each object's veracity, examples of similar artefacts and the like. Pippa knew her stuff."

Pru sniffed again; Becky appeared to produce the same reactions in her as Howarth did in Robin. "Was she equally convincing about fakes?"

Becky quickly suppressed a sly smile. "Pippa had a way with words. She could put together a document full of information which could be read two ways. On the surface of it the authenticity of the item was proven, but if you read through carefully, at no point was that veracity stated explicitly. That's why we weren't that worried about all that 'being charged with fraud' stuff."

She was evidently still not worried about it, given how she'd provided chapter and verse on the business. Fraud prosecutions were notoriously difficult to secure a conviction with, and Robin knew that on such a small scale the Crown Prosecution Service might not bother. Sian Wheatstone—or any of the other victims—might have been able to take a case to the small-claims court, but people didn't necessarily make the effort.

Robin pressed on. "And Sian Wheatstone was threatening Pippa too? Because she was the one who'd verified the objects?"

"Yes. Although part of me says she *can't* be the dead woman. Like you pointed out, she took my approach to matters and got herself out of harm's way. There was nothing suspicious at the time she went, and I'm sure I've had emails from her since then."

"Did you keep them?"

"No. Why should I?" That belligerent edge had appeared again. "They didn't contain anything important; they've been long deleted."

Conveniently so, if they held information about the fakes. "Did the pair of you plan your respective escapes together?"

"Not quite. I mean, when we were first threatened, we made a bit of a joke about how we all needed to run away, but I certainly didn't have any intention of doing so until things got nastier. Pippa went before I did."

"Not perhaps in the way you're implying," Pru mumbled.

"Sorry?" Becky gave the sergeant a withering glance.

Pru, flushing, reverted to her normal "for the tape" voice. "So, do you think she's dead or not?"

"I don't see how she can be. Where did the emails come from? You're surely not suggesting that somebody's impersonating her?" Becky rolled her eyes. "That's like something out of a film."

"I don't think *we* suggested anything." Robin was tiring of faffing around. "You were the one who put Pippa's name forwards, and then you started backtracking. Have you proof that she's still alive, other than the emails? Have you met her?"

"No, I've not met Pippa since then, not that I know of."

Not that I know of. An odd choice of words. "Can you explain what you mean by that?"

"Well, I never actually met her face-to-face in the first place. Everything was done online, and she hated posting photos of herself. I wouldn't recognise her if she were in this room."

"Are you saying you wouldn't know if she was dead or not?"

"I suppose so. It's all a bit bewildering." Becky didn't exactly sound bewildered—more like she was choosing words carefully. So used to having to keep up a pretence and being in a constant state of watching her back that it had become habitual? Irrespective, it appeared there was little further to be gained at this point. Robin reminded the witness that they were expecting her to make a full statement about the faked artefacts, and that the police would want to talk to her again when they had new information. He made a bit of an act of getting his papers together, then glanced up. "One final question."

"I thought you'd finished. You've stopped recording."

"We have. This is more for our information than anything potentially to be used in evidence. Are you selling your story to the tabloids? Or one of the celebrity magazines?"

Becky, jaw dropping, couldn't have feigned her degree of surprise. "How preposterous. Where did you get that idea from?"

"A reliable source."

"Not that reliable, then, because that's the last thing I'd do. And especially not given what I've said about being under threat. Selling stories to the media is the lowest of the low."

"That's what I suspected," Robin assured her, "but I had to check."

They delivered the witness into the local officer's care, to give as full a statement as possible about the fakes business, then returned to the interview room to debrief.

"What was with the tabloids question, sir?" Pru asked.

"I don't like things not adding up. If Becky was so scared that she'd gone to all these lengths trying to protect herself and her family, why would she risk that by selling her story? And if she *isn't* selling her story, why are people saying she is?"

"Good point." The sergeant paused, pen in hand. "There are a lot of points that don't add up, though. I'm still not entirely convinced by her reasons for returning now."

"Neither am I. Nor the story about her and Howarth restarting their business, although that's timeline dependant, I guess. If they genuinely didn't know that Sian had started volunteering at Culford, they might have taken the risk." Robin took a deep breath then exhaled loudly. "Plenty about this case bugs me. Too much pretence. Too many lies. Where's a good old domestic barney followed by hubby getting hit over the head with a rolling pin when you need it?"

"I never thought I'd be hankering for that sort of case, but it's starting to look attractive." Pru picked up her things and headed for the door. "Coming, sir?"

"In a minute. Just getting a few more ideas straight."

"Ideas? Like wondering if Agnew or his wife might have lied to us about *Hello*?"

"I've been considering that, although maybe somebody else put the rumour around and Mrs. Agnew believed what she heard. You know what the internet's like; one person says something and it spreads like wildfire. Misinformation seems to spread fastest of all."

"One of their dupes who still bears a grudge?" Pru, standing by the door clutching her bag, clearly impatient to get away and back to familiar territory, asked, "You talked about Becky keeping a low profile, but the fact she's alive is already in the public domain. Walking into our police station made it so. She can't hide completely."

"No, she can't, although the other information about her is pretty scant. Surely that's the way she'd want to keep it? The more she tells the media, the more chance there'll be of one of those dupes locating where she is." Robin pushed his chair back at last and rose to better gather his things. "I've got one dead woman. I don't want another."

"You think she's still in danger?"

"Possibly. *She* certainly gives the impression she believes she might be. You heard the list of threats—what did you notice about them?"

"That they could have come straight from the forensic report about how our dead girl met her end. And the bit about the marks on the neck didn't get reported in the media, so it can't be a case of back attribution."

"Exactly. I wonder if Howarth kept the threatening letters?"

Pru shrugged. "It wouldn't be in character, but I wouldn't have thought passing off fakes was in character, either. Shows how you don't always know somebody. Will he get charged?"

"Hard to say. Fraud's a strange area, so we'll have to hand it over to the specialists to deal with. Whatever that triumvirate have done, they've not been daft. Remember what Agnew said about not absolutely guaranteeing items? Have they actually committed any crime?" Robin reached for his briefcase, suddenly keen to wipe the dust of the interview room off his shoes. "The CPS might not think a prosecution is worthwhile. Which is why Sian may have begun making physical threats in the first place."

They started the walk back to the car park, passing the office where Becky was dictating her statement. She gave them a stony glare through the window, although Robin had little sympathy for her having to go through the process. She'd caused them enough trouble.

"What I don't get, sir," Pru said as they emerged into the fresh air, "is why Sian Wheatstone told you and Ben that Howarth and Becky were having an affair if that's not what was happening."

"Ah. She didn't actually say that, just implied it." Robin waited as Pru unlocked the car, then slung his briefcase into the back before settling into the passenger seat. "We're dealing with a very clever young woman. It strikes me that everything she told us was true, or could align with the truth. What she said she'd overheard Becky saying could apply equally well to an affair or to dealing in fakes."

Pru concentrated on reversing out of the minuscule station car park before asking, "But why mention it at all?"

"To look like she was being helpful. She's probably playing us like a fish."

Although he had a horrible suspicion that Becky Bairstow was doing something similar.

Chapter Fourteen

O ver lunch, Adam decided to take a walk into Culdover. He needed to get some cash and do a couple of other errands, but most of all he needed to have a think, because he'd identified what had unsettled him about Baxter's note. On the way to work, he'd remembered Robin getting cross that the regional radio station had got wind of the Becky Bairstow development before the news had been officially released to the media. Had that been a leak from someone at Abbotston? And if so, was it possible that the snitch had also told their media contact about Robin and him, and were they using Baxter to find out more about their relationship?

By the time he dropped into the newsagents to get the local paper, he'd decided he was likely overreacting, that the timescale was too compressed for Baxter to have been contacted directly on his account—that must have happened before the meeting, surely?—and that the local radio was just looking to dig up the usual sort of dirt.

The sight of a tabloid newspaper headline—from one of the rags whose attitude would have made the 1950s look modern—brought him up short.

Chasebury cop's gay love nest!

Chasebury had been all over the news two months previously, the location for a particularly vile child murder. The police involved had been vilified for taking so long to find the body, which had been in a cupboard at the little boy's step-uncle's house. The media too had come in for stick for having targeted one of the locals, whom they'd mistaken for a paedophile. This news story was likely an act of justification.

Adam bought a copy and read it on the way back to school, feeling sicker with every paragraph. The chief inspector leading the enquiry had left his wife while the investigation was still on, moving in with another bloke and allegedly holding wild orgies. The article had ended with some wild but carefully worded posturing, the paper proposing a campaign to "keep the public safe" by rooting out bad police officers.

While Adam didn't believe half of what was reported, it still felt like a blow to the stomach. What if one of the rotten Abbotston eggs saw that and got inspired to make mischief by serving the media up with an untrue story? You couldn't get away with homophobic remarks at work, but you could let the media kill two birds with one stone, making life uncomfortable for Robin and smearing the Stanebridge force at the same time.

While neither he nor Robin had anything to hide, the tabloids weren't always interested in the truth and even a "Gay detective's lover gets too close to the case. Again!" type headline would be a nightmare. Today's news might be next week's chip paper, but these kinds of stories had a disproportionately hurtful effect.

Adam stopped as he reached the school gates. Was he overreacting? Was there truly a threat to him and Robin? He'd have to have a word with Baxter about what *he* did or didn't say to the researcher—that would be useful advice whatever the circumstances—but he'd have to raise the issue with Robin. Finding who was leaking news to the media was a crusade that maybe couldn't wait.

Early afternoon, Robin called all his officers together to explain the developments arising from Becky Bairstow's interview. The sense of optimism in the team was still high, even though Warnock had apparently been less than helpful. He hadn't seen Pippa in ages, he'd said. She'd gone off travelling without him, and that was just one of the grudges he appeared to hold against her and life in general.

"He's a right pain, sir," Alison reported. "Never stopped whingeing. Dead sorry for himself, reckons he was stitched up over the driving conviction. We had a look at the records when we got back here, and he definitely wasn't—they didn't just have eyewitness evidence; he was caught on CCTV too—but he struck us as the sort of bloke with a whacking great chip on his shoulder. He thinks the detectorists are all up themselves and his old mate Tom has turned into a pain in the arse. The list went on and on."

"Sounds like a bundle of laughs," Robin agreed. "Nothing useful to say?"

"Not really. He definitely used to go out with Pippa Palmer—they'd been friends at university, although it didn't become more than that until later. They split about a year ago, he says. Before she went wherever she went." Alison squinted at Ben, who was wearing an unfamiliar frown. "Did I get that wrong?"

"No, spot on." Ben tapped his notepad with his index finger. "He had a chip on the shoulder about that too. Said she thought herself too good for him, especially after he got convicted of the driving offence."

"So, what's the problem?" Alison countered. "You've a face like you lost a pound and found a penny."

"What he said about Pippa. How she was a tough cookie. She didn't strike me as your typical victim." Ben looked around the team for support, but he wasn't getting any.

"Is there such a thing as a typical victim?" Pru's hackles were obviously up. "Tough women can get attacked just the same as soft ones. Anyway, I bet he only called her tough because she stood her ground. Some men wish they were back in the 1950s and women acted like Stepford Wives."

The unexpected outburst took everyone aback. Pru had never struck Robin as having a feminist streak, although he knew—and appreciated—her passion for opposing the use of stereotypes.

Fraser muttered, "Calm down, tiger."

Pru gave him a cold stare. "I'll calm down when people stop making stupid comments. Ben, all I meant was that we shouldn't jump to conclusions, not least about the reliability of a man scorned."

"Sorry, sarge." Ben raised his hands. "I was wrong to say that about victims. But if we're not jumping to conclusions, then we shouldn't automatically label Pippa as being easily led just because Becky Bairstow said she was."

"Touché." Pru gave a mock salute.

Robin brought the discussion back to the interview itself. "Did Warnock mention the fakes business?"

Alison shook her head. "Swore ignorance, sir. Said the only thing he'd had to do with old sites was when he'd had to do his Community Payback, which of course produced a rant about that. When we got him back on topic, he said if he wanted—his words—'fucking bits of old pot,' he'd go down to B&Q."

"Did he have anything to say about where Pippa is now?"

"He was distinctly cagey about that, wasn't he, Ben?"

"Yes. Clammed up." Ben shrugged. "Simply said he didn't know, but I'm not sure that's true."

"You pressed him on it?" Robin asked.

"Yes, but he just went into 'all the world's against me' mode. Complained about the police harassing innocent people."

"If he calls that harassment, he should have seen some of the things that happened when I was a young copper." Robin could have told them stories that would make their hair stand on end—not so much what he'd witnessed first-hand, but the tales of the bad old days of policing, when corruption had been rife in certain areas and where nailing a crime on someone, anyone, had been more important than making sure you'd convicted the right person. "Maybe I'll tell you about them when we've got this case sorted."

"I'm looking forward to it already, sir." Sarah grinned. "Did you get anything out of Warnock about why he comes back here?"

Ben frowned. "Sod all."

"If it *is* Pippa who was killed and he knows that, perhaps he's visiting the grave," Fraser suggested.

Pru frowned even deeper than she'd done at the "typical victim" comments. "The murderer revisiting the scene of the crime? Does that actually happen? If I'd killed someone, I'd want to get as far away as possible and keep away."

"Wouldn't that make it look as though you were guilty as sin?" Fraser countered. "Maybe it's a double bluff. 'I can't have done it, because I'm acting normally.'"

"Only Warnock's not acting normally, is he?" Sarah reminded them. "Not according to his mate in the CAS."

"If Warnock killed his ex-girlfriend, that would put the case firmly in 'domestic' territory, sir. Where you'd like it to be." Pru gave Robin a wink before explaining to Ben. "Our chief inspector here has always said you're most at risk from those you know well."

"I only say it because it's true." But did it apply here? Would Warnock as murderer work? "Let's assume Warnock has a motive—resentment about the breakup—and there are elements in the killing which would be concomitant with an argument that went too far. He'd have the means, at least to bash somebody over the head, but so would pretty well anybody." Robin picked up a large paperweight from the nearest desk. "See?"

"What about the marks on the neck, sir?" Ben enquired. "We've got to make them fit into the story."

"Do we?" Alison chipped in. "We live in the real world, not in the middle of some TV crime show where all the loose ends have to tie up. Life's not like that."

"No, but sometimes juries are." Robin hadn't served on one, although he'd heard about plenty in action. "If we've got anything we can't explain, then some clever defence counsel will pounce on it and put enough doubt into people's minds that we risk not securing a conviction. Which brings me to opportunity. How would Warnock get a body onto the Culford site? Every time I go there, I'm more convinced that you'd have to bring it in through the gate."

"Got his hands on the keys and had a copy made? The good old-fashioned strategy of a bar of soap to take an imprint?" Ben's suggestion was solid. "Although almost anyone on-site could have done the same."

"True. Okay, let's keep our minds open for the moment. We don't even know that the dead woman is Pippa Palmer. Talking of which ..." Robin looked at his constables expectantly.

"Lady Luck's smiled on us at last, sir." Sarah beamed. "We discovered that one of Pippa Palmer's relatives is already on the DNA database. That nice, middle-class family she originated from has a black sheep. Her paternal uncle was done for assault a few years back."

A murmur of approval ran round the room. They had the victim's DNA profile, although why that hadn't already been checked against the database worried Robin. Still, he wasn't going to spoil *this* meeting for a potentially vital step being missed. "Have you got Grace or anyone onto it?"

"Um." Sarah glanced nervously at Fraser. "We wanted to check with you first."

Robin took a deep breath and counted to ten. Hopefully time wouldn't turn out to be of the essence. "Get onto it as soon as we've finished here. Pru and I have work to do."

The sergeant explained that she'd been on the blower to Howarth and arranged for them to see him that afternoon, much to the bloke's chagrin, as he'd insisted that his weekends were inviolate. She'd reminded him that murder was no respecter of days off, and that he'd better make himself available.

Robin suggested the rest of the officers head off home—once they'd got the DNA comparison ordered—to get some rest, as their next step would depend on the result of the DNA tests, and he wouldn't expect that until the next day at the earliest. If any surprising developments arose, he'd call them back in.

The first surprising development—although not one that justified a recall—was Howarth arriving at the station early for his appointment.

"Sooner we've seen him, the sooner *we* can get a break," was Pru's last remark as she went to fetch him from reception, leaving Robin to go and set up the interview room. He'd noticed a distinct change in his sergeant's attitude towards her old friend these last few days—and all for the better. Now that she'd developed an appreciation for her old mate's feet of clay, maybe the smarmy so-and-so would be less able to pull the wool over Pru's eyes. Howarth was clearly taken aback by the formality of the setting, and the fact his words were going to be recorded. If Robin had been a betting man, he'd have put a tenner on Becky Bairstow having been in contact with her partner in fraud as soon as she'd made her statement. And if the prospect of a "proper" interview had unsettled him, then Pru's insistence on calling him "Mr. Howarth" must have been equally disorienting.

They went through the official procedure, Robin never having quite got to the point of it feeling like mindless routine. There was too much significance in recording a person's words to make it an everyday thing.

"Becky Bairstow has given us a full account of your business," Robin said, once the preliminaries were done. "Dealing in faked antiquities. We'd like to hear your side of the story."

Howarth gave Pru a cold glance, which she ignored. "Am I being charged with anything? If so, I'd like a solicitor present."

"We have no charges to bring at present," Robin clarified. "And as I've already said, you can have legal support at any point you choose."

Howarth looked at the officers, at his watch, and then at the officers again. "Oh, let's get this over and done with. Yes, Becky and I ran a business selling artefacts. Remember that blue file I was so keen to get back?"

"I do."

"That contained some vital paperwork concerning a range of recent transactions. You can imagine how lost I'd have been without it."

"I can. Especially if I'd picked the file up and found it crammed full of information relating to your scam."

"Scam?" Howarth's eyebrows shot up. "We were totally legitimate."

"Are you saying that you never sold any fakes?"

"No. I'm saying that our business was completely above board at the outset. And that the first object we sold of dubious provenance we sold unawares of the fact." Howarth spoke like a politician or a civil servant, weaselling his way around and through the truth to present the version of it he'd like to get across.

"Object of dubious provenance?" Pru sneered. "You mean the first fake you conned someone into buying."

"As I said, we didn't realise it was a fake at the time, given that we don't microscopically inspect everything we deal in. We just didn't have a complete history for this particular item, as we made plain to the purchaser." Howarth wore that smug grin again, the one which made Robin want to break all the rules he held so dear and punch the bloke's nose.

"Did Pippa Palmer microscopically inspect everything you sold?"

A sharp rap at the door came at entirely the wrong moment as far as Robin was concerned, allowing the witness time to think, and to further refine a story which had no doubt already been honed. Pru answered the knock, then returned to whisper in Robin's ear that he was wanted urgently on the telephone by Greg from forensics.

"Interview suspended. Chief Inspector Bright leaves the room."

He tried not to let his anger show, knowing that Greg wouldn't have had the nerve to haul him out of an interview unless the matter was vital, but given the unfriendly tones which greeted him, he must be on the warpath.

"I got a message one of your officers left me. Why are you getting us to recheck the DNA on our victim? I've already done it. She's not on the database."

"Sounds like the message got garbled." Robin tried to be sufficiently soothing; the last thing he wanted was noses being put out of joint among the CSIs or forensics crew. He'd have to replace "put a rocket up the team for not doing simple DNA check" with "put a rocket up the team for not making that message plain." "We're trying to establish if the dead woman is called Pippa Palmer. Her uncle was done for assault and is on our records, so it should be a straight comparison."

"Okay. That makes more sense." Greg seemed slightly happier. "Although I'd have thought a partial match might have shown up already. Thanks for clarifying."

"Always a pleasure. Just bring me good news, eh?"

"Can't promise that. But we'll always bring you the truth."

"I guess that will have to do."

When Robin returned to the room, the atmosphere had turned distinctly chilly. Pru, shoulders hunched and standing by the frosted window, exuded tension.

"Everything all right?" he asked.

"All ready to resume the interview, sir." Pru, with a thunderous look on her face, returned to her place at the table and restarted the recording equipment with a clipped, "Inspector Bright returns. Interview resumes."

Robin got straight down to business. "You were about to explain exactly how you got into dealing fakes."

To his surprise, Howarth spread his hands on the desk and simply said, "I wasn't, but I will." What followed was an account that matched what Becky had told them—apart from pointing the finger at himself—and no doubt contained elements that would match what she'd put in her statement when they had the chance to read it in full.

"So you see," he said finally, "you end up in a situation that's running out of control. You're where you don't want to be, but you've no way of stopping."

"Couldn't you just have said that enough was enough?" The sneering edge in Pru's voice hadn't been present earlier in the interview. "Are you really saying that you couldn't square up to two 'mere' women and say you wanted out?"

Howarth, clearly wanting to make a response but wary of saying anything that would make the situation worse, kept tight lipped.

"We're waiting for an answer," Robin said at last.

"I suppose *I* wanted to carry the business on," Howarth conceded. "We all did. It was the wrong decision, in retrospect."

"Wrong decision?"

"We thought that after a lull, people might have forgotten the kerfuffle and we could start up again. We'd reckoned without Sian."

"Oh, for goodness' sake." Pru drummed the table impatiently. "You started up again after she started volunteering at Culford. Why take such a risk?"

"I didn't know she was working there. I don't handle the details of who volunteers and where; that's all delegated to the people on-site. I'd been on secondment out in France. We have strong links with our equivalent department in Paris." Howarth appealed to Robin. "Can you imagine what it was like getting back and finding her there, gloating at us? We've been looking over our shoulders all the time since."

Robin recalled the twitchy way Howarth had reacted to Sian's arrival when he and Ben had interviewed the man on-site. "So why didn't you mention it to us?"

"Because I'd have seemed an idiot, admitting I was scared of a woman."

That avoidance of losing face certainly seemed in character, as was the patronising attitude. "You *are* scared of her? Why?"

"I didn't say I *am* scared. Only that I had been in the past. When she was making all those wild threats. Even you'd have been frightened, Inspector."

"Chief Inspector," Robin reminded him. "Was Pippa Palmer frightened of her?"

Howarth looked askance at the question. "Pippa? Of course. She wasn't daft. And that stuff about burying ourselves with our own artefacts was aimed at all three of us."

"You said *was*," Robin snapped back. "Not *is*. Any reason for that?"

"No. But we were talking about last summer, weren't we?"

Robin left the question unanswered, waiting to hear what Howarth would say if they left him to squirm a while.

"I suppose," Howarth said uneasily, when the conversational gap had gone on too long, "you're wondering whether Pippa Palmer could be the dead woman, whether Sian could have killed her, and if I knew anything about it?"

"Now, how could you surmise all of that just from my question about 'was' versus 'is'? Why don't you tell us what you know for a fact?"

Howarth sighed. "When Pippa Palmer left the business—eight months ago, I think it was—we had no reason to think that she was dead. We sort of assumed she was just trying to get out of harm's way. When the body turned up at the dig, I never dreamed it could be her. We'd still been emailing about her verifying some objects for us."

Robin looked up sharply. "When was that?"

"Last September? October? I'd need to check."

"And you're certain it was her?"

"I had no reason to doubt it. But I didn't speak face-to-face, although that wouldn't have helped. I'd never met the woman." Howarth waved his hand. "All done through email."

Both Howarth and Becky Bairstow had made a point of saying they'd never met Pippa Palmer. Was that the truth, or was there more to it? An explanation of why they wouldn't have known it was Pippa in the grave, even if her body had turned up when it remained recognisable?

Yet this still didn't add up. Yes, Robin could see Sian volunteering at Culford and getting involved with the local groups as a means of keeping up the pressure on the people she felt had been the ultimate cause of her father's death. Yes, being a keyholder there—and having seen the work done by the Community Payback volunteers—Sian might have realised she had the ideal place to hide a body should she need it. And that realisation could have been post-murder if Pippa's death had been an accident, the result perhaps of some confrontation that had turned into a blazing row.

But why should she stay on until the body was discovered? Why not do a runner when news of the planned dig emerged? Or was Sian so confident that nobody could pin this on her—and the lack of ID and few tangible things like fibres on the body showed either a very clever or very lucky criminal—that she could afford to stay and watch how things unfolded? In which case, it might be wise to have a discreet check kept on her.

"You've only answered the first of your three points," Robin said. "Is it possible that Sian killed her?"

"It's possible. Although she hasn't been acting like a murderer. She has never made any overt threat against me since she appeared at Culford. Just been there. A brooding presence," Howarth added theatrically.

"But Becky Bairstow was frightened enough to do a runner," Pru pointed out.

"Is that what she told you? I suspect she was over-egging the pudding. Trying to justify her upping sticks and creating a new life for herself with a new bloke. Otherwise it looks rather selfish, leaving her parents and going globetrotting."

Robin shared a glance with his sergeant, who wore a look of disbelief. One of these two had to be lying, but why? Had the police been studying this from the wrong angle? Although in that case, what was the right one?

"You lied about having an affair, to cover up running your fakes business." Robin raised his hand as Howarth appeared to be on the verge of interrupting. "Let me finish, please. One of the pair of you is lying about what went on before Becky Bairstow had her lottery win. Are you also lying about your involvement in murder?"

"No!" Howarth slammed his hands on the table.

Robin took a deep breath. "I can't work out if you're innocent but stupid or guilty as sin. You had good reason to want Pippa Palmer dead. She could have been as much of a threat to your reputation as Sian. More so, given that she had inside knowledge."

"That's ridiculous." Howarth, arms folded now, sat back in his chair.

"You worked closely with her. You could have been in a position to find out enough about her to access her passwords." Pru leaned closer. "So many security questions are the standard—first pet, first school, mother's maiden name. Hardly a secret if you know somebody. Do you have any Chinese rugs, by the way?"

"Chinese rugs? What the hell is this about?" Howarth flung himself onto his feet. "I'm not answering any further questions without my solicitor present. I've been honest with you about the antiquities business, but other than that, there's nothing to discuss. You can't hold me."

"We have no intention of doing so. We'll arrange to continue this interview at a mutually convenient time for all parties." At which point Robin might have hard evidence to lay on the table.

"I hope he's not gone home to dispose of his rug collection," Robin quipped as they left the interview room, only half joking.

"Don't worry, sir. We share enough mutual friends that one of them would be able to tell me if he'd ever had posh carpets. He'd not be able to stop boasting about them, for one thing." Pru grimaced. "And I bet it'd be really hard to remove every trace of them without Wendy—that's his wife—getting suspicious about why he wanted the house deep cleaned, let alone rid of expensive furnishings. What did you get called out for?"

Robin explained about Greg and the mix-up. "What happened when I was out of the room?"

"Charlie was being Charlie." Pru's frown hardened. "Asked why I was being so cold to him, when we'd been such great friends. Why the police couldn't understand that he'd not done anything wrong. Blah blah blah."

"That was all?"

"You don't miss much, do you?"

"Adam reckons I can be quite oblivious. But Howarth had changed his tune, and you looked like you wanted to thump him."

Pru leaned back against the corridor wall, rolling her shoulders. "That's because I did. Remember pointing out that perhaps I shouldn't be on the case because Charlie and I go back a long way? I thought the potential problem would be bias towards him, and I knew I could ensure that didn't happen."

"But it isn't?"

"No. Even when he was trying the 'we're old pals, Pru' line, I could handle it. But he started talking about my family. All the pride they must feel at how well I've done for myself and how nobody would have guessed the little girl with pigtails would be heading up the ladder towards Chief Constable." Pru narrowed her eyes. "Don't say anything. One quip and I swear to God I'll belt you one, whether it costs me my job or not."

"Never crossed my mind." Pru would know that wasn't the truth, but Robin wanted to sound reassuring. "He seems to have been on a course about how to get under people's skin."

"Isn't that a fact? Especially when he started going on about what my dad would say when *his* dad told him that I'd been coming down hard on his only son. I had to give Howarth a piece of my mind." She halted, taking a deep, calming breath. "How do you manage to keep objective, sir? That murder at Lindenshaw school, your Adam was involved in the investigation right from the start."

"He wasn't 'my Adam' then."

"Yeah, but I bet you wished he was." Pru was always a touch too astute for Robin's comfort. "And look at the last murder we dealt with. That ended up too close to home, as well."

"What are you getting at?"

"I'm not getting at anything. I just think you're a bloody marvel, sir. Howarth mentioned my dad and I almost lost it. Adam was threatened and you hardly blinked an eyelid."

That wasn't how it had felt at the time: when Adam—and Campbell—had been at risk, Robin had been a total jelly inside. Although he was pleased that he'd maintained a cool façade, pulling the wool over his colleague's eyes. "Did Howarth threaten your dad?"

"Lord, no. It was all schoolboy-level stuff. You know, 'I'm going to tell on you. Nyah nyah.'" Pru made a face. "I told him to grow a pair. Or else I'd be telling *his* dad what a snivelling wretch he'd turned into."

"Quite right. It did the trick too. Got him talking."

"But did he say enough? I keep thinking we're one step forwards and two steps back." Pru rubbed her forehead with both hands. "We should reconsider everything we have from Howarth and Bairstow— and Sian—making a note of inconsistencies, looking for anything that might tie them in tighter to that death."

"Get Ben and Sarah to do it. They'll bring a couple of pairs of fresh eyes. But wait until Monday. We all need to clear our minds." Robin rubbed his neck. "I wish I'd had a good rummage through that blue file of his. Makes my thumbs prick."

"Something wicked this way coming?" Pru stifled a yawn. "I have no idea what my dad would say if Howarth turned out to be complicit in a murder. It would be the scandal of the decade down our way. I'd rather it was a simple case of Sian killing Pippa Palmer and hanging around Culford to terrorise the other two."

"It's certainly the best fit we've got at the moment." Not an ideal fit, though. More like trying to put a round peg in a square hole. "I'll be happier when I know who was in that grave."

"Won't we all, sir?"

Chapter Fifteen

It wasn't often they had a proper roast dinner outside of Sunday lunchtime, but Adam reckoned he and his partner needed a treat. If Robin had to eat his later, plated up and warmed in the microwave, so be it; Adam and Campbell were having roast beef, Yorkshire pudding, gravy, the whole works. When Robin rang to say that he'd be home at a reasonable time and hopefully wouldn't have to go in again that evening, Adam opened a celebratory bottle of red wine to let it breathe. Who knew when they'd have such an opportunity again?

Broaching the subject of the "Abbotston snitch" and airing Adam's worries, might have to wait until the next day. He hid the tabloid newspaper, and some research notes he'd made subsequently inside his copy of the *Times Educational Supplement*, then tried to forget about it.

When Robin arrived—tired, hungry, but grateful to be home, or so he said—Adam suggested he loosen his tie and get himself outside of a glass of red.

"Whatever's cooking smells great. Only two places laid?" Robin asked as he slipped his tie off.

"Yeah. Campbell's having his in his basket. Room service."

"Pillock. I meant, where's Stuart?"

"Out again."

"I hope he hasn't found another woman." Robin took a sip of wine. "That would complicate matters."

"Unless he moved in with her pretty sharp." Adam tried the Merlot; it was rare to find something that fulfilled all that the label promised, but this did. "Actually, I think he's just keeping a low profile. He texted me to say he'd be taking in a film and a kebab with one of the new—male—constables at Stanebridge. Either our guest realises he's being a third wheel or he's avoiding having an awkward conversation."

"He can't avoid it forever. We'll nab him tomorrow, assuming I don't get called in." Robin launched into a résumé of the day's developments. He reached a complicated bit about DNA tests only for his mobile phone to go off. "I hope this isn't a case of famous last words." He answered the call. "Hello?"

Adam had gone past the point of pretending he wasn't listening to Robin's half of any conversations. If it proved to be something entirely confidential, one of them would leave the room.

"You don't sound your usual cheery self, Greg. Got bad news for me?" From the bleak expression that plastered Robin's face, the reply couldn't have been a welcome one. "Hit me with everything. No pussyfooting."

The rest of the conversation descended into a procession of increasingly miserable responses, ending with a, "Bloody brilliant. No chance of a mistake? No, forget I said that. Thanks anyway. Can you send the report over by email? Good, thanks."

It wasn't like Robin to drown his sorrows, but he picked up the wine glass as soon as he'd put down the mobile.

"Want to talk about it?" Adam asked.

"Not sure there's much to say. Remember I was talking about checking our victim's DNA against the bloke we thought was her uncle's? Forensic Greg has done it. They're not related."

"She's not Pippa Palmer?" For all that Adam vowed he didn't want to get involved with his partner's cases, it frustrated him that a lead he'd had a part in generating had come to nothing.

"Doesn't look like it." Robin rubbed his hands over his face. "What a bloody mess."

Adam, en route to the oven to check the Yorkshire pudding, rubbed Robin's shoulder. "DNA isn't the be-all and end-all. Have I ever told you about my best friend at school? The one who was the grandson of a missionary?"

"You've mentioned him, but I don't see how it relates."

"It was a bit like your case, in a way. Peter didn't share any DNA with his aunt because she was adopted. She didn't even have the same skin colour as the rest of the family because she'd come from an African orphanage."

"You know, that's food for thought." Robin had pulled the bottle towards him to pour a second glass, but now he pushed it away again. "What if the uncle was adopted? Or Pippa was? Am I clutching at straws?"

"I don't think so. Life's more complicated than we give it credit for. This will be about another five minutes." Adam moved from oven to hob, where the carrots and broccoli were simmering nicely. "Plenty of time for me to share another brilliant thought."

"I'm all ears." Robin inhaled the aromas that had escaped from the oven. "Apart from the bit of me that's all gastric juices."

Adam switched into a Caribbean accent and produced a calypso-style lilt. "Shame and scandal in the family."

Robin glanced at him askance. "Have you been at the wine already?"

"No, you twit. It was a song. Gran had it on vinyl. She used to play it for us, much to Mum's disgust."

Robin still looked perplexed. "Did that come out of the ark with Noah?"

"Nearly." Adam took the joint of beef—which had been resting—and placed it before Robin. "You carve. Anyway, this song was all about how this bloke fancies a girl, only his dad says that *he* is really her father—near-the-knuckle stuff for the sixties—so the son and the girl can't go out with each other. Then at the end his mum tells him that the bloke *can* get together with the girl because his father isn't really his father. If you follow me."

"I think I do." Robin, meat fork in one hand and knife in the other, paused mid-carve. "And you're quite right. It's enough to dint anyone's faith in DNA profiling."

"That's why so much is made of the maternal line," Adam observed. "Mitochondrial DNA and the like, whether it's modern tests or ancient practice. Egyptian pharaohs marrying their sisters to ensure that any royal child must have royal blood in them."

Robin nodded. "Maybe we need to do this the old-fashioned way. Get a picture of Pippa from her family, and dental records. Or a note of an identifying feature like broken bones she had in the past. I'll get Ben onto it first thing tomorrow. You're a genius, you know," he added, laying the succulent slices of beef on their plates. "It's too easy to get caught up in the flash, modern stuff. Back to basics."

"Like an old-fashioned roast dinner?"

"It's the route to a man's heart." Robin watched, with evident pleasure, as Adam laid out the rest of the meal. "Poor old Cowdrey's not likely to be getting anything as good."

"I thought he was back today?"

"Due to be, but his flight home got delayed by an air-traffic controllers' strike in France. He rang from the airport to say he wasn't sure when he'd be back and to apologise that he wasn't there to take the media off my hands. I hope nobody was listening because he also made several uncomplimentary statements about the French workforce." Robin grimaced. "The media would love that. Xenophobic remarks from a senior policeman."

Ideal opportunity to tackle Adam's worries. He settled into his seat and speared a gravy-covered carrot. "Did you ever pin down who leaked to the local radio?"

"No," Robin eventually replied, once he'd disposed of some beef. "Although I've had everyone on the team sidle up when I'm on my own to say it wasn't them."

"And you believe them? Who else could it have been?" Adam stabbed another carrot. "That bloke, Baxter, has been approached by Radio Kinechester. They say they want the detectorists' view on things."

"Tuckton will have kittens."

"He already has. He's banned the members from talking to the media. Not sure Baxter will comply, though."

"He's a mug, then. They'll misreport what he says; mark my words." Robin nodded, then tucked into another forkful.

Adam took another bite, despite his appetite ebbing away. "How much do the diehard Abbotston-ites hate the Stanebridge officers?"

"Like an Arsenal supporter hates a Spurs one. If you mean the really intransigent ones. Why?"

Adam laid down his cutlery. "Hold on. Let me fetch something."

Robin's brow wrinkled. "Okay. So long as it's not a copy of that song."

"I wish it was."

When Adam returned with the newspaper, he laid it on the breakfast bar without comment.

"Bloody hell," Robin said when he'd finished reading the story and before he took a swig of wine. "Have they got nothing better to report on? How is this in the public interest?"

"Search me. Look, I'm probably worrying over nothing, but would one of your 'intransigents' talk to the media about *us*?"

"Why should they? It's the Culford case details they leaked."

"At the moment." Adam gave his lover a sheet of paper. "I went on the newspaper website—that's not an experience I'd want to repeat—and looked at this campaign they're launching. They had a list of examples of corrupt policing. Abbotston featured in it. This is what they said."

Robin read the article, wincing. "But that case hasn't come to court yet. They might prejudice it."

"There were reports of the arrests at the time, though. Even your mate Cowdrey couldn't keep everything out of the local rags." Fortunately, Robin's previous murder case hadn't been taken up by the national press, coinciding as it did with a major scandal involving a politician and a married television cook. "I appreciate this is about corruption, but if Abbotston station's on the radar, will they dig further, especially if they have a pair of eyes and ears on the inside?"

"It's not the tabloids that have 'eyes and ears' at Abbotston. It's the local BBC. Different kettle of fish."

Adam frowned. As far as he was concerned, the media could all be as bad as each other. "Okay, but if one of your diehards at Abbotston station sees this, they might want to get revenge on you for helping air their dirty laundry. Snitch to this lot too. I can imagine a tabloid reporter"—he jabbed at the offending newspaper—"trying to dig up dirt. And making it up when he or she can't find any. What if they spied on us and thought we were in a ménage with Stuart?"

"Don't be ridiculous." Robin sniffed. "That won't happen. Cowdrey would have an officer hung, drawn, and quartered if they leaked anything personal, especially if they told a pack of lies."

"Hanging the culprit might be too late to make a difference to us." Adam jabbed the paper again. "I bet these blokes don't find it ridiculous."

"Sorry, poor choice of words." Robin sighed. "I know it's hard, but I've got enough on my plate. Try not to worry, please."

Adam bit back on his instinctive reply. He didn't want a fight, not now. "I'll try not to," he said through gritted teeth.

"Good." Robin pushed the tabloid aside, then helped himself to the little piece of Yorkshire pudding which clung to the side of the tin. "No more work talk. Chasing up the DNA and other forensics will give Cowdrey something to get his teeth into when he does get back. I'm concentrating on getting my teeth into this."

Adam forced a smile. "Your jokes don't improve."

Despite feeling his concerns had been too lightly dismissed, Adam was pleased to see a glimpse of the everyday Robin—not the man the policeman turned into when he was chasing a killer—appear again. If only he'd spare a bit of his brain to appreciate the potential danger from the press.

The next morning—planned as a leisurely one for once—Robin was on the phone before he'd even eaten breakfast. Adam could hear him detailing Ben with the job of getting the information they needed from the Palmer family. The officer could utilise the local family-liaison team or leg it up to sunny Bedford himself if need be. Robin also rang Greg; that sounded like an alert about the changed plan of attack regarding identification. The investigation was obviously full steam ahead again. After that, what Robin needed was a long walk with Adam and Campbell, and the opportunity to mull events over. There was a chance they'd talk about the case, but Adam believed that was part of his role. One of the qualities he valued in the best school governors he'd worked with had been their independence, how they weren't steeped in education-speak or education-think. How they could sometimes see things more clearly because they observed from the outside, as he himself had done over the roast beef the previous evening. Thinking of which, hopefully *he'd* get a chance to air his concerns once more over the media leaks.

Just as they got settled in the kitchen for breakfast, Anderson appeared, looking slightly the worse for wear, which he put down to a dodgy kebab.

"So long as that's all it was," Robin growled. "You don't want a drink-driving charge on top of everything."

"I had two pints maximum, honest." Anderson filled the kettle. "At least Helen can't complain that I'm always down the boozer."

Adam steeled himself. "Have you spoken to her?"

"No. I sent a text, saying I was sorry for whatever it was that I'd done and could she tell me what it actually was, because I'm only a bloke and too dumb to know without having it written in capital letters and plastered all over the shaving mirror, but she didn't appreciate the joke. All I got was the old 'if you don't know, I'm not telling you' line." Anderson stared bleakly at the kettle.

"If you can't appeal to the stereotype, what about appealing to her maternal side?" Adam suggested. "Can't you get yourself into a mess so she feels she has to look after you?"

Anderson grabbed a bread roll and started lathering it with jam. "Maternal side? I'm not sure she's got one. Anyway, are you suggesting I step in front of a van?"

"Nothing so dramatic." Although Adam couldn't think of any alternative suggestion. He made a helpless face at Robin, who just shrugged. "What about a nice simple fall and a suspected fracture? I could truss your arm up in a bandage or something."

"To be honest, Helen always struck me as having a motherly side," Robin ventured, voice unnaturally constrained. "A lot of teachers have."

"Yeah, well, not every teacher has a family like hers. Her mum's okay, sort of the type who pretends she's really modern but who'd secretly love it if we got wed so she could wear a big hat and have a posh do."

Robin gave Adam a hopeful glance. "You'd better invite us too, if it ever happens. I like a wedding. And a christening. But I can't promise I'll wear a big hat."

"It wouldn't suit you." Anderson rubbed his nose on his cuff. "Although I suppose there's no chance of either of those happening now, is there?"

Please God they weren't going to have tears over breakfast. But if tears helped to resolve the situation, maybe Adam would rescind the prayer. "There might be a chance of one or both if you get back together."

Shouldn't they just tell him the good news, and to hell with what they'd promised Helen? Surely his gratitude would be worth risking her wrath?

"Ow!" Anderson shot a foot into the air, shaking his left hand, in which part of his bread roll still lodged. "Fucking hell."

Adam leaped out of his seat. "What's the matter?"

"Your bloody dog bit me." Anderson pointed an accusatory finger at Campbell, who had retreated to his basket wearing an innocent grin, but whose chops were dotted with telltale crumbs.

"He never bites anyone. Apart from villains." Robin dashed across to give the Newfoundland a reassuring pat. "What were you doing?"

"Nothing, I swear." Anderson put down the bit of roll on the breakfast bar, then held out his reddened hand for Adam to cast an eye over.

"You must have done something to annoy him." Adam wet some kitchen roll and dabbed at the wound. "He's not a biting dog, apart from when that nasty piece of work was threatening me. Were you teasing him with that bread roll? We asked you not to."

"It's my jam and bread, not his." The change of emphasis, and the shifty expression in Anderson's eye, suggested that teasing was exactly what he'd been doing. His hand had been out of their sight, and Campbell knew he had to stay seated in his basket at mealtimes unless invited over to take a scrap.

"How does he know that when you offer it to him?" Adam pointed out.

"He needs to learn." Anderson jerked his thumb towards Campbell. "I'm not staying here with that hound. I'd rather face Helen."

Adam, about to counter the insult to Campbell, shifted tack abruptly. This opportunity was too good to miss. "You should get this wound seen to. Only not here and not at your house. Are your tetanus jabs up to date?"

"I think so. Why?"

"Shame. I was wondering if you could pop down to the Lindenshaw cottage hospital drop-in centre and have them take a look at the bite. I don't believe he's broken the skin too deeply, but it might need some sort of proper medical attention. We'll call Helen and tell her."

"He's right," Robin agreed eagerly, probably recalling how an unplanned trip to the Abbotston casualty department had been the first step in his rapprochement with Adam after a blazing row. "I'll run you down there."

"Only, be careful about what you tell the doctors." Adam took a clean handkerchief from the laundry pile, which might have been placed on the worktop for just such an eventuality rather than simply for sorting. That would work as a temporary dressing. "I'm not having Campbell investigated for being dangerously out of control."

"Say it was your own stupid fault. You know you were taunting him." The dangerous expression in Robin's eye brooked no argument.

"I'll do that." Anderson stuffed the last piece of roll into his mouth, then headed for the door.

"If the drop-in centre isn't open, we'll go over to Abbotston casualty." Robin pecked Adam's cheek. "See you when I see you."

"Here, wait a moment." Adam fetched a travel mug to pour some coffee into. "For while you're waiting. Only don't hang around too long. It won't hurt Stuart to stew in his own juice."

"Thanks." Robin grabbed the mug. "Get a strong coffee for yourself while you're at it. You've got the harder job."

As it turned out, Adam—fortified by caffeine—had an easy time of it. Helen sounded suitably concerned, and she put the blame for the incident firmly on Stuart, not believing Campbell capable of anything bad. She promised she'd go down to the drop-in centre to relieve Robin of his burden.

"Result?" Adam asked Campbell when he went to get another coffee, but the excitement must have proven too much for the dog, as the only reply was a contented snore.

Robin arrived back within a couple of hours, wearing an optimistic grin.

"How did it go?" Adam asked. "Want another coffee?"

"Fine so far as I could tell, and no thanks. I could murder a cup of tea, though."

"Go and sit in the garden and I'll bring it out."

The day was wonderfully mild, perfect for soaking up some rays and simply relaxing. Adam produced a pot of tea and a plate of decent biscuits—this could be an occasion for celebrating.

"Was Helen there when you left?"

"Yes. I didn't intend to stay for that long, but Stuart's such a wimp about anything medical. No wonder she thinks he'd get in a state about the baby. He'd probably faint in the delivery room." Robin nibbled on a chocolate digestive. "People are funny. She gave him a right tongue-lashing about being an idiot, but when the nurse came over and did much the same, Helen turned on *her*."

"That's definitely the maternal streak emerging. Mum used to do that to us if we'd had an accident. She could tell us off, but woe betide anyone else who tried. We have hope." Adam, leaning back, enjoyed the sun's rays on his face.

"Do you think Campbell did it deliberately?"

"Sorry?" Adam's eyes shot open.

"Took a nip at Stuart. Deliberately." Robin gave the dog—who'd noticed the biscuits and come to join them—an appraising look. "Maybe he'd got as fed up with him as we had. I was wondering if he'd been listening in on the pretend-fall and suspected-broken-bone bit and decided he had a better idea?"

Campbell, evidently enjoying the sunshine, was sitting with an innocent expression, making a show of cleaning his paws and occasionally glancing over to see if any crumbs had fallen to the ground.

"Who knows? I wouldn't put it past him. Dogs can get fed up as much as humans."

Robin leaned down to give the dog an appreciative pat and half a plain digestive. "As for Stuart being on his way home, let's not count our chickens. Helen may decide that he's a rabies risk, or some other thing pregnant women shouldn't encounter, and not want him back."

"I've got everything crossed." Adam took another biscuit, then weighed it carefully in his hands as though it might give him the carbohydrate equivalent of Dutch courage. "Sorry to be a pain, but could you get Cowdrey to see if he can identify your mole?"

Robin looked up from where he'd been fussing over Campbell. "Why have you got such a bee in your bonnet over that?"

"Because I can't get that Chasebury story out of my mind. Somebody's obviously got a grudge against you and they—" He halted as Robin raised a hand.

"It isn't necessarily a grudge against me or against anyone from Stanebridge. It could just be the old filthy lucre. Like it was last time at Abbotston." Robin's hackles were evidently rising, given the set of his shoulders and the way he drummed his fingers on his thighs. "As I said, Cowdrey will be trying to root him or her out, anyway. He doesn't need you to tell him his job."

"Okay. Forget I said anything." Adam took a deep breath; this was going the way of a flaming row. If Robin wouldn't do something more proactive, Adam would have to find a way to tackle things himself. "I'm not going to spoil what's been a good day so far."

"Suits me." Robin, clearly stressed, pressed his fingers against his forehead for what seemed an age before rolling his shoulders and grabbing another biscuit. "Does this count as lunch?"

Adam, puzzled, replied, "Late elevenses. Why?"

"I was thinking about that walk. I need to get some of the strain out of my system, and Campbell deserves a run up on the common and being able to rub his nose in as many disgusting things as take his fancy."

"Sounds good to me." Adam grabbed himself another two biscuits; a man needed to lay in supplies, and not just against the upcoming ramble. If Robin wasn't going to take his concerns seriously, maybe he needed to take action of his own.

"No work talk, though," Robin said. "No schools, no villains, no Ofsted, no media."

Adam forced himself to produce an enthusiastic thumbs up. "You, my son, have got yourself a deal."

The walk, followed by a sandwich, a kip, and a text from Anderson saying he might not be back until that evening, turned a good day into a special day.

Although when Robin's phone went, turning out to be one of his constables ringing in, Adam had to make an effort to shrug it off.

As Robin re-entered the lounge after his call ended, his face proved unreadable.

"Good news?"

"Not sure you'd call it good, exactly, but I think it moves us forwards." Robin, phone still in hand, as though he was weighing up who to call next, perched on the armchair. "Ben's a good lad. Gets on with things. He rustled up a sympathetic officer from Bedford to get in touch with the Palmer family."

"Must have been a nightmare for them." Adam could imagine the scene. A family maybe shocked but stoic, or perhaps suddenly frantic with worry, never having entertained a doubt that their daughter was still alive. Their world falling apart in the space of a few minutes. If he'd been in the same situation, and please God he never would be, would he have made sure in advance that he had relevant information ready and waiting, just in case the worst happened? How could one expedite confirming an identification?

"It's the part of the job I hate most." Robin ran the back of his hand across his brow. "It's never an easy conversation, and this one sounded particularly tricky. Turns out they'd known about the threats and that Pippa had been in fear for her life. The family had been complicit in her disappearing for a while and keeping as low a profile as they could, so that Sian Wheatstone—or any other aggrieved person—couldn't track her down."

"Did they know about her involvement with the fakes?"

"I believe so. Ben says they told the officer that she'd been inveigled into it by the other two." Robin rolled his eyes. "I suspect we'll never get to the truth about that racket in terms of who made who do what."

"Bad as the kids at school. 'It was his fault, sir, not mine.'" Adam did his best impression of an eight-year-old. "What happened when they mentioned the DNA?"

"Apparently Mrs. Palmer went ballistic. Accused the officer of wasting their time, of needlessly putting the family through an emotional wringer, when they knew it couldn't be Pippa. She said she'd sue the police for damages for the distress we'd caused." A rueful grin crept over Robin's face. "And then Mr. Palmer had to confess that his uncle had been adopted, something which had evidently been a family secret for such a long time he'd never told the missus."

"Blimey." What made people keep things from their loved ones? At least Helen wouldn't be able to keep the fact of her pregnancy hidden indefinitely; it was bound to show sooner or later. "Why do families get in such a state?"

"There seems to be a story behind it, and not a nice one. When the uncle was a boy he was taken from his natural parents, who were abusing him. Put into a loving family—the Palmers—and raised as their own, but before long he went off the rails." Robin wrinkled his nose. "He assaulted someone so badly that the bloke had three fractured ribs and a cracked skull."

Adam whistled. "Sounds like he really benefited from a loving upbringing, then."

"Don't be so quick to judge. Ben's a keen lad, so he'd already looked up the case notes, and it appears the uncle got a light sentence for the assault because he'd got nothing on his record and he was severely provoked." Robin shrugged. "The bloke who got beaten up had been making some pretty obnoxious statements about child abusers and how their victims brought it on themselves. I wouldn't normally have a lot of tolerance for people pleading mitigating circumstances around a crime, but in this case I've got some sympathy."

Adam could imagine how hard it would be for Robin to keep his fists under control if somebody made remarks about children who were victims of school bullies and how they'd asked for it. Those early inflicted mental wounds were still not properly healed and maybe never would be.

"But how did the family not realise it wasn't Pippa? I mean, if you only interact with somebody online it's easy to keep up a pretence, but didn't they speak to her on the phone or anything like that?"

"You should be a copper." Robin grinned. "That's what the local officer asked, but they said they couldn't. Pippa's email had been hacked already—before she went travelling—so she'd had to set up new accounts, and then she was certain her phone account had been accessed, as well. She was paranoid that Sian was trying to trace her and wanted to minimise the chances of being detected. She wouldn't even communicate via Messenger without using a VPN blocker."

Adam whistled. "Cloak-and-dagger stuff. They must all have been terrified."

"That's the impression the officer got," Robin confirmed. "Anyhow, long story short, Pippa had a couple of fractures in the past.

Broke her right leg in a skiing accident when she was in her teens, and another one—Ben did say what, but I've forgotten. He's spoken to Greg, and Greg says that matches with what he knows of the victim, but he'll get a proper comparison done first thing tomorrow. Looks like we've got a name at last."

"Now you just need the name of the killer."

Robin sighed, his body visibly racked with strong emotion that might have been relief at some light emerging or could equally have been concern that they'd taken a wrong turning once more. "With any luck, we might have that too."

Chapter Sixteen

A nderson hadn't reappeared by Sunday evening. He'd sent a text around five o'clock to say they weren't to worry—he hadn't fallen off the end of the world, and he'd be back when he was back. Adam and Robin had received that communication with cautious optimism, although not sufficient to resume romantic relations. Who'd want to answer the doorbell and let Anderson into the house when they were still in flagrante delicto?

Anderson rang first thing on Monday, before Robin had left for work, sounding tickled pink.

"How's the hand?" Robin asked.

"Sore but okay. Thank Campbell for me. He's done the job." Anderson chuckled. "After Helen gave me that rollicking—and then that poor nurse put her foot in it by doing the same—Helen apologised to both of us and explained exactly why she'd been so edgy. I'm going to be a father!"

"Wow." Robin made sure he came across as suitably amazed. "Congratulations."

"Thanks. Turn up for the books, eh?"

"Indeed it is." *So far so good.*

"The daft woman thought I'd be angry, but I'm not. Bit of bridge-building with the family needed, especially because we're not married, but nothing we can't manage between us."

Robin liked the sound of the "us." "You'll be fine. Make sure you have a big christening so both the grannies can buy a new frock and wear a big hat, and you'll be laughing."

"Just what we thought. And—assuming all goes well and we're not counting our chickens before they're hatched—we'd like you to be the baby's godfather."

"Oh. Yes. Thank you." Robin's turn to be tickled pink. "I'm not going to wear a big hat for the do, though."

"Silly sod." Anderson must be feeling chipper to address his ex-boss in so carefree a style. "I'll be over to get my stuff tonight, if that's all right?"

"Should be. Give Adam a text and check he'll be here, but I'm pretty sure he's not got parents' evening or anything on."

"Coolio Julio. Got to go. Bye."

As the call ended abruptly, Robin, stunned, stared at his phone.

"What was all that?" Adam appeared in the hallway, bag of school stuff in one hand and car keys in the other.

"I think we've got rid of our unwanted guest. Touch wood." Robin patted the banister. "Although I'll believe that when he's taken his stuff, which should be tonight. He'll contact you to make sure you're in. No guarantee I'll be home early."

"No worries. Especially if you being late means you've got a result."

Robin touched the banister again. "Let's hope so." He gave Adam a kiss and followed him out the door.

Adam had a plan. Not as bold as Campbell's supposed scheme to rid the house of Anderson, but hopefully as effective, although seeing as it involved one of the parents at the school, Rashford would need to be consulted.

The headteacher had seen the tabloid story himself, and admitted that Adam and Robin had crossed his mind at the time. "Not that you've done anything untoward, I'm sure."

"Cross my heart. But when has that stopped the press from inventing a story? Or the local radio, come to that. I want to ask Mr. Baxter to get some names for me. See if I can link them back to Abbotston nick. And," he added hastily, "I want to tell him to insist on having anonymity. And to make sure he deflects any questions about me or the school. We don't want life getting tricky for Sophie."

"I hadn't thought about that. God, we don't want her being dragged into it." Rashford ran his hands through his hair. "Just as well he mentioned it to you."

"Yep. Forewarned is forearmed."

"Can't we talk him out of speaking to this researcher? This is a murder case, after all. Sorry, sorry." Rashford, snorting, shook his head. "You know that. It's all old hat for you, I guess. But it won't be for Mr. Baxter. I wouldn't want him getting further entangled in this. It could be dangerous. For all we know one of the press is mixed up in the murder, or covering it up."

"You're quite right." One day Adam would have to tell the headteacher just how dangerous being involved with a copper could be at times, but that wasn't a conversation for today.

"I suppose I could try, but that wouldn't help solve the 'who's the mole' issue. Baxter's pretty set on the meeting too. I'd volunteer to go with him, but that would be even more likely to risk exposure."

"Very true." Rashford sighed. "Okay. I'm sure you'll try your best."

"I will. And I promise I'm not going out with my Sherlock Holmes hat and magnifying glass. I'm steering clear of crime scenes. Been there, done that, haven't I?" He wasn't promising not to ask the appropriate questions, though. He and Rashford set about the teaching observations they had planned for the morning, albeit part of Adam's mind remained on the note he'd be sending Baxter.

The Monday-morning team update was lively, despite the presence of Cowdrey, who'd dropped in to reassure the team that they were making progress and relieve them of any further need to address the media. "I'll need another bloody holiday after all this," he'd muttered before forcing a smile onto his face and joining the briefing.

He and Robin presented the new theory to the team, who greeted it with a mixture of enthusiasm and scepticism. Robin, who'd been expecting a healthy degree of doubt, had done some research on the web the previous evening to see if he could find any precedent.

"There was a case in Australia, a couple of years ago, where a victim's mobile phone was used to make it seem she was still alive. Her family were duped for ages. I'm not saying that inspired what we think happened here; I'm just pointing out that it's possible to get away with it."

"If we can identify the body as Pippa Palmer, then we'll know they got away with it," Cowdrey pointed out. "At least up until this point."

As though on cue, the phone rang; Greg, to say he was now ninety percent certain the dead woman was Pippa. He still had a DNA comparison with Mrs. Palmer to conduct—a fresh mouth-swab sample had been taken by the Bedford officers and was en route—but the picture the family had supplied was a reasonable match for what they knew of the dead woman's face and hair, and the historical broken bones, right leg and two ribs, were spot on. That tentative identification, and what had emerged in Saturday's interviews, was enough for the senior officers to justify getting Sian in for questioning.

When Robin had updated everybody and the briefing resumed, Ben said he'd gone over Sian's original statement, where she'd stated that she worked at Stanebridge library on Mondays, and he offered to ring and check she was there before they headed across.

"While I don't want to dint your initiative, I'm not sure that's such a great idea. Sian herself might answer the phone and get the wind-up." Robin blew out his cheeks. "Best just to turn up at the library and take it from there. I'm sure we could run her over to Stanebridge nick for questioning if necessary."

Pru, who'd slipped out of the briefing to answer another call, stormed out of the inner office. "Sir?"

Both Cowdrey and Robin turned round, said, "Yes?" in unison, then chuckled, although Pru's expression suggested this was no laughing matter.

"Sian's gone."

Robin leaped off the desk where he'd parked himself. "What do you mean, 'gone'?"

"Disappeared. Done a runner." Pru slumped against the door frame. "That was the manager from the library on the phone. Sian was supposed to report for work today but didn't. They rang her mobile, because she's normally one hundred percent reliable, but she's not picking up. Given that she works at Culford, they thought they should let us know. I think they were worried she'd been attacked too."

"Sorry, sir. I left it too late." Fine way to greet the boss on his return. "We should have talked to her yesterday."

"You weren't to know. I assume she'd not given any indication of clearing off up until then." Cowdrey obviously knew Robin well enough by now to understand the guilt he was feeling.

"And we didn't even have a proper ID on the victim, sir," Pru pointed out. "We'd have looked like right idiots if it turned out the dead woman wasn't Pippa Palmer. Imagine that all over the local media after we did the same thing with Becky Bairstow."

"I'd have been willing to take that risk." Robin wasn't to be mollified that easily. "I could have hauled her in as soon as we had an inkling that it was Pippa Palmer in the grave."

"And how long could we have kept Sian without charging her?" Cowdrey was the voice of reason. "A sympathetic judge might let us carry on with the questioning, but evidence was pretty thin forty-eight hours ago, wasn't it? Probably too thin to make a viable case."

"I take the point. Okay, we need to be pragmatic. Pru, get back to the library and see if anyone there has her on the 'find my friend' app. Ben, do the same with Clare at Culford." Might as well make the most of modern technology. "With any luck, she'll not have turned it off."

"Good thinking." Cowdrey nodded. "Sarah, can you go old school and get the airports-and-ports alerts up and running, along with the usual messages for forces to keep an eye out for her?"

"Will do, sir. Although if she's obtained a fake passport or has simply gone to ground on the mainland, we're stuffed."

"Then let's hope she hasn't," Cowdrey observed coldly.

"Can we put out an alert on Pippa Palmer's passport too?" Robin suggested. "It's unlikely to be at her parents' house if they think she's travelling, so there's a chance that Sian got her hands on it and will try to make use of it."

"How would she do that?" Alison asked, in a typically negative tone.

"If Pippa's like almost every woman in Britain, she'd have carried some sort of handbag or rucksack. There wasn't one found with her." Pru sounded exasperated. "Remember? Pippa might have carried her passport with her routinely, particularly if she didn't look her age and needed it for ID purposes."

Alison wouldn't let the point go. "That assumes Sian resembles her sufficiently to get through security."

"How different are they?" Cowdrey, fingers drumming his knees, seemed as annoyed at Alison's continued negativity as Robin was.

"We've only seen the one picture of Pippa, sir, and while they're not doppelgängers, they're not hugely dissimilar," Pru replied.

"Hm. Well, it's amazing what you can do with a wig and a bit of clever make-up. And luck," Cowdrey added. "When we flew out of Heathrow a fortnight ago, I had to remind the check-in girl to check my picture. I could have been anybody. Travel at a busy time, and outside the immediate aftermath of a terrorist incident when procedures have turned lax, and who knows what you could get away with. It doesn't bear thinking about."

Robin, who'd been staring at the incident board, trying to figure out if there'd been any points where they'd missed the chance to act, brought the team back to the basics. "We shouldn't ignore all the usual checks we'd normally do in the case of a mysterious disappearance. We're making the dangerous assumption that Sian's the killer, but what if she's another victim? Pru and I will get round to her house as soon as we're done here."

"Quite right, Chief Inspector." Cowdrey tapped the desk. "Very prudent. How many times does somebody go missing, and we start searches up and down the country, and then it turns out they've been done over by the nearest and dearest and stuffed behind a bath panel or buried in the garden?"

"Does Sian have nearest and dearest?" Pru asked. "I understood she fell out with her remaining family."

Robin shrugged. "Perhaps she fell in again. She has to have friends. Maybe she found somebody to replace Jerry when he gave her the push. We'll use our brains and not get blinkered." There'd been a few too many presumptions already, and Pru should know better than to fall into that trap.

"And she might simply be delayed by circumstances out of her control," Cowdrey pointed out. "Like I spent six hours at the airport because some idiots went on strike. Sian might have picked up a bug and spent six hours on the toilet, too ill to ring anybody."

That was a reasonable point but, while they would have to follow the notion through, nobody appeared convinced there was a different explanation. Surely the bird had flown the coop. Robin scanned his team's faces. "I want all of you ringing round, knocking on doors, whatever it takes to check with as many of Sian's contacts as you can. Ben, you're the king of social media. See what you can find there."

"Will do, sir, but she's not exactly got a big internet footprint. And what little there was slacked right off over the last year or so. She was keeping a low profile, maybe."

Pru, who'd been looking less than happy, murmured—loud enough for everyone to hear—"I wonder who tipped her the wink? About the net tightening."

"Not one of us," Alison protested. "Like it wasn't one of *us* who tipped off the media about Becky Bairstow."

"I'm sure nobody's thinking that," Cowdrey insisted.

Robin kicked the desk leg; remarkable how cathartic it felt, beating the crap out of some inanimate object. Better than being tempted to beat the crap out of coppers who couldn't keep their gobs shut. "Much more likely that somebody we've been questioning realised that we're homing in and has let her know, although I can't imagine Becky Bairstow doing it. Howarth's a loose cannon, though. And Jamie 'chip on the shoulder' Warnock."

"Doubt it," Sarah said. "Warnock doesn't know her personally, as far as we're aware. Only knows what Pippa told him about her."

"My money would be on Howarth." Pru nodded. "I can imagine him opening his big gob and either being overheard—you know how loud he talks—or doing something daft like saying, 'You thought you'd scare us, but we're going to sort you instead,' straight to her face. He doesn't do subtlety."

"He doesn't, but surely he's not had time to be overheard, unless they both just happened to be in the same place at the same time. Was Culford villa open yesterday?"

Ben raised his hand, like one of Adam's pupils might be doing at this very moment. "Did Sian need to be tipped off, sir? Strikes me that she's a clever girl. She'd know that we were getting close to the truth."

"Could be. And none of this gets us any closer to finding her." Robin leaped away from the desk where he'd been leaning. "Although while you're asking both Howarth and Bairstow whether they know where she is, feel free to put a bit of pressure on. They've arsed us around for long enough. Anything else to add, sir?"

Cowdrey, with his usual slightly dyspeptic, deeply thoughtful expression on his face, shook his head. "Not at the moment. I still need to get my brain round this, but it feels like you've done all the things I'd have done at the time I'd have done them. Although I don't yet know all the details." He gave Robin a smile, but it wasn't reassuring.

Had they missed their one chance?

When Robin and Pru got to Sian's house—a detached Victorian villa in Merritt's End, which was the single posh part of Culdover—there was no sign of life. Not a light on, nor a window open, no car on the gravel drive, and an empty feeling clinging to the place.

"I bet she *has* done a runner, sir." Pru's gaze swept across the well-kept facade.

Robin scanned the surroundings. The house was the last on its side of the street, adjacent to a small area of open ground which occupied all the space up to the junction with the next road. Each residential property sat in a generous plot, making it easy for someone to come and go unnoticed.

"That was always the likeliest outcome. We were clutching at straws to think otherwise." Eyes shaded against the glare with his hand, Robin peered through the window into a lounge which gave no indication of anything untoward. "No justification for us to be breaking in without a warrant. We'll take a peek round the—"

His proposal was interrupted by a cheery "Hello!" from the other side of the front hedge.

A dapper grey-haired chap peered over the greenery. "Are you looking for Sian?"

"We are indeed."

"Not seen her since yesterday. I think she's probably gone off somewhere, although she normally tells us when that happens. I'm David, by the way." The grey-haired man extended a hand, which Robin readily shook.

"I'm Robin Bright. Police." He produced his warrant card. "This is my sergeant, Pru Davis."

"Police? Is Sian all right?"

"We don't know. She's not turned up at work and hasn't made contact with anyone, so we're rightly concerned for her welfare." Which was no word of a lie.

"I have a spare key to her house. When we moved here, we asked if she'd keep one for us so she could pop in and feed the fish when we're off on our travels." David jerked his thumb over his shoulder. "She was more than happy to agree, and asked us to return the favour, not that she goes away a lot. Not like us. We're typical pensioners; always off gallivanting, and George does like his cruises."

Robin restrained a smile at the unfortunate choice of words. "Sounds like an excellent arrangement. Have you lived here long?"

"We've been here nine, ten months, I think. Might be longer. Time flies when you're our age." David's smile—which appeared to be as much of the man's apparel as his bow tie—beamed out. "Shall I fetch that key?"

"It might be a good idea. Just in case she's had an accident and needs help."

"Oh yes, quite right." Smile fading, he scuttled off, evidently keen to be of help.

"What?" Robin raised his eyebrows at Pru, who was eyeing him quizzically. "It's sensible procedure. For all we know she *might* be lying in there. Attacked by the real killer, whose identity the poor dumb rozzers have yet to work out."

"Yeah, yeah." Pru grinned. "I wonder if you and Adam will end up like David and George when you're retired? Going off cruising."

"You've got a filthy mind. Keep it on the matter in hand. Ah! Thanks." Robin gave David his most winning smile. "You've done us a real favour."

"I'm pleased to help. I just hope there's nothing nasty in there." David tried to hand the keys over, but Robin wouldn't take them.

"I'd be grateful if you'd open the door for us. You can stand on the threshold and make certain we don't trash the place." Robin smiled again, secretly pleased to see a flush creep over David's cheeks. It didn't count as flirting if the man concerned was the best part of seventy, surely?

"I trust you. Thousands wouldn't." David marched round the hedge and up the path, then worked the key in a hefty-looking Chubb lock before gingerly turning the handle and pushing open the front door. "Sian? It's David. Anyone home?"

When no answer came, Robin slipped on a pair of protective gloves, then cautiously stepped inside. There was always a fine line to be trod between what was legal—an Englishwoman's home was her castle, so no entering without proper process and all that—and what was expedient. He consoled himself with the reminder that if there was a chance Sian really had been attacked in her own home, then the police couldn't morally walk away and not double-check. Although Grace might have their guts for garters, in that case, for messing up her nice crime scene.

By the time he'd got all those thoughts clear, he'd convinced himself that the house was empty, although they'd still need to look in each room; there might be signs of a struggle, or of Sian preparing a hasty getaway. If the kitchen—unwashed dishes in the sink even though generally the place was spotless—spoke of hurried departure, the parqueted floor of the lounge was of more interest.

"Rugs!" Robin pointed like an idiot at what was obvious. "Posh Chinese rugs."

"We need to make this visit official, sir." Pru beat a careful retreat towards the front door.

"I'll do that as soon as I've checked upstairs. We said we'd come here to establish whether Sian was here," he added loudly, in part for David's benefit, "and that's what we'll do."

The brief search of the upstairs rooms produced signs of somebody having packed, but Robin refrained from delving too deeply. They needed a warrant to conduct a proper search, although would that yield anything? While he didn't hold out too much hope that the garage might still show signs of a body being stored there, Grace could sometimes work little short of a miracle.

A small black address book, on an old-fashioned telephone table in the hall, caught Robin's eye; he picked it up gingerly between two carefully gloved fingers. There could be more people listed there to contact regarding Sian's whereabouts, although they'd need one of those miracles he'd just assigned to Grace to be able to locate her so easily.

Robin thanked the next-door neighbour for his help, asked him to lock up, and enquired if he'd be around to let the forensic people gain access once all the paperwork was in place. David, clearly both intrigued and delighted, agreed at once, offering to provide Robin and Pru with coffee and biscuits while they waited.

"You're a life saver." And they wouldn't simply be taking advantage of the refreshments; David might be able to provide them with a gem of information.

They followed him into his well-appointed house, where he settled them into a well-appointed conservatory, then went to fetch the coffee.

"I can imagine you and Adam living like this in twenty years' time," Pru said approvingly.

"More like thirty if not forty, madam." Robin wagged his finger. "I wonder where George is?"

"Off volunteering for the CAB or something equally public spirited, I'd have said. Or maybe stocking up on the latest cruising information."

"No mention of cruising. Be serious."

By the time David had returned with a laden tray, Pru was wearing her most professional face and Robin was avoiding looking at the stack of P&O brochures he'd spotted on the coffee table shelf.

Over the refreshments—as tasty as Robin expected them to be—they discussed the local area. Sometime the previous year, Robin remembered, there'd been a hoo-hah going on in Merritt's End. He asked David to jog his memory.

"Oh, yes. They were going to put in a waste-recycling plant on the ground the other side of Sian's. Got planning permission for it despite huge uproar from all and sundry. Palms must have been greased to allow such a monstrosity in this area."

"Sounds likely." Recollections of the case came flooding back. "Wasn't there a councillor who had to stand down in mysterious circumstances?"

"Yes. Knuckles rapped all round. Anyway, people started selling up, particularly at this end of the road."

"But they've not built it yet?"

"Unlikely ever to. Not given that their pal's off the council. Nobody would pass it now." David winked. "And then there was rumour that the company concerned were going out of business, as

George discovered when he spoke to some of his pals who's in the know. I wish he was here to tell you, but he's had to go off and help his mother move into care."

"I'm sorry we missed him." Robin wasn't just being sociable. "You'll have to fill in the pieces."

"I'll do my best. Well, we got in and bought this house cheap as chips before the word spread too far. Some people still went ahead and moved, though—must have found better places or didn't fancy the area being invaded by hordes on granny scooters, because the current plan for that site is upmarket sheltered accommodation for pensioners."

"Did Sian snap up a bargain too?"

"So we understand. She'd not lived here long when we pitched up in July."

When they turned to picking David's brains about what Sian was like as a neighbour, he had little to offer apart from the fact that she seemed an athletic sort of girl, often out on runs, and that they'd never had any problems with her. She *had* got tipsy over drinks last Christmas and turned maudlin. There'd been a few tears on David's shoulder, but she'd soon bucked her ideas up.

"She even initiated a spirited version of the conga," David averred. "I'd never have believed George would high kick all around the garden—not with his hip—but she got us all going."

The conga. Was that what murderers got up to off duty?

"She sounds like the life and soul of the party. We imagined she led quite a quiet life," Pru remarked before sipping her coffee.

"She generally does. Rarely see many people coming and going. There's a chap sometimes."

"A chap?" Robin glanced up from where he'd been concentrating on not dropping biscuit crumbs on the carpet. "Old? Young?"

"Everyone looks young to me. Especially policemen." David's tone came so perilously close to flirting Robin knew his sergeant was striving to hide a smirk. "This lad must be in his twenties."

Not Howarth, then. "A boyfriend? Can you give us a description?"

"Couldn't say on the first. Yes to the second. Blond hair, looks as though it's been bleached. Skinny, I think, although one can't be certain with the baggy sweatshirts he wears." David stuck out his lip in thought. "Not what I'd call handsome. George says he's got a scar under his right eye, but how he's been close enough to be sure about that . . ."

Scar under the right eye. Jamie Warnock?

Robin put on a saccharine smile. "That's very helpful. You don't have a name for this man by any chance?"

"Alas, no. Sian never mentioned him, and we didn't like to ask." David stirred his drink distractedly. "Like I said, I don't even know if he *is* her boyfriend. Wouldn't she have mentioned it to us?"

"Possibly." And this opened up a whole new scenario. What if Warnock had been visiting Sian to put pressure on her, pressure that would have been ramped up since the discovery of the body? *I know what you did to Pippa. And when I've got proof* . . . Then what would he do? Kidnap her with a view to taking his revenge? But Robin was getting ahead of himself, ideas running in advance of the evidence.

"Has this bloke with the blond hair been here in the last few days?" Pru asked.

"He may have been, but we wouldn't know. We've been off gallivanting. George will be so upset he missed you. He always jokes that Sian has some deep, dark secret."

Perhaps George was right. "Really? Based on what?"

"Oh, I doubt it's based on anything. He's just very naughty. He has a theory that her opposite runs a brothel, when she's the least likely madam in the world. Mind you, she's the woman to ask if you want concrete information. She misses nothing." David's waspish expression said it all.

"We will," Robin promised.

And they did, once the refreshments were finished and they'd made their goodbyes. Pru took Sian's side of the street, Robin the other, neither confident that they'd find many people in at this time on a Monday. He was in luck, though, the woman in the house directly across the road answering his knock at such a lick she must have been watching and waiting for him.

"Good morning." Robin produced his warrant card, which was duly scrutinised. "We're making some enquiries concerning the whereabouts of Sian Wheatstone. She lives in the house opposite."

"She went off late last night." The woman rolled her eyes. "I'm Fiona Charles, by the way."

"Pleased to meet you."

"We don't get the police around here a lot. Although I've only lived here a few months."

But doubtless she already knew the intimate particulars of everyone living on the road. Robin forced a smile. "What time did she go?"

"Around half eleven. I couldn't sleep, so I was prowling around the house. I noticed lights on in Miss Wheatstone's house, which is unusual because she's not a late bird, so I thought I'd have a peep. In case there was a problem."

"Of course." Robin didn't doubt she'd have a list of excuses ready to hand for the reasons she'd been "having a peep" at her neighbours. "Was there a problem?"

"I'm not sure." Mrs. Charles's brows knit in thought, maybe a touch theatrically. Clearly, she was milking every moment of this, although that didn't mean she wasn't telling the truth. "That lad was here. He calls round a lot, and she usually gives him short shrift."

"Which lad?"

"I don't know his name. He has a scar here." She indicated her right cheek. "He's a nasty-looking piece of work if you ask me. Anyway, he entered the house, and a few minutes later they both exited. I had stayed to observe just in case I needed to call for help."

"Go on. I'm making a note." Robin continued to jot down the salient parts of the testimony.

"Well, a few minutes later they emerged. She had one of those little roll-along suitcases, and he slung it into the boot of her car."

"Thanks. Now, I need to be clear on this. Did she go willingly?"

"I don't know. He certainly seemed to be remonstrating with her before they went inside, and he was almost dragging her by the arm when they came back out." She stopped, perhaps replaying the events in her mind. "And *he* drove, even though it was her car."

"Was there any sign that this man carried a weapon?"

"No, although if he'd had it concealed in his jacket, I wouldn't have seen it. I only knew it was him because the light from the door showed his scar." She suddenly flinched, although Robin could have sworn the gesture was put on. "Is that how he got her to go with him? Waving a gun around? What if he'd noticed me? Am I in danger?" The idea didn't appear to be entirely unwelcome to her.

Two pangs of doubt nudged Robin. There was a chance Mrs. Charles was lonely—maybe widowed, or perhaps she'd poured her life into her family and had been left feeling useless now that the children had left the nest. He'd met the type before. Was this opportunity to be the centre of attention too good to resist, so the pudding was being over-egged? On the other hand, she could be genuinely scared, and with good reason. They were clearly dealing with a clever, manipulative murderer.

"The chances are you won't be in danger," he reassured her. "I'm sure you're a sensible woman, so just take the usual care in terms of opening the door to strangers. Don't even let Sian or her friend in if they come knocking. You can ring Abbotston station if you're worried, and please let us know as a matter of urgency if either of them return."

"I will do. I'll watch that house like a hawk."

Robin didn't doubt it.

He couldn't get a lot more of interest out of Mrs. Charles, although—after he compared notes with Pru—he discovered that the sergeant's pickings had been even slimmer. She'd only found two people at home, and neither had seen or heard anything suspicious over the last few days.

"Do you think things happened as your witness said, sir?"

"I think we have to assume that, for the moment. I didn't get the impression she'd make the story up. Improve on the truth, maybe, but not tell a lie."

Pru nodded. "And do we also assume that Warnock might have abducted Sian?"

"It's possible. Although if she was being coerced into leaving, why didn't she scream blue murder? Chances are somebody round here would have heard." Something didn't add up, but that had been the situation right the way through this case. "Can you contact Cowdrey and ask him to put all the wheels in motion? We've already issued the alert, but that'll need updating to include Warnock, or a man matching his description. I also think— Sorry. Cowdrey will know what to do."

"No doubt he will. We'll be staying here till we get the search warrant?"

"Yes. I'll check on the houses either side of Mrs. Charles, and then I'm going to sit in the car and have a ponder."

"About what?"

"About whether we've been looking at this upside down."

By the time Robin settled himself in the car, Pru had managed to inveigle herself back into David's house, ostensibly to update him on the developments and get the loan of his key, but no doubt to get her chops around some more coffee and biscuits. Robin, despite the pang of hunger, didn't mind; being alone was welcome.

Had they made yet another mistake, not considering that Sian could herself be a potential victim? Had Warnock worked out that she'd killed Pippa—if it *was* Pippa in the grave—and taken his opportunity to get his own back? Or had this been simply a domestic case, all along, Warnock having murdered his ex-girlfriend, and his Community Payback experience having given him the means to get rid of the body? In which case, had Sian somehow discovered the truth and Warnock been forced to keep her quiet?

Robin remembered a piece of information from the start of the investigation, when Sian had described the Community Payback men as "sweethearts" or "sweeties" or something equally twee. That must have included Warnock. And why had David called him her boyfriend while Mrs. Charles had said he'd got short shrift when he'd come calling? Was that simply because David was the welcoming sort who saw the best in everyone, while the woman across the road interpreted things more negatively?

The "sweeties" remark kept buzzing around Robin's head. He tried ringing Ben, to ask the constable to email him a timeline to show when the Community Payback people had been on-site and when Sian said she'd started working at Culford. Robin could have sworn she'd started much later, so the times couldn't have overlapped, or had they got that wrong too? But Ben couldn't oblige, being himself en route to Merritt's End, warrant in hand. Robin got Sarah on the case, instead.

When Ben arrived ten minutes later, Robin greeted him with, "Any news?" pretty certain there wouldn't be. He was right.

"We've been in contact with everyone we could think of who knew Sian, but nothing's turned up," Ben assured him. "Not a bloody sausage."

Sian had mentioned an uncle—the one who'd wanted to get his paws on the Roman coins—and Ben had managed to track the bloke down, although to little avail. The uncle hadn't heard from his niece in over a year and frankly had no interest in hearing from her again. She'd made trouble for the family, and as far as he was concerned that made her persona non grata.

"Oh." Robin drummed his fingers on the steering wheel. "The joys of family harmony."

"If those are family values, you can stuff them, sir." Ben pulled out a tube of fruit pastilles and offered Robin one. "He gave me a right earful about her. Said that for a small thing, she carried plenty of venom. Like a wasp."

"He can't have seen her in a while if he describes her as a small thing." Robin looked at the sweet in his hand. A black pastille, his favourite colour—surely that had to be a good omen?

"I had a pal who dealt with life's problems by going down to the gym. He put on pounds of muscle, so maybe Sian did the same. He said the exercise was addictive—you did one workout and you immediately craved the next."

"I wouldn't know. Gyms have never been my scene." Even though the pastille had lodged in a back tooth, its sugary, comforting taste was working its soothing magic. Somewhere very close, the clue to this whole mess was lurking, if Robin could only clear his mind's lumber room of the extraneous and irrelevant. "I've got an address book from the house. Can you work through it for anybody you've not already contacted, while Pru and I let the forensic mob in?"

As if on cue, Grace's car appeared at the end of the road, signalling the start of a period of intense activity in and around Sian Wheatstone's house. By the end of it they had evidence that Sian had packed a bag and left, taking—apparently—everything of importance, such as a passport, with her. Whether this had been under duress, they couldn't tell. But Grace had scoured the garage, taken a mass of dust samples, and pointed out some interesting features.

"There's animal poo in there. Might be rat. They're pretty common in Culdover, even in Merritt's End. Common everywhere, come to think of it. They say you're never more than a few—"

"Thanks, Grace. We get the picture." Robin shivered. He hated the things. "So our dead woman might have been placed in there?"

"Nothing so far to say that she wasn't, but we'll have a better idea when we get the samples analysed. There's a small Chinese rug in the dining room that might be made from a similar material to the one our victim had fibres from on her clothes." Grace tipped her head to one side. "Did you notice the hall carpet?"

"Not particularly. Apart from it being hideous."

"True, but that's not the point. If you lift the rug on top of it, it looks like somebody's given an area a pretty vigorous clean using something that's made the carpet pattern fade. I've taken samples, but I'm not hopeful anything survived. And it may just have been a bottle of red wine smashed."

"While they were doing the conga?" Pru asked before putting her serious face back on. "Sorry. Too flippant. Do you think we'll be able to get a link between the dead woman and this house?"

Grace shrugged. "I don't know. If it's there to be found, I'll move heaven and earth to get it, but I can't work miracles."

"That's not what Inspector Bright says." Ben flushed under the CSI's glare, but his I-wish-the-ground-would-swallow-me expression eased as Grace's frown turned to a grin.

"Really? I'll have to see what I can do."

Robin forced himself to give her a smile. Divine intervention was just what this bloody case needed.

Chapter Seventeen

Monday evening, spot on the agreed time, Anderson appeared at Adam and Robin's front door wearing something halfway between a smug grin and a sheepish one. Adam, with a wave of hospitality far in excess of anything he'd felt this last week, offered to put the kettle on for a cuppa while the sergeant fetched his stuff.

"That would be good." Anderson appeared reassured at the offer of hospitality. "Can't stay long, though. I'll just go and pack."

"That's cool. Don't worry about stripping the bed or tidying up. I'll get our cleaning lady to do it."

"If you're sure?" The added relief on Anderson's face at a job avoided almost changed Adam's mind—the bloke needed to learn to do more around the house, especially with the baby due—but he waved the offer away. Best to get the bloke packed, make sure he had a cup of tea inside him, and send him off on his merry way.

They took their tea into the lounge, with Campbell confined to the kitchen; one dose of heroics from that dog was enough for the moment. Anderson was full of the news about the baby, reiterating his invitation for Robin to be godparent and dropping unsubtle hints about a wedding at some point in the future, when said baby was old enough to enjoy it. Either the leopard had changed his spots or they'd never been quite the spots they'd been depicted as.

"We'll keep it small scale. The wedding." Once Anderson had started smiling, he couldn't seem to stop. "Helen's dad will need managing about the whole business, but doesn't he always? You guys are lucky not to have all the stress with in-laws." The smile turned sheepish once more. "Sorry. I guess now the law has changed, you've potentially got the same problems."

"Robin and I get married? I doubt the local PCC would let us. Although Neil always seems sympathetic to our relationship." What was he saying, letting his mind run on about whether his vicar—who admittedly focussed less on telling people what they shouldn't do than on reminding them of Christian service—would look kindly on any union of man with man?

"Maybe it'll happen, then. You'd love it." The zeal of the recently converted rang out.

"My mother might love it—marriage or civil partnership or whatever. She'd wear a hat the size of Belgium." He was doing it again, discussing with their erstwhile guest matters he'd not even discussed with his partner. "Anyway, I hope it all works out for you and Helen. Everybody loves a new baby in the family. Hopefully it'll be a unifying force for her dad and all the rest of them."

Better leave it there before risking letting something slip and having Anderson wonder how Adam had come to know so much about their circumstances.

Later, as the sergeant drove off, Adam watched from the window, thoughts caught up in further daydreams about his mother and Robin's having a hat off, unable to walk side by side without risking taking out anybody within five metres' range. Maybe Robin and he *would* make their union legal one day; the significance of standing up in front of friends and family, saying that they wanted to spend the rest of their lives together, couldn't be underestimated. But they'd tackle that step if and when the time became right, and that conversation would have to include a bit about children. While Adam had quite enough of the creatures during his working day, it was possible Robin harboured a hankering to hear the patter of tiny feet, despite not having mentioned it up to this point.

They mustn't let themselves end up like Helen and Stuart, making assumptions about what the other wanted. *Never assume something based on no facts or only half the story.* That's what he always told his pupils—along with "never get in a car with a stranger, even if they say your mum sent them to get you." He shuddered in remembrance of when *he'd* failed to take that vital piece of his own advice.

Don't get into a car with a stranger. Always check that people are who they say they are. People pretend to be someone else online. Adam mentally scrolled through all the advice he gave his pupils. Nonetheless, plenty of adults failed to heed that advice, with disastrous consequences, as Robin's present case showed. What a mess that had turned out to be; who knew what time he'd be returning this evening? The fretful text Robin had sent at lunchtime about his chief suspect disappearing didn't bode well for any normality of life in the foreseeable future.

Adam was back in the kitchen, halfway through the washing-up, when a plaintive whimper from Campbell, who was looking down into his empty bowl, interrupted him.

"It's no use you pretending that you didn't get any dinner, because I filled that bowl up before Stuart arrived. You might have been able to fool him, but you can't fool family."

Or could you? Could the young woman Robin believed dead— what was her name? Penny? Pippa?—really have been impersonated by somebody else so convincingly that her family never twigged? Catphishing was a heartless business at the best of times, but that was perpetrated on strangers. He'd have to air his concerns to Robin, assuming the bloke got home early enough. Not that Adam wanted to sneer at the latest line of enquiry, but he couldn't *not* make a suggestion that it wasn't the family that were being duped, but other people. The independent observer had a habit of seeing what had become wallpaper to everyone else.

In the meantime, no amount of thinking was getting the washing-up done or completing the planning for the assembly he was taking the next morning.

Adam was just letting Campbell back in from his final garden visit of the evening when they heard Robin's key in the lock. Time to dispense some TLC.

"Hard day?" Adam asked, helping his partner out of his jacket a minute later, a process inhibited by an affectionate Newfoundland attempting to lick his other master.

"You could say that." Robin pecked Adam's cheek, then scratched Campbell's ear. "Spent it locking the stable door after the horse had bolted."

"Bugger. Has your suspect upped sticks?"

"Yes. Or been forced to up them."

"Want to talk about it, or would you rather not?"

"I wouldn't mind. Because if I don't, it'll be buzzing around my head all night." They headed for the lounge and flopped onto the sofa so that Robin could relax as he gave a résumé of his frustrating day. Adam needed to bring him up to speed about the conversation with Baxter too, although he couldn't avoid the feeling it wouldn't be welcomed.

"But you're further forwards, surely," Adam said, as the account came to an end with a stream of frustration that the police still had no inkling of where either Warnock or Sian were. "The fact she's done a moonlit flit points at either her or this Warnock bloke having something to hide, and you've got the promising forensics from the house. What about the identity of the dead girl?"

"Still waiting for the absolute proof, but we're working on it being Pippa. Why do you—" Robin, weary eyed and stifling a yawn, laid his hand on Adam's arm. "Okay. What's this about? You look like Campbell when he's desperate to play fetch."

"Earlier, while I was doing the washing-up, I was thinking about your case and this woman Sian. How clever do you think she is? How devious?"

"Very clever, I'd have said. I was going back through her witness statements, and it seems like she chooses her words with a lot of care. All that stuff around overhearing the conversation about 'we have to stop' and 'we're not hurting anyone' would be in accord with whichever story Howarth and Bairstow told us. Affair or fakes."

"I have literally no idea what you're talking about, but I'll take that as a yes on both counts."

"Sorry." Robin passed a tired hand over his brow. "I forget you're not at all the team briefings."

"I'll assume that's a compliment." Deep-breath time. Was this the point at which Robin would think he'd got himself hitched to an obsessive? Or would he tell Adam to stop poking his nose in where it wasn't wanted? "I know you're knackered, but there are a couple of things I'd like to discuss."

"That sounds ominous."

"It shouldn't be." Adam slipped off Robin's shoes so he could rub his lover's feet, then steeled himself. Time to mention the other business. "Baxter came to have a word when he arrived to collect Sophie. I warned him not to go on his own when he met the local radio reporter, so he had a witness to what he said. And to make sure he saw his contact's identification."

"That all seems very sensible. And that's really good." Robin shut his eyes as Adam caressed tense muscles.

"I still have the magic touch. I told Baxter not to mention the school too. Or me."

Robin opened one eye. "Back there again?"

"Yes, we are. Baxter's worried because the newspapers have been tapping up the detectorists, as well." That made Robin open the other eye too. "Tuckton was offered a backhander by the same rag that's running the 'corrupt police' campaign. Wanted inside info on the police who had interviewed him. He told them to piss off, so I guess they're going to start offering their filthy lucre elsewhere. Like at Abbotston station."

"You're getting paranoid about the media. Ever since you saw that Chasebury tabloid story."

"I'm not sodding paranoid." Adam flung Robin's foot from his lap. "I'm watching our backs. Somebody has to." He got up. "If you want to hear what else I was going to say, then you can damn well whistle for it."

Without waiting for a reply, Adam stormed out of the room, up the stairs, and into the bathroom, where he splashed some water on his face, then plonked himself onto the side of the bath. He'd hardly had the chance to think about his next move when a tentative knocking at the door and an, "Adam?" announced Robin's arrival.

"What?"

"I'm sorry. I shouldn't have called you paranoid. I'm an idiot. I am not worthy so much as to sharpen the pencils on your table. Anything else I need to say to get you to open this door?"

Adam, stifling a grin, unlocked the door and peered round it. "Pillock. You don't deserve me sharing my bright idea with you."

"I know I don't." Robin squeezed his hand. "But you'll tell me anyway."

"Double pillock." Adam returned the squeeze.

"Is it about Baxter?"

"No." Adam pursed his lips. "Before I slander your chief suspect— although I'm not sure if it does count as slander if the victim's a murderer—how cut and dried is your case? Got stuff that doesn't add up?"

"How long have you got?" The words may have been jaded, but Robin's body language was becoming less tired, despite his leaning against the doorjamb. "I had something crop up only today. A discrepancy on timings, which meant Sian either lied to us about when she started volunteering at Culdover, which was July, or about being there when the Community Payback people were tidying up the place, which was May. Is that gobbledygook like before?"

"Not quite as much." Adam ran his hand down Robin's shirt front. "Right, this may be a load of crap, but bear with me. Is it possible that Pippa's not Pippa?"

Robin's brows knit together. "Is this another bit of 'your daddy's not your daddy' kind of thing?"

"No. Let's start with Sian catphishing. Yes, she could maybe get away with keeping up Pippa's online identity with the woman's friends, especially if she gradually drifted apart from said friends. But the more I think about it, the more I can't swallow Pippa's family falling for it for that length of time, no matter how convincing the impersonator was. Didn't anybody fly out and visit her at some point? Didn't they talk on the phone?"

"Okay, okay." Robin ran his hand over his brow. "You think we're barking up the wrong tree thinking the dead woman is Pippa Palmer."

"I'm afraid so."

"Hold on. Let me work this through." Robin's brow crinkled in thought. "If you're right—*if*—that would mean the identification was a complete coincidence, that the victim had the same accident as Pippa did. And it would have to be another coincidence that the early indications are that the body was stored at Sian's house, even if we can't fix it as being the scene of death. Isn't that stretching what's believable?"

"Perhaps not. This is the bit where you might think I've lost my marbles. What if you've got the wrong impersonation?"

"The wrong impersonation? What are you talking ab— Bloody hell." Robin stopped just short of punching the wall. "I've been blind. We've been blind."

"Don't be so hard on yourself."

"I should be. Only a couple of days back I was going over something Ben had turned up. One of Sian's family was talking to the local newspaper, after the inquest, about how cut up she'd been at her father's death. How she was such a frail little thing, he wondered if she'd survive the shock." Robin headed for the stairs, still talking. "And her uncle said that for a small girl she packed a lot of venom. Small or frail isn't how I'd describe the Miss Wheatstone who volunteers at Culford."

Adam followed him downstairs. "No?"

"No. She's built like the girls who used to wallop me on the hockey pitch." Robin reached the bottom. "Sorry, got to make a phone call or three. You brought it on yourself being a genius." He gave Adam a kiss on the head, then went to the kitchen, phone already in hand.

"What?" Adam responded to the dirty look Campbell—who'd parked himself at the lounge door—was giving him. "I know he's ringing in again, but it's all to the good. I, your dutiful master, might just be a mastermind."

Although he might simply have generated another pointless chase, if it were possible to pursue red herrings down dead ends, and that wasn't going to help Robin's temper any.

Chapter Eighteen

E arly Tuesday morning, before the whole team were in, a coterie of officers assembled in Robin's office by special invitation. If Robin was going to make a dick of himself, he wanted to minimise the number of witnesses.

He and Cowdrey were already in conflab when Pru arrived, with a few well-rounded curses aimed at the local traffic. "Any more news?" she asked, flinging her bag onto the floor and herself into a chair.

"Only that we may have used up a whole year's worth of goodwill with Greg." Robin sniffed ruefully. "I may have to buy him a box of chocolates for arsing him around so much."

"I don't envy forensics their job." Cowdrey fiddled with a paper clip. "He'll get on the trail later this morning?"

"Yes. Once I'd turned his annoyance into curiosity, he was raring to get going this morning." Greg had still been at home when Robin rang, and had been frustrated that there wasn't much he could do then. Robin went through the events of the last twelve hours, ensuring everyone had all the facts, such as they were, to hand. They'd contacted Sian's uncle—the one she'd fallen out with before any of the impersonations had begun—to see if they could get the name of the dentist she'd used before she moved to Culdover. They'd not held much hope of success, but luck had been on their side. The dentist had not only looked after all the family, he'd been golf buddies with both Wheatstone and his brother. Once his practice was open for the day and Sian's records had been accessed, the forensic people would have something to work on, something which would be augmented when the local CSI had been to take a DNA sample from the uncle.

"This time we go direct to source." Robin drummed the desk. "I'm guessing that Pippa had got her hands on all Sian's health information, then provided it to her parents, who'd naturally be in on the scam, so they'd have everything ready and waiting for us to verify that the corpse was her."

"It's possible," Cowdrey conceded. "I have a cousin who's such a hypochondriac he has a file amongst his papers with all his health records on."

"You can access them online with some surgeries too." Pru nodded. "Maybe I'm being biased, sir, and you could say I'm tarring everyone with the same brush, but I can't help thinking we should have had alarm bells about the Palmers. What with the uncle having a criminal record."

Robin shrugged. "We'd probably have said that was being overly prejudicial and pandering to stereotypes."

"Sometimes an open mind doesn't help." Cowdrey flipped his pen between his fingers. "If it turns out that your hunch—"

"Adam's hunch."

"Adam's hunch," Cowdrey corrected himself. "If it turns out he's right, this story is going straight into my memoirs. I've never known a case quite so bizarre. Any news about where Sian is? Sorry, I think we know where Sian might be. Maybe I should have asked if there was news about where 'False Sian' is."

"*False Sian*. I like that, sir." Robin managed a grin. "And no, I've not heard anything more this morning. Thank God we had that picture of her from the library personnel records to circulate alongside Warnock's. The happy couple on the run."

"A woman killing another woman and then taking over her life. How far-fetched is that?" Pru was obviously wrestling with the implausibility of it all too.

"Not as far-fetched as some cases I've read about, if not been involved in," Robin pitched in. "It's a cliché that truth is stranger than fiction, but like a lot of these old sayings, there's a pinch of reality in it."

Cowdrey said, "What strikes me is that this impersonation has got elements we haven't really considered. Chase the money. Sian Wheatstone was a wealthy young woman with little in the way of family contacts. Take over her life and you take over her wealth."

Of course. Robin should have picked that up. "She's certainly better off than the Palmer family is. If Pippa Palmer's one for taking her chances, she'd seize the opportunities to access that prosperity."

"I'm going to have to be devil's advocate, sir," Pru said. "I can see the attraction of taking the money, but why not just strip the assets and leg it? Why hang around and risk being caught?"

Robin shrugged. "The thrill of the game? Walking down the street every day knowing you're getting away with a huge scam? She'd been doing similar already—pretending to be more qualified than she was, pretending that counterfeited objects are real."

"She's been making herself into one of her own artefacts, if you like?" Cowdrey raised his hand. "Yeah, that was a bit OTT."

"Sort of thing they'd say on Radio 2, sir. Part of one of those mawkish stories listeners send in." Pru shifted in her chair. "Talking of which, maybe our pair have headed up to Gretna en route to his parents' home?"

"Given the sheer brass neck of the woman, it wouldn't surprise me," Cowdrey agreed. "Although if she's got enough gall to have held her nerve so long, what's spooked her now?"

"Got to be that impending DNA test." Was Robin the only one who thought that was obvious? "The Palmers could give the police a picture of Sian, and her physical details, but they couldn't fudge the sample from Mrs. Palmer, and that was always going to show the discrepancy. We wouldn't believe another tale of adoption."

"We could get Bairstow and Howarth back in and grill them over Pippa's whereabouts. If you think the three of them are in this up to their oxters, they might know where she's got to." Cowdrey, looking up, pointed through the window to where some of the constables had begun arriving for the day. "Young Ben's keen."

"As mustard," Robin agreed. "Get him in, Pru. Let's see what he thinks of this."

The delighted grin on Ben's face showed how much he appreciated being updated in advance of the other constables. "So, let me get this straight. You reckon it's not Pippa in that grave, but Sian herself. Presumably killed with a method that mimicked Sian's threats?"

Robin nodded. "That's how we see it. I'd still keep an open mind about whether the death was an accident that was covered up, but all the subsequent events can't be accidental."

"Absolutely, sir. She's been bloody clever too." Ben snorted. "Pippa Palmer taking over Sian's life and keeping up her own online persona. Two people at the same time."

"And in such a way that it could be interpreted as being an impersonation, if need be." Fiendishly clever, but that's how she'd been all through. "It eliminates the complication about whether Pippa's family could have the wool pulled over their eyes. They have to be in it up to their armpits, as well." Robin swung round to face his boss. "Are the Bedford police getting the Palmers in?"

"Yes. Should be around now. I've no great hope that Pippa will have gone there, as she's bound to have sussed out that's one of the first places we'd look for her. Unless she still believes she's duped us." Cowdrey shrugged. "If she's got away with things for so long, she might have become blasé, although I suspect she's too savvy for that. Mind you, I still don't get why she—or should we say 'they,' because every indication is that Warnock's in this too—moved Sian's body to Culford, knowing there was a chance she'd be found. If they'd disposed of her by weighing her down and throwing her in a lake, she could have gone undiscovered for years, leaving Pippa free to be Sian for as long as she could get away with it."

"They might have thought there was no risk of a dig. There wouldn't have been, not in the short term, if it wasn't for the sewage. And maybe she'd tried to put any diggers off." For Pru, the threads were clearly starting to weave together. "Remember those letters sent to the newspapers about Culford being a sacred site? What if Pippa sent them?"

"The first ones were sent two years ago. Unless she had this all planned in advance, that seems unlikely," Ben pointed out.

"I'm not suggesting that," Pru countered. "The first batch came from a legitimate address, right? A place that was no longer there by the time the second lot were sent. Pippa could have read the original ones and been inspired to reignite the controversy. Didn't somebody write to the university too?"

Ben nodded. "They did. It would be good if we could connect everything to her."

"Like Becky supposedly selling her story to the media?" Robin shrugged. "I know I like loose ends tied, but this girl has got them so slippery it's like tying an eel."

Cowdrey, eyes narrowed, consulted his notes. "Howarth tried to get the dig stopped, as well."

"Or get it relocated to his banjo enclosure or whatever it was. Yes," Robin agreed, "he could have been involved with trying to stop someone finding the body. I've never quite been persuaded by his explanation, although that's how I feel about a lot of what he's told us."

"I trust your judgement." Cowdrey gave Robin a tip of the head; nice to have the boss's approval. "But if he knew the body was there, he must have been shi—passing bricks for months, knowing she'd be turned up."

"Why didn't they move her before the dig started?" Trust Pru to ask the pertinent question. "I know it was short notice, but they didn't simply turn up from nowhere."

"Same applies to Pippa. If she—and whoever helped her—got the body in to the site, they'd have been able to get it out. Unless they felt too squeamish to dig up a part-rotted corpse." Ben snorted. The cool expression he wore would probably change the first time he saw a corpse "out in the field."

Robin tapped the pile of papers on his desk. "Howarth was livid because he hadn't been in the country at the time the dig got relocated, so he couldn't influence the decision. Pru, will you get him back in today so we can grill him?"

"Will do."

Robin shot Cowdrey a hopeful glance. "And perhaps, sir, you'd like to have a crack at Howarth? See if *you* can get to the truth about what he knows, because I've not managed to. Pru can sit in with you and look daggers at him."

"I'll give it a shot. I assume you'll be tackling Becky Bairstow?"

"You assume correctly." Robin drummed on the desk impatiently. "I can't get my head round that pair restarting their dodgy fakes business right under Sian Wheatstone's nose. They must have known Sian wasn't Sian."

"Do you think they were involved in the original killing?" Ben asked.

"It would certainly have benefitted all of them to have Sian dealt with," Pru agreed. "I had Warnock in the frame for the muscle man, especially as he'd been working at Culford and literally knew the lie of the land, but the same might apply to Howarth. And Becky's no small girl. If the three of them set their minds to it . . ."

"No!" Robin hadn't realised he'd spoken quite so sharply until he saw the startled reaction from his listeners. "We assumed Becky was running away from danger, but what if we misread the source of that risk? If Pippa had killed one person, would she stop there?"

"Chief Inspector Bright's making a good point. There isn't always honour among thieves. Or forgers." Cowdrey pushed back his chair. "Howarth. Let's—"

The loud ringtone of Robin's desk phone interrupted the conversation, but none of those present showed annoyance; this could be the breakthrough they so desperately needed.

"I guess that wasn't Greg?" Cowdrey asked when Robin at last put the phone down.

"No. Metropolitan police." Robin pursed his lips. "They've found Sian's car."

"Where?"

"Not at Gretna, clearly. Near Liverpool Street Station. Can people catch a train to Scotland from there?"

"No, but I bet you can get to Stansted." Cowdrey, who'd sat down once more, added, "and maybe from there to Edinburgh? You wouldn't need a passport for an internal flight."

"Ben, can you get the local force to send some officers back round to Warnock's parents' house? Pru, I hope you're doing something useful on that phone."

"Just checking where else you can get to from Liverpool Street." Pru displayed her mobile screen. "Perhaps they fancied a few days in Norwich."

"Gorleston."

A chorus of "what?" greeted Ben's unexpected outburst.

"Gorleston. It's on the coast next to Great Yarmouth," Ben explained. "If you can get to Norwich from Liverpool Street, then you can get to Great Yarmouth, I bet."

Cowdrey looked at the young constable as though he'd lost it entirely. "And the significance of Gorleston is . . .?"

Robin opened his mouth to answer before deciding he shouldn't take Ben's glory.

"Gorleston's near where Sian Wheatstone's dad either fell off or threw himself over a cliff."

"But Pippa's not Sian." Pru used a tone suitable for addressing a not-very-bright seven-year-old. "She'd have no emotional attachment to the place."

"Spot on, but Ben's got a point." Robin tapped the desk. "They also had a holiday flat there, and Pippa might have keys to it."

"That's what I thought." Ben smiled delightedly. "Shall I get the local force onto that, as well?"

"Yes. And as your first priority. The address might be in that book I picked up at Sian's house. If not, they might be able to find a note of it from when Mr. Wheatstone had his accident." This was looking promising. "If you're right, I owe you a pint."

"Bribing officers, Chief Inspector Bright?" Cowdrey, who'd risen again and was heading for the door, gave Robin a conspiratorial wink. "What sort of example is that to give?"

"I'll buy them a pint anytime, sir, if it gets us a result."

He'd willingly stand the whole station a drink if they got their hands on Pippa Palmer by the end of the day.

Later that morning, Cowdrey came out of his interview with Howarth with steam coming out of his ears. "I can see why he winds you up," he told Robin as the two of them, and Pru, grabbed an on-the-hoof lunch of sandwiches and packets of crisps. "Full of himself, isn't he?"

"Full of crap, as well." Robin attacked his packet of smoky bacon flavour. "Does he know where Sian—sorry, Pippa is?" Would Robin ever get those two women straight in his mind?

"Says he doesn't. Admitted that he'd begun to suspect she wasn't really Sian, although he's clinging to the story that he'd never met Pippa in person, so he couldn't know it was her. And he swears he didn't have anything to do with the murder." Cowdrey bit into his sandwich with gusto. "He says he tried to contact her yesterday, but he couldn't get hold of her. She's not answering her mobile."

"Trying to contact her to tell her to get the hell out of here?"

"If that's the explanation, he's not admitting it. He said he wanted to test his theory—his words, not mine—about her identity. Bloody maverick." Cowdrey took another vicious bite of his sandwich.

"You believe that?"

"Surprisingly enough, I do." Cowdrey finished his sandwich off. "And while he may have been acting full of himself, he's definitely running scared of something. Like he's suddenly realised the danger he's been under all this time. Sian making vague threats that didn't come to anything for two years, even when she appeared at Culford, is a different kettle of fish to a woman like Pippa, who's capable of committing murder and may not stop at just the one. Pru has a theory about Howarth."

Robin had plenty of theories about Howarth, but he kept them to himself while his sergeant—who up until then had been concentrating on her lunch—expounded.

"It's in character. He probably wants to show he's smarter than you in particular, Chief Inspector. You said you don't like him, and it's clear the feeling's mutual."

Robin snorted. "Go on. I can take it."

"Well, it's like he wants to be one of those amateur sleuths you get on the telly who solves the crime, then shows the dumb policemen where they went wrong. Think of how much he could boast about it down at the rugby club."

Robin could believe that. "Might explain why he's been less than helpful all this time. Doesn't explain why he tried to stop the dig, though."

"He says that was Sian's idea, sir. Or the girl he thought was Sian. He wanted to keep her sweet, so he said he'd see what he could do. He liked her idea about digging the banjo enclosures, anyway."

"So much so he claimed it as his?" Robin gave his boss a shrug; more muddying of the waters, more *He did it, she did it.* "You can't tell where the truth ends and the embroidery starts with him."

"Too right." Cowdrey shook his head. "Still, I think that if he knew where Pippa was, he'd tell us. He wants her safely locked up, where he can be sure she's not waiting for him in a dark alley."

"It certainly focusses your mind when your own neck's on the line." Or that of your loved ones. Robin learned that lesson with Adam and would never forget it. "Although if he had suspicions, chances are he guessed the truth before we did. Why not shop her to us yesterday, or whenever? If he had an inkling about what she'd done, why not get her into custody as soon as possible?"

"And when do either witnesses or suspects act in an entirely logical or sensible manner? It would make our lives a damn sight easier if they did." Cowdrey opened his crisps by bursting the packet, oblivious of making everyone jump at the noise. "What about Becky Bairstow?"

"No bloody joy," Robin confessed. "I couldn't get her on her mobile, so it was panic stations for a moment or two, but we managed to get hold of her mother. Becky and her father are out at the rifle range—he's a bigwig in local shooting circles, apparently—and she won't answer her phone when they're practicing. The mother's not daft; she said she'd get a message down there just in case there's any danger from our runaway pair, but to be frank she felt nobody was going to mess with a club full of retired men bearing firearms, albeit ones intended for sport."

"I don't think I wanted to hear that." Cowdrey laid down his crisps, only half eaten. "I want that pair banged up ready for interviewing, not splattered all over some rifle-club car park."

Chapter Nineteen

The call from Norfolk Constabulary came mid-afternoon. The retired couple who lived next door to the Wheatstones' holiday flat—and who'd been worried about such a desirable property being left empty for so long—had become suspicious when a young couple they didn't recognise arrived and made their way in. Even though the pair had keys, they'd struggled with the lock and showed other signs of unfamiliarity with the property; the neighbours were also sure that they'd not seen either of them visit when the flat had still been in regular use.

For what appeared to be the first time, somebody had instantly seen through Pippa's impersonation.

The local officers, who'd soon found the address and had been keeping a surreptitious eye on the area, didn't have the manpower to cover it at every moment so had missed the couple's arrival, but they'd moved in as swiftly as they could to make the arrests. They'd only succeeded with one, though, their arrival having been clocked. Warnock had exited at the back of the block and legged it up the road with a turn of pace the officers couldn't match. They'd got backup from another patrol car, but he'd managed to go to ground among the residential streets, probably reappearing at a walking pace half a mile away, en route for the train station and who knew where afterwards.

Pippa wasn't quite so quick off the mark, running down the stairs straight into the arms of one of the officers. She'd apparently appeared less bothered about being arrested than about her boyfriend not having given her sufficient warning when he'd realised what was going on. At first she'd not answered to her real name, but had pretty soon appreciated that the game was up. The arresting officers said she'd be on her way back to Abbotston as soon as they could arrange secure transport, but Robin forestalled them; he and Pru would make the journey to Norfolk—even if that meant contending with the bloody M25 and arriving late evening—right away. He asked them to arrange suitable accommodation in Norwich, where they'd conduct the interview. That would most likely be on Tuesday morning, unless the motorways were particularly quiet; they didn't want to risk an accusation of interrogating a witness who was too tired to give a sensible answer, let alone do the questioning when they were dog tired.

They had to get this right, the evidence being as yet so thin. By the time they commenced the interview bright and early on Tuesday, Greg should be able to say—from the dental records—whether the body discovered at the villa was that of Sian Wheatstone.

Robin informed the team of what was going on, sent Pru home to get an overnight bag, then got on the blower to Adam.

Adam, checking his phone for messages at the end of the school day, found one asking him to ring Robin when he got the chance. Either there had been developments in the case or Robin had heard about Adam's machinations behind the scenes. Please God it was the former. Robin's chipper tones on answering the returned call brought reassurance. "Hello, my favourite teacher. I just rang to say I'm nipping home."

That sounded odd. "I'm still at school. What does 'nipping' mean?"

"It means it's only a fleeting visit. Got to grab an overnight case." Robin gave a brief résumé of the day's events and explained why he and Pru would be making an unplanned overnight stay.

"Okay." Adam had to be pragmatic. "I'd offer to go home and get a case packed for you, but by the time I got back it would be pointless."

"Yeah, you're right. I appreciate the offer, though—thank you."

"Make sure you pack extra. Overnights can turn into days."

"Yes, mother." Robin sniggered. "And you brought all this disruption on yourself. Seems like your daft idea wasn't so daft."

"You'd have got there at some point." Adam, delighted, attempted not to sound too smug. "Just a matter of time."

"Maybe it would have been too late by then, though. Right, got to go. Don't forget the milk."

"Yeah, you too."

Adam ended the call, then eyed a note he'd found in his pigeon hole. Baxter was meeting the local radio researcher at the pub that evening; Adam resisted the temptation to go along and earwig. That would be courting trouble, and he'd have the answers he needed by the morning, anyway. Now his only concern was whether Sophie really believed the to and fro of letters was simply about metal-detecting business.

Tuesday morning, Robin contemplated his face in his hotel bedroom mirror, trying to focus on the day ahead. This wouldn't be the sort of interview that he relished.

He was still tired from the previous afternoon's journey, and unexpectedly aching for Adam in a way he hadn't ached for him since they'd first met and the policeman-witness protocol had made all interactions awkward. Especially when they'd been charged with sexual tension. They'd spoken on the phone that morning, and Adam had wished him luck, but it wasn't the same as being sent off to work with a kiss and a hug.

You're turning into an old married man.

The unsettling jolt his inner voice gave him with that notion would have to wait to be dealt with; he wasn't going to think the idea over until he'd completed what needed to be done here.

Pippa Palmer presented a real challenge. She was clearly an accomplished actress, and somebody for whom dissembling had become almost second nature. Clever, resourceful—a formidable opponent and one he'd soon be squaring up to. Surely between him and Pru they'd be able to spot where acting kicked in?

When they got to the police station and were led to the interview room, Pippa was already waiting, looking clean and neat as though the night in the cell had been no worse than one spent in a budget hotel.

Expression calm, she had a solicitor—the family's, not the duty one, according to the local coppers—at her side. Robin couldn't help but wonder if this was the same man who'd been involved with handling the uncle's assault case.

They began by clarifying, for the purpose of the record, that she was indeed Philippa Palmer, and once that was done, Robin could ask the key question.

"So why have you pretended to be Sian Wheatstone?"

"It's a long story, Chief Inspector, and one I'm not that proud of." Pippa gave her solicitor a rueful smile and a shrug. "I got tangled up in a chain of events that I should have broken free from but couldn't."

The same excuse the others had used. Had they planned it in advance?

"And you expect us to believe that?" Pru cut in. "After what you did to Sian herself."

"That was an accident. I swear." Pippa, face ashen, fiddled with the cuff of her blouse. "She'd asked me to her house, to talk about the fakes business, because she'd got it into her head that it was starting up again and she was livid about it. I took Jamie with me—Jamie Warnock—for backup, although he stayed out in the car. At first." A hint of a nervous glance came at the mention of the boyfriend.

"Why did you take the risk of going to her house if she'd made violent threats to you previously?"

"She'd offered to clear the air. She was as tired as me of all this stuff. At least that's what she told me beforehand. She said she wanted to talk matters through like adults and make an end of it."

"An end of it?" Pru queried.

"Yes. An end to the niggle from her side, so long as there was an end to our artefact selling."

Robin was trying to keep an open mind about what had happened in Sian's house; they'd made assumptions on this case before, and if they went down another blind alley, it could prove as disastrous as when *he'd* taken a wrong turn and ended up clobbered. Only this time it might be his career rather than his head that suffered. "So she asked you over, but things turned out different than expected when you got there?"

"Yes. She started off polite, made me a cup of tea and all that, although I only pretended to drink it." Pippa gave Pru a knowing *We're all girls together* glance. "You'll remember all that stuff at uni about watching out for spiked drinks."

"I do," Pru admitted. "I also remember being advised not to meet up with strangers in their houses. Don't you think you were being unwise?"

"I know that now, of course." Pippa, hackles clearly rising, paused to compose herself. "I realised as soon as she started ranting at me. About how we'd killed her father as surely as if we'd pushed him over the cliff ourselves. I tried to argue that we hadn't knowingly sold him anything fake—we always made certain we were covered on the *caveat emptor* bit—but Sian wouldn't have it."

And who could blame her? That would have added insult to the original injury.

"So, what happened?" Pru asked calmly enough, although Robin recognised the hard edge in her voice.

"I got up to go. Said I wouldn't stay to be insulted. That if she wanted to take her accusations to the police, she was free to do so." Pippa nodded earnestly at Robin. "You'd have known if there were charges to bring. You'd have dealt with it properly."

He ignored the attempt at flattery. "What did Sian think of that suggestion?"

"She just laughed. Like you see in a film, where there's a maniac on the loose." Pippa shuddered. "She started pushing and shoving me, trying to force me against the lounge wall. I shoved back, but I underestimated my strength and she hit her head on the end of the hearth. I didn't mean to hurt her; it was nothing more than a freak accident."

Robin recalled a vicious-looking iron trim round the old-fashioned fireplace in the lounge, although the area of carpet which had been cleaned was in the hallway. That didn't make sense. "So why not report it to us? If it was a genuine accident and you'd been acting in self-defence, we'd have been sympathetic."

Pippa's eyes flashed as a spark of anger flared, quickly suppressed. "Yes, I now realise you might have been, Chief Inspector, but I didn't know that at the time. Anyway, I panicked. We found we had a body to dispose of."

"We?"

"I texted Jamie to get him to come into the house. I didn't dare go out to the car in case I was seen. It was like living in a nightmare."

"These things do happen," Pru remarked in a deceptively calm voice. "You make one wrong decision and the longer you leave it before rectifying the situation, the worse it gets. What I can't understand is why you carried on living at Sian's house, pretending you were her."

"I didn't plan to. At first it seemed like a smart way to cover up what had happened."

"Smart? Why didn't you just wash up the cups, clean the fireplace, and then leg it?" Pru sounded as unimpressed with the story as Robin was.

Pippa sighed. "Because of Jamie, of course. He was worried that someone had spotted us. He was banned from driving, as you'll well know. He didn't want to get caught at the wheel." She sighed again, no more convincingly. "That made us panic like mad. I should have been the one to drive to Sian's, but I had a terrible headache and couldn't see straight."

The excuses were building to the point of stretching everyone's credulity. Robin, tapping the table, said, "You were either having the worst imaginable day or you're lying to us, time and again. Do you expect us to believe such an implausible catalogue of events?"

"It's not a lie." Pippa looked helplessly around the room. "Haven't you ever had a day where everything went wrong, where you wished you could rewind time because it's been a total disaster?"

"I have," Robin admitted, "but I've also learned to take some responsibility for events. If it was an accident, then you owed it to Sian Wheatstone to ensure she got a proper burial. Not steal her life in every way."

Pippa flinched. "You make me sound like a heartless cow. It wasn't like that. I swear."

Robin's patience was wearing thin. "How was it?" When no response came, Pippa simply sitting tight-lipped, he raised his voice. "How was it?"

He'd decided he had to shout it the third time when Pippa glanced at the door, then whispered, "Have you arrested Jamie yet? Is he here?"

"Answer my question, please. We can discuss Mr. Warnock in a minute."

"We should discuss him now. He's dangerous. Your officers should be told that."

"Are you saying Warnock's armed?"

"I don't think so, but I can't be sure. He might have picked something up after he ran off. He's unpredictable." Pippa's eyes flickered around nervously. "If I tell you the truth, will you help keep me safe?"

"Safe from what?" Pru asked.

"Safe from Jamie. He'd go ballistic if he knew I wasn't sticking to the agreed story."

"Agreed story?" Pru, leaning on the table, stared the witness out. "Let's get this straight. What you've told us happened isn't what actually happened?"

"No. I've been too scared to tell." Pippa compulsively rubbed her hands together. "You've seen what Jamie's like. I gave him the push ages ago, but he keeps coming back. I can't shake him off, unless it suits him—you saw how he ran away in Gorleston, leaving me to face the music. It was his idea to go there; I think I was actually relieved when you found us."

If somebody had put Robin's brain in a tumble dryer, this was how it would feel. The story had flipped once more, and in a way which accorded with what Fiona Charles over the road at Merritt's End had said, but was Pippa simply acting again, playing another role? He glanced at the solicitor, but he had his poker face firmly in place. Pru, however, wore a look of total disbelief.

"In your own words, then. What really happened to Sian?"

"It was like I said, honestly it was, up until the point where she started to get agitated. She was such a spiteful cow. And nasty with it. Do you know the detail she went into with those threats? It wasn't a case of 'I'm going to get you,' but details of exactly what she'd do to us." Pippa shuddered. "It was horrible. She started pacing up and down the room, ranting, so I had the chance to text Jamie without her noticing. Told him to come to the rescue. Now I wish I'd just got up and left."

"Go on," Robin encouraged her.

"He came to the front door and rang the bell. When Sian went to answer it, I thought I'd be able to simply slip out, but Jamie thrust her back into the hallway. She pushed at him, and then he had his hands at her throat and was shouting at her to leave off. I managed to pull him away, told him to calm down, but he'd gone mental." She looked at the solicitor. "The rest of this isn't going to look good. Should I carry on?"

As always with the breed, the solicitor urged caution. "I wouldn't advise it if you're at risk of incriminating yourself."

"But I don't think I'm incriminating myself about the murder."

"Murder?" Robin leaned forwards on the table. "You said Sian's death was an accident. When did it become a murder?"

"When Jamie killed her, of course." Pippa shut her eyes, shivering, before recommencing the account. "I pulled him off her, but he shoved me away. I fell on the floor, with a hell of a jolt, and he made for Sian again—grabbing her, shouting and swearing. There was a big iron thing in the hall. A hatstand or something."

Robin glanced quizzically at Pru—he couldn't recall seeing that in the house.

"It's not there anymore, Chief Inspector, if you're wondering. We got rid of it. Anyway, he smacked Sian's head against it, really hard. Said that was what *she'd* promised to do to us, so she was getting a taste of her own medicine."

"You didn't try to stop him?" Pru asked.

"I did, but it was too late. He'd given her such a wallop." Pippa passed her hand over her brow. "I've never seen anybody so determined."

"So you're saying that Warnock wanted her dead?"

"He said he'd only meant to frighten her, but he didn't know his own strength. He wanted her to back off and leave me alone. I'm not certain that's true. I think he intended to hurt her from the moment he came into the house. That's why I now wish I'd not texted him." Pippa produced a hankie, then took an age to blow and wipe her nose.

When she'd finished, Robin—forcing himself to sound gentle— prompted, "What happened then?"

"We checked her over, but it was clear she was dead. We got scared someone might come to the door, so we hauled the body into the garage."

"How did you know where the garage was?" Pru chipped in.

"We didn't then, obviously." Pippa bridled before visibly making herself calm down. "Sorry. Didn't mean to snap. This isn't easy. We'd spotted the garage as we parked, and we guessed there'd be an internal door. There was a bit of a mess in the hall, where she'd fallen. Blood and that. We rolled her up in a rug to make her easier to move—that was horrible—and then we had to try to clean the carpet. I don't think we were entirely successful."

Truth? Or Pippa's attempt to cover all the bases with what might show up on the forensics? "And then?"

"And then we found the kitchen and made a cup of tea. I know, it sounds ridiculous, but that's all I could think of. A nice cup of tea and trying to work out what the hell to do next."

Pru rolled her eyes. "Was this the point you decided to take Sian's place?"

"Not then, and not me. It was Jamie's idea. When he was out in the car, he'd noticed that both the house next door and the one opposite had been sold and were empty, so he wondered why. He did some Googling and discovered that they were about to build a waste-recycling facility next to Sian's house. We found a story about people selling up and leaving the area. He also found out from one of those house-selling websites that Sian couldn't have moved in that long ago." Pippa shrugged. "It meant there was less chance somebody would notice the switch of owner."

Was it far-fetched to wonder if Warnock had come into the house with that thought already in his mind?

Pru spread her hands in an eloquent gesture of disbelief. "It seems ridiculous. Simply taking over somebody else's life on the spur of the moment. The longest of all long shots."

"Actually it turned out to be pretty low risk, as you'll have to agree by the fact I was able to keep it up for so long. And we always had the option of just disappearing if it looked like we'd been rumbled." Pippa turned to her solicitor, who was shaking his grizzled head. "I know you don't want me to say all this, but I'm determined to get the truth out. I'm tired of living a lie, and I'd rather be thought of as a fraudster than as a murderess. I admit to being one, but not the other."

The solicitor glanced at Robin, shrugged in a way he'd never seen a solicitor shrug before, and let the witness continue.

"Looking back on it, things almost started as a game."

"A game?" Pru fumed. "When is murder a game?"

"Not the murder. Never the murder." Pippa furiously shook her head. "The impersonation. Jamie was pumped with adrenaline or something, and I guess I was running on fear. It all seemed so unreal, like I'd wake up in a moment and it would have been a nightmare."

Robin had experienced that feeling himself, but the explanation was coming a touch too pat. "What did you do after you'd had your cup of tea?"

"We rummaged through all her papers, and her diaries. She wrote everything down. Medical records, the lot. We discovered she was estranged from the rest of her family, and that she was pretty lax on security, leaving a list of passcodes and user IDs for all the sites she was on." Pippa rolled her eyes. "Everything seemed to be in our favour. Jamie was sure we could get away with it."

And they had, the bastards. "It couldn't have hurt that she was so well off."

"Of course it didn't!" Pippa composed herself before continuing. "Sorry. Look, I come from a family you'd describe as middle class but poor. Always been too keen to serve others and forget themselves. Very noble, but you have to look after your own. I hardly had two pennies to run together after uni—and a pile of student debt. That's why I got involved with Howarth and his business: to earn some extra cash. And that's why I didn't dob him in when he wanted things to get dodgy. I couldn't afford to."

Yet another version of the fakes-business history, one Robin had little patience with. "Plenty of people without two pennies to rub together get through without turning to crime."

"I know. But I was weak and Jamie's very persuasive. And can you blame me for taking up the opportunity of having a house of my own and some money to spend?" As the tears started to well, the solicitor produced a handkerchief, but Pru just gave a snort.

"And whose idea was it to bury the body at Culford?"

"Jamie's. Do you remember the summer storms? They shut the place to visitors, and he thought it was an opportunity too good to miss."

"How did you transport her there?"

"In the boot of my car. It was a horrible experience. Her face. While she was in the garage, she'd been— I don't want to talk about it." The witness shuddered.

"I'm afraid you'll have to talk about it," Robin said with a sympathetic tone he didn't feel.

"We left her in that garage too long." Pippa held her fingers to her brow. "Something awful had happened to Sian's face. Like an animal had got at it. When I saw that, I forgot about how violent she'd been. I felt horribly sorry for her. And the smell . . ." She covered her nose, as though it filled her nostrils afresh.

"The scent of decay," Pru remarked bluntly.

Pippa flinched. "How can you be so callous? We couldn't let her stay there, in the garage, so we took the carpet off and wrapped her carefully in some black polythene sheets. That's when Jamie suggested the disturbed ground at the Roman site. He'd got a key for the gate. Said he'd found one lying about and got a copy made. Just in case it might be useful."

"What about the mosaic?"

"The mosaic? We found that in the garage. It was one of the artefacts I'd mistaken for a real one, so I wanted to get rid of it. Two birds with one stone."

Pru, silently fuming, stared at the witness as Robin continued the questioning. "And you volunteered to work at Culford so you could keep an eye on things?"

Pippa nodded. "Not just keep an eye on things—keep an eye on her. I owed it to Sian not to let anything else bad happen."

"That didn't work, though, did it?" Pru remarked through gritted teeth.

"No. I didn't hear about the university dig until it was about to start, and that threw us into a panic. We'd already tried writing to the local papers and trying to stir up controversy, like had happened before, but that hadn't done the trick." Pippa put her handkerchief to her eyes again. "I wanted to let her rest in peace."

"You should have thought about that when you denied her proper burial."

"I know. I've beaten myself up about it time and again. But Jamie said we had to stay and ride out the storm. That if we ran, then people would know it was us."

Robin opened his mouth, then shut it. There seemed no chance of breaking this story, not until they had Warnock's side of the tale. And maybe, just maybe, she was telling the truth and *he* was the danger man.

Robin was struggling to think of the most effective question to ask next when the arrival of a constable with a message gave him the opportunity to get some thinking time. To Pru's evident surprise, he terminated the interview, leaving Pippa to either wallow in genuine pity or stew in her own juice.

Chapter Twenty

"**W**hat's up, guv?" Pru's question was out the minute they were through the door.

Robin eyed the wall of the interview room as though it might suddenly turn into a lens through which Pippa's memories could be examined clearly, rather than the present glass in which the truth was reflected darkly, if at all. "They've got Warnock. He's on the way here. And I want to get his angle on things before we talk to *her* again."

"I don't blame you."

They grabbed something to eat while waiting, being updated by the constable who'd somehow got all the gen on the arrest. The story didn't suggest Warnock was the quick-thinking genius he'd been made out to be; he'd apparently gone to the Palmers' house in Bedford, where the police, calling in ostensibly to update the family, had found him tucking into a steak-and-kidney pie—and whisked him down to the station before he'd had a chance to mop up the gravy. Although, given the way people in this case had managed to create convincing personas to hide behind, the fecklessness could be a front.

Robin was grateful they'd not have to hare up to the midlands; he needed his brain clear, and English roads weren't always amenable to that, even when travelling as a passenger. They should be able to interview Warnock later that day, traffic willing, although the chances were they'd be spending more nights in Norwich than anticipated, but as Robin had plenty of clothes packed, he needn't panic just yet. At least not about clean underwear.

"Are we charging him, sir?"

"We'll be charging them both. For as much as I can make stick. In the short term we'll go with aiding and abetting, fraud, and illegal disposal of a body, and we can increase that once we have the bigger picture." Robin, swallowing too large a mouthful of too-hot tea and immediately regretting it, avoided the amused gaze of his sergeant.

"When you've finished choking, sir, would you mind telling me which of them you think did it?"

"Cheeky mare." Robin carefully wiped his mouth. "At this point, I have no bloody idea. Maybe I could do with Campbell here. Take the two scenarios we were told, write them on paper, stick them on two lamp posts, and see which one he cocks his leg against. At the moment, it's as likely to produce the right answer as logic."

Pru giggled. "I wouldn't put it past him."

Neither would Robin, but the dog had saved the day in his two previous murder enquiries, so asking for a third intercession would be stretching credulity. A nagging voice at the back of his mind asked what would happen if they couldn't pin the murder onto either of the pair. Was there a chance one or the other could wangle being released on bail, and how much of a danger—to Howarth or Becky Bairstow or anyone else who'd got in their way—would they be in that case?

When they eventually got to interview Warnock—in the interview room only recently vacated by Pippa—it seemed impossible to believe he was the hard-nosed murderer she'd depicted him as. Although looks, as Robin reminded himself, could be deceptive; Pippa certainly didn't look like a scheming cow. Another solicitor was present, from the same firm as the one who'd represented Pippa. Had she been paid for in advance by Sian Wheatstone's money while they could still access it, assuming the Palmer family was as poor as Pippa made out?

Ben's description of the witness as having a huge chip on his shoulder was borne out by the sulky expression plastered all over his face, and the general hunched-shoulders demeanour of a man out of sorts with the world. They got the formalities over and done with, and then Robin launched straight in.

"Did you murder Sian Wheatstone?"

"No." Warnock, arms crossed over his chest, faced Robin out defiantly.

"Did Pippa murder her?"

"No."

Robin snorted. "Are you really expecting us to believe that?"

"I don't care what you believe. It's the truth."

"Okay, let's go back to the start." Robin kept his voice calm. He'd have bet fifty quid that Warnock was going to accuse Pippa, but this response had wrong-footed them. What story was the witness going to produce? "You and Pippa went to see Sian Wheatstone on the day she died."

Warnock nodded grudgingly, and Pru reminded him to answer aloud for the recording. "Yes. We did. She'd been making threats, and we wanted to ask her to stop."

"What happened when you got there?"

"She—Pippa—asked me to stay in the car. Said it would be best if only one of us tried to handle things. I waited, fiddling about on my phone." Warnock shifted in his seat. "She was in there ages. Then suddenly she was at the front window, looking like she'd seen a ghost, face all scratched. I legged it from the car; luckily, the front door wasn't locked."

Robin clasped his hands in his lap, attempting—and suspecting he was failing—to present a cool exterior. "What had scared her?"

"Sian. She'd gone loopy and turned on Pippa. It must have been some catfight—Pippa's face was all bloody." Warnock shuddered. "I hadn't realised what had been going on."

"Didn't you hear them fighting?"

"No. I had the car radio on."

Pru shook her head, obviously incredulous. "Why didn't Pippa simply run out of the house when she was attacked?"

"I don't know. She was in a right state, didn't seem to know what to do. Shock, I guess." Warnock clamped his arms tighter. "She said Sian had run out into the back garden; I could hear her screaming and shouting. I grabbed Pippa, tried to get her to move, but by the time I'd dragged her into the hall, Sian was there. She went for Pippa again."

"And what did you do?" Robin waited as the witness appeared to gather his thoughts.

"Nothing. I was sprawled on the floor, where she'd pushed me over. I'd cracked my head on the skirting board. Next thing I know there's a bloke coming through the door, telling Sian to shut the fuck up."

"What?" Pru gave Robin a *What the hell's this about?* look.

"A bloke. Barged into the house and pushed Pippa out of harm's way. Sian leaped onto his back and pulled at his hair, so he shoved her off. She reeled back and he went for her, effing and blinding and saying she was a vindictive cow and how he'd give her a taste of her own medicine. He slammed her against this fucking great iron monstrosity in the hall. Hatstand or something." Warnock leaned forwards again, elbows on the table. "One minute she was fighting like a tiger —next minute she was dead. I've never seen anything like it."

Robin shared a glance with his sergeant. What the hell was going on? "Let me get this straight." He fixed the witness with a cold stare. "You're saying that this bloke simply ran in off the street and attacked Sian."

"Not just some random bloke. A colleague of Pippa's, who'd heard she was meeting Sian and thought she might be in danger, so he came along to play the 'white knight' bit." Warnock sneered. "Charlie Howarth."

"Howarth?" Robin and Pru chorused.

"But Pippa insists—" Pru was cut off by a warning wave of Robin's finger.

"What happened next?" he asked, keeping their powder dry for the moment.

"Howarth panicked. Forced us to cover everything up."

Robin snorted. "Pippa says that was your idea."

"She what?"

"Said you were behind the cover-up." Pru, hands folded demurely in her lap, but with a voice like cold steel, kept her eyes fixed on the witness. "And you suggested burying the body at Culford."

The weighty, increasingly uncomfortable silence following Pru's statement worked. "Yes. Okay, I admit that I had a part in it. But it wasn't just me."

Pru's voice flipped into soothing mode. "We'd better hear your version, then."

"Right." Warnock took a deep breath and slightly relaxed his arms. "We were there, with this dead body and blood everywhere. Like I said, Howarth went into panic mode, and we weren't far behind.

So first thing we had to lock the front door, move the body out of the hall, and then tidy up. Once that was done we made a cuppa."

So far that part of the story tallied with what Pippa had said, even if the key elements were in dispute.

"Made a cuppa?" Robin snorted. "Rather than call for an ambulance or ring for the police and report an accident? Isn't that cold blooded?"

"There was no point in ringing for an ambulance," Warnock countered. "I've done first aid and I knew she was dead. As for the police, Howarth said if we didn't keep quiet, he'd go to you lot and tell them he'd come to visit Sian but found us with her dead body. That people would believe him, given his position, rather than us, given that I've got a criminal record. Wouldn't you have thought that one of us had done it deliberately? I'd done nothing but try to protect Pippa, and I'd ended up in this mess."

There were glasses of water on the table, which Robin would sometimes use tactically to aid thinking or create a pause. He used one now, taking a long sip while keeping his eye on the witness. "So instead, you got yourself deeper embroiled in the cover-up?"

"I was scared. Scared of what had happened and scared of both Howarth and Pippa."

Robin noticed that Pippa was now coming in for some of the blame, but he didn't interrupt.

"I realised they might have planned all this, and I'd been set up. I didn't want to get smacked against the hatstand as well." Warnock shuddered. "While I was in the car, I'd been looking up the local area, wondering why so many of the local houses were for sale or recently sold. Turned up some dodgy stuff about a waste site that was going to be built. I also discovered there was a chance Sian couldn't have lived there that long, either, according to the date the house was last sold, which got confirmed when we found things still unpacked, in the kitchen. I said the fact the houses next door and opposite were both empty might work in our favour. Less chance we'd been spotted."

"So why build up this big pretence? Why didn't you clean up, shut the door, and run?"

"I wish we had, but both Howarth and Pippa were worried someone would connect them to Sian. Because of the public threats the woman made." Warnock grabbed a glass of water and swallowed half of it at a gulp. "You know when you're nervous, you just start gabbling? Well, I developed verbal diarrhoea. A load of crap about how we could cover our tracks, including the thought that the longer we could hide the fact of Sian's death, the better it would be. By then we'd moved from tea to a bottle of vodka we found in the cupboard."

"Go on."

Warnock knocked back the rest of the water, as though it might be as fortifying as the vodka had been. "On the wall there was a picture of Sian, with her family. I made the fatal error of saying that, apart from the build, she and Pippa could have passed for sisters, certainly from a distance. Same hair colour—at the time Pippa had hers dyed auburn—and stuff like that. Then Howarth made a daft joke about how Pippa could pretend to be Sian for the next few days while we worked out what to do. I had no idea it would go on so long."

"You didn't attempt to stop her?"

"Can you imagine what it's like trying to stop her doing anything? Anyway, she realised she could get her hands on Sian's money, and she really liked that. Sian had made it too easy for people to access it." Warnock stared into his empty glass, then set it down. "The most I could manage was splitting up with her, a couple of weeks after it happened. Pippa didn't mind that—she's never found it hard to get a bloke."

Like Jerry, who seemed to have a thing for forceful women.

"Was Howarth one of them?" Pru asked, voice barely hiding her disdain.

"He wanted to be, but she wasn't having it. Said the only favour she'd do for him was covering up."

"Why did you keep coming back, if you'd split?"

"I wanted to make sure I knew what they were up to. She blows hot and cold on me, though." Warnock sneered. "Sometimes when I get back she isn't that pleased to see me. Considering all I did for the pair of them . . ."

Robin noted that accorded with what the neighbours had said, and with the overall impression Warnock had created. The rest of Warnock's story largely matched what they knew, with the addition of Howarth's involvement. He admitted he'd "come across" a key at

Culford and kept it by accident, an explanation they didn't believe but let ride for the moment. If Howarth was involved, site access wouldn't have been a problem. Pippa had taken a job at the library because it seemed in keeping with what Sian would do, and had volunteered at Culford so she could keep an eye on things there.

"Howarth had kittens when he found out, but he wasn't going to make trouble. Not given what we knew." Warnock seemed increasingly proud of what they'd done. "We tried everything we could come up with, like writing to the papers to scare people off exploring the site, but then that bloody university dig came out of nowhere."

"And you panicked again?"

"Yeah." Warnock blanched. "None of us fancied dealing with a half-rotted corpse."

"Okay. So let me get this straight." Robin spoke slowly and calmly. "Howarth killed Sian by accident, while protecting Pippa, and he forced you to help cover up the death. You came up with the impersonation idea, and Pippa found she enjoyed it so carried the deception on."

Warnock grinned mockingly. "Yeah. Got it in one."

"So why," Pru cut in, "did Pippa insist that *you* were the one who killed her."

"What?" Warnock shot out of his chair and leaned over the table before the solicitor, taking his arm and muttering about not making matters worse for himself, guided him back into his seat. "No. I'm not a murderer."

"That's not what Pippa says."

"Pippa can go to hell. Lying cow." He slumped back in his chair, crossed his arms, and glared defiance at all present. The solicitor, laying his hand on Warnock's arm in a cautionary gesture, had it swiftly shaken off.

"She says you'd got a defence agreed between yourselves that it had been an accident involving just her and Sian. That's what she told us first off, but then she changed her tune and said that story had simply been covering for you. No mention of Howarth anywhere."

"Yeah, well, that's what she's like." Warnock pressed his crossed arms closer to his chest; maybe he was trying to look threatening. "You don't want to believe a word she says. She lives in a fantasy world most of the time. Always bigging herself up to be more than she is. No wonder she got involved in talking up fakes. Ideal job for her."

And with that, Warnock told his solicitor he wasn't prepared to answer further questions. They left him to be admitted to the cells, and headed off for another coffee in the canteen, Robin muttering that he wasn't prepared to discuss anything until he'd had a chance to think.

"Bloody hell, sir." Given the amount of sugar Pru was spooning into her drink, she must have been feeling the stress too. "That came out of left field. I assumed he was going to blame her."

"So did I." Robin stared bleakly into his mug. "Could what we've just heard be the truth? I know you don't see Howarth as a murderer, but I can imagine him causing an accident and then making sure it was covered up."

"Should we ask Cowdrey to get him back in?"

"Not yet. I'll appraise him and get tabs kept on our Risca Romeo, but I'm not jumping to conclusions." He sipped his drink but found little pleasure in it.

Pru took a swig, wincing at either the heat or the sweetness of the coffee. "What if Howarth has got to Pippa? Put the fear of God up her so she's desperate to turn attention elsewhere. I didn't believe the tears and the 'poor Sian' stuff for a moment."

"Yep. I assumed she was just deflecting attention from herself. Never thought there could be a third person involved. I'd give all the tea in China for some hard evidence. Shame that walls don't have ears—and a tongue—because that hallway at Merritt's End could tell us a tale."

"That's the rub, isn't it? Unless we can pin it down on one of them, we'll run the risk of convicting none of them."

There was the rub indeed. The Crown Prosecution bods would shake their heads and say that joint enterprise was a complex enough area, and when you added in a potential plea of self-defence, there might be no strong grounds for prosecution. Lesser charges could stick, but that would put one or all of the three back out onto the streets sooner than anyone would want and maybe with an axe to grind; the thought of a vengeful Pippa Palmer on the loose wasn't a pleasant one.

Robin pushed his coffee away. "No jury would believe any of them for a moment. I suspect Warnock would testify like a shot, but a decent brief would rip him to shreds in the witness box. Same goes for Becky Bairstow. Serial liars, the lot of them."

"It's a shame your mate David didn't see anything. He'd be impressive giving evidence."

"But they weren't living there at the time. And he's not 'my mate,' just because he's gay. We don't all hang out together in one big gang."

"Sorry, guv." Pru looked suitably abashed.

"Common misconception, but I don't expect you to peddle it." Robin rested his elbows on the table and then put his head in his hands. "There's got to be something."

"Mr. Bright?" A deep female voice sounded at his back.

"Yes?" He forced his head up.

"Telephone call for you at the front desk. Chap called David, says he's from Merritt's End. The Abbotston station gave him the num—" The message bearer almost got bowled over as Robin leaped up from his chair.

"Thanks, Constable. You might have brought me the best news of the day."

"Don't count your chickens, sir," Pru reminded him.

Robin gave her an old-fashioned look but didn't respond. He wouldn't tempt fate.

They had the call transferred to an empty office; Robin couldn't quite shake off the memories of the untrustworthy desk sergeant at Abbotston.

"David. Sorry to keep you waiting. They had to find me."

"I understand. And it's not me who wants to talk to you, it's George, but he felt it would be best if I introduced him. All rather Jane Austen." David chuckled. "Anyway, here he is."

"Chief Inspector." A deep Scottish burr came down the line. "Sorry I missed you when you called. Family business."

"Is everything well?"

"As well as it can be. But it's not my mother you'll be wanting to hear about."

No indeed. "I'm assuming this is about Pi—sorry, Sian?"

"It is. I believe David referred to my little joke about her having a dark secret? He didn't believe me, of course, because I'm one for making up ridiculous stories about people."

"Then one day you find out the ridiculous story is true?"

"Aye." George harrumphed. "When David said you'd been here, and that a forensic team had been all over the house, I remembered what had started this whole 'dark secret' nonsense off. It was at a party, last Christmas. She'd been really down in the dumps. I ended up taking her into the conservatory for a paternal heart to heart. She'd mentioned about how her father had died, so I expected she'd want to let her grief out, but she barely touched on it."

That was no surprise. "What did she want to talk about?"

"Men, mainly. How they were all swine, even the ones who seemed nice, and how lucky I was to have found Mr. Right." Robin could imagine George's eyes rolling. "I said that she must have found one good apple in the barrel, at which she nodded and got sniffly again. I'd brought a bottle, so I topped up her glass, and then she said that Jamie was the best of a bad bunch."

Robin nodded encouragingly.

"That glass must have sent her one over the eight. She confessed she'd done something bad, in the past, and that her bloke Jamie—he'll be the one with the scar who comes round—had helped her cover it up."

Robin forced himself not to get overexcited. This was what he'd expected to hear from Warnock, but if Pippa had made a confession of murder to George, surely he'd have been sensible enough to have flagged it up already? "Go on."

"I was trying to dig a little deeper when a horde of folk came in. Sian bucked herself up and started leading a conga, of all things."

Robin repressed a snigger. That bloody conga was going to have to get a mention, wasn't it?

"I didn't talk about it to David, not at the time, because I wanted to find out more."

"Very sensible."

"Two days later she asked me in for coffee. She said she'd been a bit drunk and a bit silly and that she didn't want me getting the wrong end of the stick. She'd only—only!—been involved in an incident when driving the boyfriend's car, and he pretended he'd been driving as she already had points on her licence for speeding. They hadn't realised he'd end up doing community service for it."

"Did you ask her to report it to the police?"

"I did." George harrumphed again. "But she said she'd already confessed it to her priest and he'd given her penance, so it was all dealt with. She asked me to respect that. I hadn't realised she was a Roman Catholic."

"No." And Robin would put money on that being another part of the story she was weaving.

"Anyway, I decided not to mention any of the details to David, just made the 'dark secret' joke, so he's hearing this for the first time too. I hope it'll be of help."

"It will." Robin promised to get one of the constables round to take a full statement, ended the call, then briefed Pru.

"Sounds like it could be a case of *in vino veritas*, sir."

"Yep. We know she wasn't behind the wheel for that dangerous-driving offence, because Warnock was captured on CCTV. She must have almost let the cat out of the bag about Sian, then had to backtrack furiously."

"I wonder if she'd have told George everything, if that conga hadn't happened."

"Maybe." Robin shivered. "And maybe George would have ended up as another victim before he could spill the beans. And we still don't know exactly what she nearly admitted."

His phone vibrated, indicating an incoming text. Adam, whom he'd messaged briefly earlier, probably replying with a bit of affectionate banter. He was about to leave it until later, when he decided he deserved a touch of light relief.

"I'm off to the loo." Robin headed for the relative peace of one of the cubicles and once inside read the text in full. Adam wanted him to ring if he got the chance, but he'd left a message on the answerphone if that wasn't an option. Nothing to worry about, just some useful information related to Abbotston nick. Robin, both intrigued and suddenly longing for the comfort of his partner's voice, went straight through to his message service. "Hi. Got a name, two actually, for you. The local radio people who've been trying to get all the inside info on your case. A woman called Pringle—I think she's the reporter—and a young guy called Lewington, who's in production and looking at moving into front of house. Mean anything to you? Speak soon. Love you."

A young guy called Lewington. How bleeding obvious. The desk sergeant with that name at Abbotston had a son who was something to do with the local media. And as the sergeant had been first point of call when Becky Bairstow rang, he'd have been the first to be able to pass the information on to his lad. Why would he take that risk of jeopardizing both career and pension, though? Sick and tired of getting nowhere, maybe, and that was in line with what Robin had heard about the bloke. He quickly messaged Cowdrey to say he'd report back on the Culford case later, but here was a hot potato for him to get his teeth into in the meantime.

He'd have to show proper thanks to Adam, especially as he'd been so ratty at him about his "obsession" with the media. That was one problem solved; if only Palmer and Warnock and Howarth could be sorted out so easily.

Chapter Twenty-one

Pippa Palmer, with the same solicitor—and his same poker face—seemed slightly less at ease during the second interview.

By some careful timing of movement of witnesses between rooms, Robin had managed to engineer her and Warnock being in the same corridor at the same time. Once she'd seen he was in custody, Robin left her to fester with her own thoughts before calling her in for further questioning. Hopefully she'd be worrying over what Warnock might have already told the police.

"Pippa, there are several things you didn't mention in the last interview," Robin said, watching her face but observing nothing more than a narrowing of the eyes. "Was Charlie Howarth present when Sian died?"

"Howarth?" Pippa's surprise smacked of ham acting. "No, of course he wasn't."

"We need the truth, Pippa." From the tightness around Pru's mouth, it was costing her to be so compassionate. "If he's put you under pressure to cover up for him, then we'd view that sympathetically."

"The truth?" Pippa's gaze moved from Pru to Robin and back as she apparently weighed up her options. "The truth is it was Jamie's idea to come up with a story fingering Howarth to cover up what *he* did. He's clearly sticking to it while I've decided not to."

Head throbbing like a drum, Robin wished he'd grabbed a side order of ibuprofen with his coffee. "But you said that the agreed story was that *you'd* killed Sian by accident."

"That was my suggestion, but Jamie wasn't impressed with that, probably because *he* hadn't come up with it. Jamie thinks Howarth is so up himself he's coming out the other end. You want to hear him ranting on about Howarth's flash car and how he acts like he's God's gift to women. Jamie knew you'd been on Howarth's case, so that seemed an obvious direction to send you in." The handkerchief which had featured in the last interview made an encore. "I didn't want to get him into trouble; that's why I decided I'd say it was me."

"So, what was the story you agreed between you?"

"That I panicked—as if I would—and then Sian started haring round the place. Jamie came in and tried to drag me to safety, because he always enjoys the idea of being the hero, even in a made-up story. Then Sian attacked us again, at which point Howarth came steaming in. Sian went for him, and he fought her off and then went apeshit. Killed Sian and made us cover up for him." She blew her nose. "Ridiculous, isn't it?"

Ridiculous was exactly the word for it. But the account matched precisely what Warnock had said. Before Robin could respond, Pru said, "You told your neighbour that Jamie Warnock took the blame for a driving offence you committed."

"Yes." Pippa's face, which had momentarily clouded, was soon back under control. "I know it was the wrong thing to do, but Jamie was so kind about it. He wanted to help. We thought he'd have his knuckles rapped, not end up doing community service. I was mortified. That's why I said I'd help him cover up the murder. I only wish I'd been as strong at keeping his secret as he was with mine."

That wasn't how her previous interview had come across, but Robin had become used to her changes of story. "Well, there's a problem with all that, isn't there? Jamie *was* driving the car at the time of his offence. The witness statements and CCTV are conclusive."

"No, that's not right!"

"I'm afraid it is." Robin produced an envelope from the file he'd brought in. "I'm showing the witness CCTV pictures taken of Jamie Warnock driving the car the night he was arrested. You're not with him, are you?"

"I was, earlier."

"But not at the time the offences were committed," Robin persisted, to no response from the witness.

Pru broke the silence. "What did you really get upset about that evening, when you were crying on George's shoulder?"

"What? What's George been saying?" Pippa's alarmed expression was unmistakable. From the recesses of his memory, Robin remembered what Adam had said about phones and dealing with unwanted callers. How you could send them into a panic by calling their bluff. It was worth a punt. "You know that as well as I do." Robin raised a hand. "We're going to go and check over some of the things you've alleged. Interview suspended."

Before Pippa or her solicitor could respond, Robin pushed back his chair and left the room, with Pru in tow, while the suspect went back to her cell.

"What was that for, sir? I thought we were going to use what George said?"

"I changed my mind." Robin glanced over his shoulder, in case Pippa was within earshot. "One of those three is dangerous. They've killed one person, whether it was murder or manslaughter, and gone to enormous lengths to cover the crime up. Now Pippa knows that George has said something that we've picked up as important, even if she doesn't know the details."

"Oh, hell." Pru blanched. "Are you thinking she'll manage to contact someone on the outside who'll put pressure on him to keep quiet?"

"That's certainly a possibility, and I wouldn't want anything happening to either of those blokes. Or to anyone," he added hastily. "I want her to stew in her own juice for a while, wondering exactly what George told us. In the meantime, let's have another word with Warnock."

Once they were all back in the interview room, and while Pru set things up, Warnock kept looking anxiously at his solicitor, obviously urging her to speak.

"My client wishes to change his previous statement," she said after the recording started. "He admits that he was using a pre-agreed story earlier, one that doesn't reflect the reality of what happened. He'd like to amend that."

Robin nodded. "To be absolutely clear, are you saying that Howarth didn't kill Sian?"

"I am." Warnock wasn't so defiant now. His arms were at his sides, fingers drumming nervously against his legs. "He wasn't even there.

Pippa suggested we point the finger at him because he had motive to kill Sian. That's what we agreed we'd say to you. I should have known she'd go her own way."

"What really happened?"

"I don't know. Not exactly. When I got in the house, Sian was already dead. I think she'd smacked her head against that thing in the hall. Or had it smacked." He glanced at his solicitor, got a tentative nod in response, then leaned on the table. "Pippa said it was an accident and asked me to help cover it up."

"I think there's a consistent story about what happened after Sian died." That part never seemed to vary, except in who'd been present. "What we need to know is what happened in the hallway. Was it deliberate or accidental?"

Warnock shrugged. "I think it was deliberate. If I'd known that was what she had in mind, I'd never have gone with her."

Robin sat, fingers pressed together; they were so close, but still miles away from having concrete evidence. "You've got to help us, Jamie. What you think happened isn't enough; give us something we can use to prove she did it."

Warnock glanced at his solicitor again, but her quizzical expression suggested she had no idea what was being asked of her. He turned back to Robin. "Where's my phone? They took it from me when I came in."

"Then it'll be with the rest of your stuff. Why?"

"Pippa texted me, from the house, telling me to come in."

Robin, remembering Adam's old phone, cut in, "You kept the text?"

Warnock nodded.

"For the tape, please," Pru reminded him.

"I kept the text. Just in case I needed it."

A text should have a date and time stamp. Maybe they were getting somewhere.

They were waiting in the interview room when Pippa and her solicitor arrived. The suspect looked less at ease than she'd done in either of the previous interviews. Pru reminded her that she was under caution, with a curt, "As we've already said, if you do not mention something when questioned which you later rely on in court, it may harm your defence. And we mean that—ask your solicitor if you don't believe me."

"When you had your heart to heart with George," Robin said, as though the break hadn't happened, "it wasn't about covering up a driving offence. We've proved that. The terrible thing you'd done was murdering Sian, wasn't it? Wasn't it?"

Pippa opened her mouth, shut it again—like a drowning woman gasping for air—then crossed her arms tightly. "No. And if that's what he said, he's lying."

"What if you had so much to drink you can't remember what you confessed to him?" Robin let the point hang, although Pippa's exterior remained defiant.

"I don't have to say anything more. You've no evidence."

"Don't we? Do you remember texting Jamie when you killed Sian?"

"I didn't kill Sian. Why are you hounding me?"

"We're not—"

"You are. You've done nothing but make my life hell. Where were you when Sian was threatening to strangle me, smash my head in, and bury me with a piece of old pot?"

Pru shook her head. "We'd have been there if you'd bothered to tell us about the threats."

"Would you?" Pippa swept her up and down with a withering look. "Like you were there to help my uncle when he was being picked on? He had to stand up for himself because nobody else would, and look what happened to him. Nobody cares about the victims."

"You were a victim. Is that what *you* did?" Robin asked. "Stand up for yourself?"

"It's what you have to do. Not take any nonsense." Pippa's voice had grown louder; the notion of protecting one's own seemed to rile her in a way nothing else had so far. "You know, when I went to see Sian, it was like one of those scenes in a James Bond film, where the criminal mastermind starts gloating and making ludicrous threats. It was laughable."

"I know what you mean," Pru agreed. Robin forced himself not to smile. He'd always found those scenes particularly dumb.

Pippa sneered. "What master criminal would act quite so much like an idiot? Why not kill Bond outright straight away?"

"If James Bond was shot on sight, there'd not be a story," Pru countered. Robin had been about to step in and move the discussion on from films, but he let it run. Pippa was losing her cool. "Real people aren't that thick."

"Oh, do me a favour." Pippa rolled her eyes. "Sian was thick as shit. So I—we—got our own back. Made it look like she'd done exactly what she'd threatened." She stopped, face suddenly ashen. "When we did the cover-up, I mean. After Jamie killed her."

"I or we?" Robin saw his opportunity to come in hard. "Leave all that crap about Warnock out of this. You murdered her, didn't you?"

Pippa flinched, but there was no spoken response.

"I'm showing the witness a copy of the content of a text message she sent to Jamie Warnock on July the twelfth of last year at eighteen twenty-five." Robin pushed a piece of paper across the table. "Would you read it out, please? For the recording."

The solicitor, nudging her arm, shook his head.

"No, I won't. You'll pretend it was a confession."

"It certainly reads like that, doesn't it? 'I've done it. Turned the tables on the bitch. Get in here quick and help.' What did you mean by that?"

Pippa, colouring up, slammed her hands on the desk. "I told that sod not to keep anything. If his stupidity has pinned this on me, I swear to God I'll kill the bastard."

"Like you killed Sian?"

"Yes. No. Whatever." Pippa leaped to her feet, shaking off the restraining hand of the solicitor. "I killed her. Satisfied now? I killed her and I took over her life and I got a lot more out of it than she ever did. If Jamie Warnock hadn't been such a bloody wimp about moving the body again, I'd have still been doing it."

All that remained after that was a fresh reading of the caution, a charge of murder, and making plans for going home.

As Robin and Pru drove back south, he was in contemplative mood. He'd met some hard-boiled villains in his time, but Pippa Palmer had leaped straight into gold-medal position. Pru kept ringing into Abbotston, given that they still had to clear up the not-inconsiderable matter of Howarth and Bairstow and how much they knew. A team was also going through all of Jamie's devices to see if he'd kept any other evidence of Pippa's guilt, although Robin asked Pru to keep any updates for when they took a break. He couldn't trust himself to drive and talk at the same time.

Over a coffee at a service station, Pru reported that, in light of developments, Cowdrey was pulling Howarth and Bairstow in, because he had a hunch they'd known a lot more than they were letting on, a hunch seemingly confirmed when Becky Bairstow's solicitor asked if she could make some sort of deal. While neither was going to make a convincing witness for the prosecution, they might provide something in the way of solid evidence.

"Howarth's a sly dog, sir," Pru averred. "I wouldn't be at all surprised if he's kept something to use against Pippa in case things got rough."

"I'd not be surprised, either. Maybe it was in that blue file, which is why he made such a fuss about it."

Pru giggled. "If it was, no wonder it made your thumbs prick. Do you think we'll be able to charge them with more than just being a pair of grade-one pains in the arse?"

"I sincerely hope so, but don't hold your breath. If I were a betting man, my money would be on it taking a long time to wheedle out all the truth." And while he couldn't see Howarth or Bairstow as a murderer, he'd put money on the pair being Pippa's pawns after the event. Howarth's reluctance to develop Culford—whether through the university dig or the student's business plan—couldn't just be driven by the fakes business. That could be relocated anywhere; you couldn't so easily relocate a body.

Before they set off again, Robin rang Adam to say when he'd be home, apologised for how hectic life had been, and promised they'd get some time together now. When he eventually started the last part of his journey, Abbotston to Lindenshaw, further inspiration struck;

all that was needed was for a certain shop's late-night opening to extend to the time Robin had found somewhere to park nearby.

He was in luck, the bakery still open for business and with a few cakes in stock, including some of Adam's—and Campbell's—favourite varieties displayed in the window. If Robin wasn't too late to get a special message piped onto a suitably plain one, then he was in business.

"Don't forget the milk?" The woman behind the counter rolled her eyes. "You really want that message on a *cake*?"

"Every word."

When Robin got home, Adam had a bottle of bubbly chilling and a spread of the best canapés and tapas that Waitrose could provide. The cake would make the perfect dessert.

"You daft bugger." Adam eyed the cake, then gave Robin a huge hug. "What did they say at the shop when you asked for that?"

"Let's not go there." Robin didn't think he dared face returning to the bakery. The woman who'd iced the message had evidently thought it meant something pornographic—he should have settled for a simple, unambiguous *I love you*. They shared a kiss. "Will those snacks wait?"

"If I put them back in the fridge, yes. I haven't even warmed the oven for the ones that need heating."

"Good." Robin drew Adam into another cuddle, then turned him round to propel him in the direction of the stairs. They indulged in a few more kisses en route—a messy job but someone had to take the plunge and do these things, even with a Newfoundland trying to make it a three-way hug.

"Okay, you." Adam broke the clinch, better to manoeuvre the dog back into the kitchen, and shut the door on him. "He can whimper all he likes. I don't know about you, but I need more than just a bit of hurried fumbling in the hallway."

"You've read my mind. Dinner can wait; this can't."

"Too right." Adam leaned in for another kiss, then pulled back. "What if the bloody phone goes?"

"Don't answer it. Cowdrey says that, short of world war three breaking out, the team won't be called in tonight."

"Cowdrey's a legend. I always—" The chat was cut off by Robin pinning his lover to the wall. Time for talk to give way to action.

Afterwards, they'd have lain in bed longer, but Robin's rumbling stomach and Adam's swearing that his own guts thought his throat had been cut spurred them into action. By the time Robin had got washed and changed into a T-shirt and jogging pants, the savoury aromas of cooking food were wafting up the stairs and—as he found on opening the kitchen door—the Prosecco had been poured.

"We'll take it through to the dining table." Adam encouraged Robin to pick up a glass. "Make a proper celebration."

"We'll have a toast here first." Robin raised his drink in the direction of the dog basket. "Campbell. That dog deserves a medal."

"Campbell." Adam solemnly completed the toast. "For saving our bacon yet again."

The dog, an unconvincing expression of innocence plastered on his face, gazed hopefully at the tin where his biscuits were stored.

"Oh, all right, just the one." Adam produced a charcoal-black biscuit—Campbell's favourite variety. "You've earned it."

"Everybody else's Newfoundland makes heroic water rescues," Robin observed. "How did we end up with one who does marriage guidance? Because he's the most intelligent dog in the world?"

"I should cover his ears. You'll inflate his ego." Adam returned his gaze to his bubbly.

"It deserves inflating. I wish he worked on my team at Abbotston instead of some of them—it would make the setup a damn sight more efficient."

"Maybe you should take him in. He could growl at any officers he didn't think were working hard enough."

Robin chuckled. "He'd certainly make a good wingman. Shame I can't teach him to speak or use the phone."

"What's going to happen at Abbotston? Did you plug the leak?"

"Yeah." Robin knocked back his glass, then gave them both a refill. "The desk sergeant—name of Lewington, so there's the connection you found—is going through disciplinary procedures. Thanks for sorting that. I'm sorry I didn't take you seriously enough."

"You've had a lot on your mind." Adam sipped his wine. "Glad to be of help."

"I think it'll work out well. It's given everyone a much-needed reminder that Cowdrey's not going to stop until he's excised all the rot."

"Another night of the long knives?"

Robin shrugged. "We might get away with simply having a swap round of personnel with Kinechester and some of the other big stations. Split them up and see if they sink or swim. I'll be keeping Ben, though. He's almost as useful as Campbell."

"You'll get a good team in the end. You did at Stanebridge. Just needs time and patience." Adam inspected the contents of the oven. "About five more minutes and we're there."

"I should put you on my team too. Efficiency, brains, and looks. Cracking combination."

"Flattery will get you nowhere. Anyway, familiarity breeds contempt and all that. You wouldn't like to have me hanging around all day long. Think what it was like with Stuart being here. That was nearly the end of a wonderful working relationship."

"True. I said you had brains." Robin set down his glass and pulled his partner closer. "Thing is, I'm not in love with Stuart. Only you."

"Silly bugger." Adam leaned into the embrace, head on Robin's shoulder. "We're all right, aren't we?"

"Yeah. I think so." He caressed Adam's back. "And I'll never have to worry about you being pregnant and not telling me."

"Or have your mother fretting about her hat for the christening."

"She does like her millinery. We could, by all means, give her another excuse for hat shopping." Robin pulled back so he could look into his lover's eyes. "Not sure I'd be comfy with the whole wedding thing—I'm too conservative by half—but if you ever thought a civil partnership could be a goer, I'd be your man."

Adam's brow wrinkled in contemplation. "If that's a proposal, it has to be the least romantic in the history of the universe."

"Is that a 'no' then?" Robin swallowed hard; had he misread this like he'd misread so much in the Sian Wheatstone case?

"Of course it isn't, you clown. It's a resounding 'yes.' I've got a mother who wants to wear a posh hat, as well."

A rumble of delight emanated from Campbell's basket, although whether at the news or the biscuit, Robin couldn't tell. And frankly, at that point, he couldn't care less.

Explore more of the Lindenshaw Mysteries:
riptidepublishing.com/titles/series/lindenshaw-mysteries

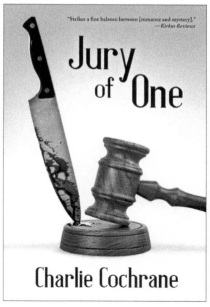

Dear Reader,

Thank you for reading Charlie Cochrane's *Two Feet Under*!

We know your time is precious and you have many, many entertainment options, so it means a lot that you've chosen to spend your time reading. We really hope you enjoyed it.

We'd be honored if you'd consider posting a review—good or bad—on sites like **Amazon, Barnes & Noble, Kobo, Goodreads, Twitter, Facebook, Tumblr,** and your blog or website. We'd also be honored if you told your friends and family about this book. Word of mouth is a book's lifeblood!

For more information on upcoming releases, author interviews, blog tours, contests, giveaways, and more, please sign up for our weekly, spam-free newsletter and visit us around the web:

Newsletter: tinyurl.com/RiptideSignup
Twitter: twitter.com/RiptideBooks
Facebook: facebook.com/RiptidePublishing
Goodreads: tinyurl.com/RiptideOnGoodreads
Tumblr: riptidepublishing.tumblr.com

Thank you so much for Reading the Rainbow!

RiptidePublishing.com

Acknowledgements

Thanks go to Cathy, who came up with the idea of the feud between the CAS and the detectorists and so kick-started the whole tale. And to Sally, who invented the murderous Pippa single-handed. Also to my editor, Caz Galloway, who always points out where I've made no sense and takes the sow's-ear bits and suggests ways of making them into silk purses.

Also by
Charlie Cochrane

Novels
The Best Corpse for the Job
Jury of One
Broke Deep
Count the Shells
Lessons for Survivors
Lessons for Suspicious Minds
Lessons for Idle Tongues
Lessons for Sleeping Dogs
Lessons in Love
Lessons in Desire

Standalone short stories
Second Helpings
Awfully Glad
Don't Kiss the Vicar
Promises Made Under Fire
Tumble Turn
The Angel in the Window
Dreams of a Hero
Wolves of the West
Music in the Midst of
Desolation

Coming soon
Lessons in Discovery
Lessons in Power
Lessons in Temptation
Lessons in Seduction
Lessons in Trust
All Lessons Learned

Paired novellas
Wild Bells
Home Fires Burning
In the Spotlight

Anthologies (contributing author)
Pride of Poppies
Capital Crimes
Lashings of Sauce
Tea and Crumpet
British Flash
Summer's Day

About the Author

Because Charlie Cochrane couldn't be trusted to do any of her jobs of choice—like managing a rugby team—she writes. Her mystery novels include the Edwardian-era Cambridge Fellows series and the contemporary Lindenshaw Mysteries.

A member of the Romantic Novelists' Association, Mystery People, and International Thriller Writers Inc., Charlie regularly appears at literary festivals and at reader and author conferences with The Deadly Dames.

Where to find her:
Website: charliecochrane.wordpress.com
Facebook: facebook.com/charlie.cochrane.18
Twitter: twitter.com/charliecochrane
Goodreads: goodreads.com/author/Charlie_Cochrane

Enjoy more stories like
Two Feet Under
at RiptidePublishing.com!

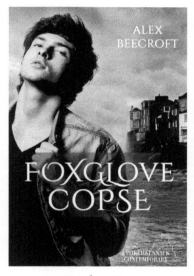

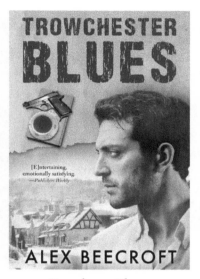

Foxglove Copse
ISBN: 978-1-62649-547-0

Trowchester Blues
ISBN: 978-1-62649-199-1

Lightning Source UK Ltd.
Milton Keynes UK
UKHW010214290721
387924UK00002B/148

9 781626 496828